MADAME POMMERY

Creator of Brut Champagne
A Champagne Widows Novel

Rebecca Rosenberg

LION HEART PUBLISHING

ISBN Numbers:
978-1-7329699-4-0 (print)
978-1-7329699-5-7 (ebook)

Publisher's Cataloging-In-Publication
(Provided by Cassidy Cataloguing Services, Inc.)

Names: Rosenberg, Rebecca, 1955- author.

Title: Madame Pommery : creator of Brut champagne / Rebecca Rosenberg.

Description: Kenwood, California : Lion Heart Publishing, [2023] | Series: A champagne widows novel

Identifiers: ISBN: 978-1-7329699-4-0 (print) | 978-1-7329699-5-7 (ebook)

Subjects: LCSH: Champagne (Wine)--Fiction. | Women vintners--France--Champagne-Ardenne-- Fiction. | Widows—France—Champagne-Ardenne—Fiction. | Franco-Prussian War, 1870-1871--Fiction. | Man-woman relationships--Fiction. | Social classes--France--History-- 19th century--Fiction. | LCGFT: Biographical fiction. | Historical fiction. | Romance fiction. | BISAC: FICTION / Historical /General. | FICTION / Women. | FICTION / World Literature / France / 19th century. | FICTION / Romance / Historical / General.

Classification: LCC: PS3618.O83245 M34 2023 | DDC: 813/.6—dc23

Subjects:
FIC014000 FICTION / Historical /General
FIC044000 FICTION / Women
FIC101020 FICTION /World Literature/ France / 19th Century
FIC027050 FICTION / Romance /Historical / General

Cover Design: Lynn Andreozzi
Interior Page Design by Femigraphix
Author's Note: Madame Pommery, Creator of Brut Champagne, is a novel blending fiction and fact.

Printed in the United States of America
LION HEART PUBLISHING

I raise my glass to those of you who try to do what others say they cannot, including Madame Pommery.

"Some take their gold
In minted mold,
And some in harps hereafter,
But give me mine
In bubbles fine
And keep the change in laughter."
~Oliver Herford

"Inevitably I find myself in a predicament where rules don't apply, or worse, they contradict each other."

--Jeanne Alexandrine Louise Melin Pommery

PART I

1858-1862

"Never imitate anyone, including yourself."
~Jeanne Alexandrine Pommery

1

EN AVOIR GROS SUR LE CŒUR

To have a big one on the heart

Reims, Champagne, France, 1858. If it wasn't for the vital volume of *Etiquette for Ladies* weighing down my lap, I would float away with my dear Louis, who I pray is knocking at heaven's gates by now. The waxy body before me is not my Louis, no longer smelling of lanolin from working the wool. His lips and cheeks are painted with embalmer's rouge in a grotesque likeness of the trollops at Le Palais Alhambra brothel.

My husband was a simple man who would have preferred his untouched body encased in a plain pine box. Why did I let Reynard Wolfe convince me to embalm and inter Louis in an extravagant casket of walnut burl inlaid with brass and pewter?

Wolfe, Louis's banker and executor, appealed to my sense of societal duty. "Madame Pommery, as the very pillar of Reims society, you would certainly be expected to maintain Louis Pommery's dignity as a respected businessman."

Dignity my eye. Louis puffed up and painted like a suckling pig? May as well have an apple stuffed in his mouth.

I've kept our two-year-old daughter in the nursery with her nanny, Lucille. No one should remember their parent in a box looking so unnatural. I shudder at the thought, and Madame DuBois wraps a shawl over my shoulders against the chill.

"*Merci.*" I pat her hand. She's been with me every moment since I started the Saint Remi Auxiliary for the orphanage. The other auxiliary ladies babble on about Louis—how steadfast, gentle, and loyal he was, never once mentioning his failing wool and wine business. I've given them all *Etiquette for Ladies*. Their words drift to the ceiling with the candle smoke, as my fingers examine the gift Louis gave me last year for my thirty-ninth birthday.

I'd hoped for canvas and paints, but he gave me a chatelaine. "Everything you ever need hanging from your belt." He'd demonstrated each item with such pride, I hid my disappointment. "Thimble, watch, scissors, and measuring tape for your needlework, a funnel for your oils, a pencil, a pantry key, a wax letter seal, and a vial of smelling salts. Uncorking the vial, I breathe in the stinging vapors of camphor, which smell like embalming fluid.

"It's time, Madame Pommery." Reynard Wolfe dons a Bavarian hat from his homeland.

My son, Louis's namesake, squeezes my hand. A flesh-and-blood image of his father with his brooding brow and broad shoulders. So grown up in his military school uniform, yet sweat beads his upper lip. Still a boy at seventeen.

As Father Pieter closes the coffin lid, I steal a last look at the man who is not really here.

"Wait." I pluck a rose from the vase and lay it on his folded hands that feel so cold.

My son helps Narcisse Greno with his coat. My husband's partner has aged overnight. His head quivers. Thick lenses enlarge his cloudy eyes. An ear trumpet sticks out from his breast pocket.

The rest of the pallbearers pull on fur-lined gloves and black overcoats over blacker mourning suits. Henry Vasnier, my husband's young apprentice, wears the same suit he wears every Sunday for church. He has a fresh cut under his long sideburns and a bit of lather behind his ear. No wife yet to help him catch those things.

Reynard Wolfe positions the esteemed Mayor Werle and Doctor DuBois at the head of the coffin. I imagine it's so the crowd outside will see these important men first in the procession.

As the widow, I am forbidden to join the procession. That bitter pill sticks in my throat. The men lift the coffin, and I jump up from my chair. The weighty *Etiquette for Ladies* falls on my foot with a sharp blow. Catching myself on the casket, the pallbearers buckle under my added weight.

"I want to go to the cemetery," I say, my foot aching.

"Madame Pommery, you of all people know only men walk behind the hearse wagon," Wolfe scolds. "I will make sure Monsieur Pommery is buried properly. Your friends will keep you company."

The Saint Remi Auxiliary ladies gape at me, shocked at my outburst. They do not expect such misbehavior from me.

I turn my head to the banker. "Please, Monsieur Wolfe, I must accompany my husband to his grave."

"You must set a good example, Madame, or all your etiquette lessons are for naught."

I grit my teeth. If I do not live by the rules I teach, my integrity is lost. "Get on with it then."

The men carry the coffin outside, and Old Greno grunts under the weight. Louis takes a wider grip, trying to help.

Limping after them on my sore foot, I watch them load my husband into the shadowy hearse wagon. A forlorn moan escapes my throat, and I bite down on my thumbnail.

The auxiliary ladies surround me, simpering and sniveling. The wagon lurches off, and black-shrouded horses slip on cobblestones. Despite the snow, townspeople line the street on both sides. Women wave black lace handkerchiefs as the hearse passes. A procession of fine carriages and gigs slog through the slippery street, wheels squealing.

My nanny, Lucille, brings out my daughter, who is flushed and tearful.

"Papa? Papa? Where Papa?" Little Louise totters to me.

"I am sorry, Madame. She will not stop asking for him." Lucille tucks dark curls into her kerchief. Even with her hair covered, the Jewess provokes the auxiliary's glares. Her cavernous eyes, perfect oval face and aquiline nose cannot go unnoticed, yet she never flaunts her beauty.

Louise presses her red rumpled face into my breast and wails. The auxiliary ladies' eyes bulge like moor fish, and they cover their disapproval with black silk fans.

Something snaps inside me. "Thank you for your kindness, ladies. You have been a great comfort to me." Hugging Louise close,

I wind my way through them and out to the carriage house.

"Etiquette can be tricky, Louise." I strap her in the gig. "Inevitably, one finds oneself in a predicament where rules do not apply, or worse, they contradict each other. When that happens, one must listen to one's heart for direction." Snapping Beau's reins, I turn him toward Saint Remi. I will not allow my husband to be buried without me.

2

Avoir la tête dans le pâté

To have one's head in the pâté

When my auntie receives my letter about my husband's untimely passing, she sends a leaflet entitled *Notes on Fashionable Mourning*. No sympathy or condolences. The rules are as treacherous as wolves in the sheep pasture. I make an appointment with Adolphe Hubinet, the mercer who sells fine fabrics and makes fashionable clothing.

Hubinet plunks the pianino with a zest that shakes the petals of late-blooming roses in the vase sitting on top. The tune is cheerful like the twitter of rock doves in my birdbath. Hubinet runs the shop for his brother, who manages the seamstresses in the workroom. The shop is my sanctuary of exquisite fabrics, exotic feathers, jeweled trims, and perusing *La Mode* fashion magazines. Hubinet knows what inspires his customers to buy, and buy they do. He keeps a leather journal at his desk detailing measurements, flattering colors and styles, and birthdays.

His slender shoulders rise as his fingers move dramatically on the keys in a final flourish.

"Sounds like Hayden," I say.

"Good guess. It was his student, Marianna Martines." He kisses *la bise* on both cheeks; he smells of spicy marigolds. "Oh, my dearest

Madame Pommery, we were devastated by your loss. Your marriage was a beacon of love to us all."

My lips clamp shut. Every time I meet someone I haven't seen since Louis died, I lose control. Surely, I can buy clothes without choking up. My fingers graze colorful bolts of taffeta, raw silks, and wools in new modern colors of purple, pink, blue, and yellow. The tempting fabrics usually set my creativity churning. Yet my weary eyes see no joy in them now.

Hubinet pours me champagne he keeps chilled for customers. His attire is bespoke with flair. Chinese brocade vest with a matching pocket square and cravat. Abalone tiepin with matching cufflinks. Pintucked shirt and herringbone suit. His leather boots never show the dust of the streets.

The icy liquid lifts my mood a smidgen—a Scottish term my friends used in school.

"I went ahead and made a dress for your approval." He leads me to the largest fitting room. The enormous chandelier shines too bright in the cheval mirrors, accentuating the hideous purple puffs under my eyes.

"I am sorry Monsieur, but I cannot abide these mirrors today. I cannot see myself as Louis would see me. He always disapproved of me wearing black."

Hubinet twists the end of his exuberant mustache. "My mistake, Madame." He takes me into a dressing room with silk lampshades, moire-silk walls, and velvet tufted chairs. Not a mirror in it.

Bridgette, the freckle-faced orphan I brought him to apprentice as a seamstress, helps me dress. I am always so grateful when I can arrange a good employer for one of my girls. For a few precious moments, I am distracted from my melancholy by elegant swaths of fabric, pintucked bodice, the beribboned waist she stitches tighter to fit. I have no appetite since Louis passed.

With no light and no mirror, I cannot tell a thing except the dress is dark. Dark as my mood. Dark as my future.

Bridgette stands back to study her work. "Does it please you, Madame Pommery?" Her voice quavers with uncertainty.

Ah, this is the first dress she has made. "The workmanship is impeccable, Bridgette." I smoothen the bodice; the pert texture of taffeta rustles against my fingers.

She opens the door, and I step out to the light.

Hubinet gasps. *"Magnifique."* He kisses his fingertips.

"Stunning, Madame Pommery," Bridgette says, clapping her hands together.

I swirl in front of the full-length mirror, the chandelier highlighting the iridescent purple and green undertones. My diaphragm clenches. "This will never do. The dress is not black. A widow is required to wear black for at least six months."

Hubinet's eyebrow arches. "Mourning attire is meant to honor the loved one who passed. Monsieur Pommery hated you in black, and now you pay him the greatest compliment by pleasing him."

"Nothing can possibly please my husband, now." My head throbs and my vision checkers.

Hubinet helps me to a chair, and Bridgette pours me more champagne. I have made her feel wretched, poor thing. But rules are rules, and rules of mourning are strict.

"That will be all, Bridgette," Hubinet says, and she returns to the workroom. He kneels before me, white-faced and apologetic. "Madame Pommery, I did not mean to upset you. It is only proper you want black. We will begin on another dress to suit your sense of decorum."

I sip the champagne, the fresh bubbles heartening. "Won't you join me, Monsieur? It is rude to drink alone."

Hubinet pours like a sommelier, thumb tucked in the punt on the bottom and fingers cradling the bottle.

"À votre santé." He clinks my glass, and we drink.

Bubbles float to the top of my glass and burst, releasing their fruity aroma. "Champagne cures all evils. Doesn't it?" Perhaps I overreacted about the dress.

"You discovered my secret potion, Madame." Hubinet curls his mustache around his pinkie. "I wouldn't sell a single dress without champagne."

"Didn't you live in Paris before here?" I finish my champagne, and he pours another.

He nods. "I was a wineseller there. I miss the bustle of a big city."

"I went to finishing school in Paris. Then later to St. Mary's in England."

"That explains it," he says. "Your style surpasses anyone in Reims. I suppose that is why I chose iridescent silk for your dress.

9

Sophisticated, yet not too showy. You would definitely see widows wearing this in Paris."

My cheeks burn. "But I am not in Paris, am I?"

"I offended you." He snorted. "And now that you're moving to your cottage in Chigny, I see this dress is entirely inappropriate."

"Who told you I was moving?" My fingers caress the amethyst buttons at my wrists.

His taps his cheek. "I believe I heard it from Monsieur Wolfe when I saw him at the Biergarten. But several clients have mentioned you leaving Saint Remi Auxiliary, and what a shame that would be for all the girls you have placed with employers."

"I am committed to the Saint Remi orphanage. If I decide to move, I will not leave the orphanage in dire straits."

"Of course not, Madame. You have dedicated your life to the orphanage." He bows slightly.

I walk to the dressing room to change, my fingers lighting on the scalloped edge on the bodice. Exquisite workmanship. A shame to waste it. In fact, I like everything about this dress, especially the iridescence like peacock feathers. I pivot to Hubinet. "I have changed my mind. I will take this dress and wear it home. Perhaps you can make me a couple of simpler frocks for work."

"You plan to work?" He wraps tissue around my old dress.

"I'm waiting for Wolfe to settle the estate." I scoff. "But it looks like I will have to support my family somehow. The thought of it petrifies me."

"I'd bet money on anything you put your mind to, Madame Pommery." He puts the old dress in a box and ties it with indigo ribbon. "I've watched you start an orphanage, train them for decent jobs, and even design your Chigny cottage from scratch."

"Kind of you to wax poetic about my talents, but my rose garden and butterfly collection do not pay very well." Taking the box, I catch sight of my new dress in the cheval mirror, and my breath hitches. "The dress is a wonder, Monsieur."

"A reflection of the woman who wears it, Madame." He walks me to the door.

"Please extend my compliments to Bridgette." Stepping out into the bustling street, I am sad to leave the warmth of his confidence.

Standing on the train platform, my heart sinks to see Louis leave so soon. He seems eager to go, though we have not shared all we could have about his father. Steam builds as the engineer stokes the engine. The locomotive quivers with life.

"It will be good for you to be back to your studies," I say. "Your father was so proud of you going to the academy."

He bounces little Louise on his hip, chanting, "Le train, tchou, tchou. Le train, tchou, tchou."

"Tchou, tchou!" she sings out and pulls the tassel on his shako and giggles. "Tchou, tchou!"

Having Louis home these past weeks has been my reason to get out of bed in the morning. The breakfast table did not seem so quiet with him here, voicing headstrong opinions about newspaper articles, or answering questions about his school routine and friends. He did not say much about his meetings with Reynard Wolfe. But I am grateful our banker took Louis under his wing and advised him to continue the military academy like his father wanted.

Now, Louis plays *jeu de la barbichette* with Louise, grabbing each other's chins. Separated by fifteen years, their blossoming relationship delights me. Louis paid her no mind before now. I suspect he was more embarrassed at her surprise arrival than anything.

"Okay, all right, you win." He grabs her chin again, and she peals with laughter.

"All aboard," the conductor with the flat gray cap calls through puffs of steam. The shrill train whistle blows three times. Louise claps her hands over her ears and frowns.

"Better go, Louis," I say, pointing toward the door. "You don't want to miss your train."

Louise clings to his neck and whines. "*Mon frère, mon frère.*" My brother.

"*La bise, Mademoiselle.*" He kisses her cheeks, and her periwinkle eyes sparkle. My heart swells to see such love between my children.

Louis joins the line of passengers without a goodbye. Pushing aside his thoughtless rebuff, I wheel *la poussette* to him, reach up and kiss his cheeks.

"Thank you for being so good to Louise."

"Lucille helped me see it wasn't Louise's fault Papa died."

"You spoke to Lucille about it?" He confided to the nanny? "It's no one's fault your father died."

He snorts. "Papa went back to work because you wanted another child."

My cheeks flash hot, then cold again, as happens too often these days.

"Louis, you have this all wrong." But what can I say? Louise was a mistake, but she brought us such joy when our lives were winding down.

Louis boards the train, and the conductor closes the door behind him. He slumps into a seat by the window and waves to Louise. Her eyes cloud over like a thunderhead ready to burst. She lets out such a horrible wail that bystanders back away from us.

The train lurches forward like an angry bull and scrapes away from the platform with a terrible shudder.

My son blames me for my husband's death. *Jeter de l'huile sur le feu.* Adding insult to injury.

Our maid, Chantal, enters my salon with a calling card on a silver tray. She's come a long way from her time at the Alhambra brothel. When she got pregnant, the head of the brothel sent her to me since I educate girls in her condition and place them as servants in good homes. When the poor girl lost her baby, I offered her a position.

A shaft of sunlight through the black crepe curtain silhouettes the visitor's abundant figure.

I squint at the card with bleary eyes. "Madame Barbe-Nicole Clicquot. Oh, my goodness." I glance down at my black dress to see if it is black enough to receive a guest.

The last time I saw the "mother of champagne" was when I placed a Saint Remi orphan at her mansion. After that, she took anyone I recommended, so vast was her need for trained workers.

"Please have Yvonne prepare a proper tea and pastries," I tell Chantal. "The best we have. Veuve Clicquot has a sweet tooth."

I rise to the looking glass on the wall. But it is covered with black organdy as dictated by the rules of mourning. I start to push the fabric aside but stop abruptly. Apparently, covered mirrors protect one from seeing the morbid grief on one's own face. Or glimpsing a loved one's ghost over one's shoulder.

When I turn, I'm startled to see the Grande Dame standing in the threshold of the salon holding a covered basket. Her majestic presence charges the air.

"Pardon me for not greeting you right away, Madame Clicquot. I am not myself."

"Of course you aren't, my dear. Nor would anyone expect you to be." She hobbles forward. "May I sit? My knees are not so good anymore."

"Of course." I gesture to the table by the hearth.

She lowers herself slowly, spreading her full gray taffeta skirt that rustles like leaves in the wind. A fringed mantle graces her Battenberg-lace blouse. Her hair still shines like copper, amazing since she must be over eighty. Her girlish finger-roll curls are topped with a lace cap. Her gleaming gray eyes have not dimmed.

"I am sorry I am late in tendering my condolences," she says. "I was at Château de Boursault when I heard you lost Monsieur Pommery."

I pat the *Etiquette for Ladies* I keep at the ready. "Visits of condolence may be made up to three months after the passing."

She flips her stocky hand toward the book. "I find that rules tend to hamper one's inner voice, don't you?"

I am unable to disagree since a host should never make a guest uncomfortable.

Chantal brings in a tray and sets it on the table. Her beautiful breasts almost fall from her chemise as she pours the tea.

Veuve Clicquot takes three lumps of sugar in her tea. "What are you planning to do now that you are on your own?"

"I haven't really thought that far ahead." I pick up my teacup and saucer.

"I always took you for an industrious sort," she says, eyeing the pastries. "You never let moss grow beneath your feet." She chooses an éclair and licks off the frosting. "Isn't there something you always wanted to do and never could?"

Her questioning galls me. "I have my family to consider," I say. "My daughter is only two."

"I'd love to meet her. I brought her a gift."

13

"She's napping." I offer her the tiered tray. "Care for another pastry? My cook makes them fresh to tempt me, but I don't have an appetite."

Her plump fingers pluck out a tall, layered pastry that gushes cream and jam from the sides. "I quite like napoleons with my tea." She takes a big bite, closes her eyes, and a rapturous smile spreads on her lips.

Veuve Clicquot's basket squeals. She pours cream in her saucer and lifts the linen cloth from her basket. A black cat leaps onto the table and upsets the sugar bowl. Noisily, he laps the cream until it is finished, and she pours more. He looks like no cat I've seen. His skinny tail has a tuft at the tip like a magic wand. His body is long and lean, with legs of a jaguar. Whiskers extend from his muzzle six inches on each side. His wild eyes glint with gold flecks.

"We are allergic to cats," I tell her before I can check manners.

"But he's not a cat, my dear. He's a matagot. Surely, you've heard of the enchanted creatures? A matagot is a good friend to have in tough times."

I don't have to consult *Etiquette for Ladies* to know what to say about an unwanted gift. "Very thoughtful of you, Madame Clicquot."

"I insist you call me Barbe-Nicole." Her forefinger presses her chin. "May I call you by your first name?"

"Of course," I say.

She tilts her head. "Should I call you Louise as your husband did, or Alexandrine?"

"He called me Louise as a family joke." I huff. "When Louis named our son Louis, he teased that we were the family of Louis, Louis, and Louise. Belonging together like that seemed sweet. When our daughter was born, he named her Louise."

Her penetrating stare peels away my artifice. "I prefer the name Alexandrine, don't you?"

I pick up my teacup, nervously. "I've been called Madame Pommery since I've been married."

"No one can dictate your name. That is for you to decide." She licks her fingertips. "What about Alex? It suits you, somehow. Modern, spirited, creative."

"My school friends called me that, but Louis never liked it," I admit.

She clucks her tongue. "Marriage is a beautiful thing, honoring your husband's wishes before your own. But now, it is important to trust the voice in your heart. When you become a widow, men line up to tell you what to do now that your husband is gone. But you must not listen to a single one. Trust your own counsel."

The matagot rubs against my arm, purring softly. His fur is softer than it looks.

"His name is Felix." Veuve Clicquot eyes the tray, looking for her next victim.

"Whose name?" My wrists start to itch, and I scratch them discreetly.

"The matagot." She pops a madeleine in her mouth and giggles. "Oh my, that's good."

By the time Veuve Clicquot leaves, my wrists have swollen with hives. I lure the matagot with a piece of cheese. Snatching him up, I march him to the back door and shoo him into the alleyway. "*Bon chance*, Felix!" Good luck.

Waking before dawn, I reach for Louis, but the hollow in the feather mattress is empty and cold. I sense a presence in the house, or rather, the absence of presence. Our half-finished conversations, the kisses I never gave him, the meals we shared, the wine Louis wanted me to taste. Echoes of our life together whisper in the walls.

Louise sleeps in a cradle beside my bed instead of the nursery. She's been so fretful lately without her father. There is a weird whine behind her. Something crawling about. I peek into the cradle for a better look. The plaintive sound comes from the black ball of fur. The longest whiskers and gold-flecked eyes. I snatch the matagot out before he suffocates my daughter. How did the creature get back inside?

Louise stretches her arms and yawns. "*Bonjour, Maman.*"

The matagot jumps into her arms. "Oh, Maman, I love him." She buries her tiny nose in its black fur, and he starts purring. "What is the cat's name?" She discovers the white star on his chest.

"Apparently, he's a matagot," I say.

"You mean like the fairytales?"

I nod. "His name is Felix."

"Felix. Felix. Felix." She giggles and squeezes him, his eyes never leaving her face.

The heavy mantle of grief feels lighter. Maybe the matagot is magic after all.

3

JETER DE L'HUILE SUR LE FEU

Adding insult to injury

As Reynard Wolfe supervises the inventory that determines the company's fate, I shuffle through correspondence in Louis's rolltop desk. Louise plays with my chatelaine tools on the Aubusson rug at my feet. She unreels the measuring tape, draws with the pencil, and winds the timepiece. My husband's gift is useful after all.

As a dozen men count bales of wool, my husband's partner, Narcisse Greno, calls out numbers in a voice shredded with age. Wolfe peers over Henry Vasnier's shoulder as he records quantities with a calm and focused demeanor. I see why Louis relied on the young man.

The warehouse is a mishmash of spindles and looms next to bottles of red wine they sold as a side business since wool sales were lagging. If I'd organized this mess, the business would have run more efficiently. But my husband did not want help, so I turned my attention to my orphanage.

Greno grabs his lower back and groans from bending over spools of twine. He was a saint to help Louis reopen the business when I got pregnant. Three years ago, when Doctor DuBois diagnosed that I was not in menopause but expecting a child, I was stunned. Pregnant at thirty-seven? When I broke the news to Louis,

color drained from his face, and he looked decades older than fifty-five years. He postponed retirement and went back to work.

Louis handled Pommery & Greno manufacturing and operations, while "Old Greno" handled sales, preferring to travel and
socialize. What is the company worth without Louis? As inventory
drags on, the impact of my husband's death tolls as unrelenting as
the Reims Cathedral clock strikes the hour.

Vasnier passes by the rolltop and playfully tugs Louise's bonnet
down over her eyes. She pops up the brim to see who did it. She
wags her tiny finger at him as only a two-year-old coquette can. A
pang of sadness Louis is not here to tease his daughter.

I'm sure Vasnier wonders what will happen to the company, as
all the workers do. What does all this counting and recounting mean?
Everyone could be out of work tomorrow, for all I know.

The workers descend the creaky plank stairs from the mezzanine, taking off their Phrygian caps and nodding their heads as they
pass me. "*Bonsoir, Madame,*" they say before they leave.

"We need to discuss these orders for wine." Vasnier hands me
a stack of papers.

"It's late. We can go over them tomorrow," I tell him. "Would
you mind taking Louise to her nanny before you go home?"

Vasnier scoops up Louise in his arms. "Let's go find Lucille,
shall we?" He glances at Wolfe before closing the door. He knows as
well as I do the fate of the company lies in the banker's hands.

"There is no easy way to say this." Wolfe slicks back his ginger
hair. "But, I think if we sell off the inventory, it should just about
cover the debts."

A sharp pain shoots through my forehead. Old Greno collapses
in a chair, focusing on his untied shoe.

I drum my fingernails on the top of the desk. "What debt are
you referring to?"

Greno clamps his cracked lips together.

Wolfe stops my fingers from drumming. "Don't worry, Madame
Pommery, I am here to help you through this."

I retrieve my hand from his grasp. "The facts please, Monsieur
Wolfe."

The lantern casts an eager glint in his green eyes, but his voice
is as monotonous as a priest giving last rites. "There is a mortgage
on this building to be paid."

"Do you know about a mortgage?" I ask Greno.

Wolfe continues. "And since Monsieur Greno owns half the business, he must be paid off first."

The Reims Cathedral bell gongs again, pummeling my eardrums.

"Madame Pommery, let me speak plainly." Wolfe speaks slower and louder. "After we pay Monsieur Greno and the mortgage, there will be very little left for you and the children." He consults his pocket watch. "Ah, time for *Mittagessen*. I think better on a full stomach."

The gall to ask for lunch while he explains my disastrous finances. But Louis trusted him, so I must as well.

The savory aroma of onion soup wafts from the kitchen. Louis started inviting Wolfe to lunch on Wednesdays since he moved to Reims two years ago. "The least we could do for the new banker, single and alone," he said. But I suspect Louis enjoyed the free financial advice the young German pontificated about over duck confit and sherry.

"Monsieur Wolfe, you'll want to wash up after inventory."

I gesture to the toilet and take Greno out of earshot. "Is selling the inventory the right thing to do? Wouldn't it be better to continue the business and pay off the mortgage?"

Greno hangs his head, his gray hair combed over his shiny scalp. "I tried to tell you at the funeral. I am leaving. The business is too much for me. My sister in Paris has room for me."

Panic riddles my throat. "You can't leave me now, Monsieur Greno. Not with Louis gone."

"Change comes whether we are ready or not." The old man shrugs his shoulders. "After a lifetime of work, I'm looking forward to coffee with friends in the morning and wine with friends in the afternoon. Art exhibits, museums, concerts. I want to enjoy the life I have left." His fist presses his heart. "Pardon my candor, Madame Pommery, but you are still young and attractive. Many men will want to take care of you. You have nothing to worry about."

His advice raises my hackles. "Monsieur, my husband is barely cold in his grave. Did he mean so little to you?"

The old man scruffs his jowl. "Louis meant the world to me, but the business has not done well for some time." He leans on the plastered wall.

"But if we liquidate the inventory, I'll be left with very little."

"You may be right," he says. "No one wants looms and spindles when French wool is not selling since Britain lowered their prices. Maybe we melt the iron equipment down for cannons."

Wolfe rejoins us, rubbing his hands together. "What's this about cannons?"

My cook, Yvonne, peeks into the dining room. "Are you ready to have Chantal serve, Madame?" she asks in her singsong voice.

It is the first time we've sat here without Louis; his chair is shrouded with black crepe. The past month has been full of first times without Louis, each one a sore reminder.

I inhale the earthy fragrance from the silver tureen to ground me. "We are in luck, gentlemen. Yvonne prepared onion soup."

Chantal serves the fragrant soup in my best china. Her black curls escape her mop cap and her black uniform hugs her lithe figure. She doles grilled cheese toasts on top of the banker's soup.

He takes a bite and closes his eyes, leaning back in his chair to savor the taste. "Ah, Chantal. *Du bist ein Engel.*" You are an angel.

She blushes and curtseys low, eyelashes fluttering like dragonfly wings, before she backs into the kitchen.

Dipping my spoon into the melted cheese and caramelized onion usually sets my mouth watering, but I can't bring it to my lips. I have so many questions about our inventory, the mortgage, and paying off Greno, but etiquette won't allow business to be discussed during meals, but I have so many questions about inventory.

Greno tastes his soup. "*Magnifique.*" He kisses his fingertips and explodes them, his old eyes dancing. "I will miss your dinners, my dear Madame Pommery."

"You are always welcome at my table, Monsieur." My voice breaks, and I swallow a sob. "I'm sorry, it's all too much at once."

Wolfe places his solid hand over mine. "I told you I would take care of you, Madame Pommery. Perhaps, if I could find the right buyer for the business, you could make more money than selling off inventory."

"If the business is doing as poorly as you say, who would buy it?" I ask. "French people are stretched to the breaking point with all of Napoleon's new taxes."

Wolfe's spoon stops midair, dripping on the linen tablecloth. "I have never heard you speak of politics." He slurps the spoonful. "Or business, for that matter."

"Perhaps there is more to me than meets the eye," I say, wiping my mouth with my napkin. How often men think us vapid because we keep our own counsel?

"I meant no disrespect," Wolfe says. "In fact, I often teased your husband how a mere merchant such as himself attracted such an educated, cultured, and fashionable woman such as you."

"Sweet words cannot disguise the bitter truth," I say. "Louis kept me in the dark about our finances. That is painfully clear." My fingernails click the oak table once again.

Chantal returns and serves coquilles Saint-Jacques, which smell of salt and sea and are brought in daily on the train from the Côte d'Azur.

Popping a scallop in his mouth, Wolfe groans in ecstasy.

"How much more could we get if we sell the business rather than the inventory?" I ask.

Wolfe chases a scallop around his plate with his fork, then stabs it. "At least double."

Greno reads his lips and opens his eyes wide. "Double the money? I could use that in retirement."

Wolfe wags his fork at him. "Minus twenty percent commission," he says and stuffs his third scallop in his mouth.

"Then we should sell the business." Greno's age-spotted hand raises his etched glass.

"So, it's settled." Wolfe smiles broadly with shreds of scallop between his teeth.

I push back my chair. "Monsieur Wolfe, if you'll excuse us, I'd like to discuss this with Monsieur Greno in private."

"But I haven't had my dessert." Wolfe's green eyes glint in disappointment.

"Stay and enjoy dessert, and we'll take Louise out for a stroll." Double the money sounds appealing, but by the time the mortgage and Greno are paid, will there be enough for my family to live on?

Greno pushes Louise in *la poussette* as we walk toward the great Reims Cathedral. Soon she is fast asleep. The soaring cathedral spires pierce through the sky, the first star twinkling.

"I always believed God hears our prayers better at the cathedral," I muse.

"Absolutely," Greno says. "But do you know why?"

I raise my eyebrows.

"It's the rock doves," Greno says. "They fly our prayers directly up to God."

I snicker. "And here I thought they were just pigeons with pretty iridescent necks."

He points at the flurry of rock doves circling the square. "God's messengers." He wags his finger. "Problem is God's answers are not always what we want."

Walking past my Smiling Angel carved into the façade of the cathedral, I pray silently for guidance.

"Tell me about Paris and your sister," I say. "Where does she live? Does she really have room for you?"

"Vallerie lives in the first arrondissement, *ma chérie*." He smiles, wistfully. "She is part of Napoleon's inner court and needs a ready escort."

"Oh, my. She must be quite connected."

Louise coos, eyelids closed, a small smile on her rosebud lips.

"Vallerie serves as a lady-in-waiting to Queen Eugenie," he says.

"What a glamorous life," I say, envisioning the art, music, architecture, and gardens of Paris. "Can't you take me with you?"

"You are welcome to visit anytime." He nods to Louise. "I have to see my godchild, you know." He takes my arm as we pass the Biergarten where men gather for beer and pretzels after work. Barmaids in German green pinafores carry pitchers to the tables. "Vallerie's apartment is on the Right Bank between the Place de la Concorde and the Louvre."

"I attended a finishing school near there," I say. "Saint Honoré for girls."

"Of course, Paris is a shambles now that Napoleon and his architect Haussmann demolished the entire city center. They're building thirty-six thousand meters of new boulevards. Can you imagine?" He snorts and puffs, grabs his chest.

"Let's sit a minute." I find us a stone bench beside the cathedral. Sitting beside him, I spread my ugly black crepe skirt, a constant reminder of the loss of my husband and life as I knew it.

"So, you really think we ought to sell the business?" I ask Greno.

He sighs. "With the extra money we'll get from selling, you can go to Chigny with your daughter and live a good life. You deserve the life Louis planned for you."

I sigh. When Louis retired, he bought the parcel in Chigny, though we couldn't afford it. The air smelled of plowed earth, ripening grapes, and roses planted at the end of grapevine rows. That night we sat on our hill and drank wine as the sun set. Our passion led to Louise.

"You said the wool business was failing, but what about the wine you sold?" I ask, grasping at straws. "Wine is a business I could understand."

"My sister is already redecorating my suite," he says, frowning.

The reality hits me like cold water. "Is there nothing that would convince you to stay?"

He strokes his goatee and shakes his head.

I turn away. That boy with the dirty face and wispy hair holds out his arms wide, offering breadcrumbs in his hands. A dozen rock doves land on his head, shoulders, and arms. Other children would shriek and run, but not him. Submersed in birds, his face lights with pure joy.

The Reims Cathedral bell tolls three.

"Ready to go, Monsieur?" I help Greno up, watching the bird boy behind him. His long fingers grab the dove, and he tucks it under his jacket and walks quickly toward Saint Remi Abbey.

I'm stunned. Perhaps the boy is hungry. The dove may be dinner. What seemed an act of kindness could be a desperate attempt to feed himself.

As we walk, Greno pats my arm. "Louis would want you to be happy."

Pressure builds behind my eyes. I was happy. I had everything. Our family. Our cottage. Our future was bright. Now it couldn't be murkier.

"When are you leaving?" I ask.

"Tomorrow morning. The social season has started, and Vallerie is anxious for an escort."

23

"Then go to her but give me time to consider whether we should sell. I don't want to make the wrong decision."

"I have enough money to tide me over until spring," he says. "That may be a better time to sell the company. With a new vintage ready for market, the winery will look more attractive to a potential buyer." He kisses me *la bise* and trudges up his walkway.

Another man walks out of my life.

The moon moves out of the clouds, and a cross forms on Louis's side of the bed. Taking it as a sign from Louis, I cross myself. We've always got more moonlight in this house than sunlight, with the cathedral watching over us. I move over to his side and bury my face in his pillow, but the linens have been changed several times, leaving only a memory of his smell.

There is no going back to sleep with all the invoices, payments, letters, and orders dancing a quadrille in my head. I put on my robe and go down to Louis's rolltop and organize the mess into piles. No excuse for not paying bills.

When I find the wine orders, I'm amazed there are so many. Especially when wine was always an afterthought. They bought grapes in the fall and crushed them to make wine. "Easy money," Louis said.

How hard can it be?

4

SE JETER DANS LA GUEULE DU LOUP

To throw oneself in the wolf's mouth

After weeks of waiting for Wolfe to close the estate, I go to him instead. Behind the counter, bank clerks count out napoleon gold coins and stack them up on long tables. More money than I have seen in a lifetime. With this much gold, they ought to have enough to pay the bills I've discovered. Nothing short of disgraceful to leave suppliers unpaid for months. What was Louis thinking?

A hunched clerk in a white shirt and houndstooth vest stands at the counter.

"I came to see Monsieur Wolfe, please," I tell him, clutching the file of bills with both hands.

The clerk shuffles back to the corner office. Wolfe comes out, combing his fingers through his ginger hair, tugging his vest down, and tightening his four-in-hand tie. "Madame Pommery. What a surprise." He opens the half-door. "Come back to my office where we can talk privately."

I hesitate, thinking through the etiquette. Is the privacy of his office too forward? But if I refuse, he will be humiliated in front of his employees. Making a quick choice, I follow him past all that gold. Can't take my eyes off the gleam, the clank, and the metallic smell of it.

He ushers me into his office and closes the door. Even more inappropriate. His mahogany paneling matches his oversized desk. Much too large for a man of his short stature. The heavy chairs opposite his desk are ornately scrolled, and gargoyles spring fiercely from the arm rests and chair backs. Obviously imported from Germany.

He takes my coat and hangs it on the coat tree. "You are looking very well. Is that purple you are wearing?" He clucks his tongue. "Already in half-mourning?"

I square my shoulders. "I came to find out about my husband's estate."

Wolfe leans against his desk, too casual in his herringbone vest with watch-fob pocket and shirt sleeves rolled up on his wrists. He's heavier than I thought. All that schnitzel from the Biergarten, I imagine.

"I have shirked my duties as the executor of Louis's will, and for that, I apologize." A lock of hair falls on his forehead. "I was hoping I could improve your situation before it became necessary to tell you."

"What situation?" I ask, girding my innards for the worst.

His mouth twists left as if he tastes something sour.

"Speak plainly, Monsieur." I clutch my handbag. "I need to know what I am facing."

He raises his small eyes to the ceiling as if asking the Almighty for the answer. Drawing a deep breath, he spews words so quickly I must concentrate to understand him.

"Last year, Louis confided that he had not saved enough for your son's education, so he asked me to invest his savings for a quick return. We invested his entire nest egg in Napoleon bonds, which were sure to double his money. But alas, Napoleon bonds have provided no dividends whatsoever." His teeth gnash at his pinkie nail.

"Are you telling me all of our savings are gone?" I clutch the file of bills.

"For the time being, yes," he says. "The French economy is in a shambles right now, due to Napoleon's grandiose ideas. Remaking Paris from scratch. Extending the railroad cross country. Expanding the postal service and the telegraph. The Suez Canal. Too much, too soon." Sweat beads in the folds of his neck. "I can't expect a woman

26

to understand such things." Wolfe sits next to me. "But you must trust me."

"Trust does not pay bills, Monsieur."

He takes my gloved hands in his. "I hate to deliver this terrible news, especially when you look so radiant today. That's why I waited so long to tell you about your finances. I wanted time to improve your investments." He bends to kiss my hand, and I pull it away.

He straightens and delivers more bad news. "The mortgage payment on your building is past due. Louis planned to sell the building when you moved to Chigny."

Fire burns in my belly. I am furious with Louis for not sharing this with me.

"Do you need me to explain more clearly?" Wolfe talks slower and louder.

"You have explained it quite well enough. I am broke."

He nods his double chin. "The only solution I've come up with is that I buy out Greno and we work together on the business."

"You want to be my partner?"

"It occurs to me there is more to life than paperwork, ledgers, and counting money." He tightens his tie. "And you will benefit from a partner to manage the business while you raise Louise."

Given the state of my finances, I'd be a fool not to take his offer. But I've made up my mind.

"I have decided to develop the winery business on my own." The folly of the notion romps in my stomach.

"A winery? That suits me even better." His fingertips press together. "Too bad a woman cannot own a business."

"Unless she is a widow," I quote Madame Clicquot. "A widow can own a business, form contracts, speak in court, and pay taxes."

He grimaces. "Madame, you must not trust your judgment right now. You have suffered a shock. And you are not a young woman." Cocking his head, he appraises me like a molting peacock.

My cheeks burn. "It is rude to discuss a woman's age."

"I am only speaking the truth," he says, admiring his buffed fingernails. "If you want a business, you need a younger man to run things for you."

I jut out my gloved palm. "I'll take my ledger now, please, Monsieur Wolfe."

"Madame, think of what I am offering. Louis can continue his schooling. You and your daughter will be provided for. Otherwise, you are alone in a business you do not understand."

"I will manage."

"My offer stands, Madame. Think it over, and I'm sure you'll see the benefits." He smiles tersely and hands over the ledger.

On the way home, I stop by my Smiling Angel at Reims Cathedral. Her sweet countenance instills in me a quiet confidence I feel deep in my bones.

I ask Henry Vasnier to drive Louise and me to Chigny to check on the cottage, so I can talk to him about my decision. The truth is, I don't want to face the cottage alone. As I direct the young man which roads to take through the sheep-covered hills and vineyards of the Champagne countryside, Louise sits between us playing with Felix on her lap.

Vasnier tips down his bowler hat, his hands tight on the reins. I didn't think to tell him to wear work-clothes for the three-hour drive on dirt roads. His Sunday suit will need a good brushing.

"Did you ship out all the orders for wine?" I ask him.

"We did, but there are still orders coming in." He stares at the road ahead, taking the drive seriously, as he does everything it seems.

"I've decided to keep the winery, small as it is," I tell him. "There appears to be potential there and seems more manageable than wool."

His brows draw together with a frown.

"What is it?" I ask. "Is there a problem I am not taking into account?"

"No disrespect, Madame, but a business is an onerous thing, even when you know what you are doing."

"Fair enough, but I can learn, and you know what you are doing."

His lips press together, and I sense his hesitation.

"Ah. You got another job. Of course, you did." I look away.

"Monsieur Wolfe was good enough to offer me a position," he says.

I huff. "I'm sure he did."

"But it is not that." He tips his head side to side. "Your husband was the winemaker. I was just his apprentice and bookkeeper. And once the wine is made, you need to sell it, and Greno is gone."

"*Ce n'est pas la mer à boire.*" Not as difficult as drinking the sea.

He chuckles and brushes his forefinger against his Van Dyke mustache, which makes him look more mature and worldly than his twenty-five years.

Beau's large hooves clip-clop on a brick road lined with the Champagne Houses of Epernay. My favorite street on earth. Yet, it's all wrong. "Oh, no, we went too far. I must have missed the turn for Chigny."

"Nothing to worry about, Madame. We'll go back." He turns Beau around.

"I don't know how I missed it." My gloved fingers press my forehead and I close my eyes. Everything's changed so much in the past month, I can't even find my cottage, let alone start a new business.

He allows me a moment, then gently clears his throat. "These mansions are astounding. Who lives in them?"

"Aren't they something?" I regain my composure. "These are the champagne houses of Perrier-Jouët, Mumm, Moët, and Boizel. The families live in them and entertain their clients."

Tall iron fences guard marble villas where maids sweep the walkways, liverymen brush fine horses, drivers wipe down carriages, gardeners trim hedges. I imagine the owners and their guests sitting down to a five-course luncheon of white asparagus, truffles, and quail paired with their finest cuvées.

"Do you like champagne?" I ask Vasnier.

"I've only had crémant at my cousin's wedding. Is champagne different?"

I nod. "Like drinking gold." My palate tingles with the memory. "The champagne they serve behind these hallowed doors dances on your tongue. When you swallow, it tickles all the way down, and infuses your entire body with happiness." The sensation sparkles through me. "Oh, here's the turn."

Louise tweaks Felix's long ears, which rotate, listening for sounds even with his eyes closed.

Vasnier glances down at them. "I've never seen a cat like that.

What do you call it, Mademoiselle?"

"Felix is a matagot." Louise lifts him by his front legs, his lanky body dangling.

Vasnier snorts and scoots away. "Matagots are known killers. You must get rid of him."

"Felix was a gift from a friend," I say, thinking back to Madame Clicquot.

"Friend or foe?" Vasnier rattles the reins.

"He's a good mouser, at least." I laugh nervously.

"Those clouds look mighty black ahead," he says. "How long will we be in Chigny?"

"Not long, I just need to check on things," I say.

Undulating forests and thickets surround the wide vineyards of the Champagne. Beau crosses the rotting wooden bridge in desperate need of repair. His hooves pummel the jutted dirt road, which needs leveling and gravel if I don't want the road to turn into a river in the next rain. The gig drops into a pothole, and Beau rears up and whinnies, wild-eyed. Louise cries out, and I grab her and Felix to my chest. It feels like our wheel broke with the jolt. But Vasnier keeps a steady hand and pats Beau's flank. Soon, he has us climbing the hill.

Through the beech trees, I catch glimpses of the cottage.

"Looks like a chalet," Vasnier says. "Tall sloping roofs, French doors."

"Louis left the design to me." A branch has fallen and broken the dining room window. Louis would have fixed that, now I'll have to figure it out on my own.

My chest tightens as Vasnier parks the gig, happiness and sadness wrestling for control. I haven't been here without Louis. Must stop thinking that: first time without Louis. Too much heartache.

Vasnier lifts Louise with Felix's basket off the gig. Walking the few steps to the walnut double doors, I insert the skeleton key and the door creaks open.

Louise runs past me holding Felix. "Papa, Papa, where are you?" She runs down the main hall, peering in each doorway. Her guileless voice punches my gut.

"Louise, come here."

She runs to me, her beautiful face pinched. "Where is Papa, Maman?"

Stuffing down my emotion, I kneel beside her. "He's in heaven, Rosebud." I take her hands and kiss her dimpled knuckles. "You know that, don't you?"

"But Papa said Chigny was heaven." She glances around.

"Ah, *mon ange*." My angel. I take her cheeks in my hands. "Papa went to God's heaven."

Her bottom lip protrudes.

"This is our heaven, where we can feel Papa around us if we try."

She tilts her head and considers my words.

I place my hand on her heart. "Can you feel him here?"

She nods fervently, and the matagot jumps out of his basket. "Felix!" She chases after him.

"Keep away from the glass," I call after her. "There's a broken window."

Vasnier and I follow them into the long salon and see there are two broken windows, one on each side of the four French doors. The tarps that cover all the furniture are stained with water and birds. I don't want to see the damage underneath.

Vasnier moves to the French doors. "This view is like a painting." He gazes out to the greening vineyards, grazing sheep, and duck pond on the hill across. "These floors are a work of art." He sweeps his boot toe across the pattern. "I would not have expected craftsmanship like this out here in the country."

"My heart was set on herringbone parquet, so Louis joked the floors were my twentieth anniversary present." I chuckle. "I asked for crown moldings, too."

His hearty laugh echoes through the empty rooms, and he covers his mouth.

"Not a problem. There's always a lot of laughter here in Chigny."

He explores the ceilings, the wrought-iron spiral staircase to the second floor, the granite fireplace. "The architecture is extraordinary."

"I made separate drawings of the detail work, and Louis found the craftsmen."

"Is there something I can use to cover that window?" he says.

"There might be tarps in the shed." I start outside for them, but he holds up his palm.

"Allow me." He heads out back.

Anxious to see how my roses fared through a year of neglect, I open the French doors which lead out to the terrace. Spiny shoots are overgrown, dotted with black spots of fungus, and crawling with aphids. "Positively disreputable," I utter. Last time we were here, Louise was an infant in a basket beside me as I pruned roses. She giggled and cooed at the butterflies flouncing from blossom to blossom.

Felix brushes past my skirt, and Louise chases him into the meadow as fast as her chubby legs will carry her.

"Stay where I can see you," I call after her.

A dark shelf of clouds roils over the vineyards like a tidal wave. The Marne and Vesle rivers turn black and choppy where they come together, transforming their charm into something sinister. A gust of wind nearly knocks me down. Splats of freezing rain pelt my face. Louise is nowhere in sight.

"Louise, we should go," I call out, but the wind steals my voice away. Raindrops splat on the terrace.

A blood-curdling shriek from the bushes.

"Louise." I run toward the scream.

She sobs and points at barren rose stems with hundreds of cocoons hanging from them.

"Coffins, Maman," she wails. Rivulets of rain pour down her face.

Indeed, the translucent cocoons resemble the organdy that shrouded Louis. "Those are cocoons. Cocoons protect caterpillars during the winter so they can turn into butterflies in the spring. Remember butterflies?"

Vasnier runs across the garden with his Sunday jacket sheltering his head from the sudden rain. "We should go, or we won't get down that road in the downpour."

A bolt of lightning splits the sky. Louise cries out and I pick her up. Icy hail pummels our heads, and her cries become screams.

Vasnier covers us with his jacket and leads us through the hail. When we get inside, Louise is wet and whimpering. Frozen hair dangles from her head in icicles, and I rub it gently with a linen towel. Tarps cover the broken windows. Vasnier worked fast.

"We can't leave yet," he says. "I'll make a fire." Setting wood in the hearth, he strikes a friction match to ignite it.

I bring Louise close to the fire and sit in one of the large tarp-covered chairs. Vasnier sets out pots from the kitchen to catch the leaks.

A shrill wind blows through the tarps and Louise shrieks anew. "Fe-e-e-lix. I want Felix."

Vasnier kneels at my feet, face to face with Louise. "Did you know that matagots are escape artists? They love to disappear. But if you have treated Felix well, he will always return to you." He takes a handkerchief from the pocket of his Sunday suit and dries her cheeks.

"But where did he go?" she asks.

He shrugs. *"Donner sa langue au chat."* I give my tongue to the cat. I have no idea.

In an hour, the sun shines bright again. We call for Felix everywhere, but he does not answer.

"We should get home before nightfall," I tell him.

"I want Felix." Louise starts to cry.

Vasnier scoops her up in his arms. "Remember what I told you. A matagot would never abandon a nice girl like you."

He puts her in the gig between us and wraps her with a blanket. She's asleep by the time we get to Epernay.

"I think I can sell the spindles and looms to Hubinet's dressmaking shop," I tell Vasnier. "That should get us started with the winery. You will stay to help me with the winery, won't you, Monsieur?"

He sighs. "I will stay to help liquidate the wool business. That will give you time to reconsider taking on a winery."

"Thank you, Monsieur." I squeeze his hand before I realize what I am doing.

5

Avoir d'autres chats à fouetter

To have other cats to whip

I slip into Saint Remi Abbey for mass with the orphans, always soothing to my soul. Children kneel on the pews, heads bowed, as Père Andre prays for them. Left on the church steps as infants, these children have never known parents. Many come from the Alhambra brothel. No place for children there. Some have been given up by parents who can't afford to keep them. Some of their parents died of sickness or war. Without parents, these children are left to learn strength and values from the orphanage. Rules that serve as the backbone of their lives.

"Your maid told me I could find you here." Madame DuBois sits beside me, smelling of lavender powder I gave her at Christmas.

"I'm sorry I haven't seen you." My shoulders fall inward, laden with guilt. "I've been trying to sort out the business. I haven't even been to the orphanage for weeks."

"That's just what I came to tell you." She pats my hand. "Madame Werle took over your duties managing the tasks for the orphanage."

A deserved blow to my ribs. "She's always wanted to be boss, and now she has her chance. What about the etiquette lessons? And servant training?"

"Don't worry about a thing. It's time to focus on you for a change."

"But how will the volunteers know my curriculum?" The nuns in front of us turn around disapprovingly.

"We've been assisting you for twenty years, Madame," she whispers.

Morning light streams through the rose window as the orphans sing a hymn.

I put my hand up to shield my mouth. "What about their lessons?"

She waves her hand. "That young teacher from Paris is teaching them reading and writing."

I lift a finger in the air. "They need simple arithmetic for service in fine houses."

"I'll make sure of it." She pats my hand. "You must take care of your family now, Madame, and let the auxiliary take care of the orphanage."

I grasp Madame DuBois's hand in gratitude. "Tell the ladies I'll be back as soon as I can."

At the end of the service, the altar boy in his long white robe snuffs out the candles. Bird boy.

"Do you know anything about that boy?" I ask her as we walk out together.

"You mean the pale boy? All I know is that he lives with the monks." She kisses my cheeks goodbye. "We will not let you down, Madame. The orphanage is in good hands."

After twenty years of creating a safe place for these children, it will pain me not to be there daily, but I must focus on the winery if I am really going to make it happen.

Leaving the bliss of the sanctuary, I walk briskly to Father Pieter's office to offer the altar boy a job.

One night, I'm reading to Louise in the nursery, while Lucille folds her laundry. We hear a loud knock downstairs, and Lucille runs to answer it. A deep voice filters up the staircase, followed by a hellish screeching.

Louise clutches my wrist, wild-eyed. Picking her up, I tiptoe down the stairs in my robe and nightcap. The horrific sounds come from behind the kitchen door. Lucille and a man argue, and that awful shrieking makes Louise clap her hands over her ears. I hold my finger to my mouth to hush her whimpering. I can't leave Lucille alone with an intruder, so I shove open the door to take them by surprise.

Lucille pours milk in a saucer on the table, while Henry Vasnier clutches a thrashing creature with a tiny triangular face. His enormous, peaked ears rivet our direction. He opens his needle-tooth jaw wide and emits the most terrifying scream.

"Felix!" Louise wiggles free and runs to him.

The matagot escapes Vasnier, leaps to the table, and laps up the milk. Louise stretches her arm up to him, and he hisses and arches his back.

"Felix, it's me."

Lucille places a chicken leg by the milk, and Felix tears into it with ferocity.

"Where did he come from?" I ask Vasnier.

"I've been going back to Chigny to find him. Today I finally caught him."

The matagot's gold-flecked eyes watch Louise as he demolishes the chicken.

I hold her back. "Stay back, Rosebud. He's wild."

"Felix, don't you remember me?" Louise asks.

He crouches at the edge of the table and springs at her.

I screen her face. "No, no, don't hurt her."

She catches him in her arms, and Felix tucks his face into her neck.

"Louise, give him to me. He's been in the country for weeks."

"He was just hungry, Maman." She hugs him. "All he needs is cream and chicken and he's a perfect gentleman."

"Don't put your face close to him, Rosebud. He's been wild and there is no telling what he'll do."

But Felix seems content and purrs on her chest, no longer a ferocious animal. Louise looks up to Vasnier with round eyes. "Thank you for finding him, Monsieur."

I scowl at him. "I'll walk you out." My slippers pad across the tile floor, his footsteps following. "You drove all the way to Chigny to find the matagot?"

"A couple times." He chuckles.

"I'm not sure I should thank you for bringing back that creature."

"Louise loved him so much I thought it would comfort her." He looks down at his bowler. "I'm sorry if I was wrong on that. I've not been around children much."

Of course, he is right, the matagot comforts her. I open the door and step out into the night air, breathing in the night-blooming jasmine that grows on our house.

"Beautiful harvest moon tonight," he says, taking a deep breath.

We watch the giant orange orb rise from the east like a sunrise.

"So, it looks like you are staying with us for the harvest?" I ask.

"I couldn't leave it to you to do alone," he says.

"If it's a good one, maybe I can make enough money to buy out Greno."

He tips his bowler. "We'll do our best."

"Well, I should go see what havoc the matagot created." I step inside and pause. "He's yours if he acts up again."

"I figured as much." He puts on his bowler and waves as he leaves. "*Bonne nuit*, Madame." He whistles a tune as he walks toward the rising moon.

Henry Vasnier and half a dozen men dance about in a large vat of grapes, singing and raising their knees high, plunging them down, spattering purple juice on the planked floor like impressionist paint- ers. The men punch each other on the shoulder, swigging wine and splashing each other in some Bacchanalian ritual to which women should never be subjected.

Rage rushes through me like a geyser. "Monsieur Vasnier, what is the meaning of this folderol? Your boss is barely in the grave, and you treat him with such disrespect as to dance in his wine?"

They look at each other, caught in the act. None of them move a muscle.

"Get out of that vat and clean this up," I tell them. "I should fire you all on the spot."

Vasnier lifts his purple-stained foot out of the vat and climbs down the side. The rest of the men watch dumbfounded, not moving. When he reaches the floor, he turns back to the men. "You heard what Madame Pommery said, mop up the floor."

They start to climb down.

"A word, Monsieur Vasnier." I gesture to Louis's office. I have a mind to grab his ear and lead him there myself, make an example of the young man. Louis told me how smart and industrious Vasnier was, hoping his enthusiasm would rub off on our son. It never did. Louis had his mind set on becoming a lawyer to fight for the working class.

"What was going on out there?" I stand behind Louis's rolltop, which is covered with stacks of papers I still need to resolve.

Vasnier clears his throat. "The harvest starts with stomping the first grapes of the season." His eyebrows arch, waiting for the facts to penetrate my mind.

"With a dance?"

"I thought it strange the first time I saw it, but it gets the men excited for the tremendous amount of work ahead of them." He clamps his lips together.

My hand flies to my forehead. "Oh. Let me go apologize."

"Oh, no, Madame. No need to apologize." He waves his hand. "We were getting carried away. Since you sold off all the wool equipment, the men have been extremely nervous whether you will close the winery. With the slump in France, jobs are very hard to come by."

Looking out of Louis's office door, I watch the crew mopping the floors. "Who oversees wine production? I should talk to the supervisor."

"Your husband was the boss, Madame, no one else. He issued the orders."

I feel so foolish and helpless. "What would Louis tell you to do next?"

"Same as you did," Vasnier says, smiling. "Clean up the mess and get ready for the next wagon load."

I nod slowly, a plan forming. "Follow me."

Standing with Vasnier on the grape-press platform, I summon the confidence to address our twenty-three *ouvriers*—the workers.

39

Faces are pinched with fear, as if I am the henchman, and they will climb the gallows. They've been worried about losing their jobs since Louis passed.

"You have been a faithful crew while I sorted through Pommery business," I say. "I appreciate your patience and loyalty through the years. I understand how difficult this has been. But things have changed. Louis is gone. Monsieur Greno has retired." My breath stutters, my lungs ache with emotion too close to the surface. I must be strong. "And the French economy is sluggish as coal tar."

Their heads drop to their chests, as if it's time to slip the noose around their necks. A few *ouvriers* start to take off their aprons.

"Wait." I hold up my palm. "I'm not finished. I am not selling the winery, no matter what rumors you've heard on the streets. But there will be changes." I point to Vasnier beside me. "Monsieur Vasnier is our new operations manager, and I will focus on sales and marketing."

One of the cellarmen, Leo Thomas, takes off his Phrygian cap and balls it up in his hands. "Henry Vasnier is wet behind the ears, and you have no idea how to make wine. All your profits will be eaten up. The shipments can be lost or stolen. Wagons can tip over. France has heavy export taxes, and each country we ship to adds taxes and fees."

"Monsieur Vasnier has assisted my husband for a couple years. I have the utmost confidence in him to manage the operation." I nod to Thomas. "But you sound like you have invaluable experience in logistics."

"Not sure about logistics, but I know how to ship wine."

"So, you read, Monsieur Thomas?"

His stubbled cheeks color. "No, ma'am."

"We could change that if you like." I raise my arms to the group. "If you decide to stay, we need to improve our efficiency and safety protocols. Including one hard and fast rule: no drinking on the job."

Les ouvriers look at each other for reactions. Grunts and sweat scent the air.

I hold up my finger. "But I will insist on wine tastings every Friday afternoon to educate ourselves and take pride in the wine we are making."

"You think I need lessons in wine after thirty years in the business?" Simon jerks his apron off and throws it on the worktable.

He points his meaty finger at *les ouvriers*. "A woman boss is twice as tough as any man, and twice as picky. I quit Veuve Clicquot because of her unreasonable standards, and I will not suffer that again." He stomps past me and out the door. Half a dozen men follow him. The rest look as if they're thinking about it.

"You may leave now if you have doubts." I gesture toward the door.

A dozen or so leave; their eyes avoid me as they walk out.

"All right, then," I say to *les ouvriers* who remain. "This is our team. This will not be easy, but I am confident we can make this winery successful."

I utter a prayer to my Smiling Angel to give me courage.

6

COÛTER LES YEUX DE LA TÊTE

To cost the eyes of your head

1859. By springtime, I've taken over Louis's office, where I can keep an eye on our crew starting to blend and bottle wine, the aromas of grapes thick in the air. I finger the worn places in the leather where Louis's arms used to rest. Did I truly appreciate all that he did for our family? Not only selling wool, but making wine to earn more money? He never complained.

Glancing at the watch on my chatelaine, I have a couple of hours yet. I suppose Louis meant the chatelaine to be a compliment: a woman in charge of her household. The only thing a woman can oversee since the Napoleonic Code prohibits women from owning a business. The only exception is that a widow can own a business. Strange consolation for losing one's husband, I'd say.

I pull the rubber thimble on my forefinger and dig into these bills. Did Louis know how many were piling up? There is a substantial outlay of cash before the wine is even bottled, let alone sold. I'm grateful Hubinet's brother purchased our wool equipment, or we'd never be able to pay these bills.

Through the office door, I see Henry Vasnier siphoning a barrel of red wine from the Bouzy vineyards into bottles. He hands each bottle down the line, though, for the life of me, I can't see why it takes seven men to bottle wine. Our production line reminds me of a bumbling puppet show I saw in Paris, mechanical and slow but amusing, nonetheless. About seven minutes, beginning to end. No wonder there is not much money in wine.

A red-mustachioed man takes an empty bottle out of a crate and hands it to Vasnier, who places it under the barrel spigot operated by our wispy-haired new employee, Damas, the boy from Saint Remi Abbey. When the bottle is full, another worker hands it off to a skinny man in torn overalls, who walks it to a short man wearing a Phrygian cap, and so on and so forth.

When the bottle finally reaches the end of the bottling line, a burly, white-bearded man stores it on a rack, telling jokes the whole time. "One guy says to the next guy: 'I slept with my wife before we were married, did you?' The next guy answers, 'I don't know, what was her maiden name?'"

As the crew slap their knees and guffaw, the white-bearded man swigs from a wine jug.

This will never do. I walk into the cellar, my boot heels clicking on the stone floor. All eyes turn to me, the laughing stops, and suddenly I feel foolish inserting myself into their brotherhood, which certainly does not include a woman. Especially a woman boss.

"Good morning, gentlemen."

The bearded man on the bottling line steps sideways to hide the jug behind him. Only, his aim is off. The jug tips off the edge of the table and falls to the stone floor. Chards of crockery fly in all directions, and red wine splashes all over my dress.

Henry Vasnier blushes red from his cheeks to the tips of his ears. "Where did that jug come from?" he questions the men.

The bearded man steps behind the others.

Vasnier stoops to pick up the shards. "Who was drinking on the job?"

The bearded man slips out the front door.

"What does this do?" I ask Damas, the altar boy. My hand rests on the curved top of the iron contraption that looks like a torture machine.

He pulls his Phrygian cap low over his eyebrows. Is he embarrassed, intimidated, or rude?

"Show me how it works," I say again.

44

Vasnier bends over, looking him in the eyes and exaggerating his words. "Madame Pommery would like to see how you use the cork machine."

Still, he doesn't answer.

"Is something the matter?" I ask.

"The boy is a deaf-mute, Madame."

I scoff. "Why didn't Father Pieter mention that when I offered the job? How is he working out?"

"He's smart. Look how he has mastered the corking machine." Vasnier sets a full wine bottle on the stand and nods. The boy pulls down the lever with two hands, and the contraption squeezes the cork into the neck. He holds up the corked bottle and grins at me with teeth rotting around the edges.

"Well done," I say, but the boy doesn't answer. I turn to Vasnier. "I thought we mostly sell wine by the barrel."

"A Frenchman can afford a bottle easier than a barrel with the French economy doing so poorly."

"What can you do to speed up the bottling line?" I ask.

He turns to the men. "You heard Madame Pommery. Let's show her our best work." The crew moves faster, several bottles in the line simultaneously. No jokes, no laughter, and their rhythm quickens.

"Excellent, Monsieur Vasnier." I throw him a thumbs up. "Let's keep up the pace."

He smiles under his lush mustache, and I know I can count on him. As I walk back to my office, I hear a strange, curdling gurgle. Damas grunts and growls and holds his eye.

I run to him. "What is it? What happened?"

The lever of the machine is broken off in his hand. But that is not the problem. His fingers over his eyes widen, revealing a cork embedded in his eye socket. He shrieks like a wild animal in a trap.

"Get a doctor," I shout to Vasnier.

"He's an orphan," Vasnier says. "He can't afford a doctor."

"I'll pay," I say. "Fetch Doctor DuBois."

By the time we get the boy settled in the window seat in the kitchen, his face has swollen around the cork. He shivers something

45

fierce, and his teeth start to chatter. I wrap a blanket around him, tucking it around his chin.

Lucille brings Louise and Felix into the kitchen for a treat.

Louise's eyes bug wide when she sees the boy. *"Enfant oiseau."* Bird boy.

He smiles lopsidedly at her, holding ice on his injured eye.

Vasnier brings in Doctor DuBois carrying his worn leather medical bag. His jaunty upturned collar and paisley cravat set off a perfectly tailored suit, unlike most frumpy doctors in Reims. After Louis died, the doctor checked on me daily for the ache around my heart. He prescribed Parfait Amour, a liqueur of curaçao, almonds, orange blossoms, and rose petals which he mixed with champagne.

"What's your name, son?" DuBois asks the patient.

"His name is Damas," I tell him. "He's deaf and mute, apparently."

"Let me take a look." DuBois tries to pry his hand away, but the boy whimpers.

Louise brings him Felix. "You want to pet him?" She takes his hand and gently strokes the matagot.

I can't help but gasp at the bruised swell around the cork. Before I know it, DuBois sure-handedly yanks the cork from the socket. But Damas still strokes the matagot.

"It's okay, Lucille, you can leave Louise with me."

She tucks a strand of black hair into her mop cap. "I'll be in the nursery if you need me."

The doctor douses a cloth with clear liquid that smells sharp and medicinal. "I'm going to clean around your eye," he tells Damas. "It will hurt, but it needs to be done to avoid infection."

Reaching for a wooden spoon, I mime biting down, and hand it to Damas. "Put this between your teeth."

DuBois bandages the eye and wraps gauze around the boy's head to hold it in place.

Louise chatters three-year-old nonsense to Damas about the magic of matagots, and he watches her as if he's listening to every word.

"I'll take him back to Saint Remi Abbey," the doctor says.

"I'll walk him back after supper. I want to tell Father Pieter."

He packs his bag and I walk him to the door.

"I need to prepare you, Madame Pommery. The boy will likely lose his eye."

My shoulders collapse. "There must be something we can do."

"Keep ice on it and pray." He huffs. "The winery business is dangerous. I told Louis he should give it up when his heart started failing."

"He never said anything about his heart."

DuBois shakes his head. "He never wanted you to worry. Especially after you got pregnant. Maybe if he listened to me, he'd still be here." He dons a stylish beaver-fur hat and strides out with a wave. "I'll be back tomorrow to change the dressing."

The weight of his words settles heavy on my shoulders as I return to the children.

Damas gazes at Louise with his good eye as if she is the magical creature.

Father Pieter answers the door to the abbey under the dwarf beech tree. "What happened to him?" The priest shelters him with his arm.

"There was an accident with the cork machine, and a cork flew into his eye," I tell him, reliving that awful event in my mind. "I am so sorry, Father." I tilt my head to the side. "May I speak with you privately?"

He grasps Damas's shoulders and speaks to him directly. "Go to bed, say your prayers, and I'll check on you in the morning."

The boy walks down the hall, then turns around and lifts his hand goodbye.

"Good night," I say, as he disappears into the shadows. "I have more bad news, I'm afraid. Doctor DuBois says he may lose that eye."

His face turns ashen. Looking up at the stars he mutters, "Lord of Heaven, have mercy."

"I'm sorry, Father. I will pay for his doctor bills, of course. And whatever else I can do for him."

"The boy has struggled with life since he was abandoned on our doorstep." Father Pieter's eyes water with sorrow. "He did not need this setback. A deaf-mute with one eye will have no chance to find a job."

I swallow the lump in my throat. "Of course, Damas will have a job at Pommery for as long as he wants."

7

AVEC UN PEAU D'AIDE DE VOS AMIS

With a little help from your friends

1860. Despite my prayers, Damas loses the eye. My heart sinks to realize the enormity of his loss when he has so little. Doctor DuBois fits him with an eyepatch and raises the looking glass for Damas. Standing behind him, I place my hands on his shoulders. His delicate fingertips pat the edges of the patch. Then, remarkably, his thin lips quirk up at the ends, like he rather approves of his dramatic new look.

Henry Vasnier takes it upon himself to teach Damas everything he knows about the actual wine making—all tasks one senses by smell and taste. Vasnier wisely keeps him away from bottling and corking so not to traumatize him about the accident. Over the next months, Damas discovers how to use his nose and tongue to great advantage in his new duties.

In December, Louis writes me a letter. He's been invited to Scotland by a classmate for the holidays. He won't be coming home. My hands drop to my lap, and I stare at his signature until it blurs.

This empty disappointment must be what Maman felt when I didn't come home for the holidays. Friends at my finishing schools would invite me to their Scottish castles with servants, elegant parties, Christmas fairs, sleigh rides, and snow-sculpture competitions. After that first trip to Scotland, I never considered a sedate Christmas with Maman and my aunties.

Louise and I spend Christmas at Saint Remi Abbey with Damas and the orphans decorating a fir tree with popcorn and apples for birds. That night, we light candles and sing Christmas carols until all the candles are nothing but puddles of wax.

The next day, I break protocol and telegraph Narcisse Greno that I am coming to visit him in Paris for the New Year.

At Greno's brownstone, Louise and I are met by a butler with a pencil-thin mustache. His nostrils twerk as if he smells something distasteful. "Monsieur Greno expected you hours ago."

"We had to take a later train," I explain. "The first one was filled." There was no way to message him of the change, but I assumed he would understand.

Louise whines and pulls my skirt, wanting me to pick her up. She's cranky from the five-hour train ride from Reims and the carriage ride from *la gare*. The butler takes our coats and goes off to tell Narcisse we've arrived.

I see why he loves it here with his sister. The apartment is old-world Parisian with tall ceilings, cream-on-cream plaster walls, and layers of crown moldings, yet the art on the walls reveal a taste for the avant-garde.

Greno steps down the spiral staircase sideways, favoring his right hip, gripping the railing with white knuckles. He looks as though he's aged a decade instead of a year. I have noticed his penmanship getting smaller and smaller on orders he sends me. And of late, the orders have dwindled entirely. I don't complain since I'm grateful he hasn't asked us to sell the business.

I kiss his ruddy cheeks three times in *la bise*.

"Two kisses in Paris, Alexandrine," he says too loudly, scowling at Louise. "You brought your daughter?"

I press my hand to my chest. "Oh, Narcisse, I thought you'd be pleased to see your goddaughter." Clearly, he is not.

"Isn't it common courtesy to let the host know you're bringing a guest?" He strokes his goatee.

He's right. I can see the page in front of my eyes, plain as day. What possessed me of late? I am ashamed not to have thought of it.

Greno bends over and tweaks Louise's nose with his knuckle. She grabs his mustachio and yanks it with her fist. "Is that real?"

"What the devil?" He jerks away and pats it back into place.

"Louise, remember what we said about your hands?" I crouch down and lace her tiny fingers between mine. "Hands are to stay by your side and not bother others."

Greno assesses her from above his half-glasses. "She has eyes like a whiting fish."

I turn his criticism into a compliment. "She does have big eyes, doesn't she?" I say, holding her close.

The butler carries one of our four trunks up the narrow spiral stairs.

Greno pokes a crooked finger at him. "Change Madame Pommery's room to the Bluebird Suite next to the nursery."

"Yes, sir," he yells and continues up the staircase with a stained-glass dome at the top.

A young footman brings in ten cases of Pommery red wine. "Where shall I put these, sir?" the youngster shouts at Greno.

"My heavens. Take them to the cellar." Narcisse scratches his long sideburn. "Are you moving in?"

"A guest is never to arrive empty-handed." I use a cheerful voice I save for cranky children and crotchety old men.

"What am I supposed to do with all that wine you brought?"

"One case for your sister, one case for you, and you can sell the rest. We need the sales, quite honestly."

He grumbles under his breath as he totters into the parlor, his exotic bamboo cane tapping the tile floor. The parlor is even more sumptuous than the foyer. Louis XV tufted settees flank a low oval table inlaid with burlwood and rose marble. Dramatic landscape paintings elevate the French countryside to dreamlike beauty. Some painting styles I recognize from past Paris exhibitions: Goyet, Rousseau, Delacroix.

"Your sister must be quite the patron of the arts," I say. "I miss our Sundays on Reims Square looking at the art, meeting the artists."

"All things come to an end." Falling into the settee, he reaches for his ear trumpet and inserts it into his ear.

Louise sucks on two fingers, staring at the strange one-horned man.

I whisper to her, "The horn makes him hear better."

"You'll have to take that wine back with you when you leave," he says loudly. "Selling wine now is like threading a camel through the eye of a needle since Napoleon raised taxes to pay for his new warship, the *Gloire*."

"Oh, Monsieur, is that what the new excise tax is all about? A warship?" Embarrassed by the sound of Louise's sucking, I take her slobbery fingers out of her mouth and hold her hand.

Greno pays no mind to us and pokes a feather wand into the horn repeatedly, then screws it back into his ear.

"Wolfe delivered a tax bill for ten thousand francs." I try to pick up the conversation. "Is there any way to avoid it?"

"I'm afraid that's just the beginning of extra taxes," he says. "Now that Napoleon has a new ship, war cannot be far behind." He gestures to the dewy ice bucket. "Would you mind pouring the champagne?"

"Ah, Narcisse, how kind of you to remember how I love champagne." I take the bottle from the silver bucket and push out the cork with my thumbs, a perfect pouf and mist of fruity fragrance.

"Why were you so late?" he says. "You've always had impeccable manners."

Louise's eyes are glued to his ear trumpet, and there's no discreet way to distract her.

"I apologize for our tardiness." I pour the champagne into the etched coupe glasses. "The train was full for the holidays."

"Didn't you tell me it was your mother who cultivated your good manners?" He takes the coupe from me.

"Upon pain of death." I laugh and wait for him to make the toast.

"*Au santé*," he says, his rheumy eyes searching for mine. "May the new year be better than the last."

Not the sunniest of toasts. He drinks, and I follow suit, the sweet, icy champagne reviving me after my first train ride, which was strange and fast compared to a carriage.

Louise tears her stare from Greno and glances around the room. The Fortuny lampshades and swagged draperies, the velvet footstools, and enameled brass peacock spreading its feathers in front of the fire. I almost see wheels turning in her brain.

"Your sister's home is breathtaking," I say. "Will she be joining us?"

"She is visiting her grown children in the Alps. We have the entire house to ourselves." He takes another sip, ear trumpet in one hand, glass in the other.

"So you were alone at Christmas too," I say. "Louis spent Christmas in Scotland. To be honest, this trip is just what we needed." I pat Louise's leg, and her delicate fingers touch the Murano glass ornaments in a bowl.

Greno frowns. "She takes after your husband with those eyes." His own eyes water as he sips from his glass.

Louis's enormous eyes were what I first noticed when my maman brought me to meet him. His warm brown eyes and quiet confidence, so unlike my Scottish friends. Louis did not need a noble title or to brag about his impressive heritage, or how much property he owned. He was an established wool merchant from Reims, a friend of a friend. A suitable match, Maman assured me, though I knew she'd do anything to marry me off. She expected me to marry a nobleman, and when it did not work out, she was humiliated. Reputation was always foremost in her mind.

Louise ventures over to the glass menagerie of animals on a round table. Greno drops his ear trumpet, pushes himself up, and moves the tray of animals out of reach.

"Mustn't touch, Louise," I scold her.

She points up to the mantel. "Felix?"

I laugh. "She has a matagot named Felix we left at home."

"Should have left Louise to tend the matagot." He chuckles.

"Narcisse, she is your goddaughter," I say.

He ignores me, fiddling with his ear trumpet, turning it this way and that.

A cheerful woman in a black uniform and pressed apron comes into the parlor and curtseys. "Good evening. I am Madame Laurent, the housekeeper. I wonder if our little miss would like a cup of hot chocolate and some madeleines in the dining room. Afterwards, I can run a bath."

"Yes, please. Yes, please." Louise runs to her, never one to ask permission, preferring to charge ahead.

The housekeeper looks to me.

"It's fine. Thank you Madame Laurent."

"She's got as much energy as you."

I finish my champagne, and would like another, but a guest is never to help themselves. "May I serve you, Monsieur?" I walk to the champagne bucket.

Like a man used to servants, he holds out his glass and I pour.

"Wolfe offered to buy out your partnership in the winery," I say, not as in control of myself as I think. "But I turned him down."

"I wondered how long it would take that Boche to circle around," Greno says. "Wolfe has been trying to buy us out for years. Like every banker who sits behind a desk and counts other people's money, he thinks our business would be a roaring success if he was running it."

His gruff tone surprises me.

"How much did Wolfe offer?" His cloudy eyes search my lips, even though he holds his ear trumpet.

"He never mentioned an amount. Why?" I ask.

He consults his pocket watch. "We have a dinner party in an hour. Can you be ready, or should I send my regrets?"

All I want is a hot bath and go to bed. "Can Louise come?"

"Alexandrine, you have been in the country too long. Paris is for adults. Madame Laurent will stay with her."

I hear them singing "Alouette" together in the kitchen.

I rise and head to the staircase. "Then, I better change." I pause on the landing. "Where is my room?"

"Second door on the right. Hurry, I don't want to be late."

Halfway up the staircase, I hear him curse. "Damn it all to hell." A thud and crack. More cursing.

Running down to the landing, I see Greno with an iron poker, pushing his ear trumpet under the crackling logs.

When I return to the parlor, Greno is dressed in his black cashmere overcoat and silk top hat, and has his ebony cane but no ear trumpet. Not a trace of his former anguish.

He holds out his free arm. "You look stunning, Alexandrine. You really do. I'm honored to be your date this evening. Every man's eyes will be on you."

The butler opens the door, and there is a burgundy and gold cabriolet carriage waiting.

"This is Paris, Alexandrine. Paris," he emphasizes with the old twinkle in his eye. "Maybe for tonight, we can dispense with the rules."

"Touché." I feel a girlish smile spread to my cheeks.

The first week passes in a scintillating blur of dinner parties at the most prestigious restaurants in Paris: Le Procope, La Tour d'Argent, Au Chien Qui Fume. Greno is in his element here.

Gossipmongers buzz about the new Paris orchestrated by Napoleon's architect Georges-Eugène Haussmann. They moved out the poor from the crowded city center and tore it down. A new Paris emerges from the rubble, making way for a rebirth of art, music, and inventions.

The bristling energy sets my mind spinning like the whirligig I buy Louise from a street vendor. How can I use my talents and education to make Pommery into something quite extraordinary?

Focused on gaining new customers for Pommery, I break another etiquette rule—never bring wine to a dinner party, because it insults the host. I wrap the bottles of my newest Pommery red wine in the finest tissue I can find and present them to every host and restaurateur we visit. They ask about Pommery: where the grapes are grown, when we harvest, the process of making the wine. They ask to visit Pommery, just a five-hour train ride from Paris.

Before the week is finished, I've sold the five cases I brought and take orders to ship. My bulging money bag will allow me to pay the new excise tax and make the next mortgage payment.

Greno is dumbfounded. "You have sold more wine this week than I sold all last year."

"We make a great team, you and I." His contacts are invaluable.

He hands me an engraved invitation with a gold bee at the top. "Can you extend your stay?"

"The Royal New Year Party at the Tuileries?" My chest tingles. "Oh my. Emperor Napoleon and Empress Eugenie? How did you get an invitation?"

"I play faro with Ambassador Casimir-Perier. He introduced me to the royal wine steward. In fact, they will be serving Pommery wine at the party."

The heel of my hand flies against my forehead. "But I brought nothing to wear, and there is no time for a dressmaker."

Greno sighs wearily. "It's all right, *chérie*. I could use the rest after this week. The holidays wear me out."

"Oh, no, Monsieur Greno, we can't possibly give up a royal party. Where is the nearest fabric and trimmings store?"

8

ÊTRE TIRÉ À QUATRE ÉPINGLES

To be dressed up to the nines

The Pavillon de l'Horloge's Roman numeral clock releases a single gong that reverberates through the ballroom. Hundreds of guests turn to the entrance to see the empress and emperor arrive, but when there are no fanfare trumpets, no guards, no royal procession, we are sorely disappointed.

I tap my jeweled toe. "They are an hour late," I tell Greno. "The guests of honor should never be late."

"You wish we ate?"

Ah, it will be a long evening without his ear trumpet. I speak into his ear. "I said, Napoleon is late."

"Royalty takes privilege, my dear." A waiter serves us coupes of champagne.

Finally, one hundred bugles announce the royal arrival. The doorman bellows through his brass speaking trumpet. "Her Imperial Excellency, the Empress Eugenie."

The crowd jostles forward, trying to get a glimpse. My first sight of the empress sends shivers down my spine. Standing atop the wide staircase, the empress gleams in gold taffeta trimmed with tassels and bold black bows. Her skirts and stiff crinolines puff out wider than Marie Antoinette's, making her waist appear as tiny as a wasp's. Her bodice falls low on her shoulders, her olive complexion is set off with strands and strands of glistening pearls. Seed pearls coil her brunette hair and wind down her bare back. The empress single-handedly revitalized fashion and extravagance of the king's courts.

I speak into Greno's ear. "Where is Napoleon?"

The empress glides into the ballroom followed by eight ladies-in-waiting in gowns in colors of sunrise, from peach to fuchsia.

I pray I am not underdressed. While the empress's gown is bold as the sun, my creation is the moon and stars. All I'd packed were half-mourning gowns, but in the trimmings shop, I searched through ribbons, laces, and trims until I uncovered a bolt of purple tulle studded with rhinestones like Scheherazade in *Arabian nights*. With needle and thread, I swathed the tulle across my shoulders and down my back like gossamer wings of a dragonfly. Next, I braided marcasite beads into my dark hair and wound it into a sophisticated chignon. I may not hold a candle to the empress, but I have attracted many a stare. *Never outshine the host.*

"The empress is stunning," I tell Greno behind my peacock-feather fan.

"Unbecoming?" he squints. "She does have a long nose, but her other qualities make up for it. Empress Eugenie is clever, educated, and an advocate for women. In fact, the two of you have a lot in common. She founded an orphanage as well."

The trumpets blare again. Napoleon marches in dressed in striking military uniform and flanked by soldiers. He trips on the royal carpet and blunders into the crowd. His soldiers pick him up and brush him off. He proceeds to the reception line and stumbles over his boots. The soldiers assist him to stand by the empress. She turns away from the crowd and orders them to remove the emperor, which they do quickly.

"What is wrong with him?" I say in Greno's ear.

"Did you see his oversized pupils? I've heard the emperor likes his opium pipe."

"It's a wonder she puts up with it."

"She is the ruler behind the ruler," Greno says. "She would not give that up."

The empress greets her guests as if nothing has happened, addressing her subjects by name and title. With her sharp nose and long face, she is not a classic beauty, but striking nevertheless.

"She comes from Spain, doesn't she?" I ask.

"Her mother was a Spanish countess," Greno offers. "Louis Napoleon saw her at a Tuileries ball. He could have chosen any foreign princess to forge a beneficial alliance, but he chose her."

The empress reaches us, smelling fresh yet mysterious. Lemon and bergamot?

Greno surprises me by kissing her hand. Bold for a commoner.

"Always so charming, Monsieur Greno." The empress smiles, exposing a crooked eyetooth. "I don't believe I have met your exquisite guest. Is this your daughter?"

"Glad I brought her?" Greno cocks his head, trying to understand.

I dip into a royal curtsey. "Her Imperial Majesty, I am honored." I rise. "I am Madame Pommery, Monsieur Greno's partner in our winery."

"Partner?" She smiles, exposing that wayward tooth. "How fascinating. I understand we are serving Pommery wine at dinner."

"You want us to sit with you at dinner?" Greno winces.

I gasp at his gaff. "My apologies, your Imperial Majesty. Monsieur Greno is not hearing so well tonight. We are sitting with Ambassador Casimir-Perier."

The empress's penciled brows wrinkle. "It seems I will have empty seats at the head table, I would appreciate it if your party would join me."

"We would be delighted," I say.

When royalty asks you to dine with them, the answer must certainly be affirmative.

"Splendid." The empress nods at me, and we've been dismissed.

Greno whisks two champagne coupes from a waiter's tray. The bubbles are strident and taste extremely sugary. Must be Veuve Clicquot, as sweet as it can be. Who can stomach the syrupy stuff? What if there was a lighter, drier champagne?

A silver-haired gentleman with a medaled sash across his chest approaches us. He reaches for Greno's hand with a white glove, but his gaze is fixed solidly on me.

"Ambassador Casimir-Perier, so good to see you again," Greno says.

"This must be your amazing Madame Pommery?" The ambassador grabs my purple gloved hand and brushes his lips across my knuckles. He lingers too long. *A hand kiss should last but a second.*

"May I present my son, Jean Paul Casimir-Perier?" he says.

The boy's cheeks color. He's Louis's age or thereabouts, awkward and reedy.

"How do you do, Jean Paul?" I shake his callused hand, yet he's no laborer.

The boy hides it behind his back.

"Do you live here in Paris?" I try to draw him out.

"We live in London," the ambassador answers for his son. "I'm here in Paris to convince the empress how these incessant wars destroy the French economy."

The young man listens intently to his father. I feel a pang of regret that Louis no longer has a father to guide him. The ambassador stares at me.

"Then you don't agree with the Austrian war," I say.

"Napoleon Bonaparte fought for the noble causes of equality, liberty, and brotherhood," the ambassador says. "But Louis Napoleon fights to pay for the reconstruction of Paris."

The dinner bell rings, and the imperial party proceeds to the Salle des Maréchaux, which is crowned with a gold-leaf dome. Portraits of French marshals, generals, and admirals hang on the ballroom walls. But I am awed by the enormous stone female figures which support the entire mezzanine. The caryatids are stunning with their strong, graceful limbs supporting heaven and earth. I wonder if the architect saw the parallel to Empress Eugenie and all the strong women surfacing in all aspects of French society. Composers, writers, artists. It gives me hope for Louise's future.

A royal valet requests us to follow him. Envious eyes watch us pass through the banquet room to the head table where the empress awaits us.

"I switched your place card to sit next to me." The empress winks a gold-leafed eyelid. "Etiquette gets in the way sometimes, don't you agree?"

I laugh. "Etiquette does not allow me to disagree with you, your Imperial Excellency."

The empress knows she's broken three rules at once:

Rule # 1 Guests of the same gender do not sit next to each other.

Rule #2 The most important guest will be seated to the left of the host.

Rule #3 Place cards must never be switched around to suit.

As it turns out, the ambassador's son is seated next to me. Greno is seated across the table, conversing with Baron Haussmann, Napoleon's city planner, over his broad-busted wife. I can't imagine how Greno is faring without his ear trumpet or me to interpret. The table is so wide I can't hear what they are saying, but whatever it is has Greno agitated.

"I should thank you for saving me from sitting by Baron Haussmann," the empress says, her gaze fixed on the ballroom at large. "I cannot afford to be embroiled in the controversy surrounding him. What is your opinion about the reconstruction of Paris?"

One must never discuss controversial subjects at a party. "I am for the beautification of Paris, Your Imperial Excellency." I high-step through a field of traps. "I only feel it is unfortunate for the thousands of citizens who have been moved out of the city." According to newspaper reports, more than three hundred thousand people have been forced out. Angry, poor people who suffer greatly from being displaced from their jobs and neighborhoods.

"I admit there were sacrifices," she says. "But when Paris is rebuilt, the world will acclaim Paris as the most beautiful city in the world." Her nostrils flare, and her icy glare demands agreement.

The stewards pour Pommery & Greno red wine, a robust blend of Pinot Noir and Meunier from the Bouzy vineyards. Alas, I can never drink red wine because it gives me an instant headache from the harsh tannins of the red grape skins.

On my other side, young Jean Paul Casimir-Perier drinks wine from a silver goblet. My fingers rise from the table to signal him. "We must wait for the toast," I say, saving him from a terrible blunder.

He lowers his goblet to the brocade table runner, and, again, I notice his callused fingers.

"Do you fly a hawk or an eagle?" I ask.

His eyelids narrow. "How did you know?"

"My son is a falconer. I felt your bow-string calluses when we shook hands. Try lanolin to smooth the skin."

He rubs the bump on his finger and makes a face. "My falcon master makes me work with a pitiful kestrel."

"You don't look happy about that."

He screws his mouth to the side. "I want to fly a white gyrfalcon. The largest, most beautiful falcon there is."

"Keep working at it, Jean Paul," I tell him. "And you will fly that white gyrfalcon, I'm sure of it."

The Empress Eugenie stands for a toast, and the trumpets blare. The buzz of conversation falls silent. Everyone stands with glasses raised.

"For our brave soldiers fighting for France, and to Emperor Napoleon for his victories! *Vive la France.*" She holds her glass high, takes a sip, and sits down.

I take my glass to my lips but do not drink, then sit beside her.

"You don't like the wine?" the empress asks. "I thought you'd be pleased we served Pommery & Greno."

Caught in a deception. "I'm afraid red wine gives me a headache."

She levels her gaze. "A winemaker who doesn't like their own wine?" She waves at a waiter. "Veuve Clicquot for Madame Pommery."

I suppress a groan as I've had enough of the sugary stuff. The server pours me a coupe of champagne. Greno raises his glass to me from across the table.

"You must have met Veuve Clicquot since you are from Reims," the empress says.

"Yes, she paid me a visit when my husband passed. A legend in her own time." I take another sip. "Her manager, Edouard Werle, was a pallbearer at my husband's funeral."

Greno strains forward to hear our conversation.

"How long ago?" The empress lifts the jeweled lorgnette and peers at my dress.

"Two years." I feel my cheeks burn. "I am in half-mourning. I know this dress does not follow the rules, but my husband hated me in black."

"Your dress is exquisite. Every eye in the ballroom followed you. Mourning gowns are so pedestrian."

Greno leans across and shouts. "Lesbian? Who is a lesbian?"

All eyes turn our way.

"Pedestrian, Monsieur Greno," I say. "The empress said pedestrian."

Greno turns scarlet. "Please forgive an old man, Your Excellency. My hearing is not so good anymore."

"No offense taken, Monsieur Greno." Mercifully, she tips her glass his way, and we all drink in relief.

The empress's butler bends to whisper in her ear. A vein on her forehead throbs, her rouged lips stretch taut, her eyelids guard like a shield. She folds her napkin and places it on the table. Without a word, she picks up her skirts and marches out.

Her butler bows. "Her Majesty is called away on an emergency of state."

Small gasps around the head table, and the ambassador waves his hand at the guests.

"Proceed with your dinner, as if nothing is amiss. We must show respect at the empress and emperor's table."

Sympathizing with the empress and the shameful way she had to leave her guests, I set down my champagne. The sugary taste turns my stomach.

"You don't seem to like this wine either," Jean Paul says. "Perhaps you are not destined to be a winemaker. My falcon master said I could never be a falconer if I don't love my bird."

"Perhaps you've not yet flown a bird that makes your heart soar." My finger circles the sticky rim of the coupe. "And perhaps I have not yet created a wine to my taste. But I'm not giving up, are you?"

Greno insists on accompanying us in the carriage to the train station, but he seems uneasy, and I'm not sure why. We certainly sold a lot of Pommery wine to his contacts, and that bodes well for the new year.

Louise plays cat's cradle with Greno across from her. The red money pouch sits safely between us. The money will go a long way toward paying expenses.

La gare lies just beyond the bridge. Wet snow weighs down the leaves and splats on the street. Fingers of fog curl around the ancient archway over the bridge, the quaint lampposts, the gargoyles, and intricate stonework.

"It seems a shame Napoleon will destroy all this," I complain. "Has he no reverence for the past?"

"Change is inescapable." Greno sighs. "One must face the future with courage."

"I'm glad you believe in change. Because I've been mulling around an exciting change this year. Pommery will stop making red wine and make champagne instead."

He drops the cat's cradle and collapses into the bench seat, his liver-colored lips trembling. "Do you know how foolish that is, Alexandrine?"

"What's wrong, Monsieur?" I help Louise untangle the string.

"You!" he sputters. "You and your harebrained ideas. I have gone along with your lark of running a winery to my own financial detriment, but it is time to sell the winery to Wolfe and move to Chigny."

Irritation ignites my spine like a torch. "And what is your reasoning? Am I only capable of tending roses?"

He waves me away. "I'm old. I have no more energy for your ludicrous ideas." He grabs his chest and wheezes.

Louise winds the string into a ball.

Greno is not well. Not well at all. How selfish I've been. "All right, Monsieur. As you wish, you are hereby released from any responsibilities at Pommery."

His jaundiced eyes flood with shame. "Alexandrine, I sold my half of the business to Reynard Wolfe."

"No." My temple throbs. "You would not do that to me." I huff. "When I offered to buy you out, you said the winery wasn't worth anything."

"Wolfe made a good offer." He shrugs feebly. "At least with Wolfe as your partner, you won't struggle for money."

I twist a lock of hair. "I'll match his offer."

He grimaces. "You can't possibly match it. And, besides, I already mailed the contract."

I cover my forehead with my hand, frustrated. I cannot allow these men to steal my winery. Taking pen and linen handkerchief from my purse, I write an agreement on the handkerchief nullifying Wolfe's offer. "Sign this and sell me your shares," I say.

"I'm sorry, Alexandrine, but I need the money now. I've been signing on credit all over town, and my accounts came due the end of the year."

I hand him the money bag from wine sales. "Take this now, and I will wire you the rest when I return."

"You are a hard woman to say no to, Alexandrine." Greno shakes his head. "But I made a deal."

Louise takes his hands and looks up at him with big violet eyes. "Grand-père Greno, please don't take away our winery."

9

Petit à petit, l'oiseau fait son nid

Little by little, the bird builds his nest

I push through the crowd to congratulate Mayor Werle on the new Reims train station. The stone depot covers a city block, three archways below, offices above, four platforms, and nine tracks.

Reynard Wolfe sidles next to me as I walk. "I always took you for an ethical person."

"Thank you, Monsieur. I try to be." By his tone I know we are headed for a public fight. Most unsavory.

"You went behind my back to buy out Greno's partnership." He sniffs his runny nose.

"Funny, I see it the other way around." I push between groups, hoping to lose him, but he ducks through.

"With me as your partner we would have capital for new equipment and could have hired an experienced winemaker," he says. "And with my contacts, we could have imported to all the states of Germany."

"Pommery will not be making wine, so I will not need your assistance." I cut through the crowd, leaving Wolfe with his mouth gaping.

The mayor cuts the wide blue ribbon, and the crowd rushes to congratulate him. I wait below the platform while businessmen and politicians shake his hand. His beard is graying, and his love of pastries has expanded his waistline. Still, he is a fashionable and formidable figure, with his long mink coat over a black suit with creamy velvet vest and silk cravat.

Whatever the city of Reims needs to prosper, Mayor Werle makes it happen. His drive and tenacity must be traits Veuve Clicquot saw in her young employee thirty years ago when she made him her partner. Now, Werle manages the entire Clicquot champagne house. Who better to teach me the champagne business?

When he descends the platform, his eyes glint with guilt. "Madame Pommery, I am remiss in not visiting you." He brushes a formal kiss on my glove.

"Congratulations on the Nord train line," I say.

"It opens up business to all of France and beyond." He looks above my head at the businessmen waiting for him.

"Speaking of business, perhaps you've heard I have taken over Pommery winery," I say. "I am anxious to learn all I can and was wondering if I could trouble you for a tour of Clicquot."

"But we make champagne," he says. "Twice as complicated as wine."

"Would tomorrow afternoon suit you?" I ask.

He clears his throat. "I'm afraid not, Madame Pommery. Our methods are proprietary, and I dare not share the techniques and protocol that took Veuve Clicquot a lifetime to achieve. So, if you'll excuse me, I must greet other guests." He steps past me and shakes hands with Wolfe.

I have no choice but to take matters into my own hands.

Our coach arrives at Château de Boursault with its towers and turrets, a high-pitched roof adorned with decorative ironwork, separate wings, arched windows with ornate pediments, all mirrored in the reflecting pool in front. Louise is beside herself with the excitement of visiting a real castle.

A short, stocky butler leads us down vast hallways that rival the elegant halls of Versailles. Several black matagots dart across the hall like ground squirrels in the vineyards. The butler ignores them, waddling through the glass-domed conservatory, outside to the veranda budding with yellow forsythia and pink magnolias. But what catches my eye is the sheen on Veuve Clicquot's gold-blonde curls, like a painter brushed on highlights at the last minute. She doesn't rise, as etiquette would demand, but sits grandly on a bentwood settee in a simple gray day dress with a fringed shawl. A raven-haired girl sits at her feet, reading to her.

"Anne, please greet our guests properly," Veuve Clicquot says. "I don't trust my knees to hold me these days."

The girl rises and curtseys with schooled grace. "Welcome, Madame and Mademoiselle Pommery," she says in a practiced tone. "I am Anne de Rochechouart de Mortemart, Madame Clicquot's great-granddaughter."

I bow slightly. "Pleased to meet you, Mademoiselle."

"Why don't you show Mademoiselle Pommery the mittens before tea?" Veuve Clicquot suggests.

Anne takes Louise's hand, and the girls skip through a wisteria archway.

"Mittens?" I ask.

"Matagot kittens. Mittens." She gestures for me to sit at the bentwood table. "How is your matagot?"

I laugh. "Felix consumes his weight in winery mice daily."

"I told you he'd be useful," she says.

"And he's a wonderful companion to Louise."

She nods. "A matagot is the best friend one can have." She looks up to the turquoise sky, not a cloud in sight. "This weather is awful."

"You don't like the heat?" I ask.

She wrinkles her nose. "Heat forces the grapevines to bud too early."

"And that affects the grapes?" I take out my journal to make a note.

"You don't know what early budbreak does to grapes?" She scrutinizes my feathered hat, my buttoned gloves, my Parisian boots.

"Pommery is a negotiant," I defend myself. "We do not grow grapes. We buy them to make our wine."

She sniffs. "I suppose you are not the type to get your hands dirty."

Trying for humor, I write in my journal. "Buy vineyards. Get hands dirty."

At least she smiles.

The butler sets an ice bucket near the bentwood table. "There you are, Gieves. Our guest is thirsty."

He pours us champagne and tea, heaping several lumps of sugar into Veuve Clicquot's teacup. I put my hand over my tea lest he ruin it.

"And have some work dresses made. Preferably wine colored so stains blend in." She holds up her coupe and toasts simply. "*Au santé.*"

I admire the clarity and lively bubbles she's achieved. But I've never seen this beautiful color. "Is this champagne pink?"

"First rose champagne ever made," she boasts.

I take another sip. "Very fruity. I taste the Meunier."

"So, you do know your wine."

I scoff. "Not like you, Madame." I question her about making champagne, taking copious notes. After a while, she stops answering and frowns.

"Something tells me this is not a social call. Perhaps, you should tell me why you came."

I take another sip for courage. "As you know, I inherited my husband's winery, but I dislike red wine. I've always loved champagne." My cheeks heat unbearably, and droplets run down the back of my neck.

"Are you all right, my dear? Is it too much sun for you?"

"To get to the point, I want to make champagne." My breath hitches. "And, I want to tour your winery, but Monsieur Werle turned me down. Now, I realize how foolish this must sound."

"Foolish, yes. Absolutely." She hands me her handkerchief. "Making champagne is the most foolish business there is. Twice as much work as wine, and twice as many things can go wrong."

Well, that settles it. She will not help me.

The girls return, and Gieves serves tea and pastries.

"No pastry for me, please." I wave them away.

"I understand you are the arbiter of etiquette in Reims," Veuve Clicquot says. "But here in the country, you are my guest. Select a pastry and enjoy it with all the gusto your tiny waist can manage."

"I'm afraid sweets don't agree with me."

"Try *la religieuse*. A perfect pastry for a religious woman such as yourself."

Gieves serves me *la religieuse*; one airy puff on top of another, filled with rich cream and drizzled with chocolate. Smooth, rich cream melts in my mouth. Eggy pastry so light I'm floating. Or maybe it's the champagne I sip between bites.

"What did I tell you?" Veuve Clicquot asks.

"Heaven." I smile and wonder if I dare raise the subject of champagne again.

The girls ask to be excused and run off to the kittens. Mittens.

"So, you are quite determined to make champagne?" Veuve Clicquot bites into another napoleon pastry.

"Yes, I am." I lick chocolate from my lips.

"*Vendangeurs*, grape pickers, are strictly a men's club," she advises. "Among themselves, they'll share information about weather, the status of harvests, new techniques, and setting prices for grapes, but they will exclude you. Pommery will suffer. But you have an older son, right?"

Gieves pours more champagne.

"Louis is getting his law degree. It was his father's dream for him to be a lawyer. I can't ask him to help me."

She sighs the heavy sigh of one who knows a steep road lies ahead. She clinks her glass to mine. "Take out that notebook of yours."

Her turnabout thrills me as I record her detailed explanation of *méthode champenoise*.

"Champagne is a blend of three grapes, not just one: Chardonnay, Pinot Noir, and Meunier. So, you are harvesting different varietals of grapes at different times when the berries mature. You must label the juice with the varietal and vineyard from which they came, so you know what you are blending in the spring."

"Proper labeling crucial for blending," I repeat as I write in my book.

"And crushing the black grapes must be swift or you'll have red champagne."

"How do you do that?" I taste her champagne, noticing the texture, the weight, the flavors on my palate like an artist's palette. The comparison makes me smile.

"You must siphon off the juice immediately and discard the skins," she says.

"So, the opposite of making red wine, where we leave juice on the skins for a robust color."

"Red wine is nothing like champagne." She holds her glass to the sunlight. "Champagne is finesse, lightness, clarity, sweetness. All of which is nearly impossible to achieve." She offers me the pastry tray. "Take one, you know you want to."

I take another *religieuse* to be polite.

She coaches me for another hour until her voice cracks with fatigue. "One last piece of advice."

"What's that?" I ready my pencil and paper.

"Don't take no for an answer." She wags a finger at me. "Never take no for an answer, and they will learn to respect you."

I consider her advice, then ask, "So, when may I tour your champagne house?"

Mayor Werle's finger scans each line of the winery ledger with the precision of a jeweler cutting a diamond. I have a hard time imagining the mayor as a German orphan, determined to learn French. Madame Clicquot said she took him on as an apprentice, and through his intelligence and hard work, he earned her confidence. So much so, she made him a partner. I almost see the gears behind his broad forehead grind to a halt as he senses my presence.

I bob a curtsey, hoping my peacock-blue day dress is appropriate for a business call. The color seems bold after two years of mourning, but Hubinet insists it complements my eyes.

"I see my opinion of you is justified," he says, locking the ledger in his desk drawer. "But regardless of my view, Madame Clicquot insisted I give you a tour of our operation. God forbid I disobey her wishes."

"I appreciate your time, Mayor Werle. I know you are a busy man."

"At least you didn't bring your daughter to slow us down." He consults his gold pocket watch. "I have a town council meeting in half an hour."

"I left her at the orphanage with Father Pieter." Mayor Werle is a major benefactor of Saint Remi.

He rises from his desk. "My wife tells me your work with the orphanage is remarkable."

I sigh. "The priests teach the boys, but girls receive no formal education. My auxiliary helps them learn to read and write, at least. Your wife is a great help."

"Reading and writing will not fill their mouths," he says. "Orphan girls must learn how to handle a mop and scrub brush so they can find a job other than the brothel." He pulls on his mink coat and wraps an orange merino-wool scarf around his neck. "Button up, Madame Pommery. It's cold in the cellars."

He leads me down into Clicquot's frosty underground storeroom with familiar smells of fermenting wine and oak barrels. A-framed racks with holes cut in them hold thousands of bottles neck down. *Les cavistes,* the cellarmen, twist the bottles a quarter turn and move on to the next.

"What are they doing?" I ask.

His jaw stiffens. "Madame, surely you do not expect me to divulge proprietary secrets."

"But why are the bottles upside down?" I ask. "And why are they turning them?"

He doesn't answer.

"I will be happy to write Veuve Clicquot my questions," I say, drawing the racks in my journal and making notes.

He exhales loudly. "The dead yeast slides into the neck of the bottle." Offering no further information.

He turns into a storeroom filled with rows of fermenting vats, twice the size of ours. When the workers see Werle, they quicken their pace. I note: observation makes work more efficient. We walk past fifty or sixty vats labeled *vins de réserve.* The cellar expands to corridors filled with barrels labeled by vineyard and year. Note: visit Bouzy, Verzenay, Verzy vineyards.

"With so many different vineyards and so many vintages, how do you know which ones to blend with each other?"

"It takes talent to make great champagne." He taps the side of his nose. "Madame Clicquot is *Le Nez.*"

"The nose?" I ask.

"Her sense of smell is extraordinary. She can identify the characteristics of the grapes, the soil, the weather, with one whiff of their bouquet. She worked with our winemakers for decades."

"So can you learn *Le Nez*?" I touch my extraordinarily ordinary nose.

He scoffs. "There will never be another Veuve Clicquot."

"I am under no presumption to take her place." But can there be a Madame Pommery?

We enter a cavern where workers release plugs from the neck of the bottle and add a liquid.

"I assume they are removing the dead yeast you talked about, but what are they pouring into the bottles?"

He tightens the scarf around his neck. "It's called *le dosage*, and the recipe varies depending on the wine we are bottling and what it needs to reach full potential."

"Can you be more specific?"

"*Le dosage* depends on when the grape leaves budded, how much sun the vineyards received, how the vines were pruned."

"But what is it exactly?"

He scowls. "Madame, you test my patience. That is like asking for the secret to soufflé." He checks his gold pocket watch. "I'll show you *les crayères*, and then I must go." He leads me through the caves, smelling like soil after a rain. "The Romans excavated chalk from *les crayères* in 1 A.D. Now they make cool storage for our champagnes."

"Mining chalk? Was it used for building?"

He picks up a nugget of chalk and crumbles it in his hand. "Too soft for that. Chalk was used for fertilizer, cleaning compounds, tanning animal hides, and mortar for bricks."

Thousands of dark green bottles rest on their sides in racks.

"Must the bottles be green?" I ask.

He harumphs. "Let me set you straight. Making champagne is not a fashionable, glamorous business suited to a woman of your obvious education. It is downright dangerous and impossible to make any money. Your husband found it difficult enough to make red wine, and champagne is another world of difficulty and investment."

His warning eats into my bones like tannery acid. "I will take that into consideration, Mayor Werle."

Suddenly, an explosion shakes the chalk walls and everything in it. On the rack next to me, another bottle explodes, pushing my shoulder against the hard chalk wall; my hands protect my heart.

Shards of glass impale my top hand like arrows to a bull's eye.

Werle rushes me up the staircase. By the time we reach the outside, blood streams down my mutton-chop sleeves.

Werle wraps my hand with his linen handkerchief embroidered with the Veuve Clicquot anchor and ties it in a knot. "Come along. I'll take you to Doctor DuBois," he says, and marches me down Rue Claire. We pass Hôtel de Ville, where a few councilmen greet him.

"Go to your meeting, Mayor," I say. "I can take myself to Doctor DuBois."

He looks up at the councilmen and back at me. "Have the doctor send me the bill." He tips his hat and climbs the steps.

Instinct tells me this will be my last invitation to Veuve Clicquot. The facts I learned swirl in my head like leaves in a storm. So many aspects to consider, and red wine is difficult enough to make. Why must I take on double difficulty?

10

Apprendre à un vieux singe à faire des grimaces

To teach an old monkey to make funny faces

The other champagne makers refuse to tutor me. So, I bury myself in the Reims library and devour every book I can find on the subject. Father Pieter arranges a visit to the Benedictine abbey at Hautvillers, where Dom Pérignon first made champagne for Louis XIV.

Yet, when wagons of grapes come into the winery, I feel skittish as a squirrel storing walnuts before a blizzard. If my first season of champagne goes wrong, which it can in dozens of ways, I will be the laughingstock of Reims: the widow who thought she knew better than her husband. Even worse, I may have to accept Wolfe's offer of partnership.

"Hurry, Maman." My little spitfire, Louise, pulls my hand toward the wagons. "Monsieur Vasnier needs my help with the grapes."

"A very important job," I tell her. "You are our number one grape taster."

"Hear that, Felix?" She wags her finger at his slinky body lying in a patch of sun. "I have a job."

I laugh, until I see Reynard Wolfe with his fists planted into his sausage waist watching my crew unload grapes.

I bend down to Louise. "Go help Monsieur Vasnier." Her tiny boots kick up her long skirt as she skips off with Felix.

Wolfe strokes his ginger stubble over a blistering red face. "Madame, I am certain you told me you would not be making wine, and therefore did not require my assistance in the winery. Were you lying to me?"

"We are not making wine, Monsieur Wolfe." I walk past him into the winery, where Vasnier supervises the crew shoveling grapes from the wagon onto the platform. Louise picks out stems and bad grapes, and Damas carries them to the grape press. A rush of pride fills me, they are working so well together.

"How did you buy a new grape press?" Wolfe's red-blond brows draw together.

"Just look at the craftsmanship." I pat the polished oak staves. I am not about to admit the new grape press is not paid for, and there is still so much more equipment I need for blending and bottling.

"It's not in your budget, I assure you." Wolfe's mouth puckers as if his sauerkraut fermented too long.

Vasnier crouches down to encourage Louise, his moss-green eyes lit with his smile. He should smile more often.

When the basket press is filled from the top, Gilbert, the *pressoir* man, turns a crank, his back muscles rippling with effort. A wooden plate lowers on the grapes applying pressure, and juice pours through vertical staves with gaps between them.

I raise my hand to stop him. "Gilbert, not so hard. I want these grapes crushed gently. I don't want any color from the skins."

"These are Pinot Noir," Gilbert scoffs. "Black grapes. The more color, the better the wine."

"We are not making red wine," I say.

The crew wrench their heads around as if I said Napoleon was wearing no clothes.

"We are making champagne," I tell them.

The crew stares at me with mouths open, except Damas, who carries baskets of grapes to the pressing platform.

Gilbert takes off his Phrygian cap and scratches his head. "All due respect, Madame, but we know nothing about making champagne."

"It takes years to master champagne techniques," says another worker. "And they keep them secret."

The morning sun streams in the double barn doors, spotlighting confusion and distrust on their grape-stained faces.

Vasnier steps to the edge of the crush platform. "Madame Pommery, forgive me for saying so, but why would we make champagne when Veuve Clicquot and Moët dominate the market?"

"You are right," I admit. "All of you are right."

Reynard Wolfe blurts a laugh. "So, all this is a joke?"

The men join his laughter with a sigh of relief. "Good one, Madame Pommery."

"Wait. Not so fast." I hold up my hands. "Monsieur Vasnier, you make a good point. But we are not going to imitate Veuve Clicquot or Moët. We will make something entirely unique: Pommery champagne."

Wolfe scoffs. "Pommery will fail, and the bank cannot afford the loss."

A cellar rat scurries across the planked floor, and Felix chases it. The banker jumps to avoid the rat, but he steps on Felix's tail. The matagot's gold-flecked eyes open wide, and he screeches a most ungodly caterwaul. He bares long claws into Wolfe's leg, springing blood through his trousers.

Wolfe kicks at Felix, who scales his corpulent body and digs up his hair like tufts of grass.

Wolfe yells, "Get this hell cat off me."

Louise stomps her foot. "Felix, come." The matagot leaps off Wolfe and runs to her.

The banker pats his hair in place above his clawed forehead. "Madame Pommery, your mortgage loan is dependent on making red wine. If you make champagne, you are taking a risk the bank cannot support. We will rescind the loan and sue you for fraud. Your winery will be closed, and these men will lose their jobs." He examines his wounds. "Is that clear?"

My crew looks daggers at me like I'm the villain here.

The Reims Cathedral bell tolls, vibrating in my bones. If I give in to Wolfe now, I will never have this chance again. "Pommery is making champagne."

Wolfe steps up to the platform and speaks to the crew. "Clicquot is hiring more workers. If anyone wants a recommendation, I'm going over to Clicquot now."

"Do we have customers for the champagne, Madame Pommery?" our caskman asks.

"We haven't made champagne yet," I say. "But we must have faith in ourselves."

"I'm sorry, Madame, but I cannot afford to stake my career on something so risky." He takes off his apron, folds it on a gunny sack of beet sugar, and leaves with Wolfe along with a dozen others.

"The door is open if you change your minds," I call after them, knowing how desperate I sound. How can I blame them? The risk is real, I can't refute it. Did I think about their welfare with this decision? Admittedly not. And look where my selfishness got me.

Henry Vasnier, Gilbert, and Damas stay. The wagons line up three deep now, more on the way. How can four of us do the work of twenty?

I roll up my dress sleeves. "Your loyalty will be rewarded. This harvest will be tough, but we can do it. Monsieur Vasnier will shovel grapes into the press."

"Please. Call me Henry," he asks. As an apprentice, Louis always addressed him as Monsieur Vasnier, while other workers went by first names.

"As you wish, Henry." I nod. "Gilbert will press the juice—gently. Three times only." I bend over to look Damas in the eye to make sure he reads my lips. "Your job is to siphon juice into the barrels quickly before the juice colors. I'll mark the barrels with the grape varietals and vineyard designations. We are making champagne!"

"Am I still the grape inspector?" Louise asks.

Vasnier picks her up and sets her on the platform near the open barn doors. "Absolutely, the most important grape inspector."

"The Crush," as we call pressing grapes, is usually a jovial time, but without my experienced crew, it is a race against time to get the grapes crushed before they spoil.

For the next two weeks, we work relentlessly. Tension crackles throughout the barn. Vasnier is anxious and exacting, grasping at fumes of knowledge he learned from my husband. When I ask him questions, he is jumpy and defensive. Damas works on wordlessly, watching our faces, trying to glean what is going on, I imagine.

To add to our chaos, Louise's nanny, Lucille, goes to Strasbourg, France, as there was a death in her family, leaving my precocious five-year-old to me. Well, not entirely. Damas watches over her as she chases Felix around the pallets of sugar I bought to make the champagne.

By himself on the grape press, Gilbert throws out his back. I bring in Doctor DuBois to examine him. He prescribes eucalyptus salve and alternate compresses of heat and ice—and a week's bedrest we can't afford right now. He insists on supervising the press, so I haul out a feather mattress from the house, and he instructs Vasnier and Damas on the grape press.

I'm forced to send the rest of the grape wagons away.

"You break the contract this year, and we're not coming back," a waggoneer tells me.

A problem to solve later. Now, we must get this fruit in barrels.

11

ÊTRE AU FOUR ET AU MOULIN

To be at the oven and the mill at the same time

April, 1861. Adolphe Hubinet grasps my elbows and kisses my cheeks. "Ah, Madame Pommery, I've missed you."

Another man I don't recognize dusts the shelves of fashion baubles—velvet flowers, jewels, and stuffed birds.

"Champagne for you?" Hubinet gestures to the dewy ice bucket.

I laugh. "It's nine o'clock. I haven't had my coffee."

He claps his hands. "Pierre, bring Madame Pommery a café au lait with extra steamed milk."

The willowy young man springs to the backroom, with duster in hand. He's wearing ballet slippers.

"I see you have a new assistant," I say. "What happened to Gustave?"

His ears redden. "Young men. You can't count on them."

As effusive as Hubinet is with his customers, he is demanding and exacting with his assistants who work in the shop by day and as companions in the evening. He must find the boys at La Perle, a glamorous refuge from disapproving society.

Hubinet offers me a fuchsia tufted chair at the mirrored table. "How are the work dresses doing for you?" He sits across from me, lacing manicured fingers on his knees.

"The work dresses are fine, but I find myself needing something entirely different."

Pierre prances back balancing a porcelain cup of steaming café au lait, exactly what I need this morning.

Hubinet flicks his wrist toward him. "Victor, go back and sweep the workroom."

Pierre grimaces.

"Didn't you say his name was Pierre?" I whisper.

"Pierre, workroom. Chop, chop."

Pierre concedes, and Hubinet turns back to me.

"Tell me what you have in that beautiful mind of yours."

My excitement bubbles up; I'm anxious to share my vision. "We started making champagne! But not just any champagne. I want to create a champagne that is entirely different. Refreshing. The most beautiful champagne in the world."

Hubinet clasps his hands. "But of course you will, *ma chérie.*"

"And I need a new wardrobe to go with my vision." I reach into my valise for the sketches I've been working on.

Hubinet studies my drawings. "Madame, your designs are reminiscent of a lost elegance. But modern somehow. Let me bring the fabric swatches."

"Nothing black." The words catch in my throat. Shrouding myself in black drained the life out of me.

He climbs the sliding library ladder and selects fabrics from the top shelf.

My fingertips graze sensuous silks, rich brocades, nubby woolens. I'm drawn to radiant shades of blue: sapphire, indigo, azure, cobalt. "Louis used to say he could tell my mood by the shade of my eyes."

"I noticed your eyes the first time we met: deep and turbulent as the ocean," Hubinet says. "A tour de force hiding under a calm demeanor."

"How you do go on." I laugh and make my selections.

"Splendid choices, Madame Pommery," he says and brings me baskets of adornments, and I sift through gleaming silk ribbons, intricate laces, multi-layered trims. My mood rises like fermenting juice in the barrels.

"Is this your secret to selling?" I ask. "Tempting and titillating the client until she believes it's her decision to buy dozens of dresses adorned with your most expensive trims?"

He lifts up on his toes, shoulders back. "I may have developed a few techniques as a wine merchant in London."

"I forgot you sold wine." A thrill runs up my spine signaling me.

"I sold only the finest wines to the toniest restaurants and bars," he says, curling a tendril of his mustache around his pinkie. "I miss my friends, the opera, the symphony, the galleries, the London theater."

Pierre returns with his feather duster, fluffing feathers all around. But Hubinet sits with his chin in his hand, lost in longing for London.

It would be a bold step, but worth the risk. "You know, Pommery would benefit greatly from a sales agent in London. One who can sell luxury items of the highest quality."

"What a splendid notion!" His hand presses his chest, eyes to the heavens. Then his chin falls to his chest. "But alas, you can't afford me. My brother pays me a percentage of sales." He whispers an absurd figure.

I gasp. "I could never afford that salary. We are just starting out."

"Not salary, Madame. Commission on sales you would never have had without my services." He shrugs. "I've tripled my brother's sales."

"Pommery just can't afford it right now, I'm afraid," I say, disappointed.

He writes up my order with his usual sparkling aplomb. "Madame Pommery, always a pleasure to serve you." He kisses my cheeks goodbye.

Walking home through the crowded streets, I cannot let go of the vision of exuberant Hubinet selling Pommery champagne in London. At my doorstep, I turn around and walk back to the shop. The bell rings cheerfully as I push open the door.

Hubinet steps through the velvet curtains from the backroom. "What took you so long?"

October each year, we celebrate Saint Remi's Feast Day, when Saint Remi baptized King Clovis in 496 A.D. with sacred oil delivered by a dove from heaven. Transformed by that miracle, King Clovis converted pagan France to Christianity.

From the pews, Louise and I watch the procession of hungry, sick, mentally ill, crippled outcasts, and harlots lined up to receive the blessed oil from Father Pieter.

"Maman, why are they so poor?" Louise asks.

"It is not their fault. Most of them are born into their class."

"Are we poor, Maman?"

"No, darling girl, we are blessed with work and food, and we must help those less fortunate than ourselves." Enough explanation for now. In time, I will explain the intricate class system which divides us by birthright, economics, occupation, politics, and religion.

The sanctuary is sweltering, smelling of despair. A tear falls on my cheek, but not for myself. Despite the new expenses of Hubinet's London office and needing new employees to replace the ones that left us, we are still blessed with my manor house on Reims Square and my winery. Humbled, I kneel on the pew, cross myself, and give thanks for my blessings, especially my children. Precocious Louise, who keeps me hopping, and Louis, becoming a man of his own.

Interrupting my sacred moment, Reynard Wolfe slips into our pew. He tips a gray Bavarian hat with gold cording and a pheasant feather. "Bonjour, Madame and Mademoiselle Pommery. Mind if I sit with you?"

"I thought you were Protestant, Monsieur."

He smiles crookedly. "I came here to drop off your donation to Father Pieter."

"What donation?"

"The one Pommery gives Saint Remi every year."

"One thousand francs?" My heart throws itself against my ribs. "I needed that money to set up our London sales office and to hire the employees you lured away."

"Shall I retrieve the funds from Father Pieter?" He tears at his pinkie nail, feigning worry.

A pregnant washerwoman in ragged clothes waddles to the altar. Behind her is a group of farmhands, out of work since the grape harvest is over.

I huff. "I can't do that now. Look at this crowd. The church must feed and clothe more citizens than ever before."

"Precisely why I assumed you'd want to continue your annual donation." The banker leans close enough for me to see his red-blond eyelashes and freckled eyelids. The smell of cloves masks his sour breath. "Of course, if I was your partner, I could access all the funds you need for the winery and your generous heart as well."

Flames of anger lick my skin. I fan myself with a hymnal. Louise kicks against the pews, causing the old man in front of us to glare at me.

"Monsieur Wolfe, next time, please consult me on any outlay of my capital. I have a new sales agent to pay, new employees to hire, and we need more space in order to age the champagne."

"Another reason champagne is a terrible idea. It takes years to age, all the while eating money. Take my advice before it's too late. Champagne is a bad investment. Surely, you've heard champagne takes twice the effort and twice as long to make any money."

"I may have heard that a time or two," I say through gritted teeth.

He pats my gloved hand. "My offer is still open. Taking me as a partner will make you very rich, and you won't have to wear gloves to hide your calluses and broken fingernails." He smiles with a shred of pig between his incisors.

"Excuse us." I grab Louise's hand and march up the aisle to join destitute men and women bowing down, heads haloed with sunlight from the stained-glass windows.

A celestial cloud of doves swirls above Father Pieter at the altar. Behind him, Damas holds a golden offering dish of breadcrumbs. Doves swoop to his dish, then whirl up in a vortex to the ceiling lit by painted windows of saints, none more glorious than Damas, with his upturned face smiling as serene and adoring as I have ever seen.

Louise points. "Maman, it's our Damas."

I lower her finger. "Ladies do not point, Rosebud."

When Father Pieter sees her, he lifts her up like the grandfather she never had and props her on his hip.

"Madame Pommery, bless you, bless you." The father rests his palm on the crown of my head. "Your generous donation and tireless work here make this mission possible."

I'm ashamed of thinking of my own needs when there is so much poverty. A notion flies into my brain like the dove of Saint Remi. What if we could help each other? "Father, I need to hire workers for my winery. Perhaps some of your flock would like a job?"

He frowns. "No one is trained in making wine."

I huff. "Then we'll have a lot in common. I will employ anyone who's willing to work. Send them to me tomorrow."

We hire ten new workers from Father Pieter. But at the end of their first week, I walk into the winery and Henry Vasnier is walking out.

"Henry, where are you going?" I call after him.

He spins around and holds his arms out. "How can you expect me to teach them when I don't know what I am doing myself?"

"You've been here for years," I say. "You know more than you think."

"I know nothing about making champagne," he says.

"One step at a time, Henry." I place my hand on his shoulder. "You and I are a team. What we don't know, we'll find out."

He scoffs and shakes his head. "You expect me to turn drunks, beggars, and whores into winemakers?" He walks away, and I catch his hand.

"Can you give our new workers a chance? It's only been a week." He looks at our hands, and I let go.

He looks at me long and hard, then snorts. We walk together into the winery, and I breathe in the aroma of new wine. "Smell that, Henry? It's champagne."

He snorts and shakes his head.

"Monsieur Vasnier, where do you want these barrels stored?" asks a tall man with coveralls.

The winery is still packed with red wines. The mezzanine is full and the cellar too.

"Ship the older wines to London, then we'll have room," I tell Henry. "We opened a new sales office there with Monsieur Hubinet. The finest salesman I have ever met."

Vasnier tugs the cuff on my dress and laughs. "Anything else up your sleeve?"

"Let me think." I press a finger to my lips and cock my head. "Would you like to accompany me to the Great London Exhibition next summer?"

"I've never been to London." He chuckles under his lush mustache.

"High time, then." I find Louise and take her with me to the telegraph office. She watches intently as the operator taps out my message to Hubinet.

Shipping wine now STOP Need space in winery STOP Sell, sell, sell STOP—M Pommery

12

ÊTRE LE DINDON DE LA FARCE

To be the turkey in the joke

London, 1862. The enormous domes and spires of the International Exhibition Hall loom like phantoms in the stormy sky. Holding the umbrella over Louise with one hand and a carpet bag of booth décor with the other, I step gingerly through the puddles, soaking my leather soles. My bowler hat slides perilously to the left, weighted unevenly by the grapevines and grape clusters on the brim.

Through the pelting rain, I barely make out Henry's and Louis's shoulders pushing trolleys of champagne ahead. Since the exhibition was close, Louis agreed to help, to my surprise, given his impudence when I started making champagne.

We are late setting up for the exhibition. Very late. Never mind it was Louise who spilled porridge on her dress, and I had to change it, which made her cranky. Made all of us cranky. And late.

Hubinet strides next to me, dashing in his London trench raincoat.

"We are not ready for this, Monsieur," I confide in him. "It's our first vintage."

He waves my fears away. "We could not miss this opportunity to be counted among the finest champagne houses."

"But our champagne has not aged enough," I say. "And we're neophytes in the business. We'll be lost among the great champagne houses."

"No one could ever miss you, Madame Pommery." He smirks and twists his curlicue mustache. "You are a rose among dandelions."

Louise jumps with both feet into a puddle and splatters me with mud. "Louise, *ça suffit!*" Enough is enough. My maman's scolding voice escapes my mouth.

Louis turns and gestures at the crowd waiting at the doors. "Well, Maman, this is your big chance to prove your half-baked scheme to make champagne is worthwhile." He pushes ahead.

Hubinet raises an eyebrow. "Your son doesn't approve?"

"I'm afraid not. He prefers red wine."

"At least he's here," Hubinet says. "He cares about you."

Thousands of black umbrellas funnel into the crystal palace which covers nearly three miles in downtown London.

"Twenty-eight thousand exhibitors from thirty-six countries," Hubinet quotes the London *Times* I read this morning. "All the best from industry, technology, and the arts."

The thought of serving our fledgling champagne to all those people makes me shudder. I chastise myself for allowing Hubinet to talk me into this.

A menacing flash of lightning strikes a tree in the park, followed by an angry thunderclap. Louise shrieks and hugs my legs. "Take me home, Maman," she howls. *Children should be seen, not heard.* She crushes her body against me. If I don't do something, she will be moody all day.

Vasnier and Louis wait at the doors with the wine carts, rain dribbling off the brims of their hats.

"The champagne needs to get on ice," Hubinet says.

"Go ahead to the booth," I tell them. "Louise and I will be along shortly."

The men take my cue and push the trolleys toward the champagne hall.

"I hear they have delicious hot chocolate at the Holland display," I tell Louise. I forgot to give the carpet bag of the booth decorations to the men.

Three strikes against me. One: I'm a bad mother for dragging Louise along. Two: Our booth will be plain and boring. Three: I'll be later than late.

If I steer clear of the manufacturing, farming, and mining exhibits, Louise is drawn to finery of every kind: diamonds and gems, stunning jewelry, sumptuous textiles, painted porcelain teacups, and golden statues. But nothing captures her imagination like the chocolate pavilion, where we stop for the best hot chocolate I have ever tasted—rich and dark.

We sit in front of a chocolate statue thirty-eight feet high. The smiling female statue is surrounded by wine jugs and grapevines. At her feet is a plaque: *Bona Dea*, a goddess I learned about in school. One of those useless bits of knowledge finishing schools teach.

"Is she the Mother Mary, Maman?"

A laugh bubbles up in my throat. "She is Bona Dea, the ancient Roman Goddess of Goodness, who protects women through changes in their lives. She represents women's traits of honesty, bravery, health, and wealth."

Louise studies the chocolate Bona Dea as she drinks. "Does Mother Mary have a chocolate statue?" She tilts her head and smiles slyly.

I nudge her nose, and she giggles. "We'll have to ask Father Pieter about that. Are you ready to go see our champagne display?"

"Most certainly," she says with a smile.

I grab the décor bag I forgot to give the men. By the time we get to the booth, the wine exhibition will have opened with none of my elaborate visions.

The crowd has grown thick in the Exhibition Halls, and it's hard to push through. I'm struck by the array of hats: shiny top hats, exotic fur caps, John Bulls, turbans, Bell Crowns, Bowrys, Derbies, and Grandees. Ornate women's hats with feathers, netting, ribbons, flowers, and stuffed birds. My wet grape vine hat feels heavy and awkward. When I finally see the Champagne Pavilion, Louise tugs my sleeve.

"Maman, I have to go to *les toilettes*." Her nose wrinkles.

"Can you hold it? We need to get to the Pommery booth."

She dances a jig. No time to waste.

"I think I saw *les toilettes* by the entrance." I lead back through the crowd, gripping the décor bag and Louise's hand. Where is the Goddess of Goodness when I need her?

The Champagne Pavilion's arched greenhouse roof should have brightened the hall with sunlight, but instead seems to bring the gloomy storm inside.

People crowd the booths awaiting their turn to taste champagne, but I stick to the center and push through. I'm not sure where the Pommery booth is, but it has to be here somewhere. My chest heaves with emotion to see the finest champagne houses, men I've known for twenty-five years since I moved to Reims as a bride. My own countrymen and friends, here on the world stage.

Yet, they could have done more to make an impression. Their tables are boring, like they represent banks or factories. Every winery looks the same, with a round tasting table and men dressed in drab suits. I wave at the owners, but they're too busy to acknowledge me. Some scowl as if I haven't been to their houses or served on charities with their wives. Mayor Werle dismisses me with a jerk of his head and turns back to his customers. What has got into these men? They're as taciturn and dour as if they're in a dentist's chair, instead of the Great London Exhibition. I'll be surprised if they sell any champagne at all.

Our Pommery table is at the very end of the hall, no booth on either side. Louis, Henry, and Hubinet stare out to the aisle. No customers.

Henry hands me a coupe of champagne. "Act like you are a customer."

Cold and refreshing but needs aging, for sure. "Not bad," I say. "Why isn't anybody at our booth?"

"They are too excited to meet with the great champagne houses," Hubinet says. "No one has heard of Pommery, yet."

"We'll just have to change that, now, won't we?" I open the carpet bag I've been lugging around. "Help me decorate." I hand Louis a bolt of brilliant-blue tulle with sparkling mica. "Hang this from our sign like a big theater curtain, will you? Make it look dramatic."

Hubinet helps him hang a long swathe of shimmering tulle over the sign. Instantly, the Pommery name looks like a marquee. Henry and I cover the table with iridescent sapphire satin and tie up the corners with silver ribbons. Louise helps me fill a copper punchbowl with ice and plunge Pommery bottles inside. We stand back to admire our work.

Werle approaches our table with other white-haired champagne vignerons behind him. How sweet of them to welcome me.

"Mayor Werle, so good to see you again." The grapes on my hat droop to my cheek. "The exhibition is a marvel, isn't it? The entire world here to taste our wine?"

"Madame Pommery, there must be some mistake. This is the Champagne Pavilion, and you make red wine." He plants his fists on his hips.

"Pommery has become a champagne house, Monsieur." Lifting a dripping bottle, I pour champagne into coupes on a silver tray. "I would be honored if you gentlemen would like to taste."

No one steps forward to take one, so I hand a coupe to the mayor. The other vignerons have no choice but to take a glass.

Werle holds it out from his body as if it smells. "The Great London Exhibition is to show the world the very best of everything. You are a novice."

"I read the exhibitor rules very carefully," I say calmly, masking my turbulence. "The rules do not mention how long you must have been making champagne."

"You, of all people, understand unspoken rules," Werle says.

"Ah, rules." My chest burns with indignation. "So many rules to learn, that to speculate about unspoken rules is a difficult task indeed. Wouldn't you agree, Mayor?"

He whiffs his champagne, and his nostrils flare. He takes a sip. The other men follow. Rolling the liquid around in his mouth, he frowns, then puckers and draws in air over the champagne. He swallows and laughs. "Madame Pommery, my dear lady." He wags his finger. "You forgot the dosage. It's too sour." He scoffs and looks to the other winemakers. "Taste that, fellows? A beginner's mistake." He tips the rest of his champagne into the dump bucket.

"Oh, but I did not forget the dosage." I hold up my glass. "I wanted a dryer champagne, so I added less sugar."

The men snigger and set their glasses on the tray.

Werle shakes his head. "Madame, champagne lovers have been drinking sweet champagne for a century. You cannot change their tastes on a whim."

"But if champagne was drier, we could drink it throughout dinner," I counter.

Werle snorts. "Champagne is not a frivolous game of *coucou*. You are humiliating yourself and us. Arrogance does not become you, Madame Pommery." The vignerons leave.

Publicly scolded by city fathers. My heart bashes against my breastbone, and blood rushes to my head.

Louise grabs my skirt. "What does arrogance mean, Maman?"

I stroke her hair, forcing myself to breathe. "Never mind, Rosebud."

Louis glares at Henry. "I knew it didn't taste right. How could you let her do this, Henry?"

"Your mother has a vision, and I think she's onto something," Henry says.

Hubinet takes a sip, and another. "Dry, sophisticated, like drinking air," he says. "The English market doesn't like sweet drinks."

"Don't humor her," Louis says. "It's arrogance, just like the mayor said."

"May I taste?" Louise's brows tangle, warning of another outbreak, and I relent. "Just a sip."

She scrunches her nose and nods. "Arrogance. Much too arrogance."

"Now you've turned Pommery into a laughingstock." Louis throws his coupe against the back wall, shattering it.

Louise buries her face in my skirt.

Louis walks out, all eyes upon him.

What does one do when judged a laughingstock by the one person who matters?

Scotsmen in kilts and their wives wearing flowered hats taste champagne at the Veuve Clicquot booth. Horrified, I recognize my old finishing-school girlfriends. I want to melt into the ground. It has been years since I've seen them, though they sent condolences when my husband passed. Rich and bright and beautiful as ever. They outshine each other in the latest London designs: tight bodices with high necks and button fronts, white lace at collars and cuffs, bell-shaped skirts. My own dress is still wet and splattered with mud.

A red fox stole slung over her arm, my oldest friend, Betty, drags her husband to the booth. "Alex! Is that really you?" she says in a playful brogue. "What are you doing here?"

Though my old nickname makes me cringe, I paste a brilliant smile on my lips. Her eyes grow misty as she kisses me *la bise,* as I taught her. For the life of me, I can't remember how to address her properly. Betty is short for Elizabeth Murray-Reid-Scott-Leveson-McDonald-Belnessie, the 8th Duchess of Abyell. Her husband is Duke George Belnessie of Belnessie Castle.

She admires my carefully curated décor: the Pommery banner, blue tulle swags, hammered copper punch bowl and trays. "Why didn't you tell me Pommery was exhibiting in the Great London Exhibition?" she scolds.

"Darling Alex, so delightful to see you," the duke slurs his words as he bows low and slobbers on my hand, exposing his thigh through his kilt. He's lost his pin along the way.

"And this young beauty must be Louise," Betty says.

Louise curtsies and loses her balance. But her dimples bloom when she smiles.

"I'm afraid I must eat my words." Betty brushes her fingertips over my blue silk tablecloth. "Remember when I told you how foolish it was to start a business after your husband passed? But seeing Pommery Champagne here among the greats is simply beyond words." She pats her initialed handkerchief under her eyes. "I don't remember you as the ambitious type, do you, Georgie?"

The duke winks behind his monocle. "More a life-of-the-party type."

I laugh it off, not keen to wax nostalgic about my spirited youth. After my father left us, Maman sent me to finishing school to meet an upper class of society. Betty adopted me as her bosom buddy and whisked me into her circle of Scottish friends with titles that hailed from centuries past. You'd think they would have ostracized a foreign commoner without a royal title. Yet, with Elizabeth Murray-Reid-Scott-Leveson-McDonald's endorsement, they were charmed by their new French friend with my French accent, penchant for style, and joie de vivre. Especially my joie de vivre, which they took as their motto. They invited me to their castles for Hogmanay, their New Year's Eve celebration with music, poetry, and bonfires. Far more appealing than spending holidays with Maman and my widowed aunties in my cheerless household.

Now the rest of the old clan gathers at the Pommery booth, kissing my cheeks and exaggerating about old times. They are all in their cups, and the noise level rises several decibels. My friends drink daily to ward off the plague, defend the body from corruption, cure roundworms, and any other excuse the Scottish concoct.

"I need a historian to remember all your titles," I joke. They hoot as if I said something uproarious.

The champagne vignerons watch us from their booths with something between shock and awe, which lifts my spirits considerably.

Henry opens bottles as fast as a timpani drum roll. Hubinet pours fresh champagne for my rowdy Scots and serves up hyperbole to match. "Your friend, Madame Pommery, is the first woman to change champagne in a generation. You can actually taste the grape varietals in every bubble."

I raise my glass. "*Lang may yer lum reek!*"

They send up a great cheer and clink each other's glasses.

Louise tugs my skirt. "What's it mean, Maman?"

"Long may your chimney smoke." I smile. "Toasting to a long, healthy life."

Betty drinks and makes a sour face.

With a flamboyant swish of silver tongs, Hubinet drops a lump of sugar into her glass, and she thanks him. He never misses a chance to please a potential customer.

"Alex, introduce us to your young men," Betty says, eyeing Henry with curiosity.

"Henry Vasnier is my winery director." My cheeks grow hot. "And Monsieur Hubinet is my sales agent."

Hubinet twists his curlicue mustache and exaggerates a bow. "At your service here at our London office." Drawing out a gold case, he hands out engraved business cards to men and women alike. Smart. Very smart.

"So, we place orders with you?" the duke asks.

"Absolutely, Your Grace." Hubinet grabs his leather order book. The duke dictates an extraordinary order while the other men look on.

My battered heart dances a jig.

Next to place his order is Lachlan Bayle, 11th Earl of Stellarmane Castle, Queen Victoria's commissioner, member of the House of Lords and president of the Royal Company of Archers. He has new kilts made every year by the finest Scottish tailors, paired with bespoke cashmere jackets with brass buttons engraved with the Stellarmane crest, lest one forgets who he is. I cannot fault his manners, following protocol to the tee, bowing and kissing my hand and addressing me by name. Yet his eyes never light on mine. I notice he's like that with women; he prefers men's company.

Helen, his wife, Countess Wallace-Gordon-Gibson-Russell-Hunter-Ferguson-Stellarmane, takes a sip and shimmies her red ringlets held with a gold hairclip of the Stellarmane crest. "Oh. Oh, my. I didn't expect that."

Taking a cue from Hubinet, Henry drops a lump of sugar into Helen's glass and refreshes her champagne.

"Oh, much better," she says. "Why didn't you become an artist, Alex? You always wanted to be an artist. You studied every painting in the museums. I could have never got through humanities without you."

While I reminisce with the ladies, Henry refills our glasses using the technique I taught him. One hand cradles the bottle while his thumb holds the punt. An engaging smile peeks from under his lush mustache. The ladies gather around him like bees on a rose bush to learn this elegant method of pouring. He helps each lady place their hands around the bottle just so. His hands on theirs. They swoon and giggle. Their overblown fuss bothers me, though I can't figure why.

"Alex, while you are in Britain, you really must pop up to Stellarmane Castle." Helen drinks. "Hmm, the second glass is so much better than the first."

"And third glasses are even better." I laugh. "Unfortunately, I can't come to Stellarmane. I'm traveling with my daughter."

"A castle, Maman?" Louise tugs my sleeve. "A real castle?"

The countess scowls at Louise.

Betty stands on tiptoe, waving a gloved hand frantically to a tall auburn-haired man standing at the back of the group. "Yoo-hoo, Sean! Sean! Come say hello to Alex."

She winks at me and gestures him to come. And, *voilà*. Baron Sean "Roderick the Turbulent" MacNeil strides toward me with those naked knees. His blue gaze jolts me like lightning. *Coup de foudre.*

He kisses my cheeks, and I'm overcome with the scent of sea spray and heather—my heart pounds in my throat. Needing to catch my breath, I turn away and pour him a coupe.

"My first champagne vintage," I say, offering the glass.

His prominent jaw moves as he drinks. How strong his jawline felt twenty-six years ago when we lie in each other's arms at Kisimul Castle. Sean took me there to show me his lost heritage. The MacNeil clan chief was forced to sell the castle and the entire Barra Island, leaving Sean without an inheritance. He vowed to change his fortuneless title no matter what it took. I never imagined his quest would break my heart.

Betty wriggles her emerald-ringed fingers at him. "Convince Alex to come to Stellarmane Castle."

He leans toward me. "Betty won't take no for an answer." His craggy voice churns up all those impassioned summers together. But his brazen blue eyes have grown stormy with tragedy. Betty wrote me about his wife: Baroness Benegal gathered wildflowers on the cliffs when the edge crumbled.

Sean finishes his coupe. "Better than Clicquot, but not quite as good as Moët."

I huff and smile. "Then, I guess I'll have to try harder."

"You should go up to Stellarmane," Hubinet says, with a meaningful glance at the order book. "In fact, I insist you take the time to renew your friendships." He laughs. "Especially after all the champagne they ordered."

"Here, here," Betty says.

"I suppose we could put off the bottling next week." I look to Henry for agreement, but he looks away, lips pressed tight. "Oh, that's right." I touch my forehead. "I almost forgot. We have tickets to the Camille Corot exhibition at *Musée des Beaux-Arts*." I turn to Betty. "We've been planning this for weeks. When is that exhibition exactly, Henry?"

He blinks his eyes. "Go ahead to Stellarmane, Madame. This is a rare opportunity to see your friends."

"Then it's settled." Sean extends his glass to Henry. "I'll try a little more of that champagne to celebrate."

Henry refills everyone's glasses, sugar lumps for the ladies.

I owe it to Pommery, I tell myself. Good for the business. Nothing whatsoever to do with Sean.

13

LA FOUDRE FRAPPE DEUX FOIS

Lightning strikes twice

When we get to Stellarmane, the nannies whisk Louise away with the other children to the far wing of the castle for their own activities. After dinner, I go check on her and say her prayers, lying down beside her until I hear her breathing grow rhythmic.

When I walk back, the sun sets low over undulating hills of greens and purples. Bagpipes wail their plaintive tune as footmen light torches along the paths. The pink sunset lights the castle outside, more beautiful than I remember. A palette of color reflects in the pond. At nineteen, I thought I'd spend the rest of my life painting these haunting landscapes. I wouldn't have signed them with a male pseudonym like women artists are forced to do, but my own signature, Baroness Alexandrine, painted in the royal blue of Sean's eyes.

How would my life be different if I'd lived this life with Sean? Standing outside the castle to take in some fresh night air, I look in at my beautiful friends. In the smoking lounge, Sean passes out cigars to the men, next to a separate parlor where the women gossip and sip Highlands cordials, separated after dinner as custom has dictated for centuries. Why are peasant men and women allowed to gather together after dinner, sharing stories by the hearth? What is it about the upper classes that strives to separate us by gender, economics, and history?

These thoughts make me long for my pillow. I'm dead tired after the days' long coach trip here, settling into my guest suite, the long cocktail hour, and longer dinner. I'm weary from acting like the high-spirited girl they knew who'd entertain them with hilarious jokes, paint their caricatures, play risqué games, or lead a moonlit romp through the heather.

I've outgrown that girl. What drives me now is the elusive process of creating the perfect champagne. Perfect to my taste, at least. My first vintage is not there yet. How could it be? And next year will be different, with changing weather and conditions. But, unlike wine, champagne is created with a unique recipe, blending grape varietals grown on different terrains, picked at different times. I have clearly missed some part of that process, or my first vintage would have been better. But what part? I spend the better part of the night thinking about what has evaded me.

After a breakfast tray of kedgeree, smoked haddock, rice, and eggs, I visit the activity den to find a sketchpad and drawing pencils. Stellarmane has all the games, sporting equipment, instruments, and art supplies one could use in a lifetime. I hike out to the pond, but I won't draw it. I face the castle, wanting to capture that timeless feeling I had last night, a building that goes back centuries and will be holding court here centuries from now. I want to capture that permanence, the elegance, the grandeur.

Sean walks toward me from the castle. He circles around and watches me draw. I try to relax my shoulders and let my hand move over the paper, first drawing the shape of the building, then the details, the tooth-shaped battlements, the contrasting stonework at the corners and windows.

"Why haven't you pursued your art?" he asks. "You could have been good."

His left-handed compliment irks me.

"Caught up in life, I suppose. The children, the house in Reims, our cottage in Chigny. So much to take care of, there was no time to focus on my art. I never thought about it." Why am I lying to him?

I sorely miss drawing, creating, making something beautiful. "In my spare time, I work with the orphanage at Saint Remi. I read to them, teach the girls to crochet, and find them work."

He watches me draw the towers. "And now you are making champagne. Do you love it as much as you loved art?"

His question punches my sternum. "Some people must earn a living. I need to support my family and pay for my son's education."

"Of course, that was arrogant of me." He touches my shoulder.

Gripping the pencil, I finish off the statue of Mercury standing guard over the castle. "When my husband died, I had no interest in taking over his wool and red wine company. But since I enjoy champagne, I thought I'd make that."

"Brave," he says. "You were always an instigator." He looks past me, lost in thought. "When my wife died, I kept living the life we always had."

I start to sketch the sad cant of his eyes, the noble angles of his cheekbones, the wrinkles across his forehead that never existed when I knew him.

"The same polo matches, same hunting trips, same weekend round-abouts get tiresome after twenty years, you know? Everyone introduces me to the same eligible women over and over like a clock's hands that circle the same numbers for eternity." His fingers run through thick auburn hair that waves off his forehead.

"Don't move, the light is perfect here," I say.

"Alex, I'm not sure I want a portrait, feeling as I do now."

I smirk. "Who says it is for you?"

The lines around his mouth quirk. "I loved your humor."

My chest tightens, but I keep sketching. "Um-hummm."

"Alex, am I alone in this feeling between us?"

I quote a poem I read him when he broke off with me.

> "You say you love; but with a voice
> Chaster than a nun's, who singeth
> The soft Vespers to herself
> While the chime-bell ringeth—
> O love me truly!
> You say you love; but with a smile
> Cold as sunrise in September,
> As you were Saint Cupid's nun,

And kept his weeks of Ember.
O love me truly!
You say you love—but then your lips
Coral tinted teach no blisses.
More than coral in the sea—
They never pout for kisses—
O love me truly!"

He frowns. "I'm baring my soul to you, and you quote John Keats."

I pack the pencils into their case. "We live in different worlds, Sean. I made the mistake once of not understanding that."

Helen rings the brass bell from the terrace, calling us to the afternoon games. Our friends gather around her, waving for us to come up.

I gather my sketchpad and pencils and start toward the house.

Sean spins me around and kisses me in full view of everyone. At first, I resist, but his soft lips dissolve my decorum. Nothing exists except the tingling warmth of our bodies together.

Our friends cheer and clap from above.

I gasp for air. "We should go."

But he holds me close, gazing at me with those turbulent eyes. Nothing has changed between us all these years. Only, everything. We have loved other people, had children, lived our lives, and yet his touch sets off a profound passion within me.

Sean holds my hand as we walk up the hill toward the castle. Clouds billow in a brilliant-blue sky. Neither of us speaks, our emotions too intense for words.

On the terrace, we are forced apart. The men will shoot skeet, and women will play croquet. I'm disappointed, but it allows me to understand my conflicted emotions. Things are moving too fast.

So strange seeing my school chums after twenty-six years, their rose-petal complexions etched with time, white croquet dresses with balloon sleeves, and white straw hats with white roses. Well-chosen husbands with well-chosen wives: Elizabeth, Araminta, Beatrix,

Gwendolyn, Jessamy, Masie, Tasmin, and our host Countess Helen. I'm thankful they don't use titles among themselves, or I would be the odd one out.

Viscountess Masie swings her mallet and sends the ball rolling over the greenest grass until it stops directly in front of the wicket. Masie has been ahead by two strokes since her first swing.

"Masie is amazing," I tell Helen, who nudges her ball forward ever so slightly.

"My husband thinks so." Helen presses her forefinger to her lips.

"The earl is devoted to you," I say.

"The earl is the perfect gentleman in public. What he does in private is his own affair, as long as he is discreet." But she sounds hurt. I would be.

She hits her ball against Masie's and sends it flying akimbo. "How was marriage to your romantic Frenchman? Was he worth jilting Sean?" She cackles like she told an outrageous joke.

"I believe it was the other way around." I hit the ball and miss the wicket by a kilometer.

Helen corners me out of earshot of the others. "Not the way I heard it. But tell me about your husband. Did you have that passion?"

"We were two sides of a coin, Louis and I. Different, but complementary. After he died, I realized how little I knew about his business." I whack my ball, and it pushes hers through the wicket.

"Thank you for that," she says, smiling with crooked white teeth. "The earl doesn't bother me with his business either, but lets me manage the house, the servants, our social calendar, and charities. Thank goodness for all the social etiquette we learned at Edinburgh, or I'd never get through it." She wipes the perspiration from her forehead with a handkerchief embroidered with her crest. "You were so good with the etiquette lessons. What a shame you have had nowhere to use it."

A jab between my ribs. "So, commonfolk have no need of etiquette, is that it?"

Helen cackles shrilly. "You know what I mean."

"Yes, I do. I know exactly." It's all coming back to me, the feeling of not measuring up to this crowd.

When Maman placed me in Edinburgh, she said I'd have to work extra hard to be accepted. She was thrilled when they invited me to their homes. She had never visited a castle, let alone stayed in one. Castles are for nobles and royals. How my orphan girls would light up to see something like this. The fairytales I read them, coming to life.

Masie hits the final post, winning the game, and we line up to congratulate her.

Feeling off kilter in their midst, I want to duck out before the next game starts. We no longer share the same vision of life. And Louis's letter this morning slapped me back to reality. I need time to think. "I'll see you ladies at the champagne tasting this evening." I blow them a kiss and wave, walking away before someone joins me.

But my walk takes me out on the bluff where the men are shooting clay pigeons, a sport Louis taught me in Chigny. I sit in the gallery behind them. They're outfitted in handsome tweed jackets with short waists. Full trousers taper at the ankles to fit neatly into tall boots. Their sporty hats have small brims. Unlike the women, they are focused on the competition, with none of the joking and gossip.

Sean glances back at the gallery where I'm sitting, grinning at me as if I came to see him. Maybe I did. He is ahead, the earl and duke tied for second. As they shoot their last round, most of their concentration has waned and they are not shooting well. But the earl and duke destroy every clay. Sean is last to shoot.

"Give me a moment, gentlemen." He walks back to me. "You've been chomping at the bit to shoot. Want to shoot my last round?"

He doesn't have to ask twice. He reminds me how to hold the rifle, and I don't object, though I've shot a thousand times. Sean's hand over mine, showing where my fingers pull the trigger. Wherever his skin meets mine sets off a shiver of pleasure.

"Shout 'pull' when you want them to send out the clay," he says. "Your eyes never leave the sight of the gun as you follow the clay through the air. When you know you have it, pull the trigger."

He backs away, his wavy auburn hair in my peripheral vision.

"Pull!" I yell, and a clay pigeon flies out. Following its arc through the gun sight, I pull the trigger, exhilaration shooting up my spine. The clay bursts into a million pieces.

"Where did you learn to shoot like that?" the duke says.

"My husband and I shot quail and grouse in Chigny." My voice shakes with unbidden emotion. "You must visit during duck season. It is quite quaint."

"We'd love to visit Chigny if you promise to cook," Sean says.

"I shoot." I laugh. "My cook cooks."

The men hand off rifles to the servants who begin cleaning them with special brushes and chamois.

We all start back.

"This is my last night, and I am hosting a champagne tasting on the terrace at five."

The duke consults his timepiece. "Two hours for my nap. Perfect."

Sean holds me back and lets the others go. "Why are you leaving? You just got here."

"I received a letter from my son," I tell him. "He says he's quitting university to come help me with the winery."

"Can't he make his own decisions?" Sean asks. "How old is he anyway?"

"He'll be twenty-one."

He strokes his chin. "Old enough to decide his future."

"He always planned to be a lawyer. I can't let him quit his dream to help me with mine." A wind gusts, and I wrap my scarf around my neck. "What if I need to sell the winery or even close the doors? He would have changed his life for nothing."

"He is a man, Alex. Treat him like one. Put him in charge of the winery and see what he can do." He kisses my knuckles. "Then, come back to Scotland." He pulls me off the path and presses my back against a tree as the rest of the crowd marches around the bend. Leaning down to kiss me, his lips move on mine, tentative at first, then unleashing his desire. All of our past passion flashes on my closed eyelids in a torrent of abandon. His smell, his touch, his breath in my ear. My hands stroke his neck, his shoulders and back, the material of his jacket becomes a hindrance. His ardent kisses erase the space between us, making my body ache for him.

"Come back to me, Alex." His breath staggers and his voice is thick. "You will love Benegal Castle. The views are magnificent. You can sketch or paint to your heart's content. We can ride, shoot, play cribbage, for all I care. So long as you are with me. We will live the life we should have lived all along."

A life with no financial struggles, no struggles to make champagne, no struggles, period. I take his rugged face in my hands—generations of seamen and pirates, the MacNeils.

"I am not the girl you loved, Sean. I am a woman with a family and a winery that needs me."

He grabs my shoulders. "You can't push me away that easily, Alex. Not this time."

Ducking under his arm, I leap onto the path, walking away. "I'll see you this evening. I must make sure they're chilling the champagne properly."

"There are servants for that," he calls after me.

I wave him off, not sure why I am running away. Sean is offering everything I've longed for. Companionship, both friendship and amorous, I can't deny the way my heart and body respond to him. His lifestyle is out of a fairytale. His wealth. I'd never have to worry about where the money will come from again.

While I dress for dinner, my mind churns with possibilities. Not much time to decide what to do since I planned to take the morning train.

Just as I finish instructing the server, Prue, on how I want her to serve the champagne, Betty enters the ballroom looking fresh and smelling of *eau de toilette à la violette*. Her blonde chignon is held with emerald hair combs. Her shoulders gleam above her evening frock, as if she read a romance novel on her divan instead of playing croquet all afternoon.

"Oh, splendid." She clasps her perfectly manicured hands. "I wanted to catch you before everyone else arrived. Why don't you and Louise come stay with the duke and me? We can invite Sean as well."

"Playing matchmaker, are you?" I ask. "I think we need champagne for this discussion." I nod at Prue, and she lifts a bottle from the silver ice bucket of chipped ice and water.

"I just thought you'd enjoy having him," Betty continues. "It will give us a proper chance to catch up, and our groom can teach Louise to ride the ponies."

Prue dries the bottle in a napkin and begins to pour slowly, so as not to burst the bubbles. A quick study, this girl.

"Louise is crazy about horses," I admit. "But my son sent a letter saying he's quitting school, and I must nip that in the bud right now."

Prue serves us coupes from a wooden tray inlaid with the Stellarmane crest.

"Louis always was a headstrong child." Betty shrugs one polished shoulder.

I'm sure she means to sympathize, but her remark rankles. I raise my glass. "*Au santé.*"

Betty gazes into the bubbles. "It's not too late for you and Sean, you know."

Sean and the rest of the crowd enter the ballroom.

"Speak of the devil," I say.

After Prue serves the champagne, I make a toast to the group, looking each one of them in the eye, saving Sean for last.

"May we have the hindsight to know where we've been, the foresight to know where we're going, and the insight to know when we've gone too far." I smile and clink their glasses, praying Sean understands and will spare me the torture of explaining further.

But Sean shows no restraint, acting as if we are already a couple, sitting beside me at dinner, whispering intimate secrets in my ear, touching my bare shoulders, arms, and hands at every opportunity. After dinner, he leads me onto the dance floor in front of the orchestra and we fall into one dance after another, our spirits exuberant and romantic. Our dancing becomes as playful and daring as we were so long ago, our bodies teasing each other. Breathless, we drink champagne between songs, finding a dark alcove to grasp each other close. The rest of our friends fade to a background, as we only have eyes for each other.

I spend the night with Sean, savoring his hungry hands exploring the sensuous realms of my body, long ignored.

After our first ravenous passion, he slows us down, allowing our bodies to remember how we move together, satisfying what we've craved and how we've changed. New ways to bring each other pleasure. Sean was my first lover and taught me this dance. To experience this again uncovers an essential part of myself long forgotten.

I lie spent on his chest, as he strokes my shoulders.

"Alex, my love, marry me," he says, kissing the top of my head.

A tingling warmth rushes from his kiss down my neck and through my spine to my core. The exhilaration unnerves me. Could it possibly last? Before I can answer him, I hear Sean's breath deepen to sleep, while I lie awake for hours on a down mattress too soft for my back, contemplating what it means.

Sean found a part of me that I had lost and presented it back to me on a velvet pillow like a diamond ring. I felt so alive having someone close to share this magical place. Such a beautiful life here. Sean and I shared an innocent love that could grow into something that suits us.

But would it? My thumb reaches across my palm and touches the calluses, signs of the life I have created since Louis passed. I miss the winery with all its foibles and challenges. I miss Damas and our crew. I miss Henry and our shared love of art.

I get up and start to dress.

"Running away?" Sean props himself up on his elbow.

I button my skirt. "I promised Henry to be back for the bottling."

"Perhaps you can visit Benegal castle after that?" His plaintive voice surprises me. He needs me to see he has made it.

"I would love to see your castle." I kiss my fingers and place them on his lips.

When the train pulls out of the station, not even Louise's gleeful chatter lifts my spirits. Why am I giving up this second chance at love? And for what? A dream too grandiose for my age and means. As Maman would say, "*Mordre trop pour mâcher.*" Biting off more than I can chew.

PART II

"Damas, we need a wine that is as dry as possible, but without rigidity. It should be soft and velvety on the palate... Above all, make sure it has finesse."

~Jeanne Alexandrine Pommery

14

JE-SAIS-TOUT

Know-it-all

1865. Louis comes home from school to "help" with harvest. His argumentative assertions, as only a lawyer can assert, interrupt our rhythm. Whenever he starts in with his ill-informed suggestions, my heart skitters like a jack rabbit and my chest flushes red hot.

But Henry has the patience of a saint and gives him all the attention he needs, never appearing frustrated. To thank him, I invite him to dinner. One dinner turns into many, discussing art and music, and sharing prized bottles of wine.

The September weather is one hundred degrees and cloudless, yet Louis measures each load of grapes like he's weighing diamonds, watching the needle jiggle one way, then another.

"Better hurry it up," Henry urges. "The grapes are going to spoil."

"Maybe if you bought the new scale I asked for, it wouldn't take so long," Louis bites back.

"Give me those grapes and move on." Henry takes the basket and gives it to Lucille and Louise to sort.

The waggoneers roll their eyes and snigger at Louis, which only flusters him more.

Damas adjusts his eye patch, waiting for more grapes to crush. The grueling heat plasters his white hair to his head like a newborn swan. He's worked his way up to *pressoir* man, and this is his first harvest. Henry and I worked with him to achieve just the right pressure to get a rich flavor, without the puckering taste of stems, seeds, and skins. I only wish Louis had the patience to learn, instead of insisting on his own methods.

Another wagon pulls behind the other three. The waggoneer joins the others who ridicule Louis watching the vacillating needle on the scale. When it finally stops, Louis painstakingly records the weight. "Now, fill out your full name, the vineyard, and your signature," he says.

The waggoneer sneers. "I no college boy. Monsieur Wolfe said I sign with X."

I'd heard Wolfe foreclosed a number of failing vineyards out from under struggling owners.

"We cannot accept an X as a signature," Louis argues. "What if you lose the money on the way back to your vigneron? What if Wolfe doesn't agree with the weight? There will be no proof of the transaction."

Stepping between them, I hand the ledger to the waggoneer. "Your X is fine."

His pencil cuts through two copies of the receipt and carbon paper between, and he grabs the money from Louis.

Louis pulls me aside. "Don't interfere or there will be anarchy."

"The only anarchy will be if you don't move this line," I tell him.

"Oh, no, please take your time," the next waggoneer jeers. "The longer you talk, the longer you cook the grapes. No matter what, you're paying us."

"You tell her, Jacob." The others snigger. "Women love to talk, don't they?"

I whisper harshly to Louis. "Approximate the weights and get these grapes to the press." My fault, I suppose. I emphasized accuracy of vineyards, dates, weights, and varietals. Never mentioned not letting the grapes spoil.

"If I am not accurate, we will pay too much," Louis argues.

"If the grapes are ruined, it won't matter if you are accurate." Grabbing an extra ledger, I go to the next wagon, recording specifics so Louis can just weigh the grapes and pay for them.

More wagons line up outside. Old, bossy waggoneers are anxious about being blamed for broiling their crop in the sun. Henry snarls and snaps at Louis to hurry, but Damas, in a silent world of his own, turns the grape-press wheel with masterful precision. Three pressings, no more.

Between the angry waggoneers, our scowling workers, and the blasted heat, the atmosphere crackles like before a thunderstorm. No time to unruffle feathers, we must get grapes pressed and in barrels. It looks like this year's harvest produced twice that of last year.

Monsieur Wolfe parades in as if he owns the winery, which he does, I suppose, until I can pay off the mortgage. "Madame Pommery, you cannot block Reims Square with your wagons."

"Working as fast as we can, Monsieur," I say in a singsong I don't feel. "Biggest crop I've seen in a decade."

Wolfe frowns. "*Eau de boudin.*" Black-pudding water. A sour mess.

Up on the grape press, Damas sways from the rising heat, his eyelids fluttering dangerously.

"Henry, can you relieve Damas? He needs a break," I say.

Henry rolls a wine-stained barrel next to the others. "Damas would be fine if Louis worked faster. He is the bottleneck."

I gesture Damas down and talk to his good eye. "Go sit in the ice box to cool down. Drink some water." He nods, and I climb up and take the wheel.

I reach across the wheel and rotate it. The round presser lowers through the barrel. Ripe grape juice sprays up at me, splattering my shirt and face, making me smile. This is the place to be. The spritzing juice, muscles straining, the glorious smell of the grapes. Soon, the tempo becomes a symphony with all the instruments in harmony.

Louis and Wolfe climb up to the grape press. "Where do you keep the cash to pay the vineyards?"

I wipe grape juice from my face with the heel of my hand. "If the pouch is empty, that's it. There is no more cash."

"If you don't pay for the grapes, the vineyards will never sell to you again," Wolfe says.

"Can you take the money from my account?" I ask.

He huffs. "No funds left after you purchased that new *pressoir.*"

117

A pang of panic. "I didn't expect such a large harvest."

"Can she use future orders as collateral for a loan?" Louis asks.

"Brilliant, Louis," I say. Finally his education works for us, rather than against.

"Orders as collateral? Highly unconventional." Wolfe strokes his double chin like a goatee. "The bank would require twenty percent interest on such a loan."

"That's extortion," Louis says.

Louise throws Felix's ball of yarn past Wolfe's shoulder, and the matagot pounces on him and climbs his back with his claws. Louise runs up to us, laughing, as if it is all a big game.

"Get him off, off." Wolfe hops on one foot, then the other.

Louise tries to pull Felix off, but his claws are stuck deep into the banker's tweed suitcoat.

Wolfe wriggles and screeches, "Take this hellcat off me!"

Louis taps his chin. "Ten percent interest, then?"

Felix yowls and jerks his claws from the fabric, shredding the fine wool and batting Wolfe's cheek.

"All right, all right," Wolfe says. "Ten percent. Get this monster off me."

Louis extracts Felix's claws from the jacket and hands him to Louise.

"I'll be adding a new coat to that loan." Wolfe stomps out, a torn swath of wool hanging from his coat like a tail tucked between a dog's legs.

"More wagons are coming," Henry says. "What do we tell them?"

"Take the grapes, and we'll find something to do with them."

Henry thrusts his hands in his pockets. "All due respect, Madame, but the grapes are too ripe now. We'll just throw out the juice. Better to save the money."

I sample the overripe grapes. The flavor has changed from green and sour to intensely rich, like grape jam. With this kind of fruit, we won't need to add sugar.

"Pommery stands by our agreements," I say. "Pay the vineyards with bank drafts, and they'll be paid with the loan."

118

After the harvest, I give everyone a much-needed vacation. Louise's nanny, Lucille, goes to visit family in London, and Louis offers to accompany her on the train to visit his university friends. Gallant of him to look after Lucille, who has become like family.

I take Louise and Felix out to Chigny. The cottage is dusty, and the gardens overgrown, but I'm too exhausted to tackle any of that just now. I need time to relax and breathe in the country air. Still, I can't resist trimming the roses. While Felix stalks field mice with a horrifying aggression, I ask Louise to hold the basket to collect the roses. The petals are vibrant and fragrant as they fall off their stems.

"What are those people doing down there, Maman?" Louise points to the wheat fields south of us.

I shield my eyes with my hand. Dozens of women and children bend over, swinging back and forth, their fingers sifting through the stubbled chaff.

"Ah, they are called 'gleaners.' After the men finish harvesting, women and children go pick up any grains the men have missed."

"Why don't the men do it?"

"They don't think it's worth the work for how little they get."

"But is it worth it?"

"All winter, the women feed their families with grain left for waste," I tell her. "They grind the wheat into flour and bake baguettes, served warm with fresh-churned butter."

Louise looks back at the gleaners as I finish the last rose bush. "Where should I put the roses, Maman?" She inhales the brimming basket, closing her dewy eyelids. Her nose touches the petals.

"What if we make potpourri from the rose petals and help the orphans make sachets? Would you like that?"

Her smile reveals a new adult tooth popping through pink gums.

We blend the petals with grated cinnamon and cloves from the kitchen and spread them out on parchment paper.

"Tomorrow, they'll dry in the hot fall sun."

We sit on the half stone wall around the terrace to watch the last rays of the sun cast an ethereal shimmer over the vineyards and fields. The gleaners carry their baskets on their heads, silhouetted against the sunset.

"What are we going to do with those old grapes Louis said were rotten?" Louise asks. "They tasted yummy to me."

I stroke her hair, gleaming in the sunset. "Well, we'll have to see how the juice tastes after it ferments. I have a notion it will make a delicious champagne."

"Then we would be gleaners, too." She snuggles under my arm.

"Out of the mouth of babes," I say, hugging her close. How often do you see something you've tried to teach your children make an impact?

15

SI CE N'EST PAS UNE CHOSE, C'EN EST UNE AUTRE

If it's not one thing, it's another

1869. In April, the fermented juice is ready for blending. The wine from last year's harvest is as bountiful as Jesus's loaves of bread. I whisper a prayer of gratitude to my Smiling Angel as my crew rolls in barrels of Chardonnay, Meunier, and Pinot Noir. We keep the late harvest separate since the juice was on the vine too long. Louis and Henry joke that they'll bottle it for the priests who are not fussy about wine.

I dip my wine thief, as we call the glass pipette, into the *cuvée* for a taste.

"It needs a fruitier flavor," I tell Henry. "Add more Meunier."

His mustache twitches, his anxiety mounting. He wants to get on with the blending, but I can't allow it until the taste is right.

Damas adds Meunier to the blend. I dip my wine thief to extract the new blend, then hold it to the light. Still gold like straw. I worried the Meunier would add too much color from the grape skins. Lifting the pipette above my mouth, I release the rubber bulb at the end, allowing the wine to flow into my palate. Tastes of tart cherry, raspberry, strawberry, and a hint of rose that will only get better with time. I nod my approval.

"What mixture should I use for the tirage?" Henry asks.

I hesitate, then give the order. "Add our regular tirage of yeast, wine, and sugar, but cut the sugar in half."

Louis scoffs. "Maman, you should have learned your lesson by now. People don't want sour champagne."

I dip the wine thief into the late-harvest barrel. "Have you ever tasted grape juice this golden? It's like liquid sunshine." I hold the wine thief over Louis's mouth and release the liquid. If I could only get him to slow down and taste, really taste the wine, maybe he could understand where I am going with this: to make a champagne that will stand out from the others. The alchemy of making champagne is like spinning gold from straw.

Louis rolls it around his mouth. At least he's tasting instead of fighting me as usual. He sees champagne as a business rather than an art.

I offer Henry a taste, and he holds up his palm. "You decide, Madame Pommery. But decide quickly so we can get to blending."

"Well, Louis, what do you think?" I ask. "Do we need all the sugar in the tirage?"

"Hubinet says to make what sells." Louis throws up his hands. "If the dry champagne doesn't sell, we can't pay the mortgage, and Wolfe will jump to foreclose our winery. Are you willing to risk everything on a whim?"

Taking another mouthful from the wine thief, I taste luscious apricots and golden raisins, plump and tender. "It is not a whim. I can taste the final champagne. It is exactly the taste I'm looking for. Light. Delicious. Sophisticated."

"Aargh!" Louis growls and tugs a lock of hair from his head. "You win. You always win."

Henry and Damas start mixing sugar, yeast, and wine according to my new recipe. "Your mother has a vision, and I for one, believe in her judgment."

"You're both on the moon." Louis throws up his hands in disgust.

Henry gives the cask of tirage to the bottling line. "Where did you find to store this vintage? As soon as it's bottled, we'll load the wagon and take it there."

I rub my aching neck. "I asked Mayor Werle to help me find

extra storage space in one of the champagne houses. But no one would help."

Henry shakes his head. "Ah, the gentlemen's club is sticking together. They can't stand to see you growing. Their employees are coming to us because you pay better wages and sick pay."

"Down at the Biergarten they say you run the winery like a charity," Louis says. "Now's their chance to get even."

We search everywhere for space: the cellar, the tasting salon, and even the mezzanine—casks and bottles everywhere.

Louis wags his finger at me. "If you didn't demand to age our champagne four years instead of two, we wouldn't have this problem. Our inventory has doubled."

I look up at him, taller than his father. "Those extra years spin gold in the bottle. Smaller bubbles and a creamier, refined taste. This quality will make Pommery champagne stand above the rest."

Henry purses his lips. "Without someplace to store the bottles, we may as well toss the champagne in the Marne River."

Both men stare at me for an answer I am helpless to give. Donning my cape, I head to the cathedral to pray for a miracle.

The Smiling Angel listens patiently as I pour out my tale of woe, pathetic when I hear it out loud. Angels and God have more important things to deal with. But finding more cellar space is essential for Pommery Champagne, and my family and employees depend on it. One last glance at her serene face, I feel certain she will work on my behalf. Having faith is the most vital part of prayer.

One foot in front of another, I wind my way through the cobbled streets of Reims. The setting sun shines ethereal rays over the city like a Delacroix painting. At the edge of town, I walk through the great stone ramparts to Butte Saint-Nicaise, a fancy name for a disgusting municipal dump yard Mayor Werle has tried to close down for years. Yet, the bourgeoisie and noblemen continue to dump their unwanted things, and poor people scour the dump for treasures.

A hunched-over woman croons an ancient folksong while she drags away a tin bathtub with rusted-out holes. Peasants, servants, and painted prostitutes pick through broken furniture and equipment—everything well past usefulness. A young man hoists out a broken plow for oxen. A mother with one child in hand and another one tied in a shawl at her breast picks out a bald doll from the fuming debris.

Recognizing a peasant woman from Saint Remi, I wave. "*Bonsoir,* Madame Auclair."

She ducks her head, then realizes it is too late to hide. "Why, Madame Pommery, I wouldn't expect to see you here." Her children pick through the rubble, their feet bare and filthy. She steps toward me, shielding them from my sight.

"I haven't seen your children lately for story time at Saint Remi," I tell her. "We're reading *Arabian Nights* after school. Would they like to come?"

Madame Auclair juts her chin defiantly. "They have no time for stories since their father went to the Army. They work at the wool mill until eight."

Now I am the one to be ashamed. Of course, they work. The woman is doing the best she can.

"I hadn't heard they were conscripting men for the Army," I say.

"They aren't. My husband enlisted when he heard they pay two hundred a month. Left for Austria the next day. Now, my Jed is the man of the family." She chucks her finger at her scrawny son dragging a bedraggled chair out of a pile with the help of his sisters.

"I'll drop by some books for you."

She holds up her palm. "Mighty kind of you, Madame. But we don't read."

Another gaff. The distance between the classes is as wide as the ocean. We barely speak the same language here in the same town.

I point to the crest of the butte. "I came to see the sunset from the top."

"Sunset?" She scoffs and looks at the poor souls scouring the dump. "Madame Pommery, this is no place for a woman without a chaperone. Isn't that what you taught us?" She clucks her tongue smugly.

My entire life I've lived by these rules and taught them to others. Now they sound haughty and ignorant.

"Would you like to see the sunset with me?"

She backs away, shaking her head like I've gone mad. She must think me a crazy bourgeoisie, walking out to see a view. And she would be right.

I climb past the dump to the top of the butte. My lungs heave and my calves twinge, but the stars piercing the deepening sky make the climb worth it. Cirrus clouds curl like fancy ribbons at the trim shop. Light glances off the Saint Remi domes and the spires of Reims Cathedral surrounded by the entire town of Reims. Beyond town, Montagne de Reims rises in undulating waves of vineyards, sheep pastures, and newly planted fields. The whirl of wind and healing toll of Reims Cathedral bells bring me a peace I haven't felt in ages.

Birds warble and twitter from the gnarled beech tree blown over to a sharp angle. An animal bounds past, and a flock of yellow-breasted chats fly out at me. Not sure if it's a weasel, polecat, or wild boar, but I start to run. My foot disappears into a soft patch of pea gravel and doesn't stop. My leg shoots down into a hole, taking my body with it.

Sharp gravel scrapes through my bloomers and stockings as I slide deeper and deeper into darkness. When I reach out to stop my descent, my palms are shredded by rough stone, and I hug them to my breasts. Lower and lower I fall into this shaft, the temperature dropping.

When my boots hit solid ground, my legs jam into my body with an excruciating jolt. Rocks slide down behind me, pelting my head. I can't move; I'm lodged between rocks. A boulder smashes the side of my skull.

16

QUAND ON Š'Y ATTEND LE MOINS

When you least expect it

Hours or days later, I gasp for air. I am awake, I think. Can't see a thing in the darkness. The pounding in my head is real, anyway. Chalk dust saturates the air, coating my tongue and throat. Still can't move. My feet seem to be covered with rocks. I dig to extract them, fingernails breaking and sending spasms up my hands. The more I move, the more stones pummel my neck. My heart jumps against my tightening ribs.

Finally, I pull one foot out and use it to push out the other. Crawling horizontally over the rocks on hands and knees, my long dress tangles between my legs. More stones fall from above. Must keep going. When my hands feel smooth surface beneath me, I squat, then push up to stand. But my ankle buckles, pain ripping through my bones. I hop along the cold, clammy floor. The darkness closes in. Can't make out anything, not even my hands in front of my face.

The black silence breaks with a terrible screeching and flapping. Bats pummel my ears like boxers. I lift my arm over my head to protect my face. They screech and churn around me, nipping at the back of my neck. Finally, they fly off with a whoosh. Oddly, the bats give me hope. If they are in here, wherever *here* is, there must be a way out.

127

I try to follow in the direction of their sound. Hobbling along with a swelling ankle, it seems an eternity until I touch a dank, dusty wall. The path slopes downward, getting colder. So much colder, goosebumps prickle my arms and legs. Hearing bats screeching in the distance, I follow the sound until my arms can touch both sides. A tunnel has to lead somewhere.

But the tunnel leads to another and another, the air getting thin and humid, making my lungs work hard. My ankle throbs as I put more weight on it, but I have no choice but to continue.

The darkness softens to shades of gray, sprouting a kernel of hope in my belly. Feeling my way around the curved expanse, I sense an enormous chamber like the crayères of Veuve Clicquot. Far above me, a pale light glows through a small square opening, stars winking. Yelling as loud as I can, my voice dissolves in the vastness, much too far away for anyone to hear me.

I've heard warnings about these shafts left by ancient Roman quarries dug a thousand years ago, leaving generations after them to fall to their death. No way to know where these sinkholes are until someone disappears into them.

Hundreds of feet above me, bats fly out of that square opening to the night sky. My heart pumps with promise. But there is no way to reach the opening.

Dampness permeates my skin. My knees and ankle ache. Sinking to the floor, I smell something sweet and rotting. Hear a rustle and squeak. Rats feasting on a fallen deer. Drawing my knees to my chest, I lift my eyes to the stars, and pray like never before.

The skeleton leers at me with a heavy brow bone and broken teeth, a welcome distraction from the searing pain of Doctor DuBois's fingertips. One of the skeleton's ribs is missing, but otherwise it is a perfect specimen that hangs in the corner of his office. Jars of formaldehyde animals line the shelves: frogs, squirrels, rats. Doctor DuBois calls them his pets.

"You may have broken your ankle." DuBois frowns.

"If it wasn't for Madame Auclair, you could have starved to death before anyone found you," Henry scolds.

"I owe her my life," I say. "Where was Louis? Why didn't she bring him to where I fell?"

"I was cleaning up in the winery and heard Madame Auclair's knock." His face colors, suspiciously, covering for Louis.

Louis is never around in the evenings, preferring political rallies and clandestine meetings of some sort. At twenty-eight, he's too old for me to object.

Henry's forefinger strokes his lush mustache, strained eyes watching with grave concern as the doctor cleans my abrasions. Henry, always there when I need him. I squeeze his hand, though it's not proper. He doesn't seem to mind. I needn't ask what he was doing at the winery so late. He always stays after everyone else, inspecting the day's work and setting up tasks for the following day, checking the fermenting barrels and riddling bottles. What would I do without him?

Henry brought back a search party with lanterns, found the sinkhole, and followed the landslide down into the cavern. He brought me directly here to Doctor DuBois's office. My dress is torn to shreds, my hands and face a fright.

The doctor's fingers reflect in his large lenses as he prods my swollen ankle, making me wince with pain. "What possessed you to be wandering around Butte Saint-Nicaise at night? An awful place even in daylight."

"I wanted to see the sunset." Sounds ridiculous now.

He clucks his tongue. "Lucky for you, your ankle does not appear to be broken, just a bad sprain."

His skillful fingers wrap my ankle with a smelly poultice of turmeric, garlic, onion, and castor oil and wraps it with a bandage. "The dump should not be allowed on the butte," he says. "It's too dangerous. People fall into the crayères all the time. And when the wind blows, it makes the city smell like a pigsty."

"Why don't they move the dump to somewhere out of the way?" A plan percolates in my brain. The crayère was cold. Perfect to store champagne.

He scowls. "I have tried to get the city council's support, but they say they have no jurisdiction since the dump is outside the city ramparts."

"Who owns the property?" I swing my throbbing ankle down from his table.

He tilts his head. "Deeds are kept at the courthouse."

Henry helps me off the table, rumpling the linens that smell of lavender water.

"Wait, Madame." The doctor reaches behind the door and hands me a beechwood walking stick. "Use this until your ankle is better."

"I couldn't," I say, meaning I won't. I don't wish to hurry old age.

Henry takes it. "Just until your ankle heals, Madame. We'll return it when you don't need it any longer."

I run my hands along the smooth handle where the doctor's initials are carved. "A cane would make climbing up Butte Saint-Nicaise so much easier." I laugh.

"As your doctor, I cannot recommend viewing sunsets from the butte."

"You can't imagine how beautiful it is up there." I smooth the linens on the operating table. "How much do you think that land is worth?"

"Three hundred acres of trash?" The doctor laughs. "The city should pay you to clean it up."

"Sold." I smile and thank the doctor.

Henry helps me into the rig. "My dear Madame, if you wish to see the sunset, I am happy to take you for a ride." He jumps in beside me.

"Henry, we could store thousands of cases down there in those crayères."

Worry wrinkles his brow. "You could have been seriously hurt." He rustles the reins, and we jerk ahead down the narrow street. The dawn brings the first signs of life in the city, storekeepers sweeping their stoops, wagons arriving from the fields to set up the market.

Henry drives on in silence, his jaw working, his eyes sunken deep in thought. His hair tousled. A stubbled beard I've never seen. His hands are scraped and bleeding. His clothes torn and dusty. I haven't thought how my fall affected him.

"Where was Louis last night?" I ask.

"You must ask him yourself, Madame." He swallows hard. "Tell me you are not serious about the dump."

I repeat, "I am not serious about the dump." I poke my tongue in my cheek.

He grins and the gloom leaves his face. "Oh, what am I going to do with you, Madame?"

"Coffee would be nice."

He laughs. "After the night we've had, coffee would be delightful."

17

PAS SORTI DU BOIS

Not out of the woods

As soon as I feel up to it, I drive my buggy to the courthouse, using the doctor's cane to walk in. The stooped clerk with lenses dangling off his bulbous nose points to a wall of wood filing cabinets smelling musty and old. The filthy paned windows on the alleyway let in very little light, so I light a lantern. I search the files all afternoon, never finding mention of Butte Saint-Nicaise, until the clerk says he's closing.

Despondent, I drive my buggy up to Butte Saint-Nicaise to say goodbye to a foolish dream. The hillside shadows the abandoned furniture and trash, but the setting sun turns Reims golden as heaven's gates. If this land is owned by someone, why would they let people dump here? Is it possible no one owns the land?

The next day, I return to the courthouse and ask to reference the Napoleonic Code. The cranky clerk points a crooked finger at a row of a hundred leather-bound books. I search the books with dry fingertips, getting dryer with each page turned. I have no idea what I am looking for.

Book II is about property: the distinction of property, of usufruct, right of common, and habitation, servitudes, or manorial services. Several hours pass, skimming pages and finding nothing about abandoned property.

On to Book III, which continues with "Property," and I find this passage in section IV:

> 811. When no person appears to claim a succession, there is no heir known, or the known heirs have renounced therein, such succession is taken to be vacant.

> 812. The curator of vacant successions may maintain possession of a property, without legal title, becomes the lawful owner if the original owner does not show up to take possession within a year.

> Killing two birds with one stone. Before anyone else beats me to it.

Louis is skeptical about taking over Butte Saint-Nicaise, until he checks his lawbooks about squatters' rights that confirms what I found. Though neither Louis nor Henry loves the idea, they concede we have no choice. Our winery is beyond capacity. As insurance, Louis quietly files a claim to the property with the city clerk.

Henry finds an old, rutted road around the back side of Butte Saint-Nicaise, so folks won't see our wagons. Then, at daybreak, before most people are about, we take our crew to clear the avalanche rubble. We take care not to draw attention and are shielded by the outcrop of dwarf beech on top of the hill.

By April, we've built a makeshift staircase thirty meters down and one hundred and sixteen steps to the bottom. Then, we move our oldest wine into the crayères, stacking the wine bottles near the chalk walls horizontally with planks of wood between.

Louis comes to me to ask for extra payment for the crew. "The work is dirty and hard, and we've worked them double shifts."

"I'm impressed with your concern for those less fortunate, Louis," I say.

"Cats don't make dogs," he says. "How else would I think, living with you all my life?"

"We should reward our crew, but company funds are held by Reynard Wolfe, and he cannot know anything about this place until it is ours."

He hangs his head. "I know we're pressed to cover expenses and payroll each month."

I huff. "And the mortgage payment. Wolfe never lets me forget that."

"But, Maman, these men support their parents, wives, and children. They've been loyal to us, while others have deserted us to work for the gentleman's club wineries."

I grasp Louis's shoulder. "I'll see what we can do."

In a couple of days, when we finish hauling the last of the older champagnes into the cavern, I send Louis and Henry to bring all fifty-three workers to the grand gallery of the crayères. I stand at the foot of the wood-slat staircase as they file into the dusty gallery. They line up before me and take off their hardhats we gave them to protect their heads from falling rocks and low ceilings. Chalk dust covers their clothes and faces, making strange white crevices in their wrinkles. I'm sure their mouths are dry and dusty like mine. They look tense and on edge, whispering tersely to each other. I only catch one word: *licencié.* Fired.

I raise my arms up, and they quiet down. "We could not have done this without you," I tell them.

Henry uses the payroll sheet to call them by name. I shake each of their hands, thanking them for all their extra work and loyalty to Pommery. Louis gives them an envelope of francs, a bonus week's pay. Money I keep under my mattress for emergencies.

With their hands waving envelopes, their jubilation bounces off the walls.

Henry brings his brass whistle to his mouth, and the men quiet down again.

"Tomorrow is my birthday," I say. "I'm giving you the day off with pay." I turn to Henry. "Even you, Monsieur Vasnier. The winery will be closed."

The crew cheers and marches out singing *"Joyeux Anniversaire."*

The next morning, I hear a knock at the door. Must be Henry for the outing he mentioned.

He stands in front of a sleek Landau carriage with a hired driver. The porch smells of springtime with fragrant baskets of yellow forsythia, pink magnolia, white almond blossoms, camellias, daffodils, narcissus.

"Oh my," I say. "What's all this?"

"The crew wanted to do something for your birthday," Henry says.

"And the Landau?" I ask, stepping toward the sleek carriage. "We said we'd take my gig."

"It's your birthday," Henry smirks. "I want you to relax and enjoy the day. And maybe we will not get lost this time."

I laugh. "I didn't mind that so much." Too forward, too much.

The jarring clip-clomp of horse hooves on cobblestones softens when we turn into a smooth dirt road between vineyards. The April air is thick with the fragrance of budding grape leaves and wild mustard between rows, making me quite giddy.

I clasp Henry's hand. "Glorious, isn't it?"

"Joyeux anniversaire, Alexandrine." He kisses my cheeks la bise with the affection of a friend, but the touch of his lips springs a deep longing for more. I hold myself back. Henry is my employee, after all, and fifteen years younger. Am I afraid he will reject me, or afraid he won't?

Gazing out to the rolling vineyards, I breathe in the heady aroma to calm my racing heart. I should be proud of my restraint, but instead I'm sorely disappointed I missed catching the brass ring on the carousel.

18

Où sont les neiges d'antan?

Where are the snows of last year?

1869. Baron Sean "Roderick the Turbulent" MacNeil invites himself to Chigny for duck season. The house will already be full, since Henry invited Reynard Wolfe in order to improve our banking relations, and Louis invited his young lawyer friend, Emile Loubet, who has been coming for years. I can hardly turn Sean down since I've casually invited him in letters over the past several years.

I brought Lucille, Chantal, and Yvonne in early to get the cottage in top shape for the Baron—no cobwebs on the rafters, fresh linens on the beds, crystal-clear French doors, my rose gardens blooming like mad.

I never visited Benegal Castle. A subject we never broach. Our missives are airy and witty. Never personal. After all, we'll both be fifty this year and have gone on to live our separate lives.

So, I'm taken aback when he arrives. The gray at his temples accentuates his brilliant gaze. His sharp-edged body has filled out nicely with a couple of pounds. He touches me every chance he gets and speaks low, sharing intimacies like we've never been apart.

The Baron, as everyone calls him now, looks very much at home here in the paneled dining room overlooking the garden: his fine manners, his elevated English, his bespoke country gentleman clothing.

I seat him at the head of the table next to me. Is it his skin or cologne that smells of a sea breeze? He grasps my hand and compliments my champagne. How long will he pretend he is an old friend?

Lucille helps Chantal serve the cassoulet in small crockery; it smells of bacon and leeks. Wolfe and Emile compliment the steaming dishes, while Louis drops his hand and caresses Lucille's leg. So that's where he spends his time.

Across from me, Henry studies the Baron with an intense scrutiny. What is he looking for?

"Bon appétit, everyone," I say, and we clink glasses of Pommery red.

Emile and Wolfe dig into the cassoulet with great gusto.

"My Lord, if you do not mind me asking, where does the 'Turbulent' moniker come from?" Henry asks the Baron.

"Ah, well, my great-grandfather was 'Roderick the Turbulent,' a ruthless and cunning pirate, who caused a great deal of trouble raiding merchant ships up and down the coast. He became so rich he shod his horse with golden shoes and decorated Kisimul Castle with fine silks and exotic woods. His trouble came when he raided Queen Elizabeth's ship. The queen posted a bounty for his capture, but no one could penetrate his castle."

"So he was never captured?" Louis takes a bite of sausage.

"Everyone knew of Roderick's great love of wine." Sean's eyes dance. "So, a greedy wine merchant sailed to Kisimul Castle and invited Roderick to taste wines on his ship, an invitation he could not resist. He sampled wines to his heart's content and fell asleep—only to awake shackled in chains and headed to Edinburgh. The great pirate had finally been caught."

"If he was captured, how did you get your title?" Henry asks.

The Baron holds up his forefinger with a mischievous expression. "We'll need some Scotch for that story."

We retire to the drawing room, where Lucille adds logs to the great hearth. The men settle into the oversized leather wing chairs, and Sean opens the Glenturret he brought, pouring glasses for everyone. I decline, asking Lucille for coffee instead.

In the chair next to mine, Henry smells the Scotch. "Subtle aromas of white pepper and bonfires."

I laugh. "You made that up." Leaning over, I smell his glass, but smell Henry instead. "I detect a whiff of licorice."

He smiles and offers me his hard licorice tin. Sean frowns.

"What happened to Roderick the Turbulent?" Emile asks.

"He was released to King James, who asked why he robbed Queen Elizabeth's ship. Roderick answered that he did it to avenge the killing of Mary, Queen of Scots. With that clever answer, King James pardoned Roderick and sent him back to Barra."

"You have to admire Roderick's shrewdness." Wolfe offers a box of cigars. "Care for the finest cigar you will ever taste? A German banker named Upmann makes these in Havana."

The men light cigars, drink Scotch, and argue about France's parliamentary elections.

"The opposition party won seventy-five percent of the legislature seats away from Napoleon," Louis says with fervor. "Rioters sang the "Marseillaise," which Napoleon banned, while they destroyed streetlamps and shop fronts."

Emile nods eagerly. "I read more than a thousand were arrested by the cavalry and infantry."

"Mark my words, gentlemen," Wolfe says, puffing black clouds of smoke. "Now that Germany sees a crack in Napoleon's power, it leaves France wide open for attack."

Why must men always talk of politics, war, and sports instead of art, literature, and music? Sean pours more Scotch all around, except Henry, who holds his hand over his glass. The mantle clock strikes eleven. The smoke and strident voices make my temples throb. I bid the gentlemen *bonne nuit* and climb the stairs to my boudoir.

Hearing footfalls behind me, I turn around.

Henry holds out the licorice tin. "For your headache."

I pluck it from his hand. "Thank you, Henry." I don't have to ask how he knew about my headache; he watches everything. It comforts me to know he does.

"That was an unbelievable story your Baron told," he says.

"Yes, unbelievable," I say. "The Baron inherited his title, castle, and fortune from his wife."

Apparently, the Baron is sleeping in. Reynard Wolfe ogles Yvonne as she serves up a Scottish breakfast of potato scones, lorne sausage, white pudding, and porridge, which I ordered especially for Sean. After breakfast, the men get tired of waiting for him. I tell them to head out to the duck pond and I'll bring the Baron later.

The fog clears in the valley before he comes down the stairs, dressed out of the pages of *The Sporting Magazine* in a houndstooth cutaway jacket, knickers, and tall buttoned boots.

"That feather bed swallowed me up." He stretches out his long arms. "Aren't the others awake, yet? We stayed up till the wee hours drinking Scotch and talking politics—never a good combination."

"They left for the pond an hour ago." I pour him coffee.

"Alone at last." He leans in to kiss me, and I turn one cheek then the other for *la bise*. "It's good to see you again, Alex."

The warm timbre of his voice prickles goosebumps across my décolleté. "Would you like some breakfast?" To cover my nerves, I take my hunting jacket off the coat rack and slide my arms in the sleeves.

"No breakfast for me." He finishes his coffee. Picking up his rifle case, he gestures to the door. "After you, my dear Madame Pommery."

I take the beechwood walking stick from behind the door and stride out toward the duck blind, Sean beside me. You'd think at fifty years of age, I'd be over the fluttery-stomach and pounding-heart nonsense. Perhaps it's fear. Sean scares me. Not Sean exactly, but the fairytale life he represents, that I once dreamed was mine.

I was so sure of our future back then, I wrote Maman that I expected Sean to propose. But then, at a grand dinner party with all our friends, his parents proudly announced that Baron Sean "Roderick the Turbulent" MacNeil was betrothed to his cousin. Our friends gasped throughout the ballroom. The shame I felt that night still stings, twenty-some years later.

As we walk, I plant the beechwood cane in the weeds. I haven't returned it to the doctor since my ankle is still weak.

"What happened to your leg?" he asks as we walk.

"Long story."

"I'd like to hear it."

"Maybe later, over a Scotch."

He knocks the heel of his hand to his temple. "Scotch is long gone, I'm afraid. Your banker talked the hind leg off a donkey about you and your winery. Acted like he owns a piece or it, and that you two are very close. Is there something I should know?"

"Goodness, no." I laugh. "I am the sole proprietor. Wolfe is interested in whatever advances him in the banking empire. He has lent us a great deal of money over the years. I could not have made it without his help."

"So, you rely on his financial assistance," Sean says.

"Which he holds over my head like a guillotine blade." I huff. My ankle is throbbing, but the duck blind is in sight. "It's just that Wolfe's bank holds the mortgage on the winery and if we default, I'd be forced to take him as a partner, or sell outright."

"That banker needs to be knocked down a notch or two." Sean swallows hard, his Adam's apple working.

"Oh, no, don't say anything." I place my hand on his chest. "Please, Sean, it will only make matters worse."

He traces my widow's peak with his fingers, trailing down to my cheekbones, and holds my chin between his fingers. "So, Wolfe is all business."

"Of course."

"So, he won't mind if I kiss the hostess." His mouth hovers mine, just out of reach. His thumb explores my bottom lip. He's teasing me, and I cannot move. Then he kisses me, I'm flooded with desire.

"Where have you two been?" Wolfe watches suspiciously as we enter the lean-to blind.

Camouflaged with reeds and cattails, the rest of the hunters scour the skies and pond. Three ducks lay in a basket.

"You've done well, I see." The dogs come to greet me, and I rough them up behind their ears.

"Thanks to Emile, we'll have dinner tonight." Louis claps his old classmate's back, and he beams.

Sean crouches down and pets the dogs beside me. "Brittanys?"

"Braques Français," I tell him, rubbing Harley's ear. "I bought puppies for my husband when he retired. Now the neighbors keep them for me."

Sean opens his case and prepares his rifle, while Wolfe spews duck-hunting tips as if everyone in the blind hasn't been hunting all their lives. Ignoring Wolfe's banter, Sean raises his sporting rifle and swiftly fires. Several ducks fall from the sky.

Wolfe drops his musket. "Criminy, is that a Scottish rifle? Takes the sport out of hunting, doesn't it?"

Henry signals the dogs to retrieve the fallen ducks, and they bound through the weeds.

"Made in Scotland by Alexander Henry himself." Sean wipes his gun barrel down. "Beautiful, robust, reliable, a rifle of the highest quality and precision."

Wolfe cups his hands around his mouth, stretches his thick neck upward, and calls ducks overhead. His squawk is loud and insistent, sounding more like a wild turkey.

"Try quieter, shorter calls," Sean says. "Ducks in a pond are attracted to the serenity and peacefulness."

Wolfe swivels around. "I'll have you know I called ducks for the Grand Duke of Mecklenburg-Schwerin."

The hair stands on the back of my neck.

"Perhaps that was in a larger body of water," Sean says. "But when hunting in ponds, every aspect needs to be brought down to size."

Henry scans the sky with binoculars in his calm and meticulous way.

Wolfe cups his hands and lets out a dreadful screech.

"Stop calling for a while," Sean suggests. "If the ducks sense we are desperate, they won't land."

Wolfe's face colors. "I'm starved. What's for dinner? I love your duck confit."

"Yvonne is preparing a very special magret de canard," I say.

"Only the finest for nobility, I see." Wolfe rocks his head affectedly. "How did you meet, anyway?"

"School friends," he says. "Alex breathed fresh air into our stuffy crowd with their suffocating Scottish sensibilities. She led us on midnight mongoose chases, was a better shot than any of the boys, and flirted like Sarah Bernhardt." His fervent gaze roils up an old version of myself that feared nothing.

Wolfe's nostrils quiver. "The Madame Pommery I know sets the standards of decorum in our town." His head cranks to me. "Which is it, Madame Pommery, are you the daring coquette or a pillar of society?"

"Monsieur Wolfe, you know Madame Pommery works tirelessly to support the town of Reims," says Henry.

Wolfe lifts his chin. "It is the Baron who is disparaging her reputation, not I. What say you, Madame Pommery?"

Nothing good can come from answering. I was a rebel at finishing school, and my friends loved it. But when I married, I abandoned my devil-may-care attitude and lived by the rules for twenty-five years.

"What is your answer, Madame?" Wolfe heckles.

Sean steps toward him. "Apparently, Prussians don't teach manners in school, so let me advise you. When a lady does not answer, she does not wish to tell you."

Louis and the others laugh.

Blood surges to Wolfe's cheeks. Riveting toward the pond, he bellows out another duck call. Ducks scatter in all directions. Sean brings out a strange-looking wooden pipe without a bowl from his hunting vest.

"Whoa! What is this contraption?" Louis steps in for a look, and Emile Loubet joins him, fingering the barrel, stopper, and reed.

"Scottish duck call." Sean blows on the pipe and emits a whine. Five ducks land among the wood decoys. He blows the call again, emitting a soft chuckle. A flock of ducks settle in. Teals, mallards, black ducks, gadwalls, wigeons.

"Finally, some ducks." Wolfe grabs Sean's rifle and positions it improperly on his collarbone, his hands loose on the barrel. He cocks the trigger and pulls, swinging the barrel in rapid fire, gunshot perforating the water across the pond. The butt of the rifle punches his clavicle again and again, thrusting his body against the log wall.

"*Verdammt. Verdammt. Verdammt.*" Damn it. He grabs his chest, eyes blazing. "What kind of weapon is this?"

"Are all Prussians as dumb as they look?" Sean grabs his rifle from the ground. "You shoot ducks when they fly, not sitting in the water."

I kneel beside Wolfe, blood staining his linen shirt. "Louis, run and get Doctor Louvell and bring him to the house."

Louis starts running along the ridge toward town. Henry, Emile, and Sean crouch down to help.

"Get your hands off me, you Jockie." Wolfe spits in Sean's face. "You tried to kill me."

Rage rises in Sean's face, his honor injured. I hand him the ducks on hooks. "Please, Sean, will you take these to Yvonne for me? The rest of us can handle Monsieur Wolfe." Though, personally, I'd love to chuck the banker in the drink.

The doctor anoints Reynard Wolfe's scratches and bruises with some foul-smelling poultice to humor the overwrought banker.

I turn away with my snicker. Serves him right to smell of a pig pen, the way he's acted.

Wolfe pleads for laudanum to ease his pain, though the wounds do not call for such medicine. He claims he'll need several days' bedrest at my cottage in Chigny. The banker is as wily as he is insistent.

If Wolfe thinks I am going to nurse him back to health, he is sorely mistaken. Tomorrow, I will leave him here while I take Sean hiking in *la montagne*.

19

COURIR SUR LE HARICOT

To run on the bean

The Baron huffs behind me in his bespoke sporting togs as we climb *la montagne* through the dwarf beech forest that teems with warbling birds taking shelter in their craggy branches.

I push back the new growth on the path. "Not too much further to the top. It's worth it." Wiping perspiration from my forehead, I peer through the leaves for the bridge my husband built. Nothing looks familiar. My skirt catches on a bright-yellow blooming bush, and angry thrushes fly out, batting my arms with their wings.

"Oh my!" Trying to jump away, I'm caught fast by the thorny bush.

Sean shoos the birds away. "Gorse bushes. We use them for sheep fodder." He offers a vibrant yellow flower to my nose and watches as I smell the aroma of coconut.

"I thought gorse bloomed in spring," I say.

"Year-round." He smiles impishly. "When gorse is out of blossom, kissing's out of fashion." His lips find mine as surely as his duck call found ducks. No quick peck among friends, but an enticing exploration, lingering onto my neck. Placing my palms on his chest, I feel his heart pounding against his ribs.

His stomach growls, and he rubs it sheepishly. *"Hunger-heartit."* Ravenously hungry.

"We'll have lunch at the top." I laugh and walk ahead. But lunch is not what I want. I want to feel his body on mine. Escape the mundane worries of the harvest, the winery, the daunting task of building out the Butte Saint-Nicaise crayères to store our champagne.

"I never asked about your name," I say, stepping over rocks that have fallen from the mountain. "I thought Sean was Irish."

"Gaelic, actually," he says. "The MacNeil's hail from Niall, first chief of the Clan MacNeil from Barra in 1049. But my grandfather lost Kisimul Castle and the entire island of Barra in 1838. That is why my parents married me off to my cousin from another branch of MacNeil's, to regain our heritage."

He gave me up for his family. I stop walking. "Why didn't you explain this to me before?"

He shakes his head sheepishly. "How could I tell you I could not marry you so my family could regain their status in the MacNeil clan?"

"Do you have any idea how I felt?" My mouth goes dry remembering the profound disappointment.

He clasps my hands in his, his face contorted with regret. "It hurt me as much as you. But I was honor bound to do this for my family."

"That is not an apology," I say.

He kneels on one knee, pressing his palms together. "I'm sorry for leaving you without explanation. It was unfair."

Now it seems silly to hold a grudge. I help him up. "Our lunch spot is just over this ravine." I point to the ancient rope bridge Louis made so long ago. It's mossy and frayed, and I test the first wooden slat with my boot, holding on to the rope rails which sway precariously under my grasp. Stepping both feet onto the bridge, I look behind me. "Are you coming?"

"Is this your idea of revenge?" Dimples tease from the corners of his mouth.

"Better hold tight." I stride across and feel Sean's hesitant steps behind.

"How deep is this ravine?" His voice quavers.

"Eyes straight ahead and you'll be there before you know it."

On the other side, I reach out to him. He runs to me, wrapping his arms around my back.

"Not so bad, huh?" I whisper in his ear.

"Not at all." He kisses my forehead, setting off a warm sensation.

When we reach the rock ledge overlooking a broad valley of vineyards, a thrill shoots up my spine as it did when I hiked here with Louis to explore this parcel for our retirement. Louis planned to retire when our son went to university. A whole new life awaited us here. A chance to indulge in our pastimes. Hunting and fishing for Louis. Growing roses and collecting butterflies for me. But, as soon as he bought this Chigny property, I began to feel queasy in the mornings. I was pregnant again. Louis's retirement went up in smoke. He went back to work to support two mortgages, our son's education, and our new family.

A profound ache lodges in my breastbone. He never lived to see Louise grow up, or his son graduate and get his law degree. Blinking away tears, I stare at the vibrant scarlet and gold vineyards, recalling a message from my Smiling Angel. *Focus on what is good in life.*

Sean stands behind me and wraps his arms around tight. "Tell me what you see, *m'eudail?*" My darling.

"I see the *vendangeurs* working all year to make the grapes the best they can be, pruning dead canes, fertilizing, trimming leaves back so the sun can kiss the grapes." I spread out the MacNeil-tartan plaid blanket he brought for me.

"Why don't you own vineyards?" he asks.

"I want to, but men won't sell vineyards to a woman, and secondly, I can't afford it yet." I set out Chaource cheese and a baguette. "Enough business." I twist the champagne bottle, the cork explodes from being jostled, and we laugh.

He touches his glass to mine; those blue, blue eyes pierce my soul. "May the sun shine on you all day long, everything go right and nothing wrong. May those you love bring love back to you, and may all the wishes you wish come true."

I drink in the luscious nectar bubbling on my tongue, without the cloying sweetness. "What do you think of this champagne? We used late-harvest grapes for sweetness and body but added less sugar to the second fermentation."

147

He cuts a piece of Chaource, pops it into his mouth, and chews very slowly, as he's wont to do. I wait for him to finish before telling me his thoughts, but he cuts another piece of cheese.

"You don't like champagne, do you?" I ask.

His forehead colors. "You can't take champagne as a serious drink, now, can you? Not like Scotch."

"You bought twenty cases of Pommery." My voice rises, and my heart palpitates.

He grabs my hand. "Don't take offense, darling. I wanted to support you." He tips his glass back, drinking it down in a single swallow. "Ah! Far superior to Veuve Clicquot, I'll give you that." He kisses me with his champagne tongue.

I try to savor his manicured hands stroking my shoulders, his warm breath on my neck. But I can't fight my unrest. He rubbished my champagne. He belittled my dream I've nurtured for a decade. I cut more cheese. For a long while, we eat with only our thoughts between us.

"Alexandrine, don't get me wrong." His brows pleat in the center. "I admire your ambition. I've never had much myself."

We laugh at his joke.

At least he sees things as they are. He's lived a life of privilege, never needing for anything. He couldn't possibly understand what building the champagne house means to me, supporting my family, trying to create something entirely new and beautiful.

Sean presses my shoulders down on the blanket. "We've waited so long to be together again. Don't ruin it." He starts to unbutton my blouse, and I don't stop him.

But the heaving and panting come from behind the rock outcrop. Henry pokes his head around, red-faced and huffing. "Ah, there you are, Madame Pommery."

"Henry." I sit up. "What's wrong?"

Henry scans the blanket, my undone buttons, Sean's awkward position.

"I was worried you hurt your ankle again when you were gone so long." He swipes his neck with his hand.

Sean tucks in his shirt. "Egad, man, you scared the daylight out of us."

"My ankle is fine," I say. "We were just enjoying our picnic and this magnificent view."

"Yes, magnificent view." The Baron glances down at his lap, props his knee up and leans on it, as if posing for a painting.

"Yvonne got worried because you said you'd be back to help with dinner," Henry says.

I check the timepiece on my chatelaine. "Oh, my. I lost track of time." I gather the food and champagne and stuff it in the pack.

"I think I'll stay a while if you don't mind," Sean says. From the looks of things, he cannot actually get up at the moment.

"Take your time." I kiss his cheeks *la bise*. "Dinner won't be until eight."

On the way down, I follow Henry's sure footing. His boot heels are worn, and his trousers are his same Sunday best. He deserves a raise when I'm able.

"Are you sure you are all right, Madame Pommery?" he asks.

"Please Henry, you agreed to call me Alexandrine. And I'm fine, now. Thank you for looking out for me." Every night when I read to Louise, I see him walking past our house. "You are always looking out for me, aren't you Henry?"

"Yes, Madame."

"Alexandrine."

He laughs. "Yes, Madame Alexandrine."

My pride got in the way up on *la montagne*. Why hold it against Sean that he doesn't like champagne? I don't like Scotch much, either. I owe him a second chance.

With Wolfe dosing off medicine in his bedchamber, I send Louis, Emile, and Henry to dinner at the tavern. A chance for Sean and me to enjoy an intimate dinner for the two of us.

Dressing in an off-the-shoulder bustle gown is hard enough without help. But when I try to clasp the pearls my husband gave me, my fingers shake. Sean's world is no closer to mine than when I met him but that is part of his allure. He clearly has something in mind for our future, making the trip from Scotland alone. He knows how much the winery means to me. I wonder if he would he stay here part of the year?

Entering the drawing room, I notice the windowpanes are painted with frosty patterns. It's cold out there, but the fire is roaring.

Sean is drinking a double Scotch and studying my butterfly collection framed on the wall. He is dressed formally in a MacNeil-tartan kilt and short jacket with gold buttons down the front and at the cuffs. My heart skips a beat.

Setting his drink on the bar, he gazes at me as if he bears no grudge about this afternoon. "You look beautiful, Alex." He takes my hand and kisses it, sending a charge through my veins.

Reaching for the champagne chilling on the bar, I pour a glass. "Brut champagne from the grapes we saw from *la montagne*." Then I remember he doesn't care for champagne, and I grab his Scotch and hand it to him.

"To each his own." I smile and toast his glass.

The candelabra in the dining room is lit, the table set with my hand-painted pheasant china and a bouquet of late-blooming roses of yellow. The color of remembrance, affection, friendship—not love. Following protocol, I sit at the head of the table with Sean on my right, looking into the drawing room with the fireplace roaring.

In mop cap and black uniform, Chantal serves the Provençal soup with squash, fennel, cannellini beans, and red potatoes from our garden. The aroma makes my mouth water.

Sean takes a spoonful, and I wait for his comment. No one makes Provençal soup like Yvonne.

"Have you ever had Scotch broth?" he says. "Lamb shank, split peas, turnips, and leeks? Delicious." He takes another bite. "My cook makes it for Guy Fawkes night." His bushy eyebrows shoot up, and he points his spoon at me.

Never point a spoon. *Etiquette for Ladies.*

"Say, Guy Fawkes is coming up November fifth," he says. "Come stay with me at the castle. It's a roaring good time. All our friends will be there."

"Now that harvest is over, it is a good time to get away. Tell me about it."

Chantal clears our soup plates. Sean has barely touched his.

"Tell Yvonne her Provençal soup was *magnifique*." I tell Chantal and kiss my fingertips.

Sean glares at the table linen until she leaves the room.

"We do not acknowledge servants at Benegal Castle." He pats his mouth with his napkin.

I couldn't feel more scolded if he'd rapped my knuckles.

"Where was I? Oh, yes. Guy Fawkes Night goes back to 1605 when a group of English Catholics failed to assassinate King James and replace him with a Catholic king." He grabs my hand. "Say you'll come. There are bonfires, moon dances, fireworks celebrating the purity of Scottish bloodlines."

Purity of the bloodlines.

Chantal backs through the door and serves us sumptuous plates of duck confit with frisée salad. I'm about to tell her how delicious it looks, but I hold back because of Sean's reprimand. She pours the rich, vintage Chardonnay I paired with the duck.

Sean's hand covers the top of his glass. "I prefer red wine."

"Of course." You'd think I'd learn not to presume. "Please open a Pommery red for the Baron, Chantal." I tell myself it is not a sin for a man to prefer a certain wine.

"I'll send a carriage for you," Sean says.

I haven't a clue what he's talking about, I'm so disconcerted.

"But I suppose a modern woman like you would travel by train, now that it reaches Reims." He wipes his pristine mouth with a napkin, and his face flushes. "You've spoiled me for anyone else, Alex. Can't you see?"

I gulp champagne, my head churning like the paddlewheel.

He reaches into his vest pocket and takes out a carved wooden box. The light of the candelabra flickers on his urgency. "It's for you, my darling."

My heart shudders to a stop. I take the box and study it. More of a treasure chest, forged from metal, engraved with Celtic symbols.

"It was my mother's." His brows pinch together.

I push the treasure chest back at him. "Oh, no, Sean. It's too precious."

He opens the box and extracts a gold necklace. "The Trinity knot honors the three life cycles of a woman. Maiden, mother, and wise crone. My mother embodied these three women at the same time, and so do you."

My chest tightens. "Sean, I..."

"To you, Alex." He toasts my glass. "And all the women in you."

I gulp my champagne. "Your mother's necklace should be kept in the family."

He smirks, his eyes dancing. "Exactly."

My stomach jumps like a fish. "Perhaps we can discuss this over cognac."

"Perfect." He kisses me so tenderly my lips yearn for more.

"I'll be right back, I just want to freshen up," I whisper. Upstairs, I slip on the fancy lingerie I had made in Paris. Tucks at the bodice and fine lace frills at the cuffs, iridescent beads at the neckline and an organza sash. Looking in the cheval mirror, I decide to leave on my pearls which glow against my décolleté. The candlelight softens the age around my still deep-blue eyes. My figure is as slim as when I first met him. He won't be disappointed.

I'm prepared for this night. The linens have been changed, the lamps filled with lavender oil and turned low. Rose petals on the pillows. We deserve this moment. Then why is my stomach in knots? I try to push aside my doubts.

But as I descend the stairs, men's voices clash like swords. Sean and Wolfe lean into each other, yelling and red-faced. With Wolfe in his nightshirt and Sean in his kilt, both with hairy legs, I have a good giggle.

Both men turn and ogle me in disbelief, and I realize I'm the spectacle in my Parisian nightgown.

"You shouldn't be up, Monsieur Wolfe," I say, taking his arm. "You've had a lot of medication."

"I am starving," he roars. "How do you 'spect me to sleep on an empty stomach?"

Sean takes his other arm to keep him upright.

Wolfe jerks away. "Take your hands off me, you Scottish pipe blower."

"You must not speak to the baron that way," I say. "I'll send a tray up to your room."

"Unnn…aseptible," he slurs. "I'll eat with you in the dining room."

I sigh. "We finished dinner, Monsieur. We were just turning in for the night."

Wolfe's eyes drop to my marabou slippers and up to my diaphanous bodice. A drop of drool seeps down his chin. He collapses into the wing chair. "I was just 'splaining to the Baron that Napoleon is not as smart as you people think. He is being lured into war by King William and Chancellor Bismarck."

"Why would Prussia want war with France?" Sean says, sitting in the chair by Wolfe.

I walk to the bar and pour myself some champagne. Why would Sean engage him when I appear in my negligee?

"Bismarck wants to unite the German states together, and what better way than war against the enemy."

"That's your laudanum talking," Sean says. "German states are too cocky to join forces."

"Let's call it a night, shall we?" I say.

"I never had dinner, and you're not polite enough to offer me a drink," Wolfe roars. "One lousy drink!"

Sean pours a Scotch for Wolfe. "You are full of sauerkraut, old chap. Napoleon won't allow himself to be bullied by Prussians. He is a master at chess. You don't play chess, do you, you conceited jackanapes?"

I gasp at the slur.

"Jackanapes?" Wolfe slams his glass on the side table. "You've done nothing but insult me since you arrived. I do not care what title you hide behind; you are intolerable." He pushes himself up. "Step outside, and we will finish this man to man."

I cross my arms around my negligee. "You are in no condition to fight tonight."

Wolfe pounds his chest. "This so-called Baron called me an impertinent ape. He insulted my homeland and my intelligence. My honor is at stake, and I demand to defend it with a duel."

"I accept your challenge," Sean says, as calmly as taking a cup of tea. "I name Madame Pommery as my Second." He holds his hand out for mine.

I throw up my palms. "This is absurd. Stop this at once."

"Too late now that he's thrown down the gauntlet," Sean says. "You know the rules, my dear Alex. Each duelist must be accompanied by a Second to ensure fair play and honorable outcome. There must be a referee as well."

The front door opens, and the others shuffle in from the tavern—Lucille dressed up in silk. Louis heads to the bar. "Anyone for a brandy?" He pours several glasses, and Emile serves them.

Henry waves him off, staring at me in disbelief. Oh, yes, the negligee.

"Excuse me." I take Lucille into the hall. "Who gave you permission to go with them?"

Her face loses all color. "Louis asked me. I assumed he asked your permission."

I scoff, flustered, but Lucille's round dark eyes reflect innocence. "Go to bed. Your own." I point to the servants' quarters beyond the pantry.

In the drawing room, Wolfe grips a snifter of brandy in his chubby fingers. "Louis will act as my Second." He tosses the liquid into his throat. "That leaves Monsieur Loubet as referee."

I wring my pearls from side to side. "Please, gentlemen. Let us agree to disagree on these issues and shake hands instead of swords."

"You of all people know once a duel is accepted, we are bound by honor to complete the challenge," the Baron snarls. "We must duel at dawn."

Wolfe jerks his chin down. "Our Seconds will prepare the swords."

Relief pools in my stomach. "Ah, gentlemen. Alas, we have no swords at Chigny. The duel must be called off after all."

Louis pulls a leather case from behind the bar, and my heart leaps to my throat.

"Louis, no." I wave my hand. "The sabers are for champagne, not duels."

He opens the brass buckles, lifts the leather lid, and shows the men two gleaming sabers with silver scrolled handles. "Will these do?"

Sean glides his finger against the saber. "The blades are so thin."

"Don't try to wiggle out of it, Scot." Wolfe sneers. "Accept my challenge or accept defeat."

"I won't allow this," I say.

Sean huffs. "The ridge at daybreak."

So much for a night of romance.

154

chaource
_____
quel — fromage

20

MENER UN COMBAT PERDU D'AVANCE

To fight a losing battle

Racking my brain all night how to save their lives and honor, I hit upon one inescapable custom that plays to my advantage. No matter the outcome of the duel, it must be fêted with champagne. As a Second, it falls to me to bring champagne. On ice. An abundance of ice. A crucial part of my plan.

It is dark and cold when we set out into the misty predawn. Lanterns swing in the men's gloved hands, smelling of whale oil. Our somber band trudges up the hill in silence, only the crunch of our boots on the rocks. My ankle starts aching again.

The Baron's MacNeil-tartan scarf is wound so tight around his neck, you'd think he'd choke. His brow is pinched, and worry etches his face. His anxious mood doesn't make sense. I've seen him fence; his trophies line the shelves of his study. I hardly think he would worry about dueling the flabby Wolfe, who sits at his desk and dines at the Biergarten most nights.

Louis and Wolfe lag well behind. I imagine the climb will have the banker puffing. Henry brings up the rear with Emile Loubet hauling the cart containing sabers and champagne. Loubet is short and strong, Henry tall and slender. A comical pair, though no one is laughing.

155

"Isn't there some way you can back out honorably?" I ask Sean through the heavy mist. "We could just make a picnic of the croissants and champagne."

He flashes a half-smile. "Always wanting to please everyone, aren't you, Alexandrine? An admirable trait. But the time for that has passed." His breath is hot in my ear. "Don't fret, darling. I won't lose."

"It's not you I'm worried about," I say. "Monsieur Wolfe is the most respected banker in Reims and holds our mortgage. The shame of losing will destroy him if it doesn't kill him."

"Then he should not have challenged a duel," Sean says, ribbons of breath streaming from his nostrils in the frigid air. "Duels are not so much to kill the opponent as to gain satisfaction. To restore one's honor by demonstrating a willingness to risk one's life."

"Promise me you won't hurt him." We've almost reached the top of the hill.

By the swinging light of the lantern, I see his flaring nostrils and the angles of his face constrict with resolve. I asked too much; he will not sacrifice his honor for me. A gust of icy miasma makes me shiver, and I clutch my cape around me. How has the situation escalated so?

The sun rims red on the horizon, casting an eerie red glow to the drifting fog. Emile and Henry park the cart. Their bare hands are red with cold.

"Emile, you will present the sabers. The rules say you must wear gloves," I lie to him. If he doesn't wear gloves, he'll discover that the sabers have been freezing in ice all night long.

Emile checks his jacket pockets, revealing a pistol to start the duel. "I don't have gloves."

"Here, use mine." I give them to him. He's small; my gloves will fit.

Hoooo. Hooo. Hooooooo. Raucous moans mocks us from the tangled foliage. Hundreds of bright orange eyes flash in the branches—angry cat-owls warning us away.

Louis and Wolfe catch up. The banker huffs and bends over with hands on his knees.

"Monsieur Wolfe is ill," Louis says. "He cannot go on with the duel."

Wolfe straightens up. "Nothing will hold me back from defending my honor. You must allow us to proceed."

The burden of honor squeezes my lungs. "Monsieur Wolfe, I beg you to abandon the duel before we must all live with the consequences. Shake hands and walk away like gentlemen."

Sean and Wolfe glare at each other without a glimmer of surrender.

"You must not interfere in matters between men, Madame," the Baron says.

His dismissal turns my heart cold. "Emile, present the weapons." I hear the angry tremor in my voice.

Emile unlocks the saber case. Steam rises from under the felt. I pray no one notices the ice packed under the sabers.

Louis and I present the frozen weapons to the duelists, and they retreat to opposite ends of the ridge. Their gloved hands grip the forged handles and swipe the sabers through the air in preparation. The rising sun casts an orange light to the haze.

Emile Loubet stands solemnly before us. "Gentlemen, take your places back-to-back to your opponent."

The Baron steps into position, his noble face hard as stone. An expression I never want to see again. Wolfe follows hesitantly and nods at me as if he's defending my honor. I shake my head in disgust.

A draft of fog obscures them from view, but Loubet's voice cuts through like the trumpets of heaven's army. "Let me remind you, you are fighting for your honor. Say your prayers, for one of you will be defeated."

By now the sun rims the horizon, clouds swirling over in a peculiar morass. Sunlight shoots through sporadically on the duelists, made stranger when snow starts falling from a dark cloud above. The flakes splat cold and wet on my face—a signal. Wake up. Stop this tragedy before it's too late.

"March five paces and turn to face your opponent," Emile commands through the snow. Their shadowy forms march away from each other and turn around.

"Louis, announce the rules of the house," I say.

He clears his throat like his father used to. "The House of Pommery has decided this duel of honor will not be fought to the death, but only until blood is drawn."

"Nonsense," Wolfe says. "That is a sissy duel. I demand full revenge."

"I agree," Sean says. "Honor is not defended by a drop of blood."

Louis comes to me, panicked. "Maman, do something. We cannot let them kill each other."

I squeeze his hand. "They won't."

Emile Loubet raises his pistol in the air, pulls the trigger, and an amber blast shoots through the snowflakes.

Snow falls so heavily; I can only hear sabers clattering. Not the sharp sound of metal on metal as you'd expect, but the frozen sabers sound like drumsticks struck against each other.

The Baron circles Wolfe, jutting his saber at him like a lion tamer.

Wolfe whacks the sword carelessly, and Sean leaps aside. Around and around they tread, sabers slicing through the air just missing their targets. My anxiety mounts with each swipe of a blade. Blood pulses in my ears. I pray to my Smiling Angel. If my plan doesn't work, our lives will be forever ruined by this day.

The Baron's stare hardens, and he raises his saber high above Wolfe's chest, hovering above his clavicle.

My heart bounds to my throat. "Sean, don't. We agreed on a scratch. Only a scratch."

Sean cocks his head, his jaw shifting, considering my plea.

But Wolfe takes advantage of his hesitation and swipes his saber across Sean's neck.

I scream and run to them.

"Alexandrine, stop." Henry holds me back.

Miracle of miracles, Wolfe's blade breaks on Sean's tartan scarf and clanks to the snowy ground. Wolfe stares down at the broken blade, bends over, and retches.

I break free and run to Sean. "Are you all right?"

The Baron wipes his neck, then stares at his hand. Only a scrape on his cheek from the saber.

I cross myself and utter a prayer of gratitude. My plan worked. Hallelujah. I dab Sean's cheek with my handkerchief.

"He's bleeding. He's bleeding!" Wolfe slaps his knees, thighs, and the soles of his boots in some sort of German jig. "I won. I won. You must declare me the victor, Madame Pommery."

I press my handkerchief on the Baron's cheek. "Your sword broke. That hardly counts as a victory," I tell him. "Louis, call the duel a draw."

"A draw?" Wolfe yells. "That is a travesty. I won and demand vindication."

Henry grabs his arm to lead him away. "Please take your leave, Monsieur Wolfe. It's over."

"I will not leave until you declare me victor," says Wolfe, stomping his foot.

The Baron walks to the banker, standing head and shoulders above him. "You are correct, Monsieur Wolfe." He extends his hand. "You won the duel."

Wolfe shakes the Baron's hand with both of his. "Hear that, Madame? Your Baron plays by the rules."

Reluctantly, I pop the cork, but Sean marches down the hill without so much as a backward glance, disappearing into the snowy fog.

My ankle is swollen again from the climb, and Henry supports my arm and waist down the hill. Reynard Wolfe boasts all the way down, the rest of us silent.

When we get to the cottage, Sean is packed and gone. His honor was lost, and that's everything to him.

I don't hear from the Baron until my birthday in April. Sean sends an exquisite music box, painted with the Scottish countryside and Ben-egal Castle, a gentleman and lady picnicking by a pond. The scene is right out of our memories as is the music box song he used to sing me: "Come where my love lies dreaming."

Of course, I write him a gracious thank-you note, post haste. But I haven't heard back.

PART III

1870–1871

"You might be passionate, but without perfection
and discipline,
you cannot attain the ultimate."

~*Jeanne Alexandrine Pommery*

21

ARRIVER COMME UN CHEVEU SUR LA SOUPE

To arrive like a hair on the soup

1870. "Madame Jeanne Alexandrine Pommery revolutionizes the champagne industry by creating first brut champagne." *The London Herald* trembles between my fingers. Apparently, Pommery has caught on like wildfire in the United Kingdom, thanks to Adolphe Hubinet's brilliant outreach to every newspaper, magazine, and circular. The dry, clear, effervescent taste of Pommery has made sweet champagnes antiquated in comparison. Pommery champagne appears on every Spiers & Pond wine list and is featured in hundreds of London hotels and elegant bars. Hubinet even managed for Pommery champagne to be showcased on the new Cunard transatlantic cruise.

Apparently, the champagne house owners are quite miffed about our success. When I see them on the street, they cross to avoid me.

I can't worry about them, and focus instead on keeping up with the demand Hubinet has mustered. We must build out Butte Saint-Nicaise for more permanent storage *tout de suite*.

Louis and Henry are too busy filling orders, so I take on the Butte Saint-Nicaise crayères myself, hiring the Nair brothers to supervise French and Belgian miners to excavate. The project is much larger than I realized with eighteen kilometers of tunnels.

Progress is excruciatingly slow. Heavy rains flood the caverns and make the work miserable and dangerous. I supervise a crew of peasants and beggars I gathered from Saint Remi to help the miners: men for the heavy lifting and shoveling, women to carry out buckets of rubbish and soil on a hoist and pulley system.

As an extra incentive for the workers, I tell them they can keep anything they find as we dig out the caverns—treasures from centuries past. Some of their finds are remarkable: silver candelabra, gold chalices, porcelain dinnerware, hand-painted baby dolls.

Thirty meters below the ground, Jerome Nair, a burly man with coal-pitted pores, supervises miners to dig out an intricate network of tunnels and vast chambers I call galleries. Their picks and axes thrust into the rock making ear-splitting pounding and chiseling. Workers complain of the chalk dust, so I have bandanas made to wear around their noses and mouths.

Jerome Nair finds me lifting pails of slag to the pulley. "Uh, Madame Pommery, there appears to be trouble outside." His overgrown eyebrows press together in a single line. "Gentlemen at the gate demand to know what we are doing here. I did not know what to tell them."

I wipe my grimy face with a handkerchief embroidered by Louise, her intricate work so much finer than my own. "Thank you, Nair. I'll see to them." My stomach twists in pain. If we lose Butte Saint-Nicaise, all these cellars would be lost, not to mention months of back-breaking work. Even if I could find a place for all this champagne, to move the bottles in the middle of fermentation would ruin the wine.

Pulling up my skirts with one hand, my wet boots slip on the mossy wood-planked stairs. Water dribbles down the steps from a morning rain. I look up at the blue patch of sky. There must be something I can say that would allow us to continue here.

Half a dozen men swarm around their fancy carriages. I brush chalk dust from my skirts, take a deep breath, and walk toward them. Rallying all the poise I can muster, I wave my hand and smile.

Reynard Wolfe stands front and center of the riled hive of men. Of course, he does. I recognize most of them: Mayor Werle, Doctor DuBois, and Doctor Henroit, wool millers, merchants, businessmen, several champagne house owners. We've attended church together, harvest parties, funerals, weddings. I know their wives and children. I know where their skeletons are buried, and I don't mean the cemetery. Despite their familiar faces, my insides rumble as I approach them.

"Good afternoon, Messieurs," I force my best lyrical voice. "What brings you outside the city gates?"

The sun shines directly on Wolfe's growing belly that shaded his checked trousers. Too many beers at the Biergarten.

"Madame Pommery." Wolfe clears his throat. "As the city council of Reims, it has come to our attention that you are poaching city property."

"Forgive me if I am wrong, gentlemen," I say. "But I recall that the council claimed the city of Reims was not responsible for cleaning up this rat-infested dump because it fell outside city ramparts."

The men exchange scowls.

Doctor DuBois strokes his goatee. "With all due respect, Madame Pommery, that does not give you the right to take the land."

Mayor Werle steps forward. "We must insist you depart immediately."

I widen my stance to gird myself. "For as long as I remember, the people of Reims have petitioned the council to clean up Butte Saint-Nicaise. The hideous stink of garbage descends on the city whenever the wind blows. Citizens worry about the infestation of rodents and spread of disease. The sinkholes injure anyone who dares climb the butte. As Doctor DuBois can attest, I, myself, fell into the crayères and sprained my ankle. Still, the mayor and city council have done nothing to clean up this dump."

The mayor pushes out his chest. "We have not had funds to dedicate."

"And, yet, you have not hesitated to tax our citizens for Napoleon's expansion of Paris," I say, scanning their angry faces. "Shouldn't the citizens get a say in how you use their money?"

"What the council does is not your concern, Madame Pommery," the mayor rebuts. Ten councilmen glare at me.

My thoughts form one second before the words escape my mouth. "Mayor, I will offer you a bargain. I will clean up this property and give city council credit, if you will move the dump somewhere safer, out of the way."

"She's trying to steal the property from under our noses," Doctor Henroit says. "We need to put a stop to this." The men huddle and talk in harsh whispers.

Wolfe pulls me aside. "Madame Pommery, you do not want to be on the wrong side of the city fathers. You'll destroy your reputation, business, and family."

"I simply need a place to store my champagne. Is that a crime?"

"You are a pillar of decorum in this town," Wolfe says. "I implore you to stop at once and make a full apology to save yourself further embarrassment." He turns back to the men.

"Madame Pommery," the mayor shouts. "You are hereby put on notice of serious consequences to your business and your person if you do not vacate Butte Saint-Nicaise immediately." The councilmen concur with stiff nods and jutting chins. "We'll return in a week to insure you have left the premises."

I watch their carriage drive toward town. "And what if I don't?"

Mayor Werle and the city council return as promised.

"Are you sure about this, Louis?" I ask as we walk down to greet them.

"I'd bet my law degree on it." He entwines his arm with mine and infuses me with confidence.

Behind us on the butte, our employees dump rocks from the hoist into a growing pile.

The councilmen cackle like a brood of hens. "Deceitful. Shocking. Outrageous."

Wolfe blocks us from the councilmen, his face splotched red. "Louis do as I say, and we can avoid violence. Take your mother home and stay there until I come."

"What is the meaning of this, Wolfe?" Mayor Werle yells. "You said you had them handled."

"We are not going anywhere," I say, waving Wolfe away. "Step aside."

He stands firm. "You are doing this deliberately to spite me."

"You cannot think we will be lenient because you are a woman," the mayor says.

I push past Wolfe. "Gentlemen, allow me to introduce my son, Monsieur Pommery." Louis blanches, but I proceed. "Explain what gives Pommery the right to Butte Saint-Nicaise."

He pulls a document from his suit jacket and hands it to the mayor. "The last owner of Butte Saint-Nicaise died more than a century ago and left this title available for a song."

I smile. "So, we sang to the city clerk and paid him a trifle."

"You will not get away with this," Wolfe says. "Will she, Mayor?"

"The deed seems real, but the method in which it was obtained is suspicious," Werle says.

"If you can find any flaw in our dealings, you can consult my lawyer," I say.

Mayor Werle looks up from the deed. "Who is your lawyer, Madame?"

I clap Louis on the shoulder. "My son, Monsieur Pommery."

Louis snatches the deed from the mayor. "You'll find a copy filed with the city clerk."

"We would love to stay, but we have work to do." We climb the hill, leaving the councilmen gaping.

"You were gloating, Maman," Louis says. "You taught us it was a sin to gloat."

"I know. I couldn't resist." I pat his arm. "You were marvelous."

The next time I see Mayor Werle, circumstances have changed, and not in our favor. In fact, the entire country has gone mad.

Seven in the morning, the jarring bells of Hôtel de Ville clang urging all Reims citizens to gather. Lucille takes care of Louise, and Louis and I rush to hear the news. Henry Vasnier catches up with us, since he was already in the winery preparing the day's work. He's put his raise to good use—he's outfitted with new coat and trousers, a handsome distinction he well deserves.

As we enter the courtyard of Hôtel de Ville, we are handed small French flags, triggering speculation. Perhaps Empress Eugenie is pregnant again or someone important has died.

Town criers in their red and gray uniforms blow their hunting horns to quiet the crowd. Mayor Werle raises a megaphone and *reads a letter from the Emperor, Louis Napoleon, addressed to French citizens.*

"Frenchmen, there are solemn moments when the national sense of honor violently imposes itself with irresistible force, dominates all interests, and takes on the destiny of the country. One of those decisive hours has sounded for France. Prussia launched on the path of invasion, provoked mistrust, necessitated armaments, promoted uncertainty and fear. Our country resented this treatment with profound irritation, and a cry for war resounded from one end of France to the other. I will place myself at the head of our valiant army for love of duty and country. France calls upon all of our men to bear arms against our enemy. May God bless our efforts!"

The crowd explodes in a frenzy of protest and panic.

I lean to Louis's ear. "This cannot be about Spain choosing a Prussian queen, can it?"

The fury in his eyes frightens me.

"That is exactly what this war is about," he says. "A power-crazed ruler who thinks nothing of killing his citizens to have his way. Frenchmen are like toy soldiers for him."

"But he's done so much for France," I say. "Secondary schools for boys, improving roads and sewer systems, transforming Paris into the most beautiful city in the world."

Louis scoffs. "At the expense of displacing three hundred and fifty thousand citizens from their homes and work and moving them as far away as possible from his palace."

The hunting horns blast again, and the town crier shouts out from the Hôtel de Ville. "The following citizens are to report here for mandatory duty, Saturday morning, nine a.m."

I grab Louis's arm. "Napoleon is conscribing men for the army?"

"I told you," he says. "We are no more than toy soldiers to him."

My ears ring from the blaring horn. This cannot be happening.

They start calling names from every family I know, each one a blow to my stomach. The crowd's cheers are replaced by anguished sobs. How can they take our men on Napoleon's whim and leave the families without a breadwinner? Every man between eighteen and forty is to leave in two days' time. How many will come home?

When they call Henry Vasnier's name, a sharp pain spears my ribs. But he's only the first of my crew to be called. Pins prick my innards like a pincushion with each crew member they call. Only Damas, who is deaf and mute, is not called, leaving me no one to work the fast-approaching harvest.

But when they call Louis's name, my vision checkers. I see baby Louis in my arms, my son waddling his first steps, his chubby arms wrapping around my neck, and smashing his lips into my cheek for a wet kiss.

"Madame Pommery. Alexandrine." I hear but cannot see. A whiff of ammonia, and Henry and Louis's faces hover over me like angels.

"Maman, it will be all right," Louis says.

"Let's get you back home." Henry takes one arm and Louis the other, and they walk me home, talking about how to prepare for the harvest that they will miss.

I stop and wriggle free of their arms. "They cannot possibly take you two from the winery before harvest. I will not stand for it. I'm going back to talk to Mayor Werle."

But the mayor's hands are tied. According to Napoleon's orders, the list of new recruits is unconditional. If one does not report for duty, punishment is prison. A fate I would not wish on anyone after I visited a girl's mother there. The dead chill of those gray walls ached in my bones for days. Rats nibbled at tin plates on the dirt floor. The poor mother handed me something through the bars with skeletal fingers. A cross necklace to give her daughter. She died of starvation or something worse. The memory makes me shiver with dread.

In two days' time, Henry, Louis, Louise, Lucille, and I crowd into the Berlina carriage and ride to the train station, the dreary downpour outside cheerier than inside. We huddle in the drizzle with the other families, hugging and crying under umbrellas, saying last goodbyes.

Louis kisses his sister *la bise*, and she bites her bottom lip, fighting tears. When it is my turn, I hug him tight and press a Saint Christopher medal in his hand.

"We'll be home as soon as we can, Maman," he says with trembling lips.

"I'll be here with open arms," I repeat what I told him as a child.

When the conductor blows a whistle, Louis enfolds Lucille in his arms, raw emotion painting his handsome face with anguish.

The young woman sobs, narrow shoulders shaking as she clings to him.

I am at once moved and shocked at the tender vision of their love. Shocked that I didn't recognize it sooner. Thirteen years ago, Lucille came to Saint Remi as a Jewish refugee, and I brought her home to be Louise's nanny. Her kindness and cheerful nature warmed me to her. When Louise grew older, Lucille stayed on as my housekeeper. She is our servant. She's Jewish. And she loves my son?

A hand encloses mine. "I'm sorry, Alexandrine," Henry says. "It wasn't my place to tell you about them."

A warm gust of train steam blankets us, leaving his face dewy. I rise on tiptoe to kiss *la bise*, but he doesn't turn his head, and I kiss his mouth, lingering, not wanting to stop. A dam of emotion bursts in me, wetting my cheeks. "I-I want you to be safe, Henry. You stay safe and come home."

"All aboard!" the conductor yells and blows three long whistles.

The shrill sound drills my ears.

Henry squeezes my hands between our chests, impassioned eyes speaking beyond words. His lips reach for another kiss. Not an accident this time, not a sad goodbye, but a kiss that could last through the darkest night.

"I'll keep Louis safe for you." He brushes my knuckles to his mouth, then turns away, leaving me yearning for him to return.

Henry and Louis board the train as the great iron wheels shimmy and squeal warming up.

Out of nowhere, Damas darts past us with a rock dove in a tiny cage and hands it to Louis. Louis takes the cage, and with a last look back, steps inside.

The engine wheezes and huffs, and the iron wheels turn. Soldiers inside press their hands and noses to the windows. Wives and lovers sniffle and wail, wiping wet eyes with white handkerchiefs. Children run with the train until the platform ends.

"When will they return, Madame?" Lucille asks. Her hand rests on her stomach, and I realize she's carrying Louis's child.

Then and there the insignificance of class and religion are crystal clear. Love and respect dissolve the human constructs of class and religion.

I reach for her hand and squeeze it. "They won't be long, Lucille. Napoleon just has to show Prussia his military muscle. As soon as he does, our men will be home."

Our men? It dawns on me I have buried my feelings for Henry for meaningless reasons of age and position, only to have them resurface with a vengeance when he is taken away. Now that he is gone, my yearning grows cavernous.

The sky is gray and leaden, but the rain has stopped, leaving an eerie glisten to the empty streets of Reims. We pass only women, children, and the elderly. A carriage stops at our door, and Monsieur Wolfe steps out in a shiny top hat and three-piece suit.

"Ah, Madame Pommery." He tips his hat. "I missed you at the train station. So many people."

"Why weren't you conscripted?" My voice hardens.

Wolfe's face colors behind his stubbly red-blond beard. "I am a Prussian citizen, Madame. There are many Prussians and Germans here in Reims—none of us were conscripted, of course."

"After all these years here, you're still Prussian?" I unlock the door. My key doesn't seem to fit, and I try another. "You must excuse us, Monsieur Wolfe, or should I call you Herr Wolfe?" The lock finally turns, and I gesture Lucille and Louise to go inside.

"Wait, Madame." Wolfe holds up his palm. "I want to offer my assistance while your men are at war. Anything I can do to help you?"

A kernel of hope. "Perhaps you can do something, Monsieur. You could put a hold on my mortgage until the war is over."

He winces. "Ooooo, not that I'm afraid. My Prussian backers would declare me a traitor if I granted the enemy a reprieve on a loan of any sort."

"So, we are enemies, then?" My stomach turns icy.

"Certainly not us, Madame. Just Germany and France. If I can do anything personally for you, I am at your service."

The energy drains from my body. "Without my crew, there will be no harvest. So, unless you plan to pick grapes, you cannot help me."

22

Avoir le cœur sur la main

To have the heart on the hand

After Louise goes to bed, I sit in front of the hearth in the salon; empty divan and chairs surround me. Firelight throws murky shadows on the stucco walls. I am bereft and lonely.

Felix jumps on my lap. "What do we do now, Felix?" I pet him, but his purr only adds to my deafening thoughts. My men gone to a meaningless war. Lucille, carrying my grandchild? The upcoming harvest. Wolfe's mortgage payment, always hanging over me like a noose.

Footfalls tread lightly on the Savonnerie rug. "May I join you?" Lucille carries in a tray with an exquisite hand-painted bottle and two glasses.

"What's this?"

"An apology, Madame." She pours the ruby-colored liquid into small, delicate glasses. "*Liqueur* de Framboise from Alsace." She offers me a glass.

I gesture to the easy chair beside me and sip the liqueur. "Humm, like fresh raspberries with a peppery aftertaste."

She smiles shyly. "My father worked at the winery where they made this, until they threw him in jail."

The shock hits me. "Jail?"

173

"They found out he was Jewish and accused him of stealing. He died in prison." She holds her glass to the light.

"I thought antisemitism was better in Strasbourg."

"Jews have been allowed to live in Strasbourg since the revolution, but that doesn't mean they are accepted. There are still extra taxes and rules to observe. People find many ways to hate Jews. Broken windows, burning their businesses, beatings, even murders." A small shiver. "Antisemitism is a plague with no cure."

Lucille has never spoken so much in the years she's worked for me, always returning to her home after work. I never asked where it was.

I pour us more liqueur. "How long have you and Louis been having this...this clandestine relationship?"

She presses her slender fingers in prayer. "Louis and I are married, Madame Pommery." Her thumb turns a ring I've never seen her wear. Oval garnet surrounded with diamonds, the ring my maman left Louis when she passed.

Shock and shame riddle my chest. "How long?" I focus on the ring, not trusting myself to look at her.

"About a year after Louis joined the winery."

"So, three years ago? You kept it secret?"

She drops her chin. "Louis said you wouldn't approve of him marrying a servant, especially a Jew. He was trying to find the right time to tell you, but it never came. Then, we were ashamed for keeping it from you for so long."

The flames die down, the oxygen sucked from the room. My own son does not trust me with his true feelings. Setting Felix down, I stir the coals and add a couple of logs. "Louis should have known I have never been prejudiced against Jews."

She looks at me, face lit like the moon. "I converted to Catholicism." Pulling out a delicate cross from under her collar, she slides it on the chain.

"But, Lucille, you were so devout."

Felix jumps onto her lap, and she lays her hand on his back. "God still hears my prayers." The rekindled fire throws golden light like blessings on this young woman who's been my constant companion. Now my daughter-in-law.

I reach for her hand, my heart overflowing. "Welcome to our family, Lucille. I am so very happy to have you with us."

She smiles. "I told Louis you had a big heart, Madame."

I shake my head. "You must never call me Madame again."

She tilts her head. "May I call you *la belle-mère?*" Mother-in-law. Sounds so lovely when she says it.

I hug her and feel her heart beating against mine. Lucille and her baby are family—we will get through this terrible war together.

My hopes of a quick resolution to the war are destroyed when Otto Bismarck, the Prussian chancellor, unites all twenty-five German states to fight against France. Samson fighting Goliath, as Father Pieter preaches on Sunday. With God on our side, France will prevail, he says. But God is God for all humanity, so I sincerely doubt he's picking sides.

The harvest won't wait for the war to end. The hottest August anyone can remember forces the grapes to ripen early. Without our men to help with harvest, we will lose an entire year's grapes. Lucille convinces me to pay a visit to the one place I never thought I'd go.

The intricate iron gate moans and clanks closed behind us; my spine riddles with doubt. Le Palais Alhambra is unlike any other house in Reims: Moorish in design, three stories high, narrow archways on the façade. Copper onion-domed lanterns burn at each window, glowing mysteriously.

Courtesans pose in the arched windows looking for passersby. But with most of our men at war, only one girl is occupied, her curtain closed. The rest of the painted ladies wave from their windows as we walk through the mosaic archway, which glitters with mica and quartz stones.

"Do you know them?" I ask.

"Intimately." Lucille smiles slyly. "I do their laundry in exchange for renting their carriage house."

"Clever girl," I say.

The courtesans dress in exotic costumes: a geisha in turquoise dragonfly kimono, a redhead with alabaster skin and a sprinkling of freckles. Even an American Indian with long, shiny black hair, fringed buckskins, and a beaded band across her forehead.

"How does Madame Scheherazade attract girls from all over the world?" I ask.

Lucille smiles slyly. "They have a costume room in the basement. Each day, the girls dress as someone new." She pulls the rope, and a gong reverberates in our ears.

A voluptuous woman opens the door in filmy harem pants and beaded bustier that encases overflowing bosoms dusted with shimmering mica powder.

"Madame Pommery, may I present Madame Scheherazade."

Scheherazade surprises me with a curtsey. "I'm honored to meet you in person, Madame Pommery. I've only seen you at Saint Remi."

My eyebrows hike.

"I wear a mantilla over my face in church, so no one recognizes me." Her hand covers the lower half of her face, leaving her enormous periwinkle eyes outlined in charcoal.

"Of course," I say. "I've seen you praying to the Smiling Angel."

"My patron saint," she says. Blue smoke wafts out of the house, sweet and cloying.

"Mine, too." I hold my chest, trying not to cough.

"Would you like to come in?" She turns and gestures inside the mirrored salon. Chiffon-garbed women lounge with half-mast eyes, sucking a *narguilé* pipe. They sigh and giggle and blow clouds of smoke. Black cats slink across the room and nuzzle their legs. A barefoot eunuch plucks an oud; the eerie sound makes me quiver.

"We'll stay out on the porch if you don't mind." Lucille takes my hand, giving me courage. "Madame Pommery has a request."

Scheherazade holds up her palm drawn with henna patterns. "We already donate to the orphanage every month—ask Father Pieter. We appreciate all you do there to help our children."

"I am well aware of your generous donations," I tell her, growing uncomfortably warm. "Actually, I have a proposition that benefits us both. The vineyards have enough peasants to pick the grapes, but Pommery needs help to make the wine. Otherwise, we'll lose an entire harvest."

She grimaces. "You're asking my girls to do physical labor?"

I blurt a laugh. "Isn't that what they do?"

She narrows her eyes. "How much?"

"I'll pay them the same as my men get."

She pushes out her bottom lip. "These girls don't know the first thing about real work."

The courtesan behind the curtain shrieks. "You-you-you pervert!" The courtesan throws his shoes out of the curtain, and they tumble down the stairs.

The man chases after them in his undergarments and slips on the stairs. Head over heels he tumbles to the bottom, grunting and cursing. It's Wolfe, all right. The courtesan throws his jacket, trousers, shirt, and vest after him, and they scatter around him at the bottom.

I need to get us out of here before he sees me and cup my hand to Scheherazade's ear. "Have the girls at Pommery at nine o'clock Monday morning."

Our old barn doors are open to the relentless rain that followed a month of scorching sun. Wagonload after wagonload of grapes come in from the vineyards in the worst shape I've seen. The grapes are blistered and moldy, disastrous for wine.

I took over logging wagons into the ledger and issuing a pay slip to exchange for payment at the bank. Yvonne and Chantal serve the waggoneers hot cider from the kitchen, and towels to dry their oil-slicked coats before they head back.

The wagon drivers are not familiar men, but young peasant women taken away from egg gathering, butter churning, and scrubbing laundry to help with the harvest.

The courtesans are not familiar, either, dressed in their oldest dresses and bandanas on their heads. Thirteen-year-old Louise, home from convent school, teaches them how to sort the grapes. The ladies are slow to catch on, taking too much time with their task, and the line backs up. So, to improve their pace, Louise leads the courtesans singing "Frère Jacques," singing each verse faster than the last. They sing along, their working hands moving with the rhythm.

Older children from the orphanage dump the bad grapes in a compost pile for fertilizer we'll use next season.

When the ladies finally fill the wheelbarrow of good grapes, Lucille hauls them up to Damas waiting at the grape press.

Damas, wispy white hair sticking out of his Phrygian cap like dandelion fronds, cranks the grape-press wheel as if he's done it all his life. He's careful not to press too hard or the wheel crushes the seeds and stems, releasing bitter tannins.

Bouffer

A burning sensation sizzles from my core to my face. *Bouffées de chaleur.* Hot flashes, again. I fan my face with my hand.

Damas siphons the new wine into casks for the first fermentation. On each cask, he meticulously records the date, vineyard, varietal of grape, and quality notes. He obviously reads and writes and understands complicated tasks and I am amazed at how far he has come. I've watched this young man grow up before my eyes, yet never really seen what he was capable of. Without Damas, I would be sunk.

At the end of a grueling week, the courtesans line up at my desk, and I pay them the same as I would my workers, yet we've crushed only half the wine. They're no substitute for the experienced crew. While I pay the last few girls, Damas cleans and organizes for the coming week. It will be a challenge preparing and moving the giant hogshead barrels to ferment over the winter months.

Damas waves goodnight at my door.

"Don't forget your pay." I gesture for him to come in and hand him his money. "There's an extra five francs in there for you, Damas. You can expect it from now on. You took over work that Henry and Louis usually do, without complaint." I reach for his hand and shake it, trying to meet his good eye, but he looks aside as usual. His reddened face nods abruptly, and he ducks out of my office. I wonder what he'll do with the extra money, since he lives with the monks at Saint Remi. He'll probably buy bread to feed the doves and pigeons in the square.

I hear someone at the side door and lock away the ledger. Maybe Damas forgot something. Then I hear the click of heels across the planked floor.

"Madame Pommery, are you in here?" Wolfe bobs his head around the corner of my office. "Ah, I hoped I'd catch you before supper." He sniffs the savory air coming from the adjoining kitchen. "Smells like beef bourguignon, am I right?" He plonks his ample derrière into the leather chair across from my desk. He's dressed in checkered trousers and belted vest, shaved and showered as if it's Monday morning.

"Could this wait, Monsieur Wolfe? It's been a long week with a new crew, and I am dead tired."

"I figured you've been too busy to read the newspapers." He presents a folded newspaper with a smirk I'd love to slap off his pudgy face. "Napoleon surrendered."

Snatching the paper from his hands, I skim the front page, scarcely believing what I'm reading. On September 3, Napoleon marched the French army straight into the Prussian trap. Thousands of Frenchmen were killed.

"Louis and Henry." Bile rises from my stomach. "My entire crew is there."

"It gets worse," Wolfe says. "Napoleon has been captured along with one-hundred thousand French soldiers. The coward abdicated as Emperor of France."

My hands drop in my lap. "Will Empress Eugenie take the throne?"

Wolfe snorts. "When Napoleon surrendered, the empress hired a yacht to take her to England."

"She betrayed her country to save herself?"

"Can you blame her?" Wolfe shrugs. "Otto von Bismarck has united the entire German states against the French. A more formidable army has never existed."

"What will they do?" I ask. "Without an army or monarch, we are defenseless."

He scruffs his beard, thinking. "Bismarck is conniving and ruthless. There is nothing to stop them from taking France. Don't worry, Madame. I am Prussian. You will be safe with me."

Tendrils of fear twist around my innards. "Go inside and join the others for dinner, Monsieur Wolfe. I have something to attend to." Grabbing my cape from the hook, I slip out to the cathedral. There's only one thing to do when fear threatens to throttle you.

Pray.

23

TOMBER DANS LE PANNEAU

To fall into the trap

1870. I hire a transport wagon and will ship as much champagne as possible to Hubinet from the crayères. As Louise directs the Alhambra courtesans and orphans pulling carts up the ramp, the ceiling and walls begin to quake, chunks of chalk raining on our heads. The thudding earth sounds like thousands of boots marching above us. Panic courses through my blood.

The Prussians? It's only two days since our army was captured. The Alhambra women gather the orphans under their arms to keep them quiet. They cannot cry or shout for fear of being heard. We are rats.

Hours pass under the shuddering ground until the massive army has moved over us toward town. My first thought is to stay here in the crayères. But there is no food or water. And the temperature is dropping rapidly.

No one dares speak as we climb the rough-hewn staircase out of the depths. But as we reach the dwarf beech tree atop the butte, our silence is broken with glass shattering, shouting, and jeering. The pillage has begun.

Our wagon and horses parked below are gone, so we creep through the back streets, glimpsing the riotous soldiers seizing each

181

café and tavern, tossing empty bottles on the cobblestone streets.

Louise grips my arm, biting the nails of her other hand.

Instinctively, I take her hand out of her mouth. "Ladies do not bite their fingernails."

"Maman, this is no time for etiquette," she says. "We need to get out of here. Go to Chigny."

"And leave the winery to the Prussians? I'm not leaving everything we have built here."

She shakes her head vehemently. "I read the newspapers, too. The Prussian army is ruthless. They set circles of fire around our French army to slaughter them. Those that survived were sent to work camps."

I shudder, thinking of Henry and Louis and the others.

My throat aches, but I must not show my fear. "Take the Alhambra women to Saint Remi; you'll all be safe there."

Louise clings to my arm. "No, Maman. I want to stay with you."

I smooth her hair back from her face. "Lucille will need your help to keep the children entertained at the abbey. You need to be brave. Can you do that?"

Her mouth purses, and she buries her face into my bosom as she did as a child.

We reach Saint Remi, and the courtesans and orphans take shelter inside.

I hug Louise and Lucille, and gesture for them to join the others. "I need to get Damas and lock up the winery and house. Then we will come back."

Another mile to Reims Cathedral. The rioting gets worse; loud, guttural, drunken soldiers make my skin crawl.

Only one block more. I'm relieved to see Monsieur Wolfe standing guard at my double winery doors.

Soldiers carry out cases of champagne from our winery.

"What are you doing, Monsieur Wolfe?" I ask. "Where are they taking my champagne?"

"Not now, Madame Pommery." He pulls me aside. "Don't interrupt the soldiers."

They load champagne into the wagon they stole from us, then return to the winery for more.

Wolfe speaks quietly, barely moving his lips. "They are taking ten cases from each winery for their victory celebration tonight at the Palace of Tau."

I scoff. "How generous you are to help them."

He puffs out his chest. "Mayor Werle assigned me to the soldiers to make sure there are no incidents. The Prussian soldiers are apt to help themselves to whatever they fancy." He slants his eyes toward me. "If you take my meaning."

The lust of soldiers after victory is a lady's worst nightmare.

"General Francis needs servers for their victory dinner," Wolfe says. "I offered your Saint Remi Auxiliary ladies."

I scoff. "Think again. The auxiliary ladies do not serve anyone, least of all an enemy army."

"General Francis was not asking," Wolfe says.

An intense heat overcomes me. "This General Francis has a lot of nerve asking our women to serve dinner to these hoodlums."

Color drains from Wolfe's face as he stares behind me.

A towering officer with a fierce red beard blocks my doorway. His pickelhaube emblazoned with a gold eagle makes him even taller. The side of his helmet is freshly pitted by gunshot. Maltese crosses secure the fish-scale chin strap.

"This house will do, Herr Wolfe." The general's uniform is laden with medals, and there's a white sash across his chest, gold epaulettes, a well-used scabbard at his waist.

Wolfe throws back his shoulders. "Madame Pommery, allow me to introduce Frederick Francis II, Grand Duke of Mecklen-burg-Schwerin. The grand duke is now our governor-general."

Grand duke? I curtsey automatically and hate myself for it. *Zut, zut, zut!*

"We are taking over your lovely city," the general says. "Monsieur Wolfe recommended your home for my headquarters since it is large and close to the cathedral."

Another *bouffée de chaleur*. "Monsieur Wolfe was mistaken. This is my house, and he had no right to take it."

"Thirty thousand soldiers are requisitioning homes in Reims," Wolfe says. "It is in your best interest to host the Governor-General and his staff."

"I'm sure Monsieur Wolfe can find you somewhere more suitable," I say.

"Madame Pommery, let me be clear," the general says. "France as you knew it is no longer. United German forces will capture Paris, and France will be ours." He studies my face. "Now then, I would like a tour of the house."

I consider rejecting him outright, but the consequences would likely be dire. "This way." I lead him through the hallway, and Wolfe follows like a faithful schnauzer.

"What are all these small rooms used for?" General Francis asks.

"In the past, this house accommodated the monks of Saint Remi," I say. "Now, the house and winery occupy the same building. Three stories above ground and two below, with the cellar extending under the street. There is a garret in the roof and two subterranean apartments. The tasting salon and counting house are on the street level."

We walk through the door to the winery. The smell of fermenting grapes hits my nose.

"Ah, amazing fragrance." The general pauses and looks around the big open space surrounded by the mezzanine.

I point out the crushing equipment and tasting salon. My throat contracts when we reach Louis and Henry's empty desks, backing up to each other. Don't even know if they are alive.

I lean over Louis's desk, fingering neat stacks of papers he touched. "My son manages the vineyards and helps with winemaking."

"Her son and all the cellarmen were conscribed to war," Wolfe says.

The general turns to me. "You haven't heard from them?"

I shake my head.

The general walks past me, smelling of gunshot. "Where are the cellars?"

We walk down the plank stairs, the temperature dropping with each step. Bottles are stacked on racks near the stone walls as we walk around the cellar. The general pulls out bottles along the way, reading the labels.

"When did you start making champagne?" He picks out a bottle from the triangular riddling rack, shaking up dead yeast gathering in the neck.

"Twelve years ago, after my husband died."

He replaces the bottle in the rack. "What was your best vintage?"

"Alas, it is all sold." I hope to convince him, but it is stored in Butte Saint-Nicaise. "1865 was the perfect year. Since the Great Comet vintage of 1811, there has never been a grape so ripe, so delectable, due to favorable weather."

"I would love to taste that champagne." His eyes narrow as if he sees through me. "If you can find a bottle."

The chill of the cellars makes me shiver. "I have a similar vintage I can serve you inside the house."

We climb to the ground floor, and the general says he'll join us after he checks on his officers.

Wolfe follows me. "You handled that perfectly, Madame. His occupation here must go well, or it will reflect badly on both of us."

At the door I block his entry. "I invited the general as my guest, but you are just the traitor who invited him to live in my house."

Wolfe's mouth drops open, then snaps shut. "It is unwise to cross me, Madame. I am the personal liaison between General Francis and Reims. Make sure the auxiliary ladies are at the Palace of Tau to serve the victory dinner."

I scoff. "Wouldn't want our guests to think they are unwanted."

I freshen up and give myself a good talking to. Creating more tension will not do us any good. I have Louise and Lucille and the rest of the household to protect.

When General Francis joins me, he has the good graces to take off his spiked helmet, revealing a balding head that makes him more human. As I open the champagne, the general walks from painting to painting. Local artists I've collected over the years, wanting to support them. But also, paintings from the sidewalks of Paris and London.

"My wife loved art." His granite eyes glisten as I hand him a flute.

"To your wife." I clink his glass.

He sips the wine and swallows, his Adam's apple thrusting up like a fist. His eyelids clench.

"You don't care for the champagne?" I sniff my glass, the bouquet fresh and pristine.

He shakes his head. "No."

I clamp my lips together.

"No, no." He waves his hand. "The champagne is fine. Your toast made me think of my wives."

Plural.

He leans against the marble mantle, his shoulders slumped. "My first wife died of consumption; my second wife died in childbirth. My third wife will be lucky if she doesn't die from our six children." He snorts a laugh.

"Six children, that would do me in, too." I sip my champagne, surprised we're talking of marriage and children under these circumstances.

"Actually, I have eight children, and my third wife just turned twenty, so I doubt she is finished." He raises his glass with a wry smile. "Any wonder I chose the military?"

I smile. "I understand you are a grand duke? Where is your duchy?"

"The House of Mecklenburg at Schwerin on the Baltic Sea, surrounded by other Prussian states. I enlisted to protect my duchy from being swallowed up by the Northern German Confederation."

He watches as I fill his empty glass. I have a feeling nothing escapes him.

"Why haven't you remarried, Madame Pommery?" He sits on the sofa facing the hearth.

"Long story." The Baron crosses my mind with more than a little regret.

"I like stories." He spreads his arms out on the back of the sofa as if he is already master of the house.

Sitting in the tufted chair adjacent, I sip my champagne. "When my husband died, my life stretched out before me like a new road. I saw the opportunity to do something completely different, something I'd love."

"But that does not explain why you didn't marry," he says.

"Touché." I hold up my forefinger. "A married woman cannot own a business on her own. But a widow can."

"Ambitious woman." He drinks his champagne and makes a face. "But you should use more sugar if you want to sell champagne to Germans."

I huff. "So people tell me."

"Germans love Veuve Clicquot. Follow her lead and keep your prices below hers, and you'll steal away sales." He strokes his wild red beard. "In fact, you should change your label to Veuve Pommery, and people will never know the difference."

Hackles rise on the back of my neck. "I have no interest in imitating anyone's champagne, not even my own. Every year Pommery Champagne gets better. My goal is to make the most delicious champagne in the world."

He chuckles. "You are a spitfire." He holds out his empty glass for more champagne, something one should never do. I pour him more, and he dives his nose into it. "Yes, definitely more sugar."

"Is Germany planning to conquer France?"

"That is not up to me, unfortunately." He arches one eyebrow. "But as long as I'm here, I plan to live like God in France."

A common German saying. Germans think we are hedonists with our fine wines and delicious food. I pour the rest of the bottle to the very top of his glass, breaking another rule. "Is there anything else you require of me? Or may I be excused?"

"Ah, yes. I require strong coffee and fresh croissants at six in the morning, a delectable French meal with wine at lunch, and an evening repast for my officers in the dining room."

"You want me to provide your meals?"

"And I require your company at dinner when I deem it necessary." He stares at the fire. "Women can soften the hardships of war." He gulps the last of the champagne.

I can only imagine what he means. "I'm sorry I cannot accommodate you. I must eat with my daughter and daughter-in-law."

"You will dine with me." His voice cracks. "And you will arrange for your auxiliary to serve at tonight's officers' dinner."

I scoff. "The auxiliary ladies are the top crust of Reims society. They do not know the first thing about serving. They are served by their servants, who have been trained by us at the orphanage."

"*Dumme Frau!*" He clunks down his flute and breaks it at the base. The stem cuts into the heel of his hand, and blood drips into a red puddle.

"Oh dear." Snatching a lace doily from the armchair, I bind his hand tightly. "There. That should stop the bleeding."

He jerks his hand away. "You don't understand what is happening. You are my prisoner and will do as I command, with no backchat. *Verstehen Sie?*" Understand? All kindness has vanished.

I am his prisoner. The thought paralyzes me. My friends and neighbors face the same terrifying reality.

He stands and turns his back to me. "You are to provide women to serve tonight's dinner. Fifty should suffice."

Striding straight to the front door, I don my cape from the wardrobe. Fifty, he said, as if it's possible. I can't think of one who would agree to serve our captors.

On Reims Square, hordes of soldiers swarm like hornets, arms slung over shoulders, spitting on the cobblestones, hooting, howling, singing German songs, swigging stolen bottles of champagne.

Pulling the hood over my head, I hurry through the back alleys to Le Palais Alhambra.

24

Donner de la Confiture aux Cochons

To give marmalade to the pigs

Prussian soldiers' old sweat reeks with the enormous fire blazing in the Palace of Tau. They wear their bloodstains and battlefield dirt like badges of victory and boast of killing and plunder to their commanders and General Francis. And Reynard Wolfe. What is the banker doing here, seated next to General Francis, talking as if they are old friends?

The irony of this night weighs on me. Prussian captors celebrate their victory over France in the Palace of Tau where French kings held coronations for hundreds of years. Ear-splitting revelry bounces off the gothic, arched ceilings, fueling their frenzy.

Giant hogshead barrels have been cut in half and filled with hundreds of bottles of champagne and wine pilfered from every winery in Reims. The soldiers do not bother with glasses but grab bottles and lop off the tops with their swords as Napoleon made popular. Another irony.

They strike a gong that echoes through the vast hall. Soldiers make their way to long tables.

Trumpets blast through their chatter. General Francis raises his fists high, pummeling the air in triumph. He starts to chant, and soldiers join him.

Victory. Victory. Victory, Victory.
And if my heart breaks in death,
You won't become a Frenchman yet.
As abundant with water is your flood,
So is Germany in heroes' blood.

General Francis gives me the signal, and I open the double kitchen doors. Scheherazade and her courtesans carry out trays high above their heads and weave through the tables. Soldiers cheer and whistle. I'm sure they never expected exotic harlots wearing colorful harem pants and bustiers to serve them.

I should be outraged by how they dressed, but how can I complain? The Alhambra came to my rescue when the auxiliary women refused to leave their houses, sending servants instead. I can't blame the auxiliary either. Our men are gone, captured, or killed, and the enemy has taken over our homes. God help us. I cross myself and take a deep breath.

Garbed modestly, Lucille and Louise pass out fresh baguettes to the tables. A soldier grabs Lucille to his lap, her eyelet pantaloons kicking in the air like a cancan dancer. The man beside him grabs Louise and smashes his lips against hers. Their comrades jeer them on.

Lifting my skirts above my knees, I run to their aid. Thrusting my arms between the men, I hoist the girls out of their grasp and accompany them to the next row.

"Don't smile. Don't look them in the eyes and stick together," I tell them. "I'll meet you at the other end."

The Alhambra girls take the soldiers in their stride, winking and blowing them kisses. The right women for the job.

The soldiers start a new chant.

Deutschland, Deutschland über alles,
Über alles in der Welt.
Germany, Germany above all,
Above everything in the world.

Lucille and Louise struggle through the men. A soldier grabs Louise around the middle, chanting, "Germany, Germany above all…"

I try to reach them, but the row is blocked by chanting men. "Above everything in the world."

Louise's arms cross over her budding breasts as they pass her stiff body through the crowd.

"Germany, Germany above all. Above everything in the world."

Louise is carried away on a wave of lust, soldiers handing her off, pinching and squeezing. I run around the perimeter, yelling at the soldiers to stop, as if they can hear me over their jeers. They volley them from table to table, their guttural jeers accosting my ears. I shoulder through the crazed mob, shoving their hands away from my body. Doesn't seem to matter to them I'm old enough to be their mother.

Bugles blare and all eyes turn to the head table. The general stands with arms raised, and with a swift command, he orders Louise brought to him.

I run to her. Louise clings to me, sobbing and shaking.

"You are barbarians," I shout at the general.

"There is one person to blame here, and it is you alone," the general says. "What were you thinking, submitting your daughters to soldiers who haven't seen women for months." He turns to Wolfe. "Take them back to the house."

"They should be punished."

"You are naïve, Madame." He speaks through gritted teeth. "We are the conquerors and you the conquered. Everything you have is ours from the moment Napoleon surrendered. Your house, your winery, your very lives are ours now."

A loud cheer goes up, and now soldiers pass Lucille from table to table, grabbing her wherever they please. Her arms cover her belly, but they pinch her breasts.

"Stop this at once," I yell at the general. "That woman is with child."

The general orders his guards collect Lucille, whose face is crumpled in on itself. She moans and pants like an animal dying.

Something is wrong. Terribly wrong.

"Accompany them to Madame Pommery's house at once," the general orders Wolfe.

There are more soldiers outside than there were inside—the lowest of low, scraped up from the gutters for the Prussian army. They ogle us, make lewd gestures, and yell vulgarities. Louise and Lucille clutch my sides for dear life, and I shelter them with my cape. Wolfe straggles behind as if he'd rather stay at the Palace of Tau.

Lucille mumbles and moans. Though she's small, it is awkward holding both girls.

"Help me," I yell at Wolfe. "I can't handle them both. Lucille is faint."

He grasps her waist and cradles her head with his hand.

I pull Louise under my arm, and we walk away from the heckling soldiers and their putrid smell.

"What will happen to the Alhambra girls tonight?" I ask Wolfe.

"Do not worry about them. Madame Scheherazade is as shrewd as they come," he says. "Tonight, they'll whet the soldiers' appetites and tomorrow charge double for their wares."

"Surely the general will protect our women. He is a grand duke, after all, not a barbarian."

"Don't be fooled by General Francis," Wolfe says. "He is notorious for his ferocity. The neighboring states are terrified by him. He spares no one to accomplish his mission, or Chancellor Bismarck would not have sent him here to occupy France."

"The Prussians cannot take over France," I say.

"They've taken over eighteen departments already." Wolfe repositions his grasp on Lucille, who flutters her eyelids, unconsciously.

I glare at him. "Whose side are you on?"

"I am on the victor's side," he smiles. "You must be also, or you will suffer. Prussians are the most ruthless of Germans."

A shrill wind blows through the vacant streets, and Louise shivers. Lucille cries out in pain and holds her belly.

"Oh, dear God." I find the house key on my chatelaine and jiggle it in the lock. "Go get Doctor DuBois."

Wolfe scoffs. "You women make such a fuss. She'll forget all about it by morning."

"I'll get the doctor, Maman." Louise runs into the alley before I can stop her.

"Couldn't you have done that? My daughter has been through enough tonight to last a lifetime."

"You are overreacting," Wolfe says, holding Lucille up under her arms and looking around. "Where do you want her?"

Every door is open, with army packs and bedrolls in each room. He drags her through the hallway as I check. "Let's put her in Louise's room." We lift her into bed. Her dress is soaked with blood.

"What happened to her?" Wolfe says.

"Your soldiers, that's what." I start to unbutton her dress. "Light the lamps, will you?" Lucille writhes and moans.

He lights the oil lamp on the bedside table. "What is wrong with her?"

"She's having a baby." Omitting that Lucille is my daughter-in-law and the baby my grandchild.

Wolfe stares at the gold star necklace around her delicate neck. "She's a Jew. In Prussia, Jews are still burned at the stake. General Francis will not stand for a Jew in the house."

"She converted to Catholicism." I unclasp the necklace and put it in a drawer.

"Jews lie. Don't you know that Madame Pommery?" Wolfe huffs. "I will not be punished for your Jew servant."

Grabbing his four-in-hand tie, I pull him so close I see his nostrils twitch. "You brought this Prussian monster to my door. It will be on your head if any of us is harmed."

Lucille groans, her brow drenched with sweat. I pour water from the pitcher into the basin.

"You should thank me, Madame," he says. "I put the general in your house so you and your family would be safe."

Lucille pitches and moans, then wails like a banshee—a sound so otherworldly, it shivers my spine. The baby is coming. She screams again, her face splotched red and white. Her fingernails dig into her belly.

I swat Wolfe's evening coat. "Go find out what happened to Louise and the doctor."

Lucille squawks and pushes for what seems like hours while I swab her face, grotesque from the pain. Blood floods from her insides, soaks the bedding, and spills to the floor. My arms and dress are covered in her blood.

When Doctor DuBois finally comes, I send Louise straight up to my room to save her from the sight.

Lucille has long stopped screaming. She lies spent and pale in a puddle of slime, the pink fetus lying on her chest.

Doctor DuBois pronounces mother and baby dead.

Scheherazade and her courtesans do not return to the winery the next day, or the next.

As I wait for Louise to come down for the funeral, Wolfe, in top hat and bespoke vest, arrives in a brand-new carriage, embodying his role as the general's attaché.

"I have reconsidered the situation and feel the best solution is for you and Louise to go to Chigny. I came to take you."

"I won't leave the winery in Prussian hands," I say, pulling on my gloves. "But I must get Louise out of here. I can telegraph Greno to collect her in Paris. Can you take us to the train station this afternoon?"

Wolfe frowns. "Too late for Paris, Madame. As soon as the army has rested, they'll be marching to take over the provisional government."

My hand presses my mouth. "Paris, too? Then, Louise will have to go back to convent school. Anything to get her away from these soldiers." I call upstairs. "Louise, darling. Come down, we'll be late for the service."

"Where are you going?" Wolfe asks. "The general will want to know."

"Am I a prisoner in my own home?"

"I am afraid you are." His lips curl. He likes to see me squirm.

"Very well," I raise my voice. "Tell General Francis, I am going to Saint Remi to mourn my daughter-in-law and grandson his men killed last night."

"Your daughter-in-law?"

"Lucille was Louis's wife," I drop my head, too heavy to hold high.

He gasps and holds his chest. "Madame, you must be joking."

"Louis did not tell me they married because he thought I would not accept a Jew in our family," I tell him. "But, now I would give anything to embrace them with open arms."

Louis, Lucille, and their son are gone. And Henry, too. My family is Louise.

She plods down the steps with bloodshot eyes and pasty complexion, somber in her black frock. Lucille, her nursemaid, friend, and sister-in-law, now gone. Her world is turned upside down, and it doesn't help that her house has been taken over by Prussians.

I must find a way to protect Louise from more tragedy. Taking her hand, we walk past Wolfe to Saint Remi Abbey.

25

La lumière au bout du tunnel

Light at the end of the tunnel

Since Yvonne and Chantal have their hands full feeding the general and officers, I take over their daily trip to the boulangerie for bread. Biting off the end of a warm baguette, I pass by Reims Cathedral to visit my Smiling Angel. The sunrise bathes her soft cheeks in serenity and hope. No matter how anxious and upset I feel, she is always smiling, offering the promise of better days. She has been through the French Revolution, dozens of kings, and wars, and still she smiles. Kneeling before her, I pray for Lucille and the baby. May they find comfort in God's arms. I pray for Louis, Henry, and our boys, hoping against hope they are alive and will make it back home. I pray for my strength and courage to keep our household, orphanage, and women of Reims safe from this Prussian occupation.

The tendrils of fear and uncertainty slowly unfurl around my heart, at least enough to hear a new beat of strength and hope.

When I return, I deliver the baguettes to Yvonne and Chantal, who are busy preparing breakfast, if one can call it that. The smell of organ meat turns my stomach.

"Heaven help us." I hold my nose dramatically, and Chantal laughs. The general calls for liverwurst and pickled onions on a baguette.

"Where's Louise?" I ask. She helps them in the mornings now, with so many more to feed.

"She left for the winery," Chantal says.

"This early?" I check my timepiece on my chatelaine as I walk down the corridor to the winery. Only seven o'clock. Since we've lost the Alhambra girls to the Prussian soldiers, there are only three of us working. At least there is less to do in the winter when the new wine is in first fermentation, transforming grape juice into wine.

The cold air makes me shiver. Louise and Damas are peering into a small wooden cage with a wire grate. Felix sits with them, flicking his tail like a metronome.

"What is it?" I ask.

Louise runs to me and pulls me to the cage. "Remember the rock dove Damas gave Louis at the train station?" she says, breathlessly. "It flew back."

My heart leaps. Louis is alive if she's right. "How do you know it's the same dove?"

"The red socks I embroidered for him."

I cross myself and utter a prayer of gratitude. Kneeling beside Louise, I smell lavender from her bath. The dove coos and puffs its iridescent neck feathers as if he's proud of his colorful socks on his spindly legs.

"Damas and Louis always sent messages back and forth with the pigeons," she says. "So I crocheted socks to hold them."

"So clever, Rosebud." I put my arm around her.

Damas reaches in the cage for the dove, his long fingers holding the wings. Louise extracts a paper from the sock. Thin and small like a cigarette paper, the missive is folded many times. The writing is so tiny, she holds it close to read.

"Damas, my friend. If this gets to you, bring it to my maman. Henry and I escaped the camp along with some of our crew. If we can make it through Germany, we'll come home. Louis."

Damas smiles and puts the dove back in the cage and locks it. He's still smiling when he climbs the ladder up the new hogshead barrel, and punches down the fermenting grape must.

Louise wipes away tears, and I rub her back. "They'll make it back," I tell her.

"He doesn't know Lucille and the baby are gone." She holds back a sob. "He doesn't know we're prisoners."

Her pain needles my ribs. I wipe tears from her cheeks with my thumbs. "They are alive, Rosebud. Henry and Louis are alive. We must focus on that."

But Louise is right. Our men don't know we are occupied by the Prussians, and worse, they are headquartered at our home. If General Francis knows they are escapees from the German work camps, will he make an example of them to keep the town in fear?

The general has taken over the mezzanine level of my winery, which unfortunately shares a wall with my bedroom. For the past two weeks, German voices permeate the wall between us into the wee hours of the night. Pulling the pillow over my head, their voices rumble through nightmares of Louis and Henry lying dead in a field somewhere or starving in a German prison.

I wake to the banging of my front-door knocker. Looking out the window, I see Wolfe and two military officers on the porch. The general and his aide walk out to meet them.

Last night after dinner, the general said he was looking forward to meeting the Mumm brothers, one of many meetings Wolfe has arranged with German descendants. Old champagne houses like Mueller-Ruinart, Bollinger, Krug, and Charles Heidsieck. Would they renounce France and help the Germans? The most important meeting would be with our mayor, Werle, who inherited Veuve Clicquot, and changed the name to "Werle et Cie, successors to Veuve Clicquot." The woman is barely in her grave, and he diminishes her legacy.

At least the general's meetings give me time to slip away to Butte Saint-Nicaise undetected. I dress hastily, grab my sketchpad and a fresh croissant from Yvonne in the kitchen. I set out walking in the opposite direction to the general and Wolfe. The murky night starts to fade, and I feel the morning dew on my cheeks.

As I near the walled gardens of Saint Remi, I breathe in the scent of clematis. The cooing doves in the garden soothe my ears.

How marvelous that nature thrives even while men perpetrate hate and destruction.

Out of nowhere, the general, Wolfe, and officers appear at the crossroads of two streets. My stomach falls. "Good morning, gentlemen."

Wolfe glares. "You must salute the general when you meet him in public, Madame."

My clammy fingers touch my forehead.

"I wouldn't expect you to be out so early," the general says.

"I am on my way to mass."

"She is the patron saint of the orphans at Saint Remi," Wolfe says.

I'm surprised at his praise.

"With a drawing tablet?" the general asks.

I raise the pad. "I love the light through the windows."

The general assesses me, then nods curtly. "Carry on, Madame Pommery."

Relieved, I walk into Saint Remi Abbey and out the side door to Butte Saint-Nicaise. Why stop the excavation if we can make progress and employ workers who have not been conscripted to war? It has been two years since we began to clear out the crayères and dig out passageways between galleries. It will be another few years before we finish. I only hope Mayor Werle and Wolfe have enough loyalty not to share my secret with the general, or the Prussians will steal my best wines.

Climbing up to the hidden entrance under the dwarf beech, I hear the clinking chisels and echoing voices, exposing the underground project. If soldiers venture near here, they will investigate.

Jerome Nair, the mining supervisor, waves at me as I pass the miners. With his long wiry hair and beard, he looks like Goliath from the Bible. His wife is one of my auxiliary ladies, as dedicated to the orphans as he is to his work.

With most men called to war, Nair hired older men who work steady and exacting. They have excavated one hundred crayères already, and by the time we finish, there will be many more. A secret world of Pommery champagne, growing more stunning as the war rages above.

As the ancient Roman crayères are exposed, they exude a stunning beauty I feel down to my bones. When I focus on creating an experience my customers will enjoy and remember forever in these crayères, my mind is released from the gnawing anxiety of Prussians camped in my home.

Opening my sketchpad, I draw up new ideas for the crayères. Each tunnel will have a wooden sign naming each city Pommery does business with. Hubinet would like that. I wonder if my letter reached him in London before they closed the postal service. Certainly, the world knows by now that France is captive. Enough. The Prussians may control my whereabouts, but they cannot control my thoughts.

I join the miners for lunch in the largest crayère gallery. They are quiet, knowing that danger lurks above. By the light of the lanterns, the white chalk walls soar hundreds of feet up to the surface, expansive and impressive as the Louvre. Perhaps we could display fine sculpture here. What about a relief carved into the wall?

When lunch is over, I start drawing ideas for a frieze. Dionysus, the Greek god of wine, celebrating harvest with the gods.

I'm lost in my drawings until Nair tells me they are finished for the day.

"Oh my." I consult my timepiece. "How did it get so late? I'll just finish this drawing and let myself out."

He leaves me a lantern, and they blow out the others before they leave.

I turn back to my drawing: cherubs, maidens, bountiful baskets of grapes, overflowing wine.

Later, I hear voices echoing in the cave. Maybe a miner forgot something. But as they draw closer, I hear Wolfe. My entire body goes rigid.

Lantern light flickers on the dappled chiseled wall. They are getting closer. "She must have smuggled the champagne down here without my knowledge," Wolfe tells someone. "Was this the way we came in? It all looks the same."

I snuff my lantern and crouch below a wine rack, holding my heart lest it jump out of my chest.

Wolfe passes by with his lantern high, followed by the general. Another betrayal; does the man have no loyalty?

"I think I feel fresh air," Wolfe says. "There must be a way out over here."

"Get me out of here," General Francis says. "I can't breathe with all this chalk dust. Why would she build a cellar under a city dump?"

Wolfe shakes his head. "She needed more space."

I sneeze. *Zut!*

Wolfe swings his lantern around, casting ghoulish shadows on their faces. "Who's there?"

I step out from behind the rack. "What are you doing here?"

"Your drawing tablet caught my interest," the general says. "After our meeting with Mumm, I asked Wolfe what you were drawing."

I hold my hands out. "This is where I age champagne. Actually, I plan to move my entire winery here, but it will take several years to complete."

The general peers into the caves with racks of wine flanking the sides. "There is a great deal of champagne down here."

"*Oui*. But if your troops discover my crayères, my champagne will be gone before month's end."

"You should not have kept this secret from me," Wolfe says, wiping the sheen off his face with a handkerchief.

"You know I have the title to this property," I tell him. "The entire city council knows that."

"The mayor has not approved the title," Wolfe says.

"Gentlemen, you don't have much oil left in that lamp," I point out. "I suggest we leave before it burns out."

"Which way?" the general says. "I am suffocating in here." He's lost all color; his breaths are shallow and weak.

I take the lantern from Wolfe and take the lead. "Tunnels connect to larger galleries."

The general stumbles and loses his balance. I steady his arm and take them through the next tunnel, smaller and with even less air.

"My lungs are burning," he says, leaning against the wall.

The lantern wick sputters and burns out. Darkness closes

around us. The general panics and runs, hitting his head. He groans and falls, screaming. The clatter of scaffolding collapsing. An appalling thud and sickening wail. Sounds like he fell below.

"General Francis?" Wolfe calls.

"Take my hand." I grab Wolfe and step carefully through the broken railing. "And watch your step. It's two feet down here, at least."

The general moans weakly, enough for us to find him on the chalk floor.

I shake his shoulder. "General Francis, wake up." No response.

We try to pick him up, but he is too heavy.

"We can't do this by ourselves," I say. "I'll get help." I stand and feel for the wall.

"You can't leave me here," Wolfe says. "It's getting cold."

"He'll wake up soon, and it's better if you are here."

A rustling of bats flies through the ceiling above our heads.

"I'm coming with you," Wolfe says.

"Then I'll stay with the general until you bring help."

"The officers will kill me if they see me without the general. We've been gone for hours, and they will think I am in on it. You planned this, didn't you? You lured us down here, so you could bury us down here, and no one would be the wiser."

"Get hold of yourself, Wolfe," I say in his direction. "You could have asked the general if he was uncomfortable underground."

"So, now I'm to blame."

"Stop arguing," I say. "Stay with the general and keep him warm."

The windows are dark in my house. Two men huddle at the front door, and I recognize Doctor DuBois and Doctor Henroit. I gasp in relief. They'll help me with the general.

Across the square, soldiers pour out of Palace of Tau, splitting into groups and pounding on doors.

"Inside, quickly. They'll never think to look here," DuBois commands in a voice I've trusted through illness and accidents, births, and deaths.

I let them into Louise's room, right by the side door, so we won't encounter any officers in the house. I light the lamp and close the door without a sound. Doctor Henroit collapses on the bed, stiff-legged and wincing. Blood spreads on his trousers soiled with ash, the smell of smoke heavy in the small room.

DuBois grips my shoulder, his eyes narrowed. "Bring your sharpest knife and a needle with strong thread. Brandy if you have it."

I tiptoe through the dark hallways, listening for soldiers, but all is quiet inside. Yvonne and Chantal must be in their quarters behind the pantry. I take a sharp paring knife from the kitchen and go to the salon for brandy and clean towels. Rummaging in my sewing basket, I find my half-finished embroidery hoop with needle and thread.

When I return, Henroit is propped up on his elbows, sweat dripping down his brow. His trouser leg is ripped to his hip, exposing a long gash on his thigh, caked with black powder and blood, a cartridge embedded deep in his muscle. Henroit flinches and grips the headboard with white knuckles.

I swab his forehead with the bar towel.

DuBois douses brandy over his hands, the knife, and the wound, then gives Henroit the bottle. He downs half.

Breaking the thread and needle from the embroidery, I hand the wooden hoop to Henroit. "Here, bite down on this."

His teeth clench the wood, his eyes bulging with fear.

"Look away." DuBois inserts the knife point next to the metal cartridge and tries to pry it out. But it doesn't budge. He tries a different angle, shimmying the knife underneath the cartridge. Henroit faints and falls back on the pillow, allowing DuBois to dig deeper and extract the cartridge with his fingers.

I wipe his bloody hands with a towel. DuBois pours more brandy over the raw opening, then takes my embroidery needle and stitches the wound with tiny red stitches of my embroidery thread. Henroit shivers in his sleep, and I cover him with a quilt.

"He'll be out until morning." DuBois tilts the brandy to his mouth.

"He'll be safe here," I tell him. "This is my daughter's room, and the general forbids soldiers to enter." I forgot the general. "Zut."

"What is wrong?" DuBois asks.

"I need your help." I grasp his forearm. "I wouldn't ask if it wasn't important."

We avoid the soldiers banging on every door, pulling men out of their homes.

"What are they searching for?" I duck through a dark alley.

DuBois huffs. "They're looking for evidence. Snipers ambushed the Biergarten."

"Prussians fired on you?" I ask.

He snorted. "We burned their barracks."

I gasp. "You did nothing of the sort."

"We had to defend ourselves," he says.

"Who is 'we'?"

"*Francs-tireurs*. Sharpshooters. Any man with a rifle."

"How can you be so foolish?" Moonlight glints on his sharp cheekbones, thin mustache, silver at his temples. "The Prussians will make our lives miserable."

"You're taking me to the dump?" he says as we climb the butte.

"The general is injured in my wine crayères."

"Not the general." He turns around, and I pull him back.

"Please, I cannot get him out alone." I light the lantern and hand it to him. "Can you take this? It's too hard to hold while holding my skirts." Climbing into the hidden knoll, I duck under the gnarled dwarf beech to the makeshift plank staircase. One foot after another, down into the cavern. I wait for him at the bottom, lantern light flickering on his anxious face.

"Follow me." As I lead him through the labyrinth of chiseled caves, a strong smell of fermented wine accosts my nose, like when we open the hogshead barrels for blending in the spring.

"Monsieur Wolfe, where are you?" My voice ricochets off the walls. No response. The soles of our boots are soaked with wine, which gets deeper the lower we go. Soon, we are wading through a flood of wine. I raise the lantern high. Barrels have tumbled down, popping off the barrel tops and releasing the wine. Years of hard work lost. This mess will take a Herculean effort to clean up, and I don't have the crew to do it.

"They must have run into the pyramid of barrels and started an avalanche."

Wolfe and the general are nowhere to be found.

26

COMBATTRE LE FEU PAR LE FEU

Fight fire with fire

General Francis reads the newspaper at the breakfast table. His head is bandaged, and his skin drawn tight and colorless as a molting snake. His aide-de-camp guards him—he's tall, broad-shouldered, blond, and blue-eyed like most of the army.

The general folds the newspaper. "You are a shrewd woman, Madame Pommery. Luring us to your dump, while your *Francs-tireurs* set the barracks ablaze. They killed at least a dozen soldiers."

I gasp. "How awful, General. I knew nothing of a fire." I'm appalled how easily the lie rolls off my tongue.

"You left us to rot there in your storehouse, tripping over old dusty barrels and bumping into racks. The disgusting smell of mold and rats. That hole is a death trap, and I insist you close it up immediately so no one else gets hurt."

"I'll have it boarded up today." Of course, in the dark, he couldn't see how much champagne is stored.

"See that you do." He glowers at me. "I'd still be in that dump if it wasn't for Wolfe."

"I'm sorry, General," I say. "I ran to the clinic for a doctor, but you were gone when we returned."

207

He scoffs. "Exactly the story Doctor DuBois told this morning when we arrested him and eight other *Francs-tireurs* hiding in your carriage house, including your son and foreman."

My heart lurches. They made it home. "That's impossible. They're not home from the war."

The general scoffs. "Your lying is pathetic. You knew your son was home. And you knew Doctor DuBois was the *Francs-tireurs'* leader." He flicks his hand at a guard. "Paper and pen."

The soldier complies, and the general slides them toward me. "I want names, Madame. Names of all the *Francs-tireurs* who set fire to the barracks."

I slide the paper slowly back to him and look squarely in his eyes. "I have no knowledge of the fire. But I can tell you, Doctor DuBois was no part of it. He came with me to help you." A devious thought occurs to me. "Have you considered why Monsieur Wolfe chose last night to show you my wine storage? Perhaps you should question him."

The general wrinkles his broad forehead. "Wolfe is German. He would never betray his homeland." His eyes search the crown molding from corner to corner, then orders his aide. "Find Reynard Wolfe and bring him to me."

The aide salutes and marches out.

"I need to see my son," I say, steadying the quaver in my voice.

"He is in no shape to see his mother." The general shakes his head. "My interrogators are overeager to punish those who killed their German comrades."

"Please, General. I must tell my son his wife and child died. He doesn't know."

"Perhaps he's better off." His jaw slackens, exhaustion over-coming him, but he squares his shoulders. "You should have thought of the consequences before you aided the *Francs-tireurs*."

Boldly, I reach for his hand and speak from my heart. "General, I promise you, I would never participate in an attack on your men."

I think I've reached him when he grasps my hand. But his fingers tighten, crushing my fragile bones. I pull away, cradling my hand like a fallen bird.

"Madame Pommery, you're mistaken to believe I would fall for your feminine wiles. Prince Wilhelm made the stakes of this war very clear. The sovereignty of my country, Mecklenburg-Schwerin, depends upon my performance here."

"Please, General Francis." My voice quivers. "I need my son and foreman to help me with the winery."

He points to the door and bellows. "Leave now, or I will throw you in prison with them."

"Yes, sir." I back out of the breakfast room feeling defeated and miserable. Louis and Henry are home, yet captives.

The tension only gets worse. Every night our *Francs-tireurs* wreak havoc on the Prussians, shooting from the rooftops into their drunken parties at the Biergarten, looting their supply tents, jumping down from rooftops into dark alleys to ambush Prussian soldiers.

General Francis imposes more restrictions each day to control the situation. Reims citizens must be in their homes by dark. Anyone caught out will be imprisoned, a problem for the *Francs-tireurs* who need a secret shelter.

I offer Butte Saint-Nicaise to Doctor Henroit for the *Francs-tireurs*. The general will never set foot in there again, and there are many crayères unaffected by their damage.

Each night, I press my ear to the wall between my chambers and the winery mezzanine, listening for news to share with the *Francs-tireurs*. Apparently German and Prussian troops have surrounded Paris. They've cut off food and supplies to the city.

Our only glimmer of hope comes from a crumbled Paris newspaper circulated among the *Francs-tireurs*. Léon Gambetta, our Minister of the Interior and War, flew out of Paris over German lines in a balloon inflated with coal gas. He floated all the way to Loire Valley and organized five new armies of more than half a million troops.

Louise and I go to the cathedral to pray for an end to the war. Soldiers occupy the front pews. Funny to think they are praying to the same God as we are. How will He choose who will win?

We sit near the back. The kneeling bench creaks behind us. The gardenia aroma is suffocating. Madame Scheherazade. I haven't seen her since Prussia invaded, as she's busy with the Alhambra.

She whispers in my ear. "Saturday night, the Alhambra is throwing a birthday party for General Francis. I'm breaking out the absinthe I save for special occasions."

Why is she telling me about feting the enemy? I consider telling her off, but she shuffles out of the pew, her purple bustle swaying as she leaves the sanctuary.

The meaning of her statement sinks in.

"Was that Madame Scheherazade, Maman?" Louise whispers as we open the hymnal to sing.

"That was an angel, Rosebud." I squeeze her hand. "A true angel."

After the service, I pay a visit to Doctor Henroit with the information.

Dressed in checkered trousers, bespoke day coat, and ascot, Reynard Wolfe sits cross-legged on a wooden crate watching me pack a shipment of champagne.

"What is wrong with your hand?" Wolfe asks. "Did you smash it with something?"

"You could say that." I try using my bruised hand, but it still hurts.

He jumps down and examines my hand. "What happened?"

"The general blames me for his fall in the crayères," I say.

Wolfe nods slowly, thinking. "The fall made him look weak, and he cannot abide that."

"Why did you have to take him down there, anyway?" I ask.

"I had no choice." Wolfe places a bottle the wrong way in the crate. "The general wanted to follow you, and demanded I take him."

"You are doing it wrong." I reposition the bottle. "Use more straw between them."

He packs a crate on his own and smiles when I nod my approval.

"The general takes an extraordinary interest in you, Madame Pommery," he says. "He is not used to women running their own business. You fascinate him."

"Ridiculous." I turn to him. "What are you trying to say? Out with it."

"I am suggesting that you treat the general nicely, and he will be easier to live with," Wolfe says. "Be practical, Madame Pommery. This war may last a long time, or tomorrow France may become another German state."

Until now, I've only prayed about war ending, but now Wolfe says Germany could win. The thought petrifies me.

"I need to check on dinner." I cross to the house door. "You can show yourself out."

"Invite me for the general's birthday dinner." Wolfe brushes straw off his trousers. "I can smooth the general's ruffled feathers and work on a visit to Louis."

It's worth a try.

Henroit told me to keep the general at his birthday dinner until eight o'clock and to serve him plenty of wine.

Candles in the chandelier, chrysanthemums on the table, five champagnes chilling in silver buckets, gleaming glasses to be paired with each course. *La pièce de résistance*. A violinist in the corner of the dining room plays Brahms' *A German Requiem*. Yvonne and Chantal prepared the dining room just as I asked.

Chantal serves quail eggs accented with caviar for *hors d'oeuvres*, and I pour a Pommery champagne for the general and Wolfe, showing off my new label. "The Cunard cruise ship serves this Pommery cuvée."

He licks his pinkie and smoothes his wily brow. "How did you sell Cunard from here?"

"My sales director, Adolphe Hubinet, is in London," I say. "I don't think there is a store, restaurant, or ship he hasn't called on."

"Madame can make silk purses out of a sow's ear." Wolfe pops a quail egg in his mouth and swallows. "The man was a dressmaker, and she made him her sales director."

Ignoring his ghastly comment, I raise my glass. "To live like God in France."

The general smiles with crinkling eyes and drinks the champagne. "Ahh." He eats the egg with caviar, then takes another drink.

I pour more Pommery and an additional glass of Ruinart champagne. "Compare these two champagnes and tell me what you think."

They taste one, then another, taking time to swirl the liquid on their palates.

"One is rich and yeasty and the other light and refreshing," the general says. "But which one is better?"

Wolfe finishes both glasses, while Chantal comes to clear the plates. He ogles at her with a seductive grin she tries to ignore.

"Do you prefer Beethoven or Mozart?" I ask.

"What?" Wolfe's face colors.

"Depends on my mood," the general answers. "Beethoven has a fiery personality, whereas Mozart is clean and precise."

"Touché, General." I hold my glass to the light, noting the size of the bubbles and color. "A composer uses a variety of keys, melodies, rhythms." I take a sip of Pommery and Ruinart. "A wine-maker uses similar techniques using different grapes, grown in different soils and weather. I blend these differing grape juices to complement each other. Like a composer." I pour the men's glasses full as Henroit instructed.

"Did you learn this from your husband?" the general asks.

"Her husband never made champagne," Wolfe says. "He was in the wool business and made a little red table wine."

I steer the conversation away from my husband. "What do you smell in this champagne?"

"I smell wine." Wolfe laughs.

The general sniffs his glass. "What do you smell?"

"The first whiff is like ripe citrus and pineapple." I smell again. "But when I inhale deeply into my palette, I smell floral notes of linden and peach."

Wolfe dips his stub nose into the glass.

"Like listening to a symphony," I tell the general. "All those flavors rolling over your tongue and down your throat. Taste the surprising mineral finish? Beethoven employs surprises in his music. He builds up the music as if leading to a crescendo, only to go suddenly soft. Ruinart is a master of a surprise finish."

Chantal, Yvonne, and Louise carry in small silver domes in their raised arms. They set them before us and lift the lids simultaneously. Savory smells of fresh grilled trout from the Marne, toasted almonds, green beans picked from the garden, all finished with brown butter.

Wolfe's hands fly up. "Oh, my. I've missed your cooking, Yvonne."

"Bon appétit, gentlemen."

Chantal fills red and white wine glasses to the brim. And we spend the next hour eating, drinking, and laughing as if we are friends instead of enemies.

"That was the best birthday dinner I can remember." The general drums his polished fingernails on his stomach. "Now I truly know what it means to live like God in France."

I check my timepiece. "Didn't you tell me you had a meeting at eight?" I ask Wolfe.

He wipes his mouth and pulls back his chair. "Time to go, General. You can't be late for the officers' meeting."

The general puts on his spiked helmet and cape. "After a dinner like that, I feel like I died and went to heaven."

Last meals always taste best, I think to myself.

I see them out and watch them stagger down the street to Le Palais Alhambra.

The next morning, we label wine bottles in the winery. Louise mixes flour and water to a sticky consistency. Damas brushes it on the labels, and I center them and press them down until they stick. The simple work keeps my mind off the midnight uproar. Angry voices, soldiers tromping on the stairs of the mezzanine, kept me awake through the night. Thank goodness Louise's room is on the other side of the house or she wouldn't sleep either.

The general and Wolfe enter the winery, looking gray and drawn. We keep working as they watch us. Wolfe clears his throat and states in a most formal tone, "Madame Pommery, the general would like a word with you."

"Go inside," I tell Louise and Damas. Wiping my hands on a towel, I join the haggard men on the receiving platform.

"Where were you last night?" The general blinks his bloodshot eyes.

"Having a birthday dinner with you?" I tilt my head and smile. "I hope the trout was memorable, even if the company was not."

He grimaces as if his head is breaking. "I am in no mood for your games, Madame. Where were you when my men and I were ambushed at Le Palais Alhambra?"

I stand straight. "After you left, Louise and I played faro by the fire. The clock struck nine, and we said our prayers. Did something happen?"

"Tell her." The general flicks his hand at Wolfe, watching my reaction.

"The Alhambra threw a party for the general and his officers. The girls were dressed up in wild costumes and performed exotic dances. Then, as a special treat, Madame Scheherazade served us absinthe, which most of us had never had. So, we were all focused on the whole ritual of the absinthe spoon with the sugar cube. Of course, all the officers drank to the general's birthday. And drank another to the German coalition. And a third to Madame Scheherazade."

He takes a deep breath, his belly bulging.

"Then zip-zap-zoom. Three bullets shattered the windows and hit three officers in the temples. The Alhambra girls screamed and ran upstairs to save their lives. I lunged at the general and pushed him to the ground."

"That's awful." My stomach roils with guilt for passing on Scheherazade's message to Henroit.

The general's steely eyes bear down on mine. "Continue, Wolfe."

"The officers ran out. Bullets flew from both sides, no gunmen in sight, just the sound of cartridges whizzing through the air and soldiers screaming in agony." Wolfe's voice crackles with strain. "Thirteen officers died without knowing what hit them."

My belly pitches forward, and I run to a bucket to retch. I heave again, my insides churning. Bending over my knees, I hold my head to stop it spinning. "No, no, no, it's not right." Feeling nausea rise, I press my fist to my mouth.

"You really didn't know, did you?" the general says.

I look up. "God help us all."

The general's expression softens. "Go rest, Madame Pommery. Women like you are too delicate for war." He climbs to the mezzanine, and Wolfe follows.

I pump water and scrub my sticky hands with lavender soap, but no amount of soap can wash away the blood on my hands. Our clever scheme now sickens me. War seems like such a cunning game of wills until people die because you won.

27

EN FAIRE TOUTE UNE MALADIE

to make a whole disease about it

The angry ranting from the mezzanine keeps me listening at my wall for several nights. I write down German words I must translate to make sense of them. When I'm confident I have it, I panic. *Morgen.* Tomorrow.

Doctor Henroit and the *Francs-tireurs* must be alerted. I slip out into the freezing night.

I pass the shallow graves on the hillside of Butte Saint-Nicaise, a grim reminder of my sins I confessed to Father Pieter. Winter rains will soon cover the mounds with new grass. I find the dwarf beech and lift the brush covering the entrance. But there is no dim light below, nor any sound of voices. The *Francs-tireurs* are not in the crayères.

Walking briskly back to the city, I consider the options. The *Francs-tireurs* could be at the stables, or the food supply wagons, or setting fire to tents.

Up ahead, windows blaze with lanterns at the long chicken houses that Prussians took over for barracks. Checking my time-piece, I see it's well after midnight, yet hundreds of German voices accost my ears.

Two soldiers guard the open doors. Behind them, I glimpse Doctor DuBois, who's been imprisoned for three weeks now. He must be dressing soldiers' wounds. The irony that we must heal the wounds we inflicted.

Gulping night air into my lungs for courage, I cross to the chicken house in full moonlight. The guards jerk their rifles at me and yell. *Halt* is the only word I understand.

Doctor DuBois runs toward me shouting, "*Sie ist meine Kranken-schwester.*" She is my nurse.

The soldiers swipe their rifles at me to go inside. The barracks reek of the sweet, pungent odor of rotting flesh. But I see no wounds, just hundreds of soldiers with their blue, green, or gray uniform sleeves rolled up, lined up between cots all the way to the far end of the chicken house, where another white-jacketed doctor works.

DuBois shuffles in front of me, barely lifting his feet. His shoulders slump forward, so unlike him. "I cannot believe you are here." His voice rasps as he explains the supplies on the cart. "Fill the tubes with medication, then insert the thumb plunger and screw in the needle."

He turns to the next soldier and cleans his arm with alcohol. He grabs a finished syringe and pushes the needle into his arm. "*Der Nächste,*" he says. Next.

"They don't understand French?"

He shakes his head. "They're from up north."

"What is the medicine for?" Carefully, I fill the glass tubes on the top tray.

"Smallpox." He gestures the next soldier forward. "General Francis noticed an outbreak and telegrammed Prussia to send vaccines."

"What about us?" I fill the last glass tubes on the first tray.

He shakes his head. "There's not even enough for them." He swabs the next soldier's arm.

"Is that Doctor Henroit down there?" I start to screw in needles and plungers. "Where are the Prussian doctors?"

"Died in the Alhambra ambush." He swabs alcohol on a soldier's arm. "They'll keep you, too, now that you're here. Why did you come?"

I lean to his ear. "The general is confiscating everyone's guns tomorrow. We need to warn everyone to hide their arms."

The next soldier's face and arms are covered with red spots filled with milky fluid. DuBois swabs him with alcohol and gives him the shot. I shrink back as he passes by.

"You must get out of here, or they will keep you," DuBois whispers. "When I distract them, run."

He holds a syringe up to the lantern light, flicking it with his middle finger. Then shooting me a glance toward the door, he jabs a shot into the soldier with force. The soldier shrieks and holds his arm, yelling and punching DuBois.

The guards run to break up the fight, and I duck out into the night, terrified they will catch me.

I knock at her window, and Madame DuBois pulls back the curtain, her nightcap askew. Moments later, she appears at the door in her nightgown.

"Madame Pommery, what are you doing out so late?" Her round face shines in the moonlight. How I've missed this face, but no time for sentimentality. I explain in no uncertain terms the task before us.

We call on our auxiliary ladies first, telling them to hide most of their guns, saving a couple to sacrifice to the army to avoid suspicion. We implore them to spread the word to their neighbors and relatives. No one refuses the call, recognizing the stakes.

The morning fog glows in the rising sun as I hug Madame DuBois goodbye at her doorstep.

"Don't forget to hide your own guns," she reminds me.

Minutes later, I unlock my side door with my chatelaine key and steal into the salon. After taking two hunting rifles out of Louis's gun case along with ammunition, I tiptoe up the back staircase, which creaks and moans; my heart is pattering. If I'm caught now, they'll know I've spied on them.

In my chambers, the sound of rhythmic breathing and the scent of lavender calms my jitters. Louise is sleeping in my bed with Felix curled in the crook of her arm. I feel a pang of guilt that she worried I was not home.

As quietly as possible, I shove the rifles between the horsehair mattress and featherbed.

Peeking through the lace curtains, I cannot see much through the early fog. Wagons of soldiers clamor through the streets, pounding fists on doors, shouting in German, citizens yelling and crying, the clank of guns thrown into wagons. Pulling the heavy velvet drapes closed, I creep into bed fully dressed, and wrap my arms around Louise.

I must have fallen asleep, because next I know there is banging at my door.

"Yes?" I answer from a dream, running through Scottish heather on the cliffs above the sea.

Louise awakes, startled. "Who is it, Maman?" She pulls the blanket over her head.

More banging. "Open up, Madame."

General Francis. My heart pounds in my throat. He's never ventured to my private quarters. Hastily, I pull my robe from the wardrobe and wrap it over my dress. Lighting an oil lamp, I open the door. The general and his aide-de-camp with the halo of curls march past me. They hold their lanterns high and peer around the room.

The aide spies a lump in my bed and whips off the covers. Felix leaps out at him, and he jumps back. Louise sits up and buries her fists in her mouth, eyes wide.

I step between her and the aide. "What could you be thinking, barging in here? Have I no modicum of privacy? You must leave." I point my arm to the door.

"What are you doing in your mother's room?" the general asks.

Louise's eyes dart to me for help.

"I did not ask your mother," he bellows.

She stares at the playing cards on the table. "I fell asleep playing cards." Her voice wavers. "Maman must have put me to bed."

The general swivels to his aide. "Search the room."

His aid opens my bureau drawer and rifles through my lingerie.

"What are you looking for?" I ask.

"We confiscated guns throughout town to stop the *Francs-tireurs*." The general narrows his gaze like sighting a rifle. "Tell me, Madame, why did everyone have their guns hidden?"

"I have no idea," I answer.

The aide pulls open the drawer of the nightstand. My husband's pistol. He was so proud of the engraved silverwork and carved ebony stocks. The aide gives it to the general and grabs my shoulders. "Put her with the others?"

Louise gasps and clings to my legs.

The general caresses the gun barrel. "Yours, Madame?"

"It belonged to my husband." I jerk my shoulder free from the aide.

"Are there any other guns in your possession?"

The aide looks under the bed. Heat ripples up my neck, triggering palpitations.

I hold my voice steady. "Just the hunting rifles in the salon."

The aide uses the bed to push himself to a stand. If he feels the rifles, my goose is cooked.

Felix pounces on his hand, claws bared.

The aide jumps back. "*Teufel.*" Devil. He wipes the bloody punctures on his hand.

"Lieutenant, take Madame Pommery's rifles," the general orders. "And dispatch the wagons to the front."

The solider salutes, and his boot heels click down the stairs.

The general examines the revolver, caressing the grip and looking down the sights. "A Lefaucheux. What would a wool merchant be doing with a revolver like this?"

"His father gave it to him," I say. "I forgot it was there."

"Then you will not miss it." He tucks it under his belt.

"You cannot take my husband's gun from me," I tell him.

"We jailed forty-three of your citizens for hiding weapons, Madame Pommery. How would it look if I allow you to keep one?"

Despite the confiscated weapons, the *Francs-tireurs* persist. They siphon off German fuel, blow up the train tracks, steal Prussian-army supplies. These activities drive General Francis mad with rage, and more men are hauled off to prison.

I volunteer the auxiliary women to cook for the prisoners. A chance to see our men. We fortify the thin chicken broth with potatoes and carrots from our gardens.

Sliding the gruel under the makeshift enclosures, I search for Louis and Henry. The chicken houses stink of ammonia and months' old body odor of unwashed prisoners. I think I see Louis lying on hay bales, but his matted hair and overgrown beard make me unsure.

"Louis, is that you?"

"Maman?" He props himself up on one elbow. "What are you doing here?" Dragging himself up in his filthy, torn uniform, he comes to the barred window.

I offer him a plate, and he takes it, our fingers touching. I want to hug him, but the fenced walls prevent me.

"Louis, I have to tell you something."

His chin drops to his chest. "Doctor DuBois told me about Lucille." His voice hardens. "You never approved of her."

"That is not true, Louis. I loved Lucille. She was always part of our family."

"As your nanny, nothing more," he says.

I reach out, and he shoves his flat palm at me. "Stay back. I may have smallpox."

"Oh, no, Louis."

He gestures behind him. "Everyone is getting it in here."

"Where's Henry?" I don't recognize any others.

"I haven't seen him since Sedan," he says.

"He didn't come back with you?" My stomach falls; I feel sick. "Do you think he's dead?"

"Most likely." He clenches his eyes closed. "The Prussian army bombarded us from all sides. They called it annihilation because they destroyed our entire military capability. By our estimate, thirty-two hundred died and fourteen thousand injured. Another hundred thousand taken prisoner and marched in heavy rain to a German work camp. They starved us there, and it was freezing. Many more died. The rest of us were sent to work on German farms, factories, and mines."

"How did you get back to Reims?" I ask.

He gestures behind him. "A bunch of us who were assigned to work on the railroads jumped a train and escaped. When we got here, we joined the *Francs-tireurs*." His red-rimmed eyes smolder with fury. "We must fight back, Maman. They are crazy for power. We cannot succumb to them." He punches a board and scrapes his knuckles. "You have to get me out of here."

"Listen carefully." I lower my voice. "The general is planning a battle in Coulmiers soon, and when they leave, we can break you out of here." I point at his untouched plate. "Now, eat that gruel. You are going to need your strength."

My heart is heavy thinking of Henry. I will not believe he is gone.

28

Coucher avec l'ennemi

Sleeping with the enemy

When the general orders his dinner served in his chambers—unusual, since he usually dines with the officers—I ask Yvonne to make it special, and she clucks her tongue.

"*Ils mangent comme des ogres.*" They eat like ogres. She cringes and shivers.

She is not wrong. The auxiliary ladies grumble how Prussian appetites are twice that of French. Our gardens are bare, and our chicken coop almost empty.

"Ask Damas to bring you a duck from Saint Remi," I tell her. "A man's stomach must be full before we ask a favor." I want him to release Louis so I can nurse him back to health.

I take time with my toilette, arranging my hair in a chignon and applying *Crème Céleste* to soften the worry lines etching my complexion. I change into one of the special frocks Hubinet designed for me. A frothy bustle dress of sapphire silk and layers of pleated ruffles. Nothing like the work dresses I usually wear.

At seven, Chantal carries his dinner tray, while I take an ice bucket of Pommery. I knock on his door. "General Francis, we brought your supper." The savory aroma makes my stomach growl, but there will be no duck for us. Only onion soup and bread since the market is meager with two hundred thousand Prussian soldiers to feed.

The general opens his door in shirtsleeves and britches, and steps aside for us to enter. How different the room looks now. The general's tall boots stand beside the wardrobe, a stack of German books on the bedstand, framed family photographs on the mantle, as if he lives here, and I am a servant. A large map of France marked with X's south of Paris covers the table.

"Oh, let me clear this." He moves the map to the sideboard. "I forgot about dinner, but the smell makes my mouth water."

Chantal sets down the domed serving dish and Limoges porcelain and silver. Nothing is too good for the general tonight. Chantal bobs a curtsey and leaves.

"Why don't you join me for supper?" He sneaks a peek under the dome.

"Thank you, but I must eat with my daughter. She is quarantined, since so many of the orphans have come down with smallpox." I twist the bottle and release the cork with a sigh. The fruity aroma drifts to my nose. "Smells rich like after harvest, birds picking at grapes left on the vine, like the 'gleaners,' the women who scrape up grain after the harvest."

"I've always thought those women were crazy."

"Oh, no," I say, pouring his glass. "They feed their families on that overlooked grain. I see it as quite noble, not wasting what God has given." I serve him his glass.

"Have a glass of champagne with me." He gestures to a chair by his desk.

"Is that an order?" I taunt, though from his frown, not a good idea.

"A request." He strokes his long beard.

I pour a glass and toast him. "*À la paix.*" To peace.

"*Zum Sieg.*" To victory. He drinks his champagne.

I notice a framed photograph of a young woman on his desk. "Your daughter is quite beautiful."

"My wife." He sighs heavily. "Princess Marie of Schwarzburg-Rudolstadt. She just turned twenty, and she's home alone with our newborn son and my other children." He drinks the rest of the coupe. "Not entirely alone, of course. She has a castle full of staff. She is not like you."

I laugh. "Yes, I am not a young, wealthy princess."

"Some people are born with titles, and some create their own," he says.

I lift the dome and serve crispy slices of duck and tiny red roasted potatoes garnished with red berries. "Duck à l'orange. The orange is from Saint Remi's sweet orange tree."

His eyes gaze at the plate like a lover, deep lines softening around his mustache. Then, he snorts.

"What is it, General?"

"The French make the best food. Why must we be enemies?" He takes a bite and smiles, his eyes brimming with pleasure.

"Precisely." Time to plead my case. "General, I have a special favor to ask. Smallpox has spread through the prisoners. I don't think Louis has it yet. I would like him to get the vaccine."

He chews slowly and takes another bite. I pour him more champagne, summoning my patience. But when he takes another bite, I cannot hold back.

"Please, General. Louis is my only son. If he dies, Louise and I will be on our own."

"There is no vaccine left, Madame Pommery. It was used up before I got it." The general drinks.

Hope drains from me and my shoulders slump.

"You look as tired as I feel," he says.

I tuck a lock of hair into my chignon. "It is never polite to tell a woman how tired she looks."

He wipes his beard with his napkin. "Also, not polite to correct a guest's manners."

Clearing his dishes, I try a last resort. "Then release Louis so he will not get sick."

The general lights a long-stemmed *Lesepfeife* of sweet-smelling tobacco. "I cannot release your son, as I have reason to suspect that he is a leader of the *Francs-tireurs*."

"Louis is not—" My voice breaks with the lie. Louis will rejoin the *Francs-tireurs* as soon as he is able. "General, my orphans are sick. The auxiliary is sick. Soon, we will all be sick." My eyelids close unwilfully. I am betraying Louis, but it cannot be helped. "Please release the doctors so they can care for us."

"Without the vaccine, the doctors can do nothing to help you." The general folds his napkin on the table. "Now leave me to my rest."

I can barely carry the tray to the kitchen, my arms feel so weak. How long can we go on as prisoners in our own city? And my own sweet home? Whatever I try to do does not work.

Glory be to Heaven. General Francis releases the doctors from the prison to seperate the sick from the healthy.

The auxiliary helps me set up the orphanage for quarantine, stripping bedding from the cots and replacing it with linens and blankets from our own homes.

After examination, the sick children are isolated in the girls' dormitory and healthy children in the boys' dormitory. I've never been in the boys' chambers as the monks take care of them. But now, I see how austere and joyless their quarters are—cold stone floors and colorless stucco walls, and quiet. Deadly quiet.

Through a row of small windows, I see Damas's white tufted head. He's bent over a boiling cauldron stirring with a paddle, ster- ilizing blankets in the monks' private courtyard. The auxiliary ladies hesitantly take wet blankets from Damas, feed them through a wringer, and hang them on a line to dry. Their lips move constantly as they throw each other comically scornful looks; the gossip must be juicy.

"Whatever they are talking about seems to have them quite entertained."

Madame DuBois blushes and pats her handkerchief on her perspiring neck.

"You know, don't you?" I say. "What is it? You can trust me."

She clucks her tongue. "They think there is something between you and the general."

My hackles spread like a peacock's tail. "Why would they think such a thing?" I wave my hand. "Was it Madame Werle who started that rumor? She always thinks the worst."

"It may have been me who started them thinking," she says. "When the guards released the doctors, they were told to report to

Madame Pommery at the orphanage." She tucks in the blanket under the mattress carelessly; it's sure to come loose.

I push it deeper. "Tuck in the blankets securely or the children will get cold at night."

"One blanket will not keep them warm," she says.

"That's all we have until those boiled blankets dry." I point through the window. "Let's help them, shall we?"

She looks at Damas. "*Il me court sur le haricot.*" He runs me on the bean. He gets on my nerves.

"I assure you he's quite—well, not normal, but smart. That's it. Damas is quite smart in his own way."

When we enter the courtyard, Damas has gone. But I notice something remarkable in the corner. A ten-foot octagon birdcage fashioned with gleaming copper wire and intricately carved sticks. The domed top is scrolled metalwork so ornate it stuns the eyes. The aviary is a work of art one would find in a museum, not a monastery. Peeking in the open door, I confirm there are no birds hiding in the grillwork. On the ground lays a rolled blanket, pillow, and crude basket of clothing and other belongings, including the tin "wine thief" pipette I gave Damas to sample wine. Heat rushes up from my heart. It can't be. I knew Damas lived with the monks, but I never knew where.

I join the other ladies wringing out the last of the blankets.

"You should keep that mute boy away from Louise." Madame Werle wags her finger. "No telling what perverted thoughts go on in that ugly skull."

"Damas is a good friend to Louise, and I trust him completely," I say. "He's saved her from more than one mishap around the winery."

Madame Werle tuts her tongue and whispers to the others as they hang blankets on the line.

"If you want to say something, tell me to my face," I say.

"Very well," Madame Werle says. "Some citizens think it is most improper for you to be living with the general in your home."

"I can assure you there is nothing between us," I say. "I would never allow myself to have an improper relationship."

"I beg to differ," Madame Werle says. "You befriended the Alhambra harlots, and they are most improper."

"I will not dignify that with a comment."

Damas returns and stands in the center of the courtyard, oblivious to anyone. He digs in his pockets and stretches out his arms, breadcrumbs in his hands. From deep in his diaphragm radiates a long throaty vibrato, accented with short grunting sounds. He turns north, east, south, and west, generating the eerie sounds all over again.

A rock dove lands on his arm and struts to his hand to feed. Another dove lands on his shoulder and another on his wispy head. Soon dozens of rock doves circle the courtyard in a flurry of flapping feathers.

The auxiliary ladies cover their heads and shriek, running helter-skelter and batting away birds. Only Madame DuBois huddles next to me, both of us watching Damas with pure astonishment.

Rock doves blanket Damas's body, cooing, strutting, bowing, thrusting their chests, and fanning their tail feathers.

When Damas is completely covered, he walks into the aviary, and the birds fly to their perches, cooing softly.

Madame DuBois holds her chest. "Astounding."

I laugh. "I'm not sure the auxiliary ladies would agree." Not a one of them is left in the courtyard.

Madame Werle sends me a message that she and her friends will not be volunteering at the orphanage until smallpox is over.

29

AIDE-TOI, LE CIEL T'AIDERA

Heaven helps those who help themselves

Damas and Louise and I check on the first fermentation of champagne at Butte Saint-Nicaise. Climbing out of the crayères, I'm blinded by the brilliant afternoon light, and I rub my eyes, not trusting them. A hot-air balloon floats languidly overhead with a billowy white canopy and sturdy woven basket. The balloonist wears a French army uniform and smart red and blue kepi. When the balloon floats closer, I see he's a fresh-faced boy not yet twenty. Damas and Louise chase after him, breathless with delight. Watching them running and laughing infuses me with joy—so little of it these days.

The balloon dips low and scatters paper like fall leaves over the hillside. Louise and Damas gather the papers from the ground as the balloon sways and bobs with the fickle air currents. The balloonist grins widely and waves a small French flag. He throws ropes overboard for us to catch and help him land.

But a sharp gust lifts the balloon up out of reach and carries it toward Reims Cathedral. The young Frenchman looks back at us and throws up his arms.

On Reims Square, Prussian soldiers gather and point to the balloon. More soldiers pour out of the cathedral. As the balloon reaches the square, soldiers raise their rifles.

"Will he be all right, Maman?" Louise asks.

I put my arm around her shoulder.

A Prussian officer shouts from a bullhorn, and hundreds of rifles blast like cannons. The billowy canopy wavers and hisses over the square. Soldiers engulf the balloon.

Damas and Louise stare with mouths open.

"Hurry, pick up all the flyers," I tell them.

They search the ground while I read the flyer. Léon Gambetta, our Minister of Interior and War urges all French men to join the army at Le Mans to battle the Prussians and Germans who have surrounded Paris and cut off supplies.

"Give me the flyers," I tell the children. "Go back to the winery and look busy if officers are there. If they ask about the balloonist, you never saw him. If they want to know where I am, tell them Saint Remi orphanage."

"And where will you really be, Maman?" Louise asks.

"Saint Remi orphanage." I wink and shoo them away. I must get word to the doctors and *Francs-tireurs*.

In the morning, the battalion of Prussians marches out. Impervious in their fearsome pickelhaube, officers ride muscled horses stolen from our stables. Hot breath spews from their mouths like fire dragons.

The formidable enemy terrifies me for our shabby *Francs-tireurs*. Dejected, I trudge to Saint Remi to cook the prisoners' dinner. They need something more substantial than gruel.

By noon, the fog has lifted, and the last of the army has left. The Reims Cathedral bells tolls, and it feels liberating without all those hostile souls among us. I wonder how long the army and *Francs-tireurs* will be gone and leave us in relative peace. I wheel the tall soup pot and bowls across the alley to the prison; the familiar Prussian guard eyes me suspiciously. We have never been on talking terms, but I sense a new hostility as he opens the door.

All the barred cell doors stand open and not a prisoner inside. Reynard Wolfe and the Prussian lieutenant examine the locks.

"Where are the prisoners?" I ask Wolfe.

"*Wo sind sie?*" the lieutenant shouts at me.

Wolfe steps out of the cell. "The lieutenant asks the same question. The general will punish him with his life when he finds out the prisoners escaped. Do you want his blood on your hands?"

I lift the lid on the pot, and the savory aroma fills the dank empty jail with rosemary, thyme, butter, and onion. "Would I have made coq au vin if I knew the prisoners were gone?"

Wolfe sticks his face over the steaming pot and inhales. "Prisoners are not allowed this type of fare."

"The prisoners are weak and sick. They need more than gruel."

The lieutenant lifts the ladle and smells, then speaks crossly to Wolfe.

"He wants to know why you made chicken stew for the prisoners if they are not here," Wolfe asks.

I can't help but laugh. "My thoughts exactly."

"The prison key was missing from the drawer where the lieutenant keeps it." He wags his stubby forefinger. "Where is the key, Madame Pommery?"

I show him the keys dangling from my chatelaine. "I have only my house keys."

He snorts and tells the lieutenant something. "Then you won't mind us searching your home."

The lieutenant talks too fast to translate. Wolfe turns.

"The lieutenant orders you to take the coq au vin to the officers' quarters immediately."

"My pleasure," I say. I don't know who did it or how, but Louis is out of prison and with the *Francs-tireurs*. Not sure which fate is worse.

Before Christmas, the Prussian army returns from the Loire battle victorious and thirsty. They loot our champagne stocks again, and the general doesn't stop them. The gloves of diplomacy are off, and the Prussians quench their greedy thirst with our champagne as if devouring us.

The *Francs-tireurs* have not returned. I don't know if they were killed, captured, or escaped. I'm fraught with worry. When the general retires to the salon after supper, he helps himself to Scotch

Sean brought me from Scotland. I stoke the fire and ask him about the battle, trying to find out anything about our men.

"We captured Orléans in two days." General Francis gazes through his crystal glass at the fire, as if talking to himself. "Nothing short of miraculous."

"What were the casualties?" I ask.

He sucks and puffs on his pipe until the smoke rises, sweet and cloying. "By our count, the French army lost twenty thousand, and we lost only fifteen hundred."

Pain sears through my temples, and I rub them. Louis and my countrymen could be dead. "You are talking about men."

"Why, yes, of course, what else would I be talking about?" He sits back in my leather chair, relaxed and content.

I scoff. "You could have been talking about winning chess the way you talked." My voice deepens, my cheeks blazing hot. "You sit here in my home and boast about killing twenty thousand of my countrymen?"

He inhales his absurdly long pipe until I think his lungs will burn, then just as slowly, he exhales. "Do not mistake my attitude as lack of grief. I grieve for thousands of good men's lives lost recklessly and without meaning. I repent over my own killings, which I cannot bear to count." He catches a cinder on his beard, and I imagine it bursting into flame.

"Yet tomorrow, you and your murderous army will demand a Catholic service at our cathedral." My tongue tastes bitter.

"War is not God's game, it is man's," he says. "God does not condone war; he grieves for his children no matter their country. But I am a man. And I must protect Mecklenburg-Schwerin from enemy attack, whether from Frenchmen or the German countries that surround us. I must prove to King Wilhelm and Otto von Bismarck that I can handle my own in the new world they are creating. German countries unified under Prussia. If I fail, Mecklenburg-Schwerin will be swallowed up as soon as this war is over. Thousands of years of my family's history will be wiped out by my inadequacy. I must do whatever it takes to save my country."

"Do you know anything about our townsmen?"

"I heard nothing about them," he says. "But if they return, they will be imprisoned."

I trudge upstairs with his words weighing on me. His stakes to win the war are stronger than I could ever imagine. Fighting for his heritage, his title, his ancestors, and his descendants. A lofty birthright deepens the difference between noble and bourgeoisie classes. Whereas my responsibilities lie with myself and my family, his includes generations going back hundreds of years. The higher one's class, the more responsibility. A heavy load indeed.

Late one night, Damas delivers a message with his fingers sticking through raveling knit gloves. Drunken Prussian soldiers pass by, slapping each other on the back, speech slurred, and Damas darts away.

Louis's scrawling handwriting. I try to hold my trembling hands steady. He's hiding with the *Francs-tireurs* at Butte Saint-Nicaise and urges me to stay away.

Pulling on my cape, I put the hood over my head and walk briskly through the moonlit streets, sticking to the shadows. I keep hearing sounds of footsteps or leaves crunching. Each time, I turn and there's silence, except for my heart pounding in my ears.

Finally, I reach Butte Saint-Nicaise. The stars glisten like diamonds and hearten me. My son is alive. Moving aside the tumbleweed disguising the entrance, a thorn pricks my finger, drawing blood. I suck my fingertip as I climb down the rudimentary stairs.

A hundred or more men mill about in the crayères speaking in hushed tones. I'm shocked to see how large the *Francs-tireurs* have grown. Their dull gray uniforms and wool kepis make it hard to distinguish one from another. I turn left into a tunnel to get a better view and locate Louis below. Cold wind whistles through from outside. Folding my arms over my chest, I search for familiar faces. Army blanket rolls, packs, and Chassepot rifles are piled against the wall a hundred yards away.

A man with long black hair strides toward me with an unmistakable gait. Louis. My throat chokes up. Climbing the ramp to the tunnel, he shakes his head, eyebrows furled, half-grinning, half-frowning. "Maman, I told you not to come. It's too dangerous."

He stinks of gunpowder, soil, and sweat, but I don't care. I grab him to me and hug him tight, my eyelids clenched against tears. "I had to see you. Had to talk to you. Come home, Louis. I will convince the general to let you stay with us." My dammed-up emotions gush out in sobs. "You have to come back with us."

"Henry is here," Louis whispers.

My eyes fly open in shock. Henry stands behind Louis, smiling warmly under his mustache, his moss-green eyes shining. Older, thinner, but so dear.

I grab him to us, his beard rubbing my cheek. "I thought you were dead."

"I wrote you letters all the time," he says, "but never found a way to send them."

"What happened to you?" My hand grasps his neck as if he might disappear again.

"I've been fighting Germans." He folds down his collar that I've flipped up, and the simple move chokes me.

Tears flood my face. "You're alive, you're alive, that's all that matters." I pull both of their heads to mine. "You need to come back with me. I'll handle the general."

A loud rifle shot hits the ceiling of the crayère and sends a shower of rocks down on the *Francs-tireurs*.

Henry pulls me into the shadows of a side tunnel, his heart beating against my back. "They found us."

A dozen Prussian soldiers point needle-guns at the soldiers below, striding boldly down the stairs. The *Francs-tireurs* run for their Chassepots, and the Prussians raise their rifles, blazing.

Bullets whiz past, hitting men and stone walls. Soldiers wail and yell. Louis signals Henry to run for their rifles across the chamber.

"We'll be killed if we run for our weapons," Henry says.

"Looks like we don't have to," Louis says.

The *Francs-tireurs* close ranks, loading and shooting as they advance on the small group of Prussians. The front line takes the brunt of the *Francs-tireurs'* fire. They grab their wounds and tumble down the stairs.

The next line runs up the staircase, dozens of *Francs-tireurs* chasing them.

"Arrogant bastards, starting a fight with a handful of men," Henry says. "We have to get Alexandrine out of here."

"No way out except the stairs," Louis says.

"This tunnel leads out to the back road behind the butte," I say. "You can hide at Saint Remi."

At dawn the next morning, the Reims Cathedral bells ring out in a riotous discord.

"What is it, Maman?" Louise asks.

"I'm not sure, Rosebud." We don our coats and step out on the square.

Wolfe stands with the priests, the bells peeling as if for a holiday. Throngs of citizens join us in the chill morning air, our breaths mingling in great puffs. People waving, laughing, chattering, a festive feeling in the air, like Bastille Day. Could the war be over? Has our new Third Republic negotiated peace? Someone starts to sing the "Marseillaise," and we all join in.

Louise's cheeks turn rosy in the chill of a December morning. So beautiful, my girl. Soon, too soon, I will be looking for a fitting suitor and I will lose her.

Bugles blow and the singing stops. General Francis prances his powerful black steed into the square. His pickelhaube frames his fierce red beard. Armor covers his double-breasted uniform. Officers flank the general on either side, their horses snorting and pawing as if ready to charge.

Bugles blare again. Prussian guards prod bayonets between the shoulder blades of *Francs-tireurs* prisoners, hands bound in rope behind their backs. My stomach moils with fear. My mind goes numb. I pull Louise under my arm wanting to take her home, but Prussian guards surround us.

Doctor Henroit and Doctor DuBois are first among other neighbors and countrymen: Hubinet's brother, the dressmaker, *vendangeurs*, husbands of my auxiliary ladies, stablemen, even the undertaker. I look for Madame DuBois in the crowd, but don't see her sweet face, thank God. I could not bear to watch her suffer this horror.

At least a hundred *Francs-tireurs* are lined up three deep against the stone wall adjacent to the cathedral. I search for Louis and Henry, and other *Francs-tireurs* I left at Saint Remi. Did they return to battle? I'm relieved not to see a one of them, yet a cold realization creeps through my veins. The general called us out of our beds to witness this. It cannot be good.

Prussian soldiers march in opposite the prisoners. A dove flies to the bell tower and the *Francs-tireurs* follow its flight, uttering last prayers. The baker falls to his knees begging for his life.

General Francis raises a despotic arm and shouts, "*Fertig.*" Ready.

The infantry braces their strong stance.

I cover Louise's eyes, and she pushes my hand away.

The general yells, "*Zielen.*" Aim.

Fifty needle-guns aim at the prisoners.

"*Feuer!*" Fire!

The flash and blast of rifles, the sickening sound of bullets into flesh. Our brave *Francs-tireurs* run from the line and are gunned down, collapsing into heaps on the ground.

A blood-curdling scream. Sobs and wailing from the crowd.

Smoke mixes with the fog, the acrid burn of gunpowder in our nostrils.

An arm rises from the ground and falls again.

Mothers and wives cry out and run to their loved ones but are stopped by the soldiers.

The atrocity scours me out like drinking the vinegar and salt we use to clean the floors. Louise sobs into my breast, shaking violently. I protect her under my arm and weave through the crowd to Saint Remi.

Leaving Louise with the orphans, I search for Louis and the rest of the *Francs-tireurs*. I find Damas in the inner courtyard, birds clinging to his wispy white hair and shoulders as he stacks small wood cages by the towering aviary.

"Where is Louis?" I ask.

He digs in his pocket and hands me a folded tissue. I recognize Louis's hasty penmanship.

Dear Maman,

I cannot shirk my duty. Henry and I and the others are joining up with General Gambetta and the Third Republic Army.

Do not worry about us. We are disguised as German merchants buying looted goods from German troops. We'll get more information that way. My German is paying off at last.

By the New Year, we will sing the "Marseillaise," victorious over our German oppressors. Please extend my apologies to General Francis for leaving him to deal with your grit and courage alone. He has no chance.

I'll send a message by Damas's doves if I'm able.

Your devoted son.

Angry and sad and proud at the same time, I watch Damas feed the birds, trying to sort out the next move. I cannot go home to face the general after what they did.

"I cannot shirk my duty," Louis's letter said, and I must not either.

I call on Madame DuBois. In the kindest words I can summon, I tell her what happened to her husband and hold her in my arms.

30

TU DONNES TA LANGUE AU CHAT?

Do you give your tongue to the cat?

1871. By the end of December, there is still no news from Louis or Henry. General Francis's battalion joins the other German armies surrounding Paris. Feeling empty and helpless, all I can do is light candles and pray to my Smiling Angel and believe they will come home safe.

Frost settles on the vineyards throughout the Champagne, threating to kill the grapevines with no *vendangeurs* here to save them. If the vines die, there will be no wine and no money to replant. Every winery and champagne house will be affected by this enemy we cannot fight—or perhaps we can.

Even though it is New Year's Eve, I call the auxiliary ladies together to save the vineyards, a cause we all rally behind, even the haughtiest of ladies, for we all depend on wine for our economy. Even Madame Werle joins our cause. We make torches to warm the vines through the night and prevent them from freezing.

Damas and Louise gather the supplies to make torches, and when we're ready, I call the auxiliary to the winery. They bring their children, and we welcome the help. I smile at their beautiful bustle dresses they wear for our grubby task, but we offer winery aprons to protect them against the worst of it.

241

First, we wrap long bones with linen, then soak them in lime and sulfur that sting our noses. Finally, we coat the linen torch with yellow wax. It feels good to be working together without the Prussians around. Even Wolfe and his Prussian troop leave us alone, spending afternoons at the Biergarten, nights at the Alhambra, and mornings recovering.

In proper mop caps and uniforms, Yvonne and Chantal serve the auxiliary ladies and their children a hot supper of onion soup and fresh baguettes.

After supper, we load torches onto three wagons piled high; other wagons carry women and children. We drive out to the valley, where the low vineyards are most vulnerable to frost. Louise and the children pass out torches to the ladies, who thrust them into the soil between the rows. Damas walks behind and lights the torches with his own torch, his pale face and wispy hair illuminated like an angel.

We work through the night this way, a caravan traveling from vineyard to vineyard.

Louise bends for another torch. "My back hurts, Maman."

"Mine, too, Rosebud, but we can't give up. The vines will die without our help." I start singing "Ce n'est qu'un au revoir"— It's just a goodbye—thinking of our men returning to us. One by one, the auxiliary ladies and children join in throughout the vineyards.

> Do we have to leave without hope,
> Without hope of returning,
> Do we have to leave without hope
> Of seeing each other some day
> It's only a goodbye, my brothers
> It's only a goodbye
> Yes, we will see each other again, my brothers
> It's only a goodbye
> Let's make with our hands held together
> At the end of this day,
> Let's make with our hands held together
> A chain of love.
> Because God who sees us all together
> And who will bless us,
> Because God who sees us all together
> Knows that we will meet again.

When all the torches have been lit, the ladies and children return to the wagons, still singing. The valley glows with torches burning bright, sending our fervent prayers to heaven. I grasp the hands of Madame DuBois and Madame Werle, who reach out to others. Louise and Damas do the same. Soon we are all holding hands in a circle, singing under the infinite starry sky. The ladies improvise harmonies, clear and crisp as the falling temperatures. The children's cheeks grow bright, their smiles radiant as the glowing torches. Their faces shine in unity, and hope dispels my darkest fear that life will never be good again.

On the ridges surrounding the valley appear dark silhouettes of horsemen. We keep singing, refusing to succumb to their terror.

They ride down into the vineyards with rifles held high, Wolfe leading the front line.

"We saw the fires all the way from Reims," he bellows. "Where are the *Francs-tireurs?*"

I shake my head. "We set the fires to prevent the vines from freezing."

He glares at the torches across the vast valley. "You take me for a fool? Where are they?"

Louise spreads out her arms. "Monsieur Wolfe, you are mistaken. We are here to save the vineyards."

Wolfe sneers. "Madame Pommery, instruct your daughter how to address an officer."

I scoff. "You are a banker, Monsieur Wolfe. These women are your customers, every last one of them. If you wish your bank to stay open, I suggest you thank us for saving the vineyards from freezing and allow us to go home and rest."

Wolfe orders the guards to search the vineyards, and they disperse.

"You are chasing ghosts," I tell him. "The *Francs-tireurs* have not returned."

His narrowed eyes peer over the burning vineyards, his lips are pressed together, anxiety contorting his features.

"Let us go," I tell Wolfe. "The ladies are cold and tired, and have much to prepare for *le réveillon*—New Year—celebrations tomorrow."

He shakes his head.

Madame Werle steps forward. "Release us immediately, or my husband will be the first to withdraw our business from the bank."

His eyes shift side to side, no doubt calculating how to save face. "Load up your wagons; we'll escort you back to town." He shoots his rifle to the sky, and the soldiers return.

Watchful for movement in the vineyards, they ride beside our wagons. When we reach Reims Square, Wolfe wishes the auxiliary ladies Happy New Year as if an armed escort was the gentlemanly thing to do.

A blizzard blows in from the west, and Felix drags in a dead bird and lays it at my feet. Not just any bird, but a rock dove with a bright green legging.

"Joshua!" Louise drops her crochet needles and runs to the prostrate bird. Her tears fall on his tattered and bloody feathers.

"Louise, don't touch it, it may be sick," I say.

"Joshua is one of the doves Louis took with him." Louise blows on the dead bird's body, trying to revive it. "He's our best courier."

"So you think there is a message?" I ask.

"Most likely."

Hands shaking, I pull down the green stocking and pull out the long, thin tissue like before. Unfolding the sheet, I see his writing and gasp. "Can you read it to me?"

She takes the tissue.

"*Dear Maman and Louise, We made it to Versailles, where the government fled from Paris. The Germans are bombarding Paris with howitzers. It will be a miracle if anyone survives. The only way in and out is through the catacombs tunnels. The general has assigned us to deliver a message to Jules Favre, who is traveling to Germany to negotiate with Otto von Bismarck. Pray for France.*"

I sigh. "What's the date?"

She studies the letter. "December eleventh."

"Twenty days ago," I say. "And they are still fighting in Paris. When will it end?"

Felix bats the dove gently between his paws. Suddenly, the bird quivers and flies up to the drapery rod, blinking down at us.

"I want to send a message back to Louis."

Louise huffs. "That letter was three weeks ago. Joshua won't know where to find him."

Disappointment hollows my stomach. "Help me get Joshua down, and we'll take him to Damas."

After the new year, another pigeon with a fuchsia legging arrives in much better shape. "Women always survive better," I quip to Louise, as she unrolls the message from under the stocking.

"Bon Courage Maman and Louise, I pray you are safe. Henry and I made it through the catacombs into Paris, passing walls of skulls and femurs. After we delivered the message, we joined the Paris commune in Montmartre to support the poor and starving people Napoleon moved out of Paris to create a city for the rich and powerful. They are forced to eat cats and rats. But the elite of Paris are not faring much better. The finest restaurant, Café Voisin, served zoo animals for le réveillon. Elephant consommé, bear chops, stuffed donkey's head, marinated kangaroo, and rats. We will stay as long as we are needed."

Louise lays her head on my arm, whimpering softly. I smooth her black hair, which smells of castile soap and lavender.

"They should be safe in Montmartre. The Germans will target the Tuileries, far enough away." I kiss her head, then ruffle her hair and get up. "Let's go check on the fermenting champagne in the crayères and make sure it's not freezing."

By the end of January, Germany is bombing Paris schools, churches, hospitals, apartment buildings, and train stations. The city hasn't had food and supplies for five months. No more doves make it to us, and it's all I can do to keep a brave face. Sales have dropped to nothing. Mail has been cut off with payments from England, yet I still have payroll and expenses.

Wolfe enters the winery bouncing on his toes. "I have brought you very good news."

I close my ledger of unpaid bills. "I could use some good news now."

He taps his fingertips together like a child. "King Wilhelm of Prussia was crowned Emperor of Germany in a ceremony at Versailles."

"Enlighten me." I throw up my hands. "How is a German emperor in Versailles good news?"

"Now that all German states are under Prussian rule, they'll leave France alone."

I shake my head in disbelief. "But now that they have France by the throat, why won't they just take France, too?"

"That was never the goal, apparently," he says. "Bismarck only wanted to unite Germany under Prussian rule, and the war accomplished that. If they took over France, the rest of Europe would rise in protest. Even the most radical German nationalists didn't want to annex all of France."

"So, the war is over?"

He snorts. "There is still a peace treaty to negotiate, and Prussia has already demanded the Alsace-Lorraine region and a war indemnity of five billion francs." He counts on his fingers. "When you add that to France's own war costs of thirty-six billion, France could go bankrupt."

I shove my ledger into my desk and lock the drawer. "So, this is your good news? Hurray, the war is over, but France is bankrupt?" I wave him away. "If you'll excuse me, I need to get back to work."

He grins. "You will need my help when France goes bankrupt."

"I don't think so." I open the door wide, waiting for him to leave. "My agent, Monsieur Hubinet, has opened accounts and warehouses all over Europe, and if the war is truly over, he will be begging me to ship champagne."

Wolfe shows no sign of moving, so I take his arm and escort him out. "I'd consider moving back to Germany if I were you, Monsieur Wolfe."

31

C'EST DE LA FOLIE DE PARLER DE PAIX AVEC UN LOUP

It is madness for a sheep to talk of peace with a wolf.

By February, the postal service starts delivering mail again, and I receive a thick envelope of orders from Hubinet. Unwanted tears spring to my eyes, the war straining me more than I realize. Hubinet, my friend and ally, has stood by me since that first time in his brother's dress shop.

My dear Alexandrine,

I hope the new peace is settling on you like a cashmere blanket, for I know how cold the Reims winters can be. Great Britain is heaving a great sigh of relief at Prussia's victory over France.

I pick at a hangnail. I never thought Great Britain would side with Prussia over France. Finding my cuticle scissors on my chatelaine, I snip the nuisance. Tidy fingernails, tidy mind. Another silly dictate from *Etiquette for Ladies*. I must really burn that book.

I pick up the letter.

Ever since Napoleon's revolution, the Brits have wanted to squash France, and now Prussia has done it for them. That is not to say the Brits would trade French champagne for German Sekt. Goodness, no. Now that the war is over, the Brits have deluged me with orders. They will pay premiums to get shipments quickly. Tell Louis and Henry to ship all the champagne they can via cargo wagon or train the fastest way possible. Not to worry about the cost.

My throat aches. Hubinet doesn't know they never returned from the war. Perhaps they will never be back. I push the thought away and start preparing to ship: cleaning bottles, labeling, foiling the corks, and packing crates—all tasks for a staff I don't have.

I'm organizing supplies to fulfill Hubinet's orders when the winery door opens, and Henry Vasnier drags in a trunk. I drop everything and run to him. My hand strokes his sunken cheek; he looks as if he hasn't eaten in weeks. His mustache is peppered with gray. His eyelids droop from witnessing carnage no one should have to.

"Oh, thank God, you made it home safe." I hug his bony shoulders and look behind him. "Where is Louis?"

"I'm sorry, Madame." He sighs. "Louis stayed with the Communards to fight the French government."

My lungs constrict. "Oh, no, he couldn't have."

"I tried to convince him to come back," he says. "But Louis wouldn't forgive himself if he didn't fight for the lower classes."

"Why didn't you stay with him, Henry?" I ask. "You two have been so close."

He drops his head and wipes his brow. "I don't believe it's right for Frenchmen to be killing each other, especially after we lost the war."

"I wish Louis felt the same." I glance at his trunk. "What's this?"

He shrugs. "My landlord figured I'd died and rented my flat to someone else. Luckily, he kept my belongings. I was hoping I could stay in the winery until I find a place."

"Absolutely not," I say. "We have a house full of empty rooms now that the Prussian army is gone. Stay with us. Yvonne will fatten you up again."

"Thank you, Alexandrine. I'll find a room as soon as I can."

"Please, Henry, you'd be doing me a favor," I say. "The house echoes without people in it. Stay as long as you like."

He looks around the winery. "Everything looks so orderly. Must be no business."

"There is now." I hand him the pile of orders. "Hubinet wants these as soon as we can ship. Can you take care of it? I'm late blending wines this spring."

He rifles through the orders. "Do we have enough champagne for all these orders?"

"We'll have to bring some in from the crayères," I say. "The Prussians cleared out most of our stock here in the winery, but they never touched the crayères. Odd, because the general knew it was there." Then it dawns on me. The general protected my champagne.

"Is our crew back from the war?" he asks.

"Just a few, but I think I can get you workers. I'll see who I can round up." I give him another hug, though it's not called for. "I can't tell you how good it is to see you, Henry." My emotions heat my neck and cheeks, and I pull away before I lose my decorum.

The next morning, I laugh to see Henry's eyes fairly pop out as we pass out aprons to the new crew I recruited from the Alhambra. Rouged lips and kohl-rimmed eyes; flimsy tissue dresses float over their voluptuous figures.

"What are you thinking?" Henry asks.

"I am thinking we need workers, and the Alhambra girls need the money since the Prussians left."

His cheeks tinge red. "But, what will people say?"

I hand out another apron. "Maybe they will say we made honest women out of them." I scruff his grimace with my knuckle.

The blending room looks like something between a chapel and a chemist's laboratory. Light beams down the chiseled chalk walls from the window a hundred feet above. Shelves carved into the wall hold beakers, carafes, and tasting glasses. Horizontal barrels line the tunnels leading out into more tunnels, that lead to more chambers that we have yet to excavate.

Louise and Damas follow closely as I point out the barrel markings of grape varietals and vineyard designations. "Chardonnay from the Côte des Blancs, Pinot Noir from Montagne de Reims, Meunier from the Marne Valley."

"Louise, copy the barrel notations on these labels, and Damas can hang them around the necks of the carafes."

I take glasses off the shelves and set them on the long tasting table.

"When do we get to taste the wine?" Louise nudges Damas and his lips quirk up at the ends.

"First, we have to steal wine from the barrels." I present each of them a long glass dropper gleaming like Merlin's wand. "Behold the calabash, otherwise known as the wine thief."

Damas's long fingers glide down the glass dropper.

"The secret to winemaking is joy," I tell them. "The joy of crushing the grapes to get the best wine. The joy of blending wines so they taste even better than they would alone. To be a good winemaker, you must quiet the chatter in your mind." I tap my temple. "And listen to what the wines are telling you."

Louise grins at Damas with dancing eyes. "Are you ready to listen to the grapes?" He nods enthusiastically.

Damas holds the ladder steady, and Louise climbs up, dips her wine thief into the opening, and withdraws a pipette of wine. I hold up the carafe, and she releases the Chardonnay into it, wafting the fresh aroma of orange blossom.

I pass them the carafe. "What is your first impression? Breath it in and capture this essence of the grapes in this particular year and season."

Damas hovers over the carafe, opens his nostrils, and closes his eyes, stepping back.

Louise inhales. "Ah. The juice smells rich and buttery."

"Yes. Because we were occupied with the war, we left the grapes on the vines three weeks longer than usual."

"Oh, Maman, how amazing!" Louise says. "Will it be the same for the other varietals?"

"You tell me."

Damas dips his wine thief into the Pinot Noir and fills the carafe.

Louise inhales. "Smells like picking raspberries in the summer."

"What else?"

She breathes in and shakes her head, impatient.

"Remember the mushrooms in the forest?" I ask her.

She inhales again and nods. "That earthy aroma of the forest floor."

"Now for the Meunier," I say.

"Why do we need three varietals of grapes?" Louise asks.

"Each varietal brings a distinct flavor to the wine," I say. "Just like our team at the winery. People do different jobs that combine to make a delicious wine."

Louise fills the carafe with Meunier and smells. "Lavender and roses."

"The aroma gives us that first impression of a wine, and first impressions are important," I tell them. "But have you ever had a first impression of someone that changed later?"

Damas nods, his wispy white hair standing out like a dandelion frond, intelligence sparking his eyes.

Louise nods with new realization. When we met Damas, he was dirty and skittish as a rat. The entire town took him for an imbecile. But under the care of the monks, and a meaningful job, he's become a part of our family and a valuable employee.

I pour a small amount of Chardonnay in their glasses and hold the glass to the light. "First, look at the wine. Is the wine cloudy or clear? Is it bright as day or twinkling like the stars? Is the color like straw or gold?"

"The Chardonnay is clear, but bold as a sunflower," Louise says.

"Precisely." I look at my glass. "That intensity comes from those extra weeks on the vine. Now we taste."

They take cautious sips.

"Swish along your tongue," I tell them. "Does it taste like it smells? How does it feel in your mouth? Is the texture light or rich? Silky or crisp?"

We taste the Pinot Noir and Meunier and discuss the nuances of each grape.

"Now is the fun part," I say, setting the three varietals in front of them. "Experiment with different amounts of each wine, remembering the characteristics of each varietal."

"What if I am wrong?" Louise grimaces.

"Wine is the winemaker's creation," I tell them. "Just like a painting—there are many ways to paint the same subject. You want to create wine that pleases your taste."

Soon all of us are lost in our creations.

Louise has chosen mostly Chardonnay with a hint of the red wines, while Damas selected equal parts of three wines.

Damas tries my blend first, making a terrible face, and grabs his throat.

Louise sips and her nose crunches. "Too sour, Maman."

What do I expect from a fourteen-year-old who loves French pastries?

Louise tries Damas's blend. "That is delicious."

She has a point. The wine is round with flavor, not too sharp, and not bland. The aftertaste leaves me wanting more, and the subtle nuance and finesse are impressive. The boy has a talent for this. Perhaps his senses of smell and taste have compensated for his lack of hearing and speech. I cannot wait to tell Henry about this.

Henry struggles to teach the Alhambra girls to use the corking machine, paste labels straight, wrap the foil well, and pack champagne so it will survive the long trip to London.

Two weeks later, the shipment leaves to our agent, Adolphe Hubinet. He should be thrilled to receive his first champagne since before the war, and I'm excited when I receive a letter postmarked from London.

I call Henry into my office. His cheeks are not quite so gaunt, and he has a healthier color to his skin.

"A letter from Monsieur Hubinet." I hand it to him. "Open it. You deserve all the credit of getting that shipment out with all the trouble you had with the girls."

Henry reads it to me.

"*Our biggest customer complained the champagne was corked badly and demanded a refund. This quality is not acceptable. I know the past year has been rough, but you must live up to standards your customers expect."*

Henry lets the letter fall to his lap. "I let you down."

I watch the Alhambra girls work outside my office. "Are they getting better?"

"A couple of them, but most of them will leave as soon as their business returns to normal."

"Any news from Louis?"

Henry shakes his head. "I read that the Communards dragged two hundred and fifty cannon up to Montmartre. When the French army tried to take them back, they executed two generals."

I scoff. "What is wrong with the French, Henry? Can't we live without war? No sooner do we get out of the Prussian-Franco war than we start another among ourselves."

"We need a strong king again," Vasnier says. "The revolutionary spirit must be controlled."

"So you don't approve of the Communards?"

"How could I? They are fighting against the French government."

"But from what I read, they are fighting for good things: women's rights, children's rights, worker's rights."

"You sound like Louis."

I huff. "I'm sorry, Henry. I'm just trying to understand why he stayed."

Vasnier sits back in the chair. "When we went to fight Prussia, all Louis talked about was his beautiful Lucille and their new child coming. He wanted to buy a small house close by, so you could help with the baby."

A tear falls to my cheek, and he wipes it away.

"Louis can't face coming back without them here," Vasnier says.

I squeeze his hand. "I need fresh air. I'm going to take the rig out to check on budbreak in the vineyards." Taking my coat from the rack, I have second thoughts. "Would you like to come with me?"

In May, General Francis arrives at my front door, two officers at his sides. The general is commanding in his red wool uniform with gold braid epaulettes, cordons on his chest, and a gold sash. Several large Iron Cross medals hang around his neck in gold, black, and red, each one engraved with a battle fought and won in the Franco-Prussian war: Toul, Beaune-la-Rolande, Beaugency, and the Siege of Paris. He takes off his pickelhaube and holds it.

I gesture to his medals. "You've been well rewarded for your war performance, I see." I don't bother to hide my snide tone.

"My reward is to return to my Grand Duchy of Mecklenburg-Schwerin." The old spark in his eyes is hooded with drooping eyelids.

"Would you like to sit?" I offer him the leather Louis XIV chair, but he refuses.

"We will not be staying," he says. "It is a ten-day march to Berlin, and if we stop here, the soldiers will never leave. They got too comfortable in your charming town."

"Then, why did you come? Did you leave something here?"

He signals the officers to step outside. "I found something that belongs to you and wanted to return it." His overgrown mustache hides a slight smile.

"And what is that?"

Henry Vasnier runs down from his chambers, scowling. "Is everything all right, Madame Pommery?"

The soldiers drag in Louis, dried blood on his bruised face, his uniform tattered and filthy with gunpowder, stumbling feet that cannot connect to the ground. He groans like a madman, his teeth chattering.

"Louis." I lunge to him, but the general holds me back.

"Don't touch him," he says. "Brain fever is contagious. Half the Communards have it."

"What can we do for it?" My arms long to hold him, swab his weary forehead.

"There is nothing you can do but make him comfortable for his last days."

"Where do you want us to put him, Madame?" the guard asks.

"Henry, will you show them the chamber across from yours?"

He leads the soldiers down the hall.

"Surely there is something we can do."

"He's past treatment." The general shakes his head sadly. "We shipped the Communards to Caledonia but sent the sick ones to potter's field to die. I recognized your son and figured you would want to bury him yourself."

"Bury my son?" My knees give out, and I lean on the nearest chair.

His guards return, and the general puts on his helmet. "I suppose it is in bad form to say I enjoyed my time as your guest," he says.

"Manners are never in bad form," I say.

The general nods, and they march out the door.

Henry returns. "You should not go in there, Madame. He is too far gone, and we cannot lose you, too."

A knot settles in my throat, and I force it down. "Louis will fight his way back, Henry. Since he was two years old, he demanded to have his way, no matter the consequences. He has the strongest will I have ever known."

But over the next few days, Louis will not accept food or water and yells gibberish. Felix is the only one who he does not seem to mind, curling his long body in a ball at Louis's stomach, purring. Louis tosses and turns, sucked into a nightmarish fog, grabbing his head, moaning, yelling at demons only he can see. I agonize for some way to reach him. He must remember who he is and come back to us.

Feeling helpless, I cook a Provençal stew he loved as a child. Surprised to see me in her kitchen, Yvonne helps me. First, we make a chicken broth with bones, vegetables, and a handful of Herbes de Provence. Then, I braise chicken thighs and onions in olive oil, stirring in a dollop of Dijon mustard, and add it to the broth with carrots, potatoes, and celery. We let the stew simmer until the aroma is impossible to resist. A last splash of champagne enlivens the flavor.

When we enter the room, Felix looks up with gold-flecked eyes. Louis stops groaning when he smells the stew, his nostrils quivering. He makes no move to feed himself, so Yvonne quietly sits on the bed and feeds him spoonful after spoonful.

Felix leaps off the bed and runs down the hall to the kitchen. I know what he wants. I make him his own bowl of chicken, payment for his vigil over my son.

After that, Yvonne makes the stew every day with fresh-baked baguettes and sweet, churned butter. Before she serves, she takes off her mop cap and brushes her hair in the round hall mirror.

Each day she stays a bit longer, and soon I hear them talking and laughing. Love is a powerful healer.

PART IV

(1872-1878)

*"I wanted this Estate to be like an open book, facing the world and time.
Leave your imprint on it, as I have left mine, for posterity."*
~Jeanne Alexandrine Pommery

32

LA NUIT, TOUS LES CHATS SONT GRIS

At night, all the cats are grey

1872. We climb Butte Saint-Nicaise to show Adolphe Hubinet the crayères, though the wind whips our faces with sleet. Hubinet's beaver-fur coat should keep him warm enough, but his velvet pantaloons are meant for the London opera instead of a hike in the snow.

"So, this is the city dump?" he asks.

"*Was* the city dump," I assure him. "We cleared the land and now it is ours."

Hubinet's patent leather slippers slide on the ice underneath the snow. Louis and Henry support his arms to keep him steady.

Hubinet glances at them, his glossy hair brushing against his shoulders. "Oh, my. Twin gods come to save me from danger." He turns to Henry. "Are you married? All the best ones are married." Hubinet's laughing eyes make his long, horsey face handsome. The past decade in London has intensified his conviviality, his panache and humor. Another reason Pommery sales have grown.

"Why did we have to come up to the butte in this weather?" Louis says.

"You'll see," I say, not about to spoil the surprise. "Monsieur Hubinet's visit is a perfect time to make an announcement." The curtain is about to go up on my vision, and I need all of their support if we are to succeed.

I am especially anxious about Henry's opinion. I've come to appreciate him even more this past year. Now that he lives in the house, we spend evenings in the salon playing piquet or belote. I suspect he lets me win sometimes. We've made a habit of popping a bottle of our competitor's champagne and critiquing it ruthlessly for our own guilty pleasure. On Sundays, we take in a local art show or exhibit at *Le Musée des Beaux-Arts*. I admire Henry's intense curiosity, always researching champagne and art, art and champagne. Both expressions of individualism.

Hubinet frowns at his black patent slippers, now scuffed and muddy. "My goodness, this is quite a long distance, isn't it? Couldn't you find somewhere closer to the winery to store your champagne?" He blows on his buffed fingernails; his fingers are red from cold.

"You haven't seen the worst of it," Louis says, lifting the beech tree branch out of the way of the entrance.

I duck into the steep staircase, followed by Hubinet, Henry, and Louis in the rear.

"Uoff." Hubinet hits his head on the low tunnel ceiling and bends over.

"I forgot you were so tall," I say.

He rubs his head. "I'll wait up here. I'm not much for the dark unless it's a theater or a boudoir." He laughs.

"Please Monsieur," I say. "I can't wait to hear what you think of the new crayères. I've always counted on you to be my arbiter of style."

Henry squeezes my shoulder from behind. "Perhaps Monsieur Hubinet should accompany you down the stairs, Madame."

"Quite right, Henry." I thread my arm through Hubinet's. "I could use the support."

"Oh, my. Oh, my." He steps down cautiously. "It looks like the dwarves' mine down there." Hubinet blows in and out with ballooning cheeks. "How many stairs are there?"

"One hundred and sixteen," Louis says. "Thirty meters below ground."

Hubinet grips tighter as the tunnel narrows. "Oh, my. Oh, my." He huffs faster and faster.

"Are you all right, Monsieur Hubinet?" I ask.

His voice rises an octave. "Ignore it, my doctor says. Put it out of your mind. He calls it claustrophobia—when one is anxious in tight places. Had it all my life, and they just discovered it. The doctor says the simple solution is not to go in tight places, so no narrow hallways, closets, or low ceilings. Can't abide low ceilings. Avoid tiny taxicabs at all costs." Hubinet turns around and starts back up.

Calmly, Henry takes his other arm. "Not to worry, Monsieur. Two more steps, and we'll be in the gallery."

We step down into the first gallery, and Hubinet gasps. The chiseled chalk walls have been polished to a glow and soar up to the single window to the sky. Hundreds of gleaming candle lanterns twinkle from hooks, illuminating the chamber as if it's Christmas Eve.

Hubinet bends back to view the towering walls, arms outstretched and voice echoing through the chamber. "The hallowed grounds of Pommery Champagne."

"When did you have time for this?" Henry asks me.

"I had help." I gesture to the tasting table where Damas turns bottles of champagne in a half-barrel of ice, and Louise polishes glasses.

"How big are these crayères?" Hubinet says. "With sales flourishing, we'll need all the space we can get."

"We've excavated twelve kilometers of tunnels so far," I tell him. "Each tunnel leads to these extraordinary galleries. And there are many more crayères to excavate."

Henry smiles at me with shining eyes. "We estimate we can store twenty million bottles of champagne."

Hubinet's laugh rings like carillon bells.

"Louise, darling, will you open the champagne for a toast?" I ask.

Her delicate fingers lift a bottle from the ice, strip the foil, and wind off the wire cage.

Louis strides over to her. "Here, let me help you with the cork."

I hold up my palm. "Your sister has it down to an art."

Rotating the bottle with one hand, she twists the cork with the other and releases a perfect sigh.

"Bravo." Louis holds out a coupe as she pours with her thumb in the punt on the bottom. "When did you grow up?" he says while she serves the rest of us.

Hubinet raises his glass to us. "If life brings you troubles, drink some bubbles."

Louise giggles. "You rhymed, Monsieur Hubinet."

"A habit I'm trying to cure," he says, studying his glass by candlelight. "The color is like spun gold and the aroma is heaven. If it tastes as good as it looks and smells, I will sell twenty thousand cases."

"Now for my announcement," I say.

"This wasn't the surprise?" Louis asks.

I raise my glass. "With the horrible war over and all of us together again, Pommery Champagne is going to build the most beautiful winery in the world." I toast each of their glasses.

Louis scoffs. "Nice thought, Maman, but it would take more than candles to make people want to visit a cave under a dump."

Patience is a virtue, I remind myself. "Allow me to explain. This is the main gallery where winery guests will be greeted to go on a Pommery crayère tour."

"People come to a winery to taste wine, not tour old chalk mines," Louis says. "They are certainly nothing special. Reims has hundreds of them."

I hold up a finger. "But no other winery uses crayères as tasting galleries. We will create a whole new experience presenting the intricate process of making champagne. Elevating it to an artform. Our guests will experience the effort, techniques, and painstaking steps Pommery employs to create a champagne that is only the very finest quality."

"Isn't your home more gracious for sampling wines?" Henry asks. "The general seemed to like it."

"I have to agree," Hubinet says. "Trudging through the bowels of a dump does not encourage customers to buy wine. I have designed our Pommery tasting salon in London to be as sumptuous as the Grosvenor Hotel. Customers crave beauty and luxury."

"And they shall have it," I say. "We will make these crayères an experience they will never forget, a gallery of fine champagne and fine art."

"They won't forget it because they'll catch pneumonia down here." Louis folds his arms against his chest, shivering. Out of nowhere, Felix leaps into his arms. "Where did you come from?" Louis strokes him, and Felix purrs, the two of them inseparable since Louis's sickness.

Louise pours more champagne for everyone. "Maybe our customers should wear fur coats like Monsieur Hubinet?"

I laugh.

"Not a bad idea, Mademoiselle." Hubinet chuckles. "And serve champagne in Baccarat crystal."

"Actually, the project starts next week," I say with as much confidence as I can muster. "I have hired a fine sculptor, Gustave Navlet, to carve the story of Bacchus, the god of wine, into the walls. It will be a wonder to all who visit."

"Customers buy champagne, not art," Louis says.

"Ah, but art elevates champagne, and vice versa," I say, trying to reason with him. "Everyone in the Champagne makes champagne—some better, some worse. Pommery will become a destination visitors will travel here for and tell all of Europe."

"It is just not the right time to expand when France teeters on bankruptcy paying off the Prussians," Louis says.

"Louis, if there is one thing I learned from that wretched war, it's that we can't always follow the rules. Sometimes breaking the rules is exactly what is called for."

Louis thrusts his thumb up. "We can certainly agree on that, Maman."

Henry raises his glass. "To your remarkable vision, Madame Pommery. That vision has brought us this far, and I trust it will take us as far as you can dream."

"To Madame Pommery," Hubinet says, and everyone raises their glasses.

Henry gazes keenly over the rim of his glass, setting off realizations I have ignored for too long. Firstly, our relationship is so much deeper than boss and manager. Secondly, my tingling limbs have nothing to do with the champagne.

A fresh layer of snow dazzles in the midday sunlight as Hubinet climbs into the open gig with his thigh-high boots, beaver coat, and red cashmere scarf.

He rubs his palms together. "Another day in paradise."

Louise snaps the reins, and we take Hubinet on a tour through the Champagne vineyards on the way to Butte Saint-Nicaise.

He regales us with plans to take Pommery to the top of the wine menus of every restaurant and bar in the United Kingdom and wherever his wanderlust takes him. His sales plan sounds more like the *Arabian Nights* and lifts our spirits in the brisk January air.

"Chardonnay grows here in the Côte des Blancs," Louise points out as we pass through the rolling hills, then gestures to the river. "And they grow Meunier grapes in Vallée de la Marne."

"She's a sponge for details, my girl," I brag to Hubinet. "Louise knows each vineyard and varietal by heart."

Hubinet laughs. "*Telle mère, telle fille.*" Like mother, like daughter. "Was there much of a harvest when the war was going on?"

I grimace. "We were very late picking grapes. But we're encouraged with how it's tasting."

Hubinet camps a grin. "Perhaps I can sneak a taste so I can tell customers what to expect?"

"We'll have to wait four years for it to age," I tell him.

"Four years is a long time to wait." He clasps his hands in prayer. "Can I try it now?"

"The new cuvée blend is in the crayères," Louise says. "What about your claustrophobia?"

"One should never let fear ruin one's thirst for knowledge," he grins. "Or one's thirst for champagne."

Louise turns the gig around, and the horses head north through the leafless vineyards.

When we get to the butte, Hubinet ducks his head as we enter the staircase, which is lit with lanterns on hooks.

"I'm beginning to appreciate your idea here, Madame." He huffs in and out. "Climbing down into ancient caves definitely captures one's imagination."

He hums a marching tune on the way down. "Curiouser and curiouser," he says as we enter the blending chamber. "So this is where the magic happens?" His long fingers glide over the barrels lined up against the wall, vineyard and grape varietal names written on the tops. "Something tells me this is your work, Louise."

The lantern on the table lights her proud expression.

Hubinet lounges on a barrel chair as if he's in a fashionable nightclub rather than a cold damp room in the caves. "So what are we tasting?"

I open a bottle and smell the whiff of yeast and fruit. "I am experimenting with a drier champagne again."

"You should stay with the champagne you are known for, Madame," he sniffs the glass with a curled lip.

"My friends in Scotland bought my dry champagne at the London Exhibition," I say. "And they keep buying."

"They pitied you because you were just starting out," Hubinet says. "And, they kept buying because you went back to a sweet dosage as I recommended."

I watch the bubbles rise by the lantern light. "This wine is completely different than my first experiment."

"How so?" He sniffs his glass.

"Since the harvest was late, the grapes were on the vines much longer than usual," I tell him. "I thought the champagne would be ruined, but it turned out that the extra maturity made for a richer taste." I raise my glass. "*Au santé.*"

Hubinet takes a swallow and makes a sour face. "You can still add more sugar, can't you?"

"That would ruin it." I inhale the bubbles bursting out of the wine. "Can you smell the apricot? Two more years of aging and these flavors will taste like apricot jam on butter croissants."

He scoffs.

"What do you think, Monsieur?" Louise asks, her beautiful face riddled with worry.

Hubinet pours his glass into the dump bucket. "Frankly, this champagne goes down like swallowing razor blades."

Louise grabs my sleeve. "Oh, no, Maman. Maybe more sugar would help."

A cold doubt creeps into my chest, and I taste it again. "The flavor is there, I know it's there."

"Louise, you must not listen to me," Hubinet says. "Listen to your mother. Madame Pommery has always had the vision to do things others have not. And she believes in her vision." He takes out a gold sovereign from his pocket and holds it in front of Louise's pert nose. "I'll bet you that in two years it will taste exactly as your maman predicts."

"But how can you be certain?" Louise asks me.

"How does an artist know what a painting will look like when it's finished?" I say. "They start with an idea and work on it until it becomes real. This champagne is my idea. In a couple of years, I am certain this wine will please palates."

"Meanwhile, Louise, I will be spreading word that dry champagne is all the vogue." Hubinet spins the gold coin in front of her. "And in a couple of years, it will be true, and they heard it first from me." He passes his hand over the coin, and it disappears.

"How did you do that?" Amazed, Louise holds her hands out, and the coin drops in her hand.

33

CE N'EST PAS LA MER À BOIRE.

It's not as if you have to drink the sea.

1873. Chalk dust hovers in the crayère netherworld as sculptors tight rope across scaffolding, chipping away at the chalk rock. Dust coats my throat and nose, making it hard to breath. The men wear kerchiefs over their faces as they haul out carts of dirt.

I try to soothe my jittery nerves by holding Felix; his purring always seems to calm me. Perhaps I moved too fast, too recklessly, on the crayère project.

The short, swarthy sculptor, Gustave Navlet, stands in the middle of the chaos waving his arms like the conductor of a cyclone. For the life of me, I cannot see how these gauges and holes will ever add up to the Bacchus scene I envisioned, and it is costing a fortune I do not have. We should have started small instead of this ambitious tableau fifteen meters long. I thought my idea was inspired, but perhaps it was merely arrogance.

Henry and Louis descend the crayère steps, brows furrowed with concern.

"The men do not look happy, do they Felix?" I nuzzle his neck, which is vibrating under my fingers.

I yell to Louis and Henry over the deafening noise. "Astounding."

267

"Pounding?" Henry raises his voice over the din.

"Confounding," Louis shouts. "She said confounding."

I take them into an alcove where it's quieter.

"When will the sculptors be finished?" Henry nervously brushes his mustache with his forefinger.

I haven't the courage to tell him I've commissioned more sculptures already.

"There is no more room in the winery," Louis says. "And now we can't put wine down here. Harvest starts this month, and we'll have new wine to store. Where do we put the wine?"

"I'm sure you two will figure it out," I say, since I have no solution.

He huffs; a vessel pulsates on his forehead. "When you decided to age the champagne four or six years instead of two, did you consider the extra years to store the champagne?"

Reynard Wolfe pops into our alcove uninvited. "And those extra years deplete your bank account."

"Monsieur Wolfe, this is a private meeting," I tell him.

Wolfe's chubby hand revolves around him. "Excuse me, I did not see a maid to present my calling card."

My temples throb with anger and lack of oxygen. "State your business, Monsieur." I hold Felix across my chest.

"This sculpture is putting your company in peril, Madame," Wolfe says theatrically. "I have to wonder what you are thinking, or if you are thinking at all."

Henry steps forward. "You must not speak to Madame Pommery that way."

Wolfe sticks out his double chin. "Louis ordered me to pay the sculptor's invoice, but if I do, Pommery will not have enough to pay for the grape harvest." He wheezes in dust. "If you don't pay the vineyards, then Pommery is finished. Done. Kaput."

My pulse throbs under my ear, and Felix kneads the spot with his paws, rumbling a deep vibrato like symphony oboes.

"Pay Gustave Navlet," I tell Wolfe.

"Then how do we pay the vineyards?" Louis says.

Navlet interrupts. "Madame Pommery, if you can move your guests, we're ready to set the blast." He holds his fingers up with a gold-toothed smile. "Small blast."

"We'll move to the stairs." I gesture them ahead.

A skinny miner inserts a stick of dynamite into the drilled hole and strikes a match.

Henry whispers in my ear. "What are they doing?"

"We're opening up a tunnel to the next gallery, so they are dynamiting."

"This is madness, Maman," Louis shouts. "Pure madness."

Wolfe claps his back. "Louis, you must take charge. Things are out of hand."

They stop at the foot of the stairs, and I hold up my palms.

"Gentlemen, all this tumult does no good," I tell them. "Ship the 1870 vintage to Hubinet right away, and he can sell it before harvest."

Louis gasps. "No, Maman. Hubinet hates that dry brut champagne. He'd quit before he'd tarnish his reputation."

"Ship the brut, Louis, and I'll write Monsieur Hubinet how to present it to customers."

Wolfe shakes his head. "When will you have the money to pay the vineyards?"

Looking up at the chalk ceiling, I calculate how long until we receive payment. Three months at least. "Tell the vineyards we will guarantee payment before—"

An explosion blows me sideways into the wall, with a sickening crack in my shoulder. Felix leaps out of my arms with a screech. Wolfe and Louis run up the staircase.

Henry shields me with his arms and back, holding my head to his chest as rocks pelt the wall like shrapnel.

Thousands and thousands of mice pour out of the exploded wall, and Felix chases them.

Gustave Navlet shouts deep and urgent. "Run! Run! The ceiling is falling."

Miners and sculptors trample past us to the stairs, pushing and elbowing to get ahead.

Henry lifts me into his arms and walks swiftly and surely up the side of the staircase, protecting me from the stampede with his broad shoulders. Hanging onto his neck, I inhale his smell as the world falls down around us.

The next day, my entire left side throbs, my shoulder is swollen, and I can't move it. I worry what happened to Navlet's crew. And what happened to Felix? Louise brings me coffee and a baguette, and I tell her I'll be working from my chambers.

Hobbling to my writing desk, I write Hubinet a letter to accompany the shipment today. I just sign it when Louis knocks at my door and peeps in.

"How are you feeling?" He sits next to my desk, his eyebrows peaked with worry.

"My age. I'm feeling my age," I say, holding the bruise on my hip. "Were any men hurt?"

Lowering his chin, he shakes his head slowly. "They are still digging them out of the rubble."

My shoulders slump inward. "They haven't found them all?"

"I'll let you know when we know more." He lays his hand on mine. "Maman, we almost lost you. Last night, I thought how you always help people who have less than we do, like the orphanage and maternity fund."

"We all do our part, Louis."

He holds up his hand. "Let me finish. When I was with the Communards, I saw firsthand how poor people live, starving and freezing in the streets. I realized I took for granted the roof over my head, good food on the table—and what you have sacrificed for us. And how when Papa died, you started Pommery Champagne so I could finish university." His voice breaks, and he presses his lips together.

I squeeze his hand, realizing the gift he is giving me. When does a child ever understand what their parents try to do for them?

"You have always had a soft heart, Louis," I tell him. "I was worried you wouldn't come back from the Communards."

He sniffs. "Is that the letter you are sending Hubinet? He's not going to like receiving the brut champagne."

"Read it," I say and he opens the letter.

"My dear Monsieur Hubinet, Do you remember ten years ago, when Monet's paintings drew outcries and mockery from art critics? But Monet and the other Impressionists did not let that stop them from pursuing their vision, and now Impressionism has transformed the way the viewer experiences art."

Louis nods, seeming to understand.

"Pommery Brut will change the way champagne is experienced, no longer as a dessert wine or a sweet ladies' drink, but a fine wine that can be enjoyed any time by men and women alike."

Louis sighs.

"Tell our customers that instead of picking immature grapes and masking the harshness with sugar, we allow the grapes to ripen and sweeten naturally on the vine. The taste of Pommery Brut is like nature intended. I believe in Pommery Brut, and once again, I'm asking you to believe in me."

Louis smiles with that crooked eyetooth like his father's. "I believe in you, Maman. But customers don't know you like I do," he teases, and I swat his arm playfully.

"What does that mean?"

"It means you are relentless with your vision of how things should be." He chuckles.

"And so should you, Louis," I say. "You have such deep feelings about the poor and less fortunate, especially our workers. How would you feel about heading up a medical fund for Pommery workers?"

"How would it work?" he asks.

"That's for you to figure out," I say. "Have Wolfe set it up and earn his keep for a change."

"I'll do that," Louis says. "Henry asked to see you next."

Glancing in the oval looking glass, I touch the bruise on my cheekbone. It will be a week before it fades. "Not today, Louis."

His eyebrows pinch together. "Is there a problem with Henry you are not telling me?"

"Yes, I'm not telling you. And no, there isn't a problem." I purse my lips together.

"Mysterious." His grin grows hesitant. "There is a concert tonight, and I'd like to take Yvonne, if you have no objections."

"Perhaps take her to dinner as well?" I smile playfully.

"Henry will be here if you need anything." He kisses my cheeks.

"Seeing my only son happy is all I need."

"Same to you, Maman." He closes the door behind him.

What does he mean by that?

Sitting at my dressing table, I apply lavender oil to my bruises, breathing in the herbal fragrance too complex to describe. Like the champagne that will be my masterpiece someday. I brush my hair one hundred times as I have every night for fifty-five years. Hardly any gray, I notice with the sin of pride.

Piano music drifts up the stairs, a bright silvery sound like moonlight dappling on the Marne River. No one plays our piano since Louis passed. I tie the belt on my indigo silk dressing gown and go downstairs, the piano concerto getting louder as I go.

Henry plays the keys of the Pleyel piano that has become a sideboard instead of an instrument. The song is evocative and sensuous, but simple at the same time. I pour two etched glasses of sherry at the bar and sit beside him on the bench.

He sings to the haunting tune, and my heart swells.

> The air is filled with the ravishing perfume of lilac
> That flowers from the top of the wall to the bottom
> Replete with the fragrance of golden tresses.
> The sea in the sun is all ablaze
> And, over the sand that it comes to kiss,
> It rolls with dazzling waves.
>
> Oh sky that reflects the tint of her eyes;
> The breeze that sings to the lilacs in flower
> To return with everything scented;
> Streams that moisten her dress,
> Oh footpaths of green,
> You that quiver beneath her dear little feet,
> Make me see my belovèd.

I hand him the sherry. "I wear lavender oil, not lilac."

He sips it with a sidelong look. "I guess Boucher did not know that when he wrote *Flower of the Waters*."

"Henry, I wanted to talk to you. I don't think—"

"Alexandrine, don't say it." He turns to me, his licorice breath on mine, moves his thumb and forefinger to my chin. "I know you're about to tell me some rule we must not break or boundary we cannot cross." He caresses my bruised cheek with his other hand. "But why do you think I've stayed here sixteen years?"

I laugh nervously. "Champagne?"

He strokes my chin and sends chills down my neck. "I never even drank champagne until you, and then you taught me to taste

272

it like I enjoy a painting or listen to music, with all the nuances and intricacy."

"Henry, I don't think you—" I seize his lips with mine, kissing him deeply with the yearning I've held back for so long.

"Please, Alexandrine." He leans closer, his lips hovering over mine until I reach for him, kissing him without reserve. "We deserve to be happy, no matter what rules we break." He kisses me long and slow, until I gasp for air. "Did I hurt you?" he says, searching my face.

I shake my head. "May I speak now?"

He leans back, and I see he's steeling himself for the worst.

"Henry, I just came down to tell you, I don't think you have been properly acknowledged for the leadership you have given Pommery. As of now, I am promoting you to director of the winery, with twenty percent of the profits and stock besides."

He looks down at the keyboard, strangely disappointed. "That's what you came down here to tell me?"

"That, and to invite you up to my suite." Smiling seductively, I stand and hold out my hand to him.

34

L'AMOUR EST AVEUGLE

Love is blind

1874. After two years of rained-out harvests, the fall of 1874 is the largest harvest in a decade. We can't get all the grapes crushed as quickly as we should in our old, cramped winery, and we can't use the crayères yet because Nair and Navlet are still working, with no end in sight.

Seven wagons of grapes are still lined up around Reims Square. If we don't get the grapes crushed today, they will be a horrible mush, good for nothing but fodder. Expensive fodder, for which I have already paid a premium.

Louise directs the wagons where to unload the grapes, her gleaming black hair pulled back in a ribbon matching the trim of her work dress. When she waves her arm, the next waggoneer shakes his reins and lurches forward. The young man ties up the horses and jumps up to the platform to steal a minute with Louise while the crew unloads the crates. His confidence is too bold for a peasant. He throws back his blond locks and laughs as if she said something hilarious.

Thinking back to when I was seventeen, I attended fine finishing schools and vacationed with nobles; I dreamed of becoming a mistress of those castles. Naïve and beautiful dreams. What a different life I provided her. I must introduce Louise to society, but I've been remiss in my social obligations, and out of touch.

Louis supervises the workers loading grapes onto the scales while Henry records the weights and orders the crates to be emptied on the tables. Nearly a hundred employees now scurry about in a beautiful dance of precision and excellence. So different from when we started.

The new mayor pays us a call, his thin mustache twitching side to side like a caterpillar trying to escape.

"Monsieur Gosset, don't you love this time of year?" I ask him. "The harvest is the biggest I've ever seen, so bountiful and beautiful."

He clears his throat. "Madame Pommery, you are blocking traffic on Reims Square and it's market day. The farmers cannot get their wagons in and set up their booths." Taking off his top hat, he wipes his brow. "Why are you so late with harvest? It was over weeks ago." He grimaces at our women sorting the grapes, their hands deftly picking out overripe grapes and tossing them into a basket to feed the hogs.

"I'm sorry, Monsieur, but I'm afraid it will take us a few more hours to bring in all the grapes. It's a huge crop this year."

"You'll pay a fine for blocking the square." He pulls out a pad of tickets.

I thread my arm through his and walk him to the house. "Tell me more about that award your son won for architecture design?"

While he expounds on how his son won the architectural contest for the new Théâtre de Reims, Chantal brings fresh croissants, churned butter, and apricot preserves. I make a special show of preparing his café au lait, adding a shot of calvados and extra cream.

"Alphonse needs to get into an architecture firm but is having trouble without a degree," he says, biting into his croissant.

"I have a project which may interest your son," I say.

His eyes light. "Anything to get a start in the business."

"Let me get my drawings." I go out into the winery to fetch my drawing pad.

Louise is still talking to that handsome waggoneer who stayed after his delivery. I really must get her out visiting the right families, or she'll find a husband without any input from me.

Returning to Monsieur Gosset, I present my art pad. "This is the Pommery winery we will build on Butte Saint-Nicaise."

He huffs and brushes crumbs off his vest. "Are you joking or insulting me?"

"I assure you I am most serious. Could your son draw plans for this?"

"A castle with turrets and towers?" he says. "No winery looks like this, and not nearly this large." He stands and puts on his top hat.

"Monsieur, your son must be very talented to win the architectural contest. I would like to show him my drawings and see what he has to say."

His caterpillar mustache twists. "If you are serious, this would be quite a coup for my son's first building."

"When may we call on you, Monsieur? I will bring my daughter, as she's coming out this year, and I want her to meet all the right families, such as yours."

When I return to the winery to tell Louise, she is laughing with the blond waggoneer.

I'm finishing my café au lait in the breakfast room when Louise carries in Felix. A single tendril escapes her night cap, so beautiful and fresh. But her peaceful expression changes when she sees our blank walls, darker rectangles where our paintings had been.

Her long, delicate fingers trace the outlines on the wall.

"Were our paintings stolen, Maman?" she says. "The ones painted by women—Berthe Morisot, Mary Cassatt, and Marie Braquemard." Her voice trembles. "Who would have done such an atrocious thing?" She hugs me and sobs into my neck.

Suddenly, my selfishness astounds me. I never thought they meant much to Louise.

I rub her back. "True confessions?" Our game since she was little. "I sold the paintings to the pawn shop."

Louise gasps and holds her chest. "Are we poor? Oh, Maman. Why didn't you tell me?"

I take her hands and smile to allay her fears. "Nothing like that. It's just that I needed to pay the *vendangeurs* and the miners at the same time, and we did not have enough money to pay them both."

"Because our brut wine is not selling?" Louise pours her café au lait.

"Where did you hear that?"

"Louis said the brut would ruin Pommery's reputation, and Henry defended you."

I slice a baguette lengthwise and spread it with hazelnut paste. We dip it in our café and savor the toasty flavor.

"So, be honest with me, what is your opinion of the brut?" I ask.

She tilts her head. "Personally, I rather like tasting grapes rather than the sugar. And I don't miss that underlying bitterness of unripe fruit."

I nod. "You are not humoring your old maman, are you?"

She reaches across and squeezes my hand. "You always taught me to trust my instincts."

"I did say that, didn't I?" I tweak her pert nose.

"Now, my turn for true confessions." Her eyes spark with mischief. "I met a young man I really like, Maman."

I smile. "Alphonse Gosset, our new architect? You never said much after your carriage ride."

She waves her hand. "Not him. He just took me riding because he's working for you." She leans closer, her eyes sparkling. "It's the waggoneer at Beaumont vineyards."

"The tall blond one?" Panic rises in my throat. "What's his name? Who is his family? How old is he?"

"I don't know his last name, but his first name is Guy. He's older than me and has a Breton accent."

"How were you introduced? We know nothing about him."

"No one introduced us, or I would know his name," she says. "The first time I met him he was riding through the vineyards, supervising the *vendangeurs*." Her eyes brighten. "Then I saw him when they delivered grapes. He stayed later, and we went to a concert with Yvonne and Louis."

"I better meet this Monsieur Guy."

"He left after harvest." She pouts. "He said his family studs horses in Brittany, and he had to get back."

I sigh and ruffle her hair. "I've been remiss. It's time to take you visiting friends and neighbors, let you meet people. And maybe a debutante party."

"Maybe Guy will come back next year."

"Maybe," I say. "Or maybe you ought to allow Alphonse Gosset another carriage ride."

"Oh, Maman." She tilts her head and smiles the sweet smile that I'm sure drew Monsieur Guy like a hummingbird to a rose. My perfect rose.

I walk to the bank with a certain bounce to my gait, waving at neighbors and singing "Alouette." I can't carry a tune, but no matter, I am singing. This morning's mail held three big checks from Monsieur Hubinet for the brut champagne, for which he begrudgingly congratulated me.

Wolfe accepts the checks with sarcasm. "This will not come close to paying for the sculpture in the crayères, let alone the winery you want to build."

"I brought you the drawings from our architect. Once you see them, I'm sure you'll be as excited as I am." And want to finance the building.

Wolfe is aghast. "This is a castle, not a winery. Who would draw such a thing?"

"Alphonse Gosset. Doesn't it take your breath away?"

"That boy who won the Théâtre de Reims competition? He only won because his father is mayor."

"I admire how he captured my vision."

"What could you possibly need with all this space?"

"It will be our production facility to crush the grapes and start the fermentation. See these arched entrances? It will be so much easier to receive grape wagons than on Reims Square."

"But the elaborate entryway and stone turrets are ostentatious and grandiose. And why do you need this grand tower?"

"From the tower, you can see the entire town of Reims, Montagne de Reims, and the rolling hills of the Champagne. Visitors will have the experience of a lifetime and never forget Pommery Champagne. And this is just the beginning. After we receive guests in the production facility, we will take them down into the crayères."

"You need to see a doctor." Wolfe presses his palm on my forehead. "You have delusions of grandeur, a symptom of hysteria, quite common in women your age."

I scoff at his insult. "This is not a delusion, and you know it. Twenty years ago, I told you I wanted to build the most beautiful champagne house in the world, and you smiled and nodded and happily took my business. Now that I am on the threshold of manifesting my dream, you balk. Where is your loyalty?"

"You were a widow with an impossible dream. Every year since then, you have pushed the bank beyond the limits of supporting you."

I turn over the new checks from Hubinet. "The British are buying Pommery Brut and the 1874 harvest was spectacular. I believe this is all the collateral you need to extend me a loan for the new winery?"

"The bank cannot possibly finance such hideous architecture. It will be the laughingstock of the Champagne."

"You are insulting the two greatest castles in Scotland, the Stellarmane and the Argyle. Both friends of mine from finishing school."

"No one claims the Scots are great architects."

I grab his ink pen and dip it into the well. "Write the check, Monsieur, or I will not hesitate to take my business elsewhere."

35

IL EST TEMPS D'ÉCOUTER SON COEUR

It's time to listen to your heart

1877. The last loads of grapes come in from the vineyards. Louise checks in the wagons and supervises the women sorting the grapes away from stems. Then, Louis takes them to Damas working the basket press. I sent Henry over to Butte Saint-Nicaise to sort out a problem at the construction site, and I'll follow him as soon as I pay the last vineyard for their grapes.

Louise talks and laughs with that waggoneer with wheat-blond hair and broad shoulders. What did she say his name was? He's not cleaned up yet from working the vineyard, his boots caked with mud, torn peasant shirt, and grape-stained trousers. Yet, Louise doesn't seem to notice his unkempt appearance. A smile lights her face, her blushing cheeks indented with dimples, her laugh clear as bells. She never looked this happy on our social visits. While every eligible bachelor asked for a second meeting, she never showed more than a passing interest, especially for my architect, Alphonse Gosset.

The waggoneer's eyes follow her every move as if he's watching a ballet.

"Louise, are you finished there?" I ask, irritated at her mistaken attention. "Help the women sort those grapes, so we can get them crushed before they spoil."

"One moment, Maman." She turns back to the waggoneer.

I gesture for his boss, the vineyard owner, to join me. "I can pay you in my office, Monsieur Beaumont."

Louise whispers something in the waggoneer's ear. I point to her. "Louise, sorting table, please."

She frowns and gives her suitor an apologetic shrug, before she joins the women.

Beaumont waits in my office. "I hope you are right to wait so long to harvest these grapes, Madame Pommery. The entire Champagne is laughing at us, you know."

"Let them laugh, Monsieur Beaumont." I lift the 1874 vintage out of the dewy ice bucket and pour. "This is the first late-harvest champagne. What do you think?"

He holds the glass to the lantern. "Color like a buttercup." His nose hovers over the glass. "Spritely bubbles. Full of life."

"*À votre santé.*" I touch my glass to his, and he takes a sip.

"May I speak frankly?" he says.

"You don't like it?" I take another sip.

"I do like it, Madame. Fresh and bold at the same time."

I lean forward. "But what?"

"But it's like silk when you wanted wool. Not bad, just different." I start to pour more, but he holds up his hand. "Can you afford to waste years convincing champagne drinkers they'd prefer dry champagne, when for a hundred and fifty years they've been taught champagne is sweet?" His eyes cut to the checkbook on my desk.

"Oh, let me pay you." I write out the check and set the wet ink with lavender powder.

He looks at the check. "I feel guilty taking this, knowing the wine won't sell."

I walk him out to the winery. The waggoneer is pointing out good grapes from the bad to Louise as if she needs help after seventeen years of harvests.

"What can you tell me about your waggoneer?" I ask Beaumont.

"Guy? Don't know much, except he's a good worker. He's shown up for harvest three years in a row, ready and willing to learn everything I can teach him."

"Where does he come from?"

"Coast of France, he says. He comes here to learn more about champagne."

"So you trust him?"

"Not particularly. *Vendangeurs* blow in for a couple weeks a year, then disappear with a fistful of money. You don't see most of them again. Why? Have you had a problem with Guy?"

"Not yet." I say and shake his hand. "Thank you for sticking with Pommery, Monsieur. I know other champagne makers want your prime grapes."

He whistles to his crew and waves them to the empty wagon. Several men exchange words with the women before they leave.

Guy walks directly to me, and I cannot turn away. His stained clothes, frayed straw hat, and crude bandana don't seem to fit his dashing demeanor and Breton accent. "Pardon me, Madame, I would really appreciate the opportunity to learn about crushing the grapes. Would you mind if I stay and help?" He glances back at Louise, who smiles. "I would not expect to be paid, of course."

A million thoughts flash through my head like a zoetrope in motion. Louise is a rose to a hive of bees. I owe it to her to make the best possible match. We have appointments this week to meet Doctor Henroit's son who just joined his father's practice, and the DuPont's son who is a lawyer. She should at least marry someone of our own bourgeoisie class, not some migrant worker. Am I too late to give my daughter a better life? Is she to marry a *vendangeur*? Not if I can help it.

"Perhaps another time," I tell him. "We must get these grapes crushed or they'll be mush. We don't have time to teach."

"Then let me haul grapes to the basket presses, at least. I'm strong, and it requires no teaching."

I scoff, but what can I do, we are wasting time. "Check in with my son, Louis, over there. He'll tell you what to do."

I take Louise with me to taste the juice and mark the barrels before they roll them into the cellar. Despite trying to separate the two of them, their eyes search for each other throughout the afternoon.

"Come with me, Louise," I tell her. "Monsieur Vasnier needs us at Butte Saint-Nicaise."

"I'll stay and finish here," Louise says.

"You will come with me." I take her hand and drag her to the gig.

"I want to remind you of our social calls this week with the Henroits and DuPonts," I tell her as I snap the reins.

"You are the worst kind of hypocrite, Maman," she says.

I gasp, holding a sudden pain in my chest. "Louise, it is my job to protect you."

"All my life, I've watched you care for the poor and treat people with respect, no matter their station. Yet, the moment a mere *vendangeur* shows interest in your daughter, you panic." She crosses her arms. "You don't even know Guy, Maman. You must give him a chance."

"What do you know about him? What kind of life can he give you?"

She laughs. "He hasn't asked for my hand. He just wants to take me horseback riding."

If I don't let her go, it's all she'll want. If I do let her go, she may fall in love. As Emily Dickinson wrote, "The heart wants what it wants."

I feel my resolve crumbling. "Where does he want to take you?"

"I told him about our cottage in Chigny, and he said he'd like to see it."

A compromise. "Very well. Have him meet us at Chigny on Sunday, and I will chaperone."

As we drive the gig to the foot of the butte, the pink sunset illuminates the new Pommery Champagne like a fairytale castle. The blue plaster exterior and red brick accents over arched windows and doorways make the Elizabethan neo-Gothic castle even more unique. Romantic turrets with slate roofs, donjon towers, and crenellations will surely inspire even the most boring imagination. The H-shaped configuration opens the castle to the world, inviting guests to visit us.

A boisterous crowd outside the doors yell and jostle about.

"What's happening, Maman?" Louise asks.

"Doesn't look good, does it?" I step down from the gig and we climb the butte.

Miners and builders surround my sculptor, Navlet, and my architect, Gosset. Only Henry's hands planted firmly on their chests keep them apart. My contractors jousting like knights.

"Let's settle this like gentlemen," Henry says. "There is too much to do to get the winery ready for the opening gala."

"You are a narcissist," Gosset sneers, and his builders jeer.

"You are an idiot," Navlet shakes his fist.

"You want a fight, old man?" Gosset darts at Navlet, goading him, then jumps back and darts to the other side.

Navlet tries to follow his sparring. "You are a child, and a child should show respect for a master."

The miners shake their fists in the air.

I see where this could lead: a huge fight between them.

Henry clears the path for Louise and me, pushing through the crowd. "Make way. Make way for Madame Pommery."

"What is the problem here? Why can't you men get along? You are not even working in the same place. Monsieur Navlet is the boss of the crayères, and Gosset is boss of the castle. What is so difficult?"

They both start talking with raised voices, pointing fingers at each other.

"Navlet's gnomes drag stone and dust—"

"Their saws and levies shake the earth—"

"Great clouds of chalk dust—"

"Trembling, causing cracks—"

"Right where we are trying to lay brick—"

"This child has the audacity—"

"Only a fight will settle it."

Henry waves his arms high. "Enough. We've heard enough."

"You are not barbarians, who must kill or be killed," I say. "We can and will talk this out and settle this as adults. Is that understood?"

Young Gosset looks sheepish. Navlet pulls on his beard.

"This has been difficult with two enormous projects going on at one time," I say. "But we are three months to the grand opening gala. Surely, we can find a way to the finish line together."

"The old man is impossible." Gosset turns away and crosses his arms.

Navlet wags his finger at me. "If this child continues his pounding, you will end up with a pile of rubble down there instead of a masterpiece."

Navlet's jaw is immobile, and Gosset's chin juts stubbornly. Their workers stand behind them like opposing armies. What makes men defend their territories with might and violence?

"I think I see the problem here," I say.

"It's him."

"It's him."

They point to each other.

"Monsieur Navlet, may we take Monsieur's construction crew on a tour of the crayères?"

"They can't touch anything."

"If you want this finished in three months, we don't have time for tours," Gosset says.

"We will make the time," I say. "I'd like each miner to take a construction worker down into the mine so you can point out details, and when we finish the crayère tour, we will come up and explore the castle."

The miners and construction workers stare at each other.

"Come on, men, let's do what Madame Pommery suggests." Henry holds out his elbow for me. "May I escort you, Madame?"

In front of everyone? Henry is waiting, and I make a quick decision. "Of course, Monsieur Vasnier. I would love to see the progress."

Curious now, with this unexpected tribute to their work, miners and builders pair up and follow Henry and me down one hundred and sixteen stairs.

"What are you hoping to gain by this exposition?" Henry asks, popping a licorice pastille.

I lean into him, smelling the licorice. "Respect."

He offers me the tin. "You know you want some."

I take a few small candies to give me strength.

The dark gallery is cold and damp. Henry lights more lanterns and illuminates the crayère. The builders gasp in wonder at the chiseled chalk gallery looking like the inside of a giant eggshell.

"Look." A miner gestures up to a square opening to the sky. A rock dove flies into the crayère to her nest in a crevice, feeding worms to her tiny squabs.

Men laugh and point, the hostile ice melting between them.

"Our very own miracle," I say to Henry, stealing his pastilles case.

"You can keep it," he says.

But I give it back with a smile. "I'd rather share."

The builders' hands glide over the polished walls, and they ask miners about their techniques. Conversations spark between groups, asking questions and answering in kind.

Navlet points out the angles of the vaulted ceilings and the perfect archways leading to tunnels.

Henry whispers to me. "How did you know this would work?"

"They speak each other's languages, just a different dialect."

Next, Alphonse Gosset leads the group on a tour of the castle. Henry and I inspect the work on our own. While the stone and brick exterior has been exquisitely crafted, and the gleaming black slate roof is finished, inside is bereft as a barn. No stucco walls, no hearths, no gas lanterns. Only the massive oak beams.

I'm aghast at how much they have yet to do. And fall is quickly turning to winter. This enormous castle will be another year of work at least.

The builders and miners shuffle past, lifting their hats to me as they go. Their comradery warms my heart, but twilight is dwindling and so is my hope to meet my goals.

Henry and I stand alone in the dark citadel, facing my failure.

"Brilliant idea, Madame," Gosset says. "The crews admired each other's work and sympathized with the problems and will work together on solutions."

"That's all very good, Monsieur, but I don't see how you will finish the inside of the production facility before the opening."

He slicks back his hair nervously. "We've been trying to get the stonework and roof done before the weather stopped us. Now, I'm afraid it's too cold to set plaster."

"Perhaps you can delay the party," Navlet says.

I shake my head. "The invitations were sent out early since many guests are traveling from Scotland and England. They've booked their ships and train passages and made reservations."

"I'm sorry, Madame." Gosset shrugs. "I've moved mountains to get this castle built against all odds."

My heart palpitates. "I invited all the people who fought me when I took over the city dump. I invited all the champagne houses who said we couldn't do it. I've invited the hotels, the restaurants, all the vineyard owners who spread rumors we were bankrupt." My voice rises and hot tears pressure my eyes. I know what I'm asking for is unreasonable, but I can't stop somehow. "Hubinet has hired a train car for the top restaurateurs, hoteliers, and sommeliers in London, and the London *Times* editor."

Navlet and Gosset exchange wild-eyed looks and peer longingly toward the massive doors that came from an old Scottish castle.

"If I may comment?" Henry brushes his mustache with his finger. "Madame, the most important thing I've learned from you, is that good things are worth waiting for, like our brut champagne."

My hand flies to my forehead. "That is just it, Henry. The Pommery Brut 1874 is the most delicious champagne we have ever created. I plan to serve it at our opening."

"Your castle will stand for a thousand years, Madame," Gosset says. "You can postpone the party."

"If we postpone the party, we'll disappoint hundreds of customers," I tell him. "And, the entire Champagne will boast loud and long that we could not finish what we started."

The men scratch their chins, look down at their shoes, cross their arms trying to stay warm. Twilight has become night, no moon to dispel my disappointment. I shiver uncontrollably.

"Let's go home and sleep on it," I tell the men. "Things always look brighter in the morning."

Henry helps me to the gig, and things look brighter already. One must count one's blessings and having Henry with me is at the top of my list.

I am pruning the roses in the Chigny garden when Louise's *vendangeur* gallops in, wheat-blond hair flying back off his shoulders, his horse swirling up a dust storm. But what a horse. Sixteen or seventeen hands high with well-formed muscles, dappled as a stormy sky, the stallion follows the subtle commands of his master's hand. Not the typical horse a *vendangeur* would ride.

"Your horse is quite handsome," I say.

He snorts. "For a *vendangeur*, you mean? Madame Pommery, I

am not going to apologize for what I do. I do a fine job, and it is honest, rewarding work."

"I meant nothing by complimenting your horse," I say. "It's just that one doesn't see many horses like that here in the Champagne."

He strokes the horse's neck. "Manny is a Percheron, the finest breed in France, in my opinion. My family raises Percherons. I bring him with me when I come over for harvest." He swings his leg down and dismounts. He stands proud and tall as he strokes his horse. His bright eyes and square jaw are wickedly handsome, like I always imaged Sir Lancelot in stories.

"Where is home, exactly?"

"Guidel on the coast. We grow grapes and verbena. We sell the grapes but use verbena to make our own Verveine du Velay." He rustles in his tooled saddlebag and pulls out a curious bottle of chartreuse green. "I brought you some to try."

"How gracious of you." I suppress a grimace at the sickly-looking brew. One must be parsimonious with honesty when it comes to etiquette.

Louise opens the glass-paned door in a gray wool riding dress with diagonal piping and ebony buttons. Her short top hat sports a wide red satin ribbon, bringing out the blush of her cheeks. "Monsieur Guy, I didn't know you were here. I hope you didn't wait long."

"Your maman was asking about my family and where I come from."

"Don't let her questions scare you away. I'll meet you here in a minute." Louise laughs and walks toward the barn.

When she's out of earshot, I turn to Monsieur Guy. "I expect you to have Louise home by three o'clock, so you can ride home by dark."

His smile disarms me.

"You don't approve of me, do you, Madame Pommery? Is it the fact that I am a lowly *vendangeur* or that I come from somewhere other than the Champagne?" He studies me, and I feel my face heating.

"Neither," I say. "Or both, I guess. How can one trust a *vendangeur* when they come in for harvest and leave when it's over, with no reputation or responsibility to worry about?"

"Then, you'll be relieved to know I am neither free of responsibility nor reputation." His shoulders slump forward. "I have plenty of both to guide my behavior, believe me."

His openness arouses my sympathy.

Louise rides her bay out of the barn. Reaching into her saddle-bag, she pulls out a bottle of 1874 Brut. "I thought we'd take some refreshment at the summit."

"What a treat," he says. "You went out on a limb with this brut champagne, Madame Pommery. I never took you for a gambler."

"She's ruthless at faro." Louise makes a face. "Let's go, Guy."

"Be sure to stay on the ridge where the horses know the path. It gets too rocky down in the valley. I expect you back well before sunset."

Louise tosses up her hand in a wave as she takes off in a canter which quickly accelerates.

"Don't worry, Madame. Your daughter is safe with me." Guy gallops after Louise.

I watch them ride onto the ridge. Louise's hair flows out behind her, and Guy leans forward in his saddle, trying to catch her. She's taunting him, which makes me laugh, and at the same time brings a pang to my heart.

Bringing in the last of the root vegetables from the Chigny garden, I dump them into the sink and pump water over them, scrubbing with a brush. "Turnips, parsnips, and potatoes. These should be good for your stew tonight," I say to Prudence, our Chigny cook whenever the family is in residence.

"How many for dinner, Madame?" She tucks her curls into her mop cap and scrubs mud off the vegetables.

"I suppose I must ask Louise's guest for dinner, since it is almost dark," I say.

"Mademoiselle has a suitor?"

"Oh, I would not call him that. He's a *vendangeur* from the Beaumont vineyard."

Prudence clucks her tongue. "You know what they say about *vendangeurs*."

"No, I don't."

"Picking grapes in September, delivering babies in June." She laughs.

"Prudence, there will be no June babies," I say. Leaving her to the cooking, I find myself at the bar, studying the bottle of Verveine du Velay. I pour a glass of the sticky green stuff and take it out to the veranda to wait for them. Sitting on my porch swing, I swing only as far as my rocking feet allow. The Verveine is good, tasting of lemons and herbs. The sun sets and lights up the entire valley. I stand to see horses coming, but no one is on the ridge. An owl hoots low and lonely.

Prudence sticks her head out of the doorway. "What time shall I serve dinner, Madame?"

"They should have been back by now," I tell her. "I'll let you know when I see them coming." I smile, but my lips feel tight.

"It is freezing out here, Madame. You'll catch your death. Come in by the fire."

"I can't see the ridge from inside. It can't be much longer."

She clucks her tongue and disappears inside, returning with a crocheted blanket that she lays across my shoulders.

"You are shivering," she says.

"Just a few more minutes."

The stars pop out of hiding. There is no moon to see the ridge. Waves of fear pump into my chest. Unable to feel my fingertips, I rub my hands together. Louise is in trouble. The ridge is too narrow to follow with a gig, and I haven't ridden a horse for years. My ears start drumming with my heartbeat, louder and louder.

"Maman, Maman," I hear Louise yell. Opening my eyes, I see her dark silhouette on a horse galloping toward me.

I run to meet her. Her smart riding dress is torn and filthy with black dirt.

"Oh, Louise. Are you all right? What did he do? What did that man do to you?"

"Guy's hurt. A skunk spooked his horse, and he tumbled off the ridge and threw Guy off. Oh, Maman, you must help me."

Adrenaline surges through me. "What about you?"

She nods. "I tried to climb down there, but the slope was too steep, and I kept slipping. I realized I couldn't carry him out by myself, so I climbed out. What do we do?" Her teeth clack against each other, and her shoulders quiver.

291

I help her down from her horse and tie him to the fence. "Come inside, and we'll figure something out." I put my arm around her and take her in.

"We have to help him, Maman." Louise talks between sobs. "I love Monsieur Guy. He proposed to me out on the summit."

My heart falls to my stomach. I settle her in the large wingback chair by the hearth, swaddling her with the crochet blanket.

Prudence pops her head in. "Dinner, Madame?"

"There's been an accident, Prudence. The young man fell into the ravine."

"Down by the Blanchets?" she asks.

"I suppose they would be the closest, wouldn't they? Can you bring Louise some hot tea, and I'll see if the Blanchets can help."

Louise throws the blanket aside. "I'm coming with you."

The Blanchet boys take Guy to the next town for a doctor to set his broken leg. Madame Blanchet serves us napoleon pastry and café au lait. It turns out that since her husband died last year and left their sons vast sheep ranches, she has wanted to find them wives.

When the boys return, Guy is not with them. The Blanchet brothers say the doctor told Guy he needed to stay immobile for three months, so he booked passage on a traveling coach to take him home.

Louise is heartbroken. But Madame Blanchet takes it on herself to change that, inviting Louise to help her with the church bazaar for the week.

While Louise is away, the traveling coach stops at the Chigny cottage. The driver helps Guy down with his crutch under his arm.

"We thought you had left," I tell him.

"The doctor wants my injuries to heal before the long trip," he says. "May I talk to Louise?"

"I'm afraid she's not here," I say, not wanting to give details.

"I asked Louise for her hand in marriage."

My eyebrow arches. "You should have asked my permission."

"I should have," he says. "The moment just washed over me, and I asked her."

"Impetuousness is not a trait I condone."

"There was nothing impetuous about it," he says. "For years I have watched Louise grow into a fine young woman. And I would be honored to make her my wife."

So many things I could say: all of them rude. "Go home, Monsieur Guy. Heal your leg. A *vendangeur* without two good legs is a waste of a good laborer."

"Good laborer." He winces. "Would you slough me off if I was gentry? Owned a castle and land?"

"Monsieur, go home and we will discuss this when you return."

The driver helps him into the coach, and he groans. "I hope that doctor knew what he was doing. My leg doesn't feel right."

"It's always worse before it gets better, I'm told. Bon voyage, Monsieur."

"Tell Louise I meant everything I said," he says through the window. "I'll be back as soon as I can."

"I will." By then, Louise will be engaged to one of the Blanchet boys, if not married.

36

BATTRE LE FER TANT QU'IL EST CHAUD

Strike while the iron is hot

1878. Henry looks up from his desktop and catches me looking at him. I lift my hand with a small wave. We moved his desk into my office to make more room for wine until the new winery is finished. Or that's what I said.

I come behind him and hug his shoulders and nuzzle his neck.

Louis bursts in and immediately covers his eyes. "Oh, my goodness. Sorry to interrupt."

I wave him in and return to my desk.

He opens the London *Times*, grinning broadly. "Pommery changes champagne forever!" he reads the headline.

"Oh my goodness." I reach for Henry's hand and squeeze it.

Louis continues, "Pommery 1874 Brut Nature fetched the highest prices ever paid at the London auction. Until now, the prevailing taste has been for sweet champagne, up to one hundred and forty grams of sugar per liter favored by the Russians. But since 1868, Madame Pommery has worked to create a wine that is dry but not harsh. She experimented with a later harvest date and longer fermentation for an exquisite champagne that is mellow, velvety, and well-balanced. Pommery Champagne has transformed the Brits into staunch champagne lovers."

"Hubinet ordered a railcar of Pommery as soon as possible." Louis hands me his letter. "He wants to invite more people to the grand opening."

I throw up my hands. "Absolutely. Invite anyone who will come."

"But the castle won't be finished," Louis says. "It will be months before we can open."

I take their hands in mine. "This is the moment we've worked for for two decades, when all the stars align, and all our hopes and dreams hang in the balance. This is the time to break all the rules and expectations. We created a champagne against everyone's judgment, and now we will invite them to our new spectacular castle and make the world take notice."

"But how?" Louis scoffs.

"I don't know how we will do it," I say. "I just know we will."

Henry smiles under his lush mustache. "Perhaps this is the right moment to tell you Navlet has agreed to join forces with Gosset to double the effort on the castle."

I clasp my hands together. "See, Louis? That's how we're going to do it."

"Only one problem," Henry says. "Reynard Wolfe said we can't afford the double salaries. He suggested taking a partner."

"Of course he did," I say. "Tell Wolfe to forget it."

Louise wasn't the least bit interested in the Blanchet boys and continued writing Guy, much to my dismay. But she hasn't skimped on planning the grand opening festivities, organizing the reply cards into stacks on her desk in the stone turret of the castle. Even with fireplaces in every room, the stone feels cold. I'll need more than tapestries and velvets to warm up these rooms.

"What is the latest count?" I ask. Now that the party is less than a month away, I am starting to panic.

"Way more people are coming than we can accommodate," Louise says.

I look at her guest list, impressed with her detail: guests' names, when they arrive, where they are staying, and for how long. Pages and pages of entries.

"Over a thousand?" I clutch my throat. "I never thought so many would respond."

"Perhaps we can have different parties for the suppliers and vineyards?" Louise says.

I shake my head. "The vineyards and suppliers are the most important since they are the people who stuck by us through the difficulties."

"We can't possibly feed that many people," Louise says. "And what will we feed them? The usual fare of strawberries, sweetmeats, and pastries taste terrible with the dry brut." She squinches her nose and shimmies her head like when she was a little girl.

I pour us glasses of brut. "What foods would pair well with brut?" I touch my glass to hers. "We have one chance to make an impression."

She swirls the champagne on her tongue. "The brut crispness will cut through rich sauces." She takes another sip. "Also perfect with runny camembert and kumquat jelly."

I let the bubbles tickle my nostrils. "Something savory and sensuous: oysters, foie gras, caviar."

"And smoked trout from the Marne River." Louise's cheeks flush. "I think I understand what food we need now, but how can we get enough staff to serve?"

"Leave it to me." I salute her playfully.

But the truth is, a party this size would overwhelm the service girls I've placed from the orphanage. There is only one place to get more women who know how to please a crowd.

Chantal brings me a calling card at eleven in the morning.

"The Marquis de Polignac," I read aloud. "Charles Marie Thomas Étienne Georges de Polignac? Polignac, Polignac—one of the oldest families in France. Did he say what he wanted?"

"He is an older gentleman, Madame. Quite elegant," she says. "He is accompanied by that *vendangeur* that Mademoiselle Louise likes."

"Monsieur Guy?" I turn the card over in my hand—the family crest of Polignac, a fearsome knight in armor centered on red flourishes. The address: Kerbastic Castle, Guidel, Morbihan, France. The town Guy is from.

"Bring our guests to the salon," I say. "Offer them coffee or tea. And bring a cold bottle of champagne, of course. The 1873 is very good."

I go up to change into something more fitting to meet the Marquis of Polignac. Something sapphire, I think, laughing because I always choose sapphire since my old friend Hubinet insisted it went with my eyes.

The two men put down their cafés au lait and rise when I enter. Monsieur Guy steps forward, limping, and it pains me he has not recovered from the accident.

"Madame Pommery, may I present the Marquis Charles Marie Thomas Étienne Georges de Polignac," he says.

The marquis takes my hand and kisses it in the old way. His sideburns billow out from his jaws to side-whiskers, extending below his cravat. He wears a resplendent suit and shawl-collared vest, and a tucked shirt with cufflinks of the Polignac crest.

"My Lord," I bow my head. "I am honored to make your acquaintance. Please sit down."

The marquis clears his throat. "Please call me Monsieur de Polignac. Titles are antiquated since France has no king."

"I suppose you are right," I say. "Though it seems a shame to lose that part of our history."

With the shock of greeting a marquis, I'm doubly surprised to see Guy dressed as elegantly as the marquis. Instead of his Phrygian cap, rough peasant shirt, trousers, and apron, he is wearing a fine wool suit with his hair tied back. Does he work for the marquis?

"May I offer you champagne?" I say, gesturing to the ice bucket. I wish we had used my silver one to serve the marquis.

"How can I resist when I come to Champagne so infrequently," he answers.

I begin to unwind the wire around the cork, wishing Chantal had used the embroidered linens instead of plain. No time to prepare for the visit, and that is not right.

Guy stands and limps toward me. "May I help you with that, Madame?" He turns the bottle in his hand until I hear the slightest sigh from the release.

"Very good." I pour the coupes on the silver tray and offer one to the marquis, then Guy. Felix rubs against Guy's leg as if they are old friends.

Sitting across from them, I arrange my skirts around me.

"*Au santé.*" I raise my glass and look each of them in the eyes, and we drink together.

"Guy has been telling me about your technique of harvesting later to get a fuller flavor without so much sugar," the marquis says. "It takes courage to change the way things have been for two hundred years." He takes another sip. "I understand you went to finishing schools in Great Britain."

"How did you know that?" I look from one to the other. I certainly never shared that fact with Guy.

"Your lovely daughter, Louise, was kind enough to tell me a bit more about your background," the marquis says. "I am duly impressed with what you have created here."

Putting down my glass, I fold my hands on my lap. "Perhaps you should tell me the nature of your visit."

The marquis looks at Guy, who bends to pet Felix.

"What is it?" I ask. "Where is Louise? Is there something wrong? Is she all right?" I slide to the front of my chair. "What aren't you telling me?"

Guy straightens up. "First, Madame Pommery, allow me to introduce myself properly. My name is Lord Guy de Polignac. I only go by Monsieur Guy when I work as a *vendangeur.*"

"So, this is your father?"

The marquis nods. "Yes, Madame. I am Guy's father, and I did not approve of his working the vineyards. But he wanted to learn everything he could about champagne making."

I've been duped. "You lied to us."

He shakes his head. "I wanted to be treated like the other workers."

I press my fingers to my forehead, remembering how I treated him. In a flash of lucidity, I know why they are here.

"Reynard Wolfe sent you, didn't he? Well, I am not selling Pommery winery. I have worked twenty years to bring it to this point, and I will not stop now." My heart pounds in my throat; flames of heat roar up my chest.

Guy turns his glass around and around. "Actually, I purchased the vineyard from the Beaumont's, where I have been working."

"So now you'll need a winery, but it won't be mine." I stand and point toward the entryway, rudely. "Now, if you'll excuse me, I have work to do."

"Madame Pommery," the marquis says. "If you will please sit down and give my son a chance to speak. His proposition may not be so abhorrent to you."

"I prefer to stand." I cross my arms against my chest and brace for his "proposition," the word itself repugnant.

Guy starts hesitantly. "Your daughter has consented to marry me."

My mouth opens stupidly, and I bite down on my tongue with a needling pain. "Does she know who you really are?"

"Does it matter so much?" He opens his palms in supplication. "All due respect, Madame Pommery, you did not like me as a peasant, and now you do not like me as a noble."

I turn away and stare at the fire. "From my experience, it doesn't pay to wish for a station in life that does not belong to you." Grabbing my handkerchief, I wipe my eyes lest they betray me. "What did Louise answer?"

He huffs. "She said I needed to ask her mother. So here I am, humbly asking permission for your daughter's hand."

"But you will take her away to Kerbastic Castle, and I will never see her." I hate the whine in my voice. "She'll be a *marquise*." Everything I wanted at her age, but I was rejected by the noble class. What if her station in life catches up with her? What if Guy regrets marrying lower than his class?

"I cannot condone lying," I say. "It is against everything I stand for."

"My son just wanted to be treated like everyone else," the marquis defends Guy. "If the *vendangeurs* knew who he was, they wouldn't have taught him so much. They would not have trusted him."

I nod. "Precisely why I cannot trust you now," I tell Guy. "I must turn your proposal down. How can I give my daughter's hand to someone who deceived us?"

37

La goutte d'eau qui fait déborder le vase

The water drop that makes the vase overflow

1878. Louis joins me in the tower over the *porte cochère*, peering down at the procession of carriages arriving for the grand opening gala. Spring green vineyard hills overlap each other to the distant horizon. Cottony clouds glide like angels in the brilliant-blue sky. I squeeze Louis's hand.

"What is Damas putting in the entryway?" he asks me.

"Aren't the aviaries genius?" I clasp my hands together. "Louise and I thought they would surprise guests when they enter the castle, preparing them for the champagne they will taste."

"Who made them?" he asks.

"I thought you knew," I say. "Damas makes them for the rock doves. He is amazing with those birds. I would have thought you were dead during the war if not for those messages."

Louis scoffs. "I hope Louise didn't bring Felix. He'll make a feast of the doves."

The carriages stretch all the way to Reims Cathedral.

"Looks like you got your wish, Maman," Louis says. "People are streaming in from all over the world. Paris, London, Brussels, the South of France."

"Exciting, isn't it?"

"Disastrous, if you ask me." His voice cuts through my joy. "The newspapers are mocking our audacity, building a castle on a dump."

"I thought you'd change your mind once you saw how beautiful the winery turned out," I say, not allowing him to ruin this day.

"This castle winery is an embarrassment we will never live down, just as audacious as inventing a new champagne."

"You may not care for Pommery Brut, but surely you see there is a market for dry champagne."

"Arrogance." He flails his finger at me. "Arrogance in believing your own fairy tales, or is it stupidity to believe you can turn everything and everybody into what you wish them to be? Which is it Maman?"

"Louis, please calm down. How we present ourselves will make all the difference in how our guests perceive Pommery." I try to take his hand, and he pulls away.

"See what you did there?" he says. "You use society rules to manipulate people to see things the way you want them seen."

"Actually, Louis, there was a time I thought all rules were made to be broken. And then, society's rules broke me." I press my thumb and forefinger on the bridge of my nose to relieve the pressure.

"I have no idea what you are trying to say."

I take a deep breath. "Rules are important, and we must understand them to get along in this world, but if we never think beyond the rules, we will miss a lot of opportunities."

"Like Henry Vasnier?" Louis smirks.

"Like Yvonne," I volley back. "You deserve to be happy."

Louis stares out at the carriages, rigs, and wagonettes, and lets out a long sigh. "Perhaps I felt guilty not being here to help you in those early years. Maybe I felt you didn't want me to or didn't believe I could."

"Why should I have insisted you change your dream to help with mine? I wanted you to do what you wanted to. You were getting excellent grades. Traveling Europe with your friends."

He tears up. "When I came back, you'd already forged a direction."

"This winery would not exist without you, Louise, and Henry. Your knowledge of languages, customs, and legal matters opened doors for us in places I never imagined." I grasp his shoulder. "The future of Pommery is in your hands. Yours and Louise's."

He covers my hand on the rail. "Don't say that, Maman."

"None of us knows how many years we have left. We have only today, and today the world is seeing the Pommery of the future, and you and Louise are the faces of our winery."

We walk down the spiral staircase to the balcony where Louise waits for us, tapping her satin slipper toe peeking from under her bustle ballgown of velvet resplendent with beadwork.

"Where have you been?" she says. "Guests are waiting for us."

"Don't worry, sister, dear." Louis kisses her *la bise*. "You kept their attention. You are as beautiful as you can be."

The three of us wave at the cheering crowd below, then proceed down the stairs to welcome them.

"Pommery Champagne is your heritage," I tell them. "Enjoy today, for it is the only day we have."

"Pinch me, Louis." I gaze out at the guests, their voices like millions of champagne bubbles bursting in my ears. The sound of happiness.

Our attention to every detail manifests before me like an elusive dream that finally comes true. The greeters, the docents, the servers, the tour guides—each employee was trained for their job and practiced it to perfection.

As guests arrive, greeters retrieve their calling cards and check off their names from the guest list.

Our docents, handsome in their sapphire wool jackets trimmed in gold satin, give guests souvenir treasure maps of Pommery Castle, the towers, turrets, barrel room, offices, drawing room, and special tasting salon. They share the history of Pommery and the painstaking process of making our champagne.

An orchestra plays Beethoven's *Ode to Joy* to set a festive mood as guests walk into the grand barrel room flanked by two dozen giant hogshead barrels. The aroma of fermenting grapes is intoxicating.

There, guests are offered Pommery champagne poured by the enthusiastic Alhambra courtesans, disguised for the night as winsome maidens in toned-down makeup, watered taffeta blue dresses, and elbow-length gloves to hide their painted nails. The Alhambra has made Pommery their house champagne, and their patrons become Pommery customers as well. I can always tell an Alhambra patron by the color of his cheeks when I ask him where he tasted Pommery. Invariably, he can't remember, but purchases a case or two to take home to his wife.

Every detail is as I planned. Limoges plates, Belgian linen napkins, silver toothpicks. I chose the flute glass over the popular coupe that disperses bubbles and causes the champagne to go flat. Appetizers are passed among the crowd by waiters with silver trays: oysters, cheese gougères, escargots, veal croquettes, and tiny ham croissants, all expertly prepared to accentuate the Pommery Brut.

The world has come to wish us well, or to watch us fall face first into a vat of grape juice. The English have come with their lace and daring décolleté. The Scottish with their kilts. The gentry and bourgeoisie have spared no expense for the occasion with their fine suits and silk dresses. The peasants are dressed in laundered and pressed Sunday best.

The Marquis de Polignac and Guy de Polignac stand at the base of the staircase, dressed in dove-gray suiting with ivory vests and cravats, boutonnières pinned on their lapels. Guy looks anything but relaxed with his stiff jaw and clenched arms, upset I refused his proposal.

Louise tried to reason with me, but when I did not relent, she stopped talking to me. To her credit, she continued to work on the party but would not discuss the Polignacs.

She joins me now on the balcony, her eyes searching the crowd for Guy. When she finds him, their yearning gaze burns in my gullet. If I forbid this marriage, I may lose Louise, and for what? Am I jealous that she would get her nobleman when I did not? I glance at Henry to my left. Of course not. Then what right do I have to protest her choice?

Louis signals Damas above us, and he jumps up to ring the great bell in the bell tower. The resonant sound draws everyone's eyes to the balcony. We have practiced our brief speeches projecting into the vast room, but having a thousand people before us is another thing entirely.

I step forward to the railing and wait for the guests to quiet down. "Welcome ladies and gentlemen." People cup their ears to hear. "It is our great honor to welcome you on this special day to launch our new Pommery Champagne winery. I want to introduce you to my daughter, Mademoiselle Louise Pommery, my son, Monsieur Louis Pommery, and our esteemed director, Monsieur Henry Vasnier, who has been with us from the beginning."

I gesture for Henry to step forward. My quiet, debonair Henry, his mustache woven with gray. My pillar, the one I count on to sustain me in business and in life.

Henry leans over the railing and his strong, assured voice booms over the crowd. "I have had the honor and pleasure of working with Madame Pommery for twenty years, and in that time, we have come to produce half a million champagne bottles a year."

The crowd gasps and applauds, and Henry directs their praise to me.

"Madame Pommery's goal was to build the most beautiful winery in the world, and she never let anyone stop her from achieving that dream. We owe our success to her vision. Without further ado, we want to commemorate this momentous occasion by sabering a nebuchadnezzar bottle of our 1874 Pommery Brut."

Several cellarmen roll in the cart holding the giant nebuchadnezzar containing one hundred glasses of champagne. A gasp of awe arises from the crowd, looking at each other in astonishment. Damas hands me the saber, and I motion for Louise to join me, but she steps back, gazing forlornly at Guy below.

My vision blurs and everything around me fades except Louise's beautiful face marred with heartbreak. My rosebud. I cannot hurt her like this.

I bend over the railing. "I'd like to ask Lord Guy de Polignac up to the balcony."

He pushes through the crowd and strides up the spiral staircase.

I take Louise aside. "You are sure this is what you want?"

Her eyes light as she grabs my hands and nods passionately. "More than anything, Maman."

Guy reaches us and smiles at her with undeniable love.

I whisper to him, "Lord de Polignac, I accept your request for my daughter's hand on one condition. Never lie about who you are again."

"But you never let me tell you the whole story," he says.

I look out at the crowd. "Can it wait, Monsieur?"

He leans forward. "I'm afraid not. I must confess the Polignac's are not wealthy. The Kerbastic Castle takes a fortune to maintain. That's why I was learning to make champagne—to restore Polignac castle."

The crowd watches us, gossiping behind their hands. "Louise, what do you say now, if Marquis de Polignac has no money?"

She takes his hand. "I thought you were a *vendangeur*, so, I say yes. Yes, I will marry you."

I signal Damas to sound the bell, which resonates through the hall. I hold their hands high and project my voice over the crowd. "I wish to announce the engagement of Lord Guy Polignac and my daughter, Mademoiselle Louise Pommery."

I hand the saber to Louise and Guy, and together they glide it against the seam of the bottle. The cork shoots off across the barrel room, spraying the guests with golden bubbles.

Our guests congratulate me, impressed at Louise's engagement and asking how I arranged such a prestigious match. I wonder what they would say if I told them Guy de Polignac is a *vendangeur*.

"My dear Alexandrine." I hear his Scottish accent before the familiar cologne hits me. "Congratulations on your daughter's fiancé, a marquis, no less."

Sean kisses me three times on the cheeks, his cologne heavy and cloying. How I loved it when I was nineteen, the tall, handsome baron that smelled of heather. Now the slender Sean of my youth has grown a paunch and his hair clumps like cauliflower.

"You look surprised to see me," he says, still holding my hand.

"I thought something came up so you couldn't come," I lie—it's the cauliflower hair that surprises me.

"We're all here," he says. "We couldn't miss it. The castle is just as you drew it."

"You remember?"

"How could I forget you drawing Scottish castles? They became something magical." He gestures up to the massive beams, the intricate leaded windows, enormous tapestries on the walls, huge fireplaces blazing at either end. "I should have known you would create your own castle one day. You didn't need me, after all."

His last comment throws me. What can one possibly say to that? Henry saves me from having to answer.

"Excuse me, Madame, but the press conference is starting," he says.

I am taken aback by the contrast between these two men I've loved. My solid and reassuring Henry, or the eccentric baron with his plaid kilt and sunburned face from too many cricket matches.

I look at my timepiece. "Oh, my, please excuse us. We're late for the press conference."

"Where can I find you afterwards?" the Baron asks.

"I'll be leading tours through the crayères," I say, taking Henry's arm.

"Sounds romantic. I wouldn't miss it." He smiles with teeth stained from his pipe I used to think was so distinguished.

Henry and I hurry off to the grape-pressing platform, and I push aside emotions impossible to grapple with at the moment. My daughter is engaged to a noble pauper, my first love has grown old, and a hundred reporters wait to pummel me with questions.

Henry's strong stride reassures me. "I never thought we'd see the Baron again after the duel." He steals a sidelong glance. "He's still quite taken with you."

Rounding the corner, the grape press comes into sight. Reporters crowd around Reynard Wolfe holding court as if he is king.

"Why aren't Louis and Hubinet here with the reporters?"

"After Madame Pommery's husband died, I advised her to go into making champagne." Wolfe sticks his thumbs in those ridiculous striped suspenders. "Pommery has been a steady success since then."

"So it was your idea to make champagne?" A red-haired reporter scrawls in his notebook.

"I've been Madame Pommery's business advisor, banker, and closest friend."

"Can you give us your full name for print?"

"Reynard Wolfe, from a noble Rhineland family."

Finally, Louis and Hubinet appear, walking to the stage from the opposite side.

A fellow with a feather in his hat asks the next question. "How was Madame Pommery able to finance such an operation during the Franco-Prussian war?"

"Business is not Madame's strong suit," Wolfe says. "She is a talented champagne maker, but the instability of winery finances is something I juggle constantly."

"That loathsome rat," I say between clenched teeth.

"Is that why she arranged her daughter's marriage to the Polignac family?" the reporter asks. "To keep the winery afloat?"

Henry and I climb the platform stairs just as Louis and Hubinet do. "Thank you, Monsieur Wolfe. We'll take over from here." I gesture to Louis and Henry. "Please escort Monsieur Wolfe to his carriage."

Louis and Henry stronghold Wolfe, and there can be no mistake what is happening. Reporters scrawl furiously on their pads.

"I'm sorry I'm late, gentlemen." I gesture to my side. "This is Monsieur Hubinet, Pommery's sales agent from London. We can answer your questions."

"What about the marriage to the Polignac family?" the reporter asks again.

"I would never offer my daughter's hand to finance our winery. Nor would my daughter allow it. She is a modern woman with a mind of her own."

Hands go up, and I choose the front-row reporter with slicked-back hair and an old-fashioned stock tie.

"What position does Monsieur Wolfe hold at Pommery?"

"Reynard Wolfe has no position in Pommery, past, present or future." I scan the crowd with a commanding stare. "If there are questions about champagne, I am happy to answer them."

Hubinet and I answer questions about harvesting, how weather and terroir affect the taste of the grapes.

"I wanted to make a champagne that can be partaken as an aperitif or throughout dinner," I say. "You'll never go back to sticky sweet champagne."

A reporter blurts out, "How do you respond to competitors who say Pommery Brut tastes like razor blades slitting your throat?"

Hubinet reaches into his pocket for newspaper clips. "Let me read a few headlines. 'Pommery starts a revolution in Champagne.'" He goes to the next clipping. "No one will drink the sweet stuff after tasting Pommery Brut." He pulls out a third. "Pommery's dry champagne corners the English champagne market." And a fourth. "Madame Pommery takes Europe by storm." Hubinet glances at me. "I can assure you that in one hundred years, champagne will be forever changed because of Madame Pommery's vision." He waves in servers with trays. "And if you don't believe me, try another glass and educate your palate to tasting champagne as it was meant to be. Like a beautiful woman naked in the moonlight."

"Oh, I like that analogy." I smile at the reporters.

Hubinet and I take the reporters to the crayères, where my old Scottish group greets me with *la bise*. Elizabeth, Helen, Isla, Frieda, Grace, and Olivia are all now duchesses, marchionesses, or countesses, as they were bound to be. Hubinet introduces each noble couple to starstruck reporters who write down their names carefully on their pads.

Sean brings over a lovely young woman, close to Louise's age.

"Madame Pommery," he says. "I would like you to meet the Baroness of Stellarmane."

"So wonderful to meet you, baroness," I say. "Your father and I are old friends."

She swallows hard and turns bright red, staring hard at Sean.

"I believe you misunderstood," Sean says. "The baroness is my wife."

My fist flies to my mouth. "I beg your pardon. I knew you had a daughter, I assumed—"

Henry comes to my aide, holding my cape. "Shall we go down? Several groups are exploring the crayères already." He drapes the cape around my shoulders.

"We must find our people." The baroness drags Sean away.

"What gave her a hornet in her corset?" Henry takes my arm and starts down the hundred and sixteen stairs, lit by torches licking the walls with their flames.

"I will tell you later," I whisper. "Are you sure Navlet finished in time?"

His grimace looks ghoulish lit by the torches. "He's angry you're showing his sculpture tonight, when it won't be finished for years."

"But he let you see it?"

"He refused to show it to me." His mouth quirks. "And he didn't come tonight, either."

A chill draft from below creeps up my skirts, and I shiver.

"Don't worry about it." Henry slides his arm under my cape and squeezes my waist.

"Better," I say and continue down.

The group giggles and babbles joyously as we lead them down into the belly of the butte.

At the bottom of the stairs, Alhambra courtesans serve glasses of champagne, and our sapphire-suited docents lead groups through the tunnels, giving commentary along the way.

"There are eighteen kilometers of tunnels connecting the galleries." The docent points to the hand-lettered street signs. "Each tunnel is named for new markets where Pommery champagne is sold: Amsterdam, Buenos Aires, New York, Brussels, London, of course, Timbuktu."

"What a splendid surprise." Hubinet claps his hands together. "Gives me incentive to open more markets."

"Wait until you see our *pièce de résistance*," I tell him.

We join the rest of the party in the dark, vast gallery. Alhambra girls refresh guests' champagne glasses for the big unveiling. The enormous bas-relief is shrouded in black like when my husband died.

"I asked them to cover it with muslin, not black crepe," I tell Henry. "It's like a funeral shroud."

"No one will remember the color of the shroud."

Damas and the miners light the lanterns under Navlet's immense tableau, and Henry and I take our places on either side of the sculpture. The crowd quiets in anticipation.

I smile at our guests. "For ten years, we've been excavating these ancient Roman crayères to store our champagne. I commissioned the renowned sculptor, Gustave Navlet, to create this immense sculpture in these hallowed crayères to represent the joy of champagne, which we will unveil now. Pommery presents *Fête de Bacchus*."

Henry and I pull off the shroud and it takes me a moment to register what I am seeing.

Gasps of outrage ricochet off the walls, followed by a backlash of silence.

"Oh, my heavens." The baroness faints into Sean's arms, and docents carry her up the stairs.

My eyes must be playing tricks on me. The sculptured mural *Fête de Bacchus* portrays a drunken revelry of nude gods and goddesses. Entirely naked except for the occasional swath of organdy, voluptuous women shamelessly flaunt prominent breasts and wide hips with a stunning sensuality. A maiden pours wine from a vessel. A cherub plucks a harp, and another blows a pan flute, while other cherubs nibble grapes from each other's hands. A bevy of nude women adorn the god Bacchus with a grape crown and grapevine sash, drinking wine and dancing around him. Looking more closely, I recognize the faces of Alhambra courtesans, and I'm torn between wonderment and shock.

"It's beautiful, Alexandrine. So beautiful." Henry kisses my cheeks in congratulations or consolation. I'm not sure which.

I look up again at *Fête de Bacchus*, a euphoric gathering of gods and goddesses enjoying champagne, for once, totally free of daily responsibility and woes. Champagne has lifted the weight of the world from their shoulders. The music, the dancing, the laughter, free-flowing affection, celebrating this joyful moment in life. Navlet captured what I've been striving for with champagne.

"What do you see?" Henry asks me.

"Joy and lightness," I say, clinking his glass. With new conviction, I raise my glass to the stunned crowd.

Hubinet steps forward, applauding wildly. "Bravo, Bravo!"

The reporters join him, howling and clapping. Then my Scottish friends shout out their bravos. French friends and neighbors thrust their fists into the air and cheer. A triumphant noise like a million birds chirruping in a grand oak tree.

Their joy is mirrored in the *Fête de Bacchus* sculpture for eternity here in this magical underground sanctuary.

Gustave Navlet steps into the light dressed in a formal black suit and black ascot. I go to him and grasp his hand, bowing several times. The applause starts all over again.

PART V

1889-1890

"God, daily life is so lovely!"
~Jeanne Alexandrine Pommery

38

SCANDALEUX, COMME DES CASSEROLES ATTACHÉES À SON DERRIÈRE

Scandal-ridden, like pans tied to her behind

1889. After Louise delivers my first grandchild, Melchior de Polignac, and Guy takes over the vineyards, Pommery Champagne grows by leaps and bounds, under Henry's wise and steady leadership as director.

We do not care what people say about us not being married; it has never come between us. If I married, my husband would own the winery by law, and Louis and Louise would not inherit Pommery. Henry's sacrifice makes me love him all the more since our love is about us, not possessions. Besides, Henry is generously compensated as director. Money is no longer the issue it once was.

We begin planning our dream home on Butte Saint-Nicaise. No effort will be spared to make our Villa Demoiselle a jewel of art nouveau architecture. We meet with the greatest artists for stained-glass windows, sculpted fireplaces, wood carvings, custom furniture, murals, and chandeliers. We travel Europe visiting Pommery Champagne accounts and shopping for art and furnishings for our exquisite Villa Demoiselle.

But I don't have my usual energy while we are window shopping at the most prestigious art galleries in Paris. My chest is congested, and I can't get Wolfe's slander out of my mind. After we pulled our accounts from his bank, he's been spreading rumors that Pommery is going bankrupt. Never mind that our sales have exploded. The more successful we are, the more Wolfe dishonors us with our vineyards and suppliers.

"You seem distracted," Henry says. "Perhaps you'd like a café au lait or glass of champagne?"

"Oh, Henry, let's go in. This is the best gallery in Paris." I pull open the door, and a bell rings. "I'm just upset we lost three vineyard contracts because of Wolfe's malicious lies."

"You must not let that man get you so riled up." Henry holds the door for me. "Guy is buying more vineyards for Pommery. Then we won't have to worry about what Wolfe says."

"You are welcome to look around," the art dealer greets us, holding his finger up in the air. "I'm just finishing up here." Then he turns back to his client.

We stroll from painting to painting, but I'm oblivious to what I'm seeing. My cough turns into a fit. All I can think is how to get Wolfe to stop spreading lies.

"He is ruining the Pommery reputation," I whisper. "If people think we don't pay our bills, the good things we've done for the community and our employees will seem like a fraud."

A tall man in cowboy boots shakes the art dealer's hand and leaves.

The dealer's pencil mustache twitches in distaste as he tucks an envelope into his vest. "It's a shame that American will steal away a French treasure." He gestures to a huge painting. "The Louvre wants it but can't afford the opening bid."

"*The Gleaners*," I say. "By Jean-François Millet."

"You know it?" he says.

"Only by reputation. My daughter and I used to watch gleaners in the fields." I study the painting, feeling that grip in my chest for women doing whatever it takes to feed their families.

"*The Gleaners* is a rare painting, indeed." The dealer adjusts the lamp to illuminate the brush strokes. "Paintings this large usually depict royalty or religious figures, never peasants working in the fields. Here Millet depicts the peasants' intimacy with nature, as opposed to bourgeoisie or noblemen."

"Please excuse my ignorance, but what does *The Gleaners* refer to?" Henry asks.

"Gleaning is the act of scouring the field in search of crops missed during the first harvesting," he says. "These peasant women are raking up the scarce remains of grain, a task only the poorest and most desperate of society would lower themselves to."

"Look at the meager sheaves in the women's hands compared to the abundant stacks gathered by the male farmers in the background," I point out to Henry.

"That American was only interested in investment," the dealer says.

"What did the American bid?" I ask.

He scoffs. "I cannot tell you that in a secret bid."

"But could you suggest what the painting will go for?" I tilt my head and smile.

"Let me check, Madame." The broker goes to his office.

Henry leans into my ear. "Are you thinking of the painting for Villa Demoiselle? It is not art nouveau, of course."

"I'm moved by what Millet is saying with this painting," I tell him.

"It looks like peasants harvesting to me." Henry squints at the painting.

"Millet is making a bold social statement. Look at his brutal portrayal of these hunched women paupers scraping up kernels to feed their families. I understand that."

Henry squeezes my hand. "Your heart extends to your taste in art."

The dealer returns. "I think a bid of three hundred thousand francs would secure the painting."

I start coughing into my handkerchief.

Henry rubs my back. "That is a lot of money for a social statement, Alexandrine."

"You are right, Henry." I tap my forefinger on my lips, contemplating a brash and perfectly ludicrous idea.

Henry narrows his eyelids. "What's going on in that beautiful mind?"

I clear my throat as delicately as possible. "How does one make a secret bid?"

Newspapers report that an American won the secret bid on the famous French painting *The Gleaners*. A couple of days later, I'm in the salon when Henry brings me a telegram with a different story entirely. We message our family to join us.

Henry opens a bottle of cold champagne. "Let's see how the 1885 vintage is tasting."

Louise takes off her wine-stained apron and perches on the footstool by my chair. "Is everything all right, Maman? How's that cough?"

Guy and their son arrive. Melchior runs to me, breathless. Ah, to be ten years old again.

"We got here as soon as we could." His large brown eyes scan my face. "Do you feel all right, Grand-mère?"

I open my arms. "I'd feel a lot better with a hug." Closing my eyes, I smell his head as I did when he was a baby. A hug from Melchior is all I need to celebrate this day.

A warm hand touches my shoulder, and I open my eyes. Louis stands above me, his brows drawn together. "What's wrong, Maman? Are you worse?"

"Actually, I'm feeling much better today." I gasp for breath. "Henry and I have an announcement."

Louise covers her mouth like she swallowed a fly.

I point to her and smile. "It is not what you are thinking." She's such a romantic—she wants us to get married, though we've been over that.

Henry serves champagne and we raise our glasses. "We are celebrating the fact that we won the silent bid for the rare painting *The Gleaners*."

Guy toasts our glasses. "Congratulations, that's wonderful."

Louise grimaces. "But the newspaper reported an American won."

Henry smiles. "The art dealer said the American boasted to reporters before the winner was selected." He gazes at me. "The owner preferred *The Gleaners* stay in France."

Louise kisses me on both cheeks. "Congratulations, Maman. I remember our afternoon watching the gleaners. I know how much it means to you."

"Where will you hang it?" Louis glances at the walls covered with art we've collected. "You'll have to wait for your new house to be built."

I reach for Henry's hand. "Actually, I'd like it delivered directly to the Louvre."

"But you love that painting," Henry says.

"In the Louvre, the rest of France can see it," I say. "And we can visit anytime we like."

"A generous donation, Madame." Guy raises his glass to me.

"The donation is not entirely selfless." I smile mischievously. "Soon all the newspapers in Europe will report that Pommery donated a rare treasure to the Louvre. And Reynard Wolfe will never again be able to spread lies about our finances."

Louis hoots. "Touché, Maman."

I drink my champagne, which is the only thing that relaxes my constricted chest.

Henry bends down to kiss me. "You are a constant surprise, Alexandrine."

39

CHAQUE JOUR DE TA VIE EST UN FEUILLET DE TON HISTOIRE QUE TU ÉCRIS.

Every day of your life is a sheet of the story you write.

1890. Melchior visits my bedchamber carrying a bouquet of roses tied with string.

"What have we here, Melchior?" Henry asks.

"I picked them for Grand-mère up at Pommery Castle," he says, sitting on my bed. His face crinkles with worry. "I figured if you can't walk up there with me, I'd bring the roses to you." He holds my hand, and it feels warm and callused from winery work.

"Very thoughtful, Melchior." It's difficult to talk now, but his sweet face keeps me trying.

"Grand-mère, I was thinking that empty field up at Butte Saint-Nicaise would make a nice sporting park for the children of Reims," he says.

"Maybe your grand-père could help you with that."

He turns to Henry. "There are people out on Reims Square who want to celebrate Grand-mère's birthday."

"My birthday is not for a month yet," I tell him.

"They want to celebrate early," Melchior says, eyes brimming with tears.

Henry peeks behind the window shade. "You are going to want to see this." Pulling the cord, he rolls up the shade.

The Reims cathedral bells begin to peal. The sun streams in on the quilt the auxiliary ladies brought me when I fell ill.

Outside the window, the entire square is filled with people holding bouquets.

"Oh, my goodness, Melchior. What a heavenly birthday surprise." But, in my heart I know why they are here.

Henry raises the window, and I hear the sweet voices of the orphanage children singing "Joyeux Anniversaire." He props pillows behind my back, and I pick out familiar faces of my friends, family, employees, the auxiliary, Saint Remi volunteers, our vineyards, and suppliers.

One by one, each person walks up and waves and presents their bouquet of roses on the porch and in the garden, and when those are full, they pile them onto the walkways and street. Hundreds of bouquets.

"Happy birthday, Grand-mère." Melchior smiles with perfect, white teeth.

In my excitement, that dreaded cough starts, wracking my aching lungs. Henry helps me drink some water.

Melchior wipes tears from his cheeks.

"You mustn't cry for me, Melchior." I stroke his hand. "I have had the most beautiful life with my family." I squeeze his fingers the best I can. "And now I have you to carry on Pommery Champagne and pass it down to your children when the time comes."

Melchior nods and smiles through his tears. "The most beautiful winery in the world."

— THE END —

EPILOGUE

Madame Pommery, Creator of Brut Champagne, is a novel blending fiction and fact.

Jeanne Alexandrine Pommery died on March 18, 1890, in Chigny-les-Roses, near Reims. She was the first woman to receive a French state funeral. Twenty thousand people gathered in the streets of Reims to honor her great contributions to the Champagne industry and the city. A tribute was given by French President Jean Casimir-Perier who issued a decree changing the name of Chigny, her country home, to Chigny-les-Roses, in an ode to her love of roses.

After Madame Pommery died, her daughter Louise ran the House with husband Prince Guy de Polignac. The Polignac family continued to run the business until 1979. The brand continues the Pommery family traditions today. The connection with art continues through support for artists and exhibitions, both local and worldwide, and fun, contemporary branding through the Pommery POP collections.

Today, the Pommery Estate is owned by Belgian entrepreneur Paul-Francois Vranken and holds more than twenty million bottles in the 18km of underground chalkpit caves. More than 120,000 people from around the globe visit this magnificent property in the heart of the city of Reims annually and equally enjoy the exhibition of contemporary art set up in the caves.

Henry Vasnier continued as director, and Louis and Louise were managers of Pommery Champagne. Louise attended to the activities of the champagne house, but when Henry Vasnier and her brother Louis died the same year, 1907, her son Melchior de Polignac took the direction of the Champagne house.

Melchior de Polignac became head of Pommery in 1907. He used his wealth to support the city of Reims, building Parc Pommery and sporting facilities, which he made available to the people of the city.

Polignac financed the building of Reims Athletic College. In 1921 he became an original member of the International Olympics Committee Executive Board and worked with the Organizing Committee of the 1924 Olympics. After Melchior de Polignac's death in 1950, the Polignac family remained the owner of Pommery until the end of the 1980s and is now owned by the Vranken-Pommery-Monopole.

Henry Vasnier was director of Pommery after Madame Pommery died. He went on to build Villa Demoiselle, an original collaboration between himself and Madame Pommery. This tribute to Art Nouveau and Art Deco architecture was constructed in 1909 on Reims' Boulevard Henry Vasnier by the architect Louis Sorel (1867-1934). The Villa is set on magnificent grounds designed by Edouard Redont, also the designer of the famous Parc Pommery that made Pommery Champagne France's foremost patron of sports.

The project brought together stained-glass windows by master glazier Auguste Labouret; sculpted fireplaces and wood carvings by Camille Lefèvre; furniture by Tony Selmersheim; paintings by Georges Picard; murals by Félix Aubert; chandeliers from the Baguès workshops. No effort was spared to make the Villa Demoiselle a jewel of Champagne's architectural heritage.

Adolphe Hubinet is lauded as the foremost wine agent in London during the late nineteenth century. His marketing techniques catapulted Pommery Champagne to the top of the champagne market. He invented the idea of "house style" and the creation of dated vintage champagne as an exclusive branded product. He continued to raise the prices of Pommery champagne and limit distribution to create the illusion of scarcity. He advertised Pommery Champagne lavishly in European newspapers and periodicals of the day to promote the brand.

ACKNOWLEDGMENTS

My toast of gratitude:

"Here's to the magic of bubbly wine
An evening with friends so true
There's none I'd rather enjoy them with
Than you, and you, and you!"

Thank you to Sofie Landry, Head of Heritage and Patronage at Vranken - Pommery Monopole for your patience with my persistent questions.

Thank you to my editors, Barbara Henderson and Rachael Mortimer.

Thank you to my friends, readers, bloggers, reviewers, and fabulous Review Crew! No one would ever see this novel without you!

Thank you to my publicist, Cindy Conger, who keeps everything rolling!

I'd love to pop a bottle of Pommery with all of you right now!

Please post a review for *Madame Pommery, Creator of Brut Champagne* on Goodreads, Amazon, Bookbub, and your favorite book retail site. Sign up for Rebecca Rosenberg's email list on her webstie.

Connect with Rebecca:

Website: http://www.rebecca-rosenberg.com

Facebook: https://www.facebook.com/rebeccarosenbergnovels/

Amazon Author Page https://www.amazon.com/stores/Rebecca-Rosenberg/author/B075WGKJ3Y

Goodreads https://www.goodreads.com/rebeccarosenberg

BookBub: https://www.bookbub.com/profile/rebecca-rosenberg

Pinterest: https://www.pinterest.com/rebecca7487

MADAME POMMERY
READING GUIDE:

1. When Madame Pommery's husband dies, why doesn't she retire to her country cottage as everyone advises her to?

2. What were Madame Pommery's advantages and disadvantages in starting a winery?

3. Who were her greatest supporters and who were her greatest critics?

4. Why is champagne such a unique wine? Why is it more difficult to make?

5. What was Madame Pommery's vision for champagne? How was it different than her predecessor's, Veuve Clicquot?

6. What revolutionary things did Madame Pommery do to accomplish her vision of champagne? How long did it take her to succeed?

7. What were the obstacles impeding Madame Pommery's success in her winery?

8. Who were Madame Pommery's adversaries, and how did she overcome them? Who was the worst adversary?

9. Who had surprising talents that ended up helping Madame Pommery? Who was the most unlikely person that helped her?

10. What lessons does Madame Pommery learn about the class system of Nobles, Bourgeoisie, and Poor? What did she want for her daughter?

11. What was the Franco-Prussian war all about? How did it cause a civil war between Communards and the French government in Paris?

12. What was Prussia's goal in baiting Napoleon III to declare war on them? Did they want to take over France, or was there something more secretive? Did they accomplish their goal?

13. Madame Pommery had many interests and passions. What legacy did she leave behind?

Other Books by Rebecca Rosenberg

CHAMPAGNE WIDOWS
Publisher's Weekly BookLife Prize
Historical Novel Society's Editor's Choice

Champagne, France, 1800. Twenty-year-old Barbe-Nicole inherited Le Nez (an uncanny sense of smell) from her great-grandfather, a renowned champagne maker. She is determined to use Le Nez to make great champagne, but the Napoleon Code prohibits women from owning a business. When she learns her childhood sweetheart, François Clicquot, wants to start a winery, she marries him despite his mental illness.

Soon, her husband's tragic death forces her to become Veuve (Widow) Clicquot and grapple with a domineering partner, the complexities of making champagne, and six Napoleon wars, which cripple her ability to sell champagne. When she falls in love with her sales manager, Louis Bohne, who asks her to marry, she must choose between losing her winery to her husband, as dictated by Napoleon Code, or losing Louis.

In the ultimate showdown, Veuve Clicquot defies Napoleon himself, risking prison and even death.

Buy now at https://www.amazon.com/Champagne-Widows-First-Woman-Clicquot-ebook/dp/B09D2HTJY9/ref=sr_1_3?crid=2OWI9RB6NK8T4&dchild=1&keywords=champagne+widows&qid=1629994623&s=digital-text&sprefix=champagne+widows,aps,190&sr=1-3

Champagne Widows

"This effervescent historical novel paints a richly detailed portrait of the enterprising Veuve Clicquot. The twinned plots of Clicquot and Napoleon Bonaparte's rise and fall are filled with detail that give life to this far-off time. The prose is light, yet detailed, and peppered with moments of wry humor. Napoleon's characterization is well-crafted and give his character new life. Clicquot's character is charming, and readers will love getting to know her. Rosenberg has a superb eye for blending humor with drama."
-*Publisher's Weekly* BookLife Prize

"Barbe-Nicole is a captivating main character, particularly with her inheritance of 'Le Nez' and the effect on her life. From grapes to pigs, the adventures she gets into with her nose are fascinating and are described in detailed and engaging ways. The champagne empire she builds is admirable, as is her relationship with Francois and its challenges."
-*WRITER'S DIGEST 2022*

"Barbe-Nicole is a strong, determined woman, who defies Napoleon to make her business a success. Fascinating details about winemaking and everything that goes into it: the soil, climate, barrels, glass bottles, and the various blends of grapes. All these things and more affect the smell and flavor of the wine. I felt I could smell the wine along with Barbe-Nicole, because Rosenberg's descriptions are so vivid. Barbe-Nicole's narrative is interspersed with brief chapters about the rise and fall of Napoleon, and the evil

advisor known as the Red Man, a devil figure disguised as a coachman, who encourages him to conquer Europe. Some of the most moving parts are the scenes where Barbe-Nicole harvests the grapes along with other women who were widowed by Napoleon's wars."
-Editor's Choice, Historical Novel Society

"**Vivid, lively, and packed with psychological and social inspection,***Champagne Windows* is highly recommended for women who enjoy passionate stories of friends, fine wine, and the delicate lines between personal and political empowerment." ~Donna Donovan, Senior Reviewer, *Midwest Reviews*

"**These first known women of Champagne/Sparkling winemaking** may not have even realized how strong they were until they had to learn and do it all to survive for themselves and their wineries!" ~Penny Gadd-Coster, ExecutiveDirector of Winemaking, Rack & Riddle

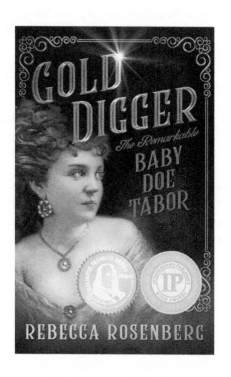

GOLD DIGGER: THE REMARKABLE
BABY DOE TABOR

DOUBLE GOLD for GOLD DIGGER! 2020 IBPA and IPPY Awards for fiction! One look at Baby Doe Tabor and you know she was meant to be a legend of the Wild West and Gilded Age! She was just twenty years old when she came west to work a gold mine with her new husband. Little did she expect that she'd be abandoned and pregnant and left to manage the gold mine alone. But that didn't stop her! She fell in love with an old married prospector, twice her age. Horace Tabor struck the biggest silver vein in history, scandalously divorced his wife, became a US Senator, and married Baby Doe at the US capitol with President Arthur in attendance. Though Baby Doe Tabor was renowned for her beauty, her fashion, and even her philanthropy, she was never welcomed in polite society. Her friends were stars they hired to perform at their Tabor Grand Opera House: Sarah Bernhardt, Oscar Wilde, Lily Langtry, opera star Emma Abbott. Discover how the Tabors navigated the worlds of scandal, greed, wealth, power, and politics in the wild days of western mining.

Gold Digger: The Remarkable Baby Doe Tabor

"**10 out of 10!** An engaging and beautifully written story, this fact-based novel celebrates the endurance of the human spirit in one woman's determination to survive." -*Publisher's Weekly* BookLife Prize

"**...An accomplished and absorbing novel**...Rosenberg brings forth a fine historical inspired by Elizabeth McCourt Tabor, better known as Baby Doe whose rags-to-riches and back to rags again story made her a famous figure in history. The skillful plotting and richly crafted characters get readers immediately drawn in. Rosenberg's poignant account delivers a stunning historical, and the open-ending climax makes readers wait eagerly for the next installment." -*The Prairies Book Review*

"**A gripping story of female grit and resilience.** Baby Doe has a wonderful, indomitable spirit, and Rosenberg brings her physical and emotional challenges vibrantly to life."-*Historical Novel Society*

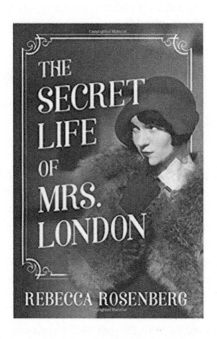

THE SECRET LIFE OF MRS. LONDON
IPPY Gold Medal Award

San Francisco, 1915. As America teeters on the brink of world war, Charmian and her husband, famed novelist Jack London, wrestle with genius and desire, politics and marital competitiveness. Charmian longs to be viewed as an equal partner who put her own career on hold to support her husband, but Jack doesn't see it that way... until Charmian is pulled from the audience during a magic show by escape artist Harry Houdini, a man enmeshed in his own complicated marriage. Suddenly, charmed by the attention Houdini pays her and entranced by his sexual magnetism, Charmian's eyes open to a world of possibilities that could be *her* escape.

As Charmian grapples with her urge to explore the forbidden, Jack's increasingly reckless behavior threatens her dedication. Now torn between two of history's most mysterious and charismatic figures, she must find the courage to forge her own path, even as she fears the loss of everything she holds dear.

The Secret Life of Mrs. London

"**An impressively original and exceptionally well-crafted novel** by an author who is a master of character- and narrative-driven storytelling, Rebecca Rosenberg's *THE SECRET LIFE OF MRS. LONDON* is an inherently riveting and thoroughly reader-engaging story from beginning to end and feature[s] many an unexpected plot twist and turn." -*Midwest Book Review*

"**Interesting, and based on the actual lives of the participants** ... Learning more about Jack London was enjoyable, as well as seeing early feminist examples."-*Historical Novel Society*

. . . . . .

"... **Rosenberg paints an immensely intriguing portrait of a marriage** and tells it in an accomplished lyrical prose that captures each moment with poetic intensity." -*Prairies Book Review*

. . . . . .

"**Women of all ages and historical fiction fans will love this book.**" -*Online Book Club*

Excerpt from *Champagne Widows*

The Nose

Reims, Champagne, France 1797. Grand-mère sways over the edge of the stone stairs into the cavern, and I step between her and eternity, dizzy from the bloody tang of her head bandage.

"Let's go back. We'll come another time." I try to turn her around, so we don't tumble into the dark crayère, but she holds firm. "There won't be another time if I know your maman and her heretic doctor."

They drilled into Grand-mère's skull again for a disease they call hysteria. The hole was supposed to let out evil spirits, but the gruesome treatment hasn't stopped her sniffing every book, pillow, and candle, trying to capture its essence, agitated that her sense of smell has disappeared.

"This is how you know you are alive, Barbe-Nicole." She taps her nose frantically. "The aromas of brioche fresh from the oven, lavender water ironed into your clothes, your father's pipe smoke. You must understand. Time is running out." Her fingernails claw my arm, the whale oil lamp sputtering and smoking in her other hand.

"Let me lead." Taking the stinking lantern, I let her grip my shoulders from behind. Grand-mère shrunk so much, she's my height of five feet, though she's a step above.

For as long as I remember, she has tried to justify my worst fault. My cursed proboscis, as Maman calls my over-sensitive nose, has been a battle between us since I was little. I remember walking with her through town, avoiding chamber pots dumped from windows, horse excrement paving the roads, and factories belching black gases. Excruciating pain surged to my nose, making my eyes water and sending me into sneezing fits. Maman left me standing alone on the street.

From then on, my sense of smell swelled beyond reason. Mostly ordinary odors, but sometimes I imagine I can smell the stink of a lie. Or the perfume of a pure heart. Or the heartbreaking smell of what could have been.

Maman complains my cursed sense of smell makes me too par-ticular, too demanding, and frankly, too peculiar. Decidedly troublesome traits for a daughter she's tried to marry off since I was sixteen. But why must the suitors she picks have to smell so bad?

Grand-mère squeezes my shoulder. "It is not your fault you are the way you are, Barbe-Nicole; it's a gift." She chirped this over and over this afternoon until Maman threatened to have the doctor drill her skull again.

The lantern casts ghoulish shadows on the chalk walls as my bare toes reach for the next stair and the next. I'll have hell to pay if we're caught down here. Part of me came tonight to humor Grand-mère, but part of me craves more time with her. I've witnessed her tremors, her shuffling feet, her crazy obsessions, which now seem to focus on my nose.

As we descend, the dank air chills my legs; feathery chalk dust makes my feet slip on the steps. The Romans excavated these chalk quarries a thousand years ago, creating a sprawling web of crayères under our ancient town of Reims. What exactly does Grand-mère have in mind bringing me down here? The lantern throws a halo on grape clusters laying on the rough-hewn table.

Ah, she wants to play her sniffing game.

"How did you set this up?" My toes recoil from cold puddles of spring water.

"I'm not dead yet," she croaks. Taking off her fringed bed shawl, she ties it like a blindfold over my eyes. "Don't peek."

"Wouldn't dare." I lift a corner of the shawl, and she raps my fingers like the nuns at St.-Pierre-Les-Dames where Maman sent me to school before the Revolution shut down convents.

"Quit lollygagging and breathe deep." Grand-mère's knobby fingertips knead below my cheekbones, opening my nasal passages to the mineral smell of chalk, pristine groundwater, oak barrels, the purple aroma of fermenting wine.

But these profound smells can't stop me fretting about Maman's determination to marry me off before the year is out. I told her I'd only marry a suitor that smells like springtime. "Men do not smell like that," she scolded.

But men do. Or one did, anyway. He was conscribed to war several years ago, so he probably doesn't smell like springtime anymore. His green-sprout smell ruined me for anyone else.

Grand-mère places a bunch of grapes in my hands and brings

it to my nose. "What comes to you?"

"The grapes smell like ripening pears and a hint of Hawthorne berry."

She chortles and replaces the grapes with another bunch. "What about these?"

Drawing the aroma into the top of my palate, I picture gypsies around a campfire, smoky, deep, and complex. "Grilled toast and coffee."

Her next handful of grapes are sticky and soft, the aroma so robust and delicious, my tongue longs for a taste. "Smells like chocolate-covered cherries."

Grand-mère wheezes with a rasp and rattle that scares me. I yank off the blindfold. "Grand-mère?"

"You're ready." She slides me a wooden box carved with vineyards and women carrying baskets of grapes on their heads. "Open it."

Inside lays a gold tastevin, a wine-tasting cup on a long, heavy neck chain.

"Your great Grand-père, Nicolas Ruinart, used this cup to taste wine with the monks at Hautvillers Abbey. Just by smelling the grapes, he could tell you the slope of the hill on which they grew, the exposure to the sun, the minerals in the soil." She closes her papery eyelids and inhales. "He'd lift his nose to the west and smell the ocean." She turns. "He'd smell German bratwurst to the northeast."

Her head swivels. "To the south, the perfume of lavender fields in Provence." Her snaggletooth protrudes when she smiles. "Your great Grand-père was *Le Nez.*" The Nose. "He passed down his precious gift to you."

Here she goes again with her crazy notions. "Maman says Le Nez is a curse."

Grand-mère clucks her tongue. "Your maman didn't inherit Le Nez, so she doesn't understand it. It's a rare and precious gift, smelling the hidden essence of things. I took it for granted, and now it's gone." Her wrinkled hand picks up the gold tastevin and christens my nose.

A prickling clusters in my sinuses like a powerful sneeze that won't release. I wish there were truth to Grand-mère's ramblings; it would explain so much about my finicky nature.

"You are Le Nez, Barbe-Nicole." She lifts the chain over my

head, and the cup nestles above my breasts. "You must carry on Grand-père Ruinart's gift."

"Why haven't you told me about this until now?"

"Your maman forbid it." She wags her finger. "But I'm taking matters into my own hands before I die."

I feel an etching on the bottom of the cup. "Is this an anchor?"

"Ah, yes, the anchor. The anchor symbolizes clarity and courage during chaos and confusion."

"Chaos and confusion?" Now I know the story is a delusion. "Aren't those your cat's names?"

"I have cats?" She stares vacantly into the beyond, and her eerie, foreboding voice echoes through the chamber. "To whom much is given, much is expected."

Holding her bandaged head, Grand-mère keens incoherently. The lantern casts her monstrous shadow on the crayère wall; her tasting game has become a nightmare.

"Let's get you back to your room." I try to walk her to the stairs, but her legs give out. Lifting her bird-like body in my arms, I carry her as she carried me as a child, trying not to topple over into the crayère.

"Promise you'll carry on Le Nez," she says, exhaling *sentir le sapin*, the smell of fir coffins.

My dear Grand-mère is dying in my arms. Now I know Le Nez is a curse.

About the Author

Rebecca Rosenberg lives in Sonoma Valley, California, where she first fell in love with methode champenoise. Over decades of delicious research with family and friends, she has explored the wine caves and cellars of France, Spain, Italy, and California in search of the essence of fine champagne. So when she discovered the real-life stories of the Champagne Widows of France, she knew she would dedicate years to telling the stories of these remarkable women who suffered through losing their husbands, laws preventing women from owning businesses, and the ravages of wars, to take the champagne industry to new heights. Rebecca is a champagne historian, tour guide, and champagne cocktail expert for Breathless Wines.

Follow the CHAMPAGNE WIDOWS blog at rebecca-rosenberg. com or on Facebook at rebeccarosenbergnovels.

Made in the USA
Monee, IL
23 May 2023

34418559R00204